FEMALE

INTELLIGENCE

Female Intelligence

This is a work of fiction. All of the characters, names, incidents, organizations, and dialogue in this novel are either the products of the author's imagination or are used fictitiously.

iUniverse books may be ordered through booksellers or by contacting:

iUniverse
1663 Liberty Drive
Bloomington, IN 47403
www.iuniverse.com
1-800-Authors (1-800-288-4677)

ISBN: 978-1-4401-5676-2 (sc)

Printed in the United States of America

iUniverse rev. date: 04/09/2012

FEMALE INTELLIGENCE

JANE HELLER

An Authors Guild Backinprint.com Edition

iUniverse, Inc.
Bloomington

FOR MY EDITOR, JENNIFER ENDERLIN,

WHOSE INTELLIGENCE—AND HUMOR—

PROVED INVALUABLE

DURING THE WRITING OF THIS BOOK

ACKNOWLEDGMENTS

This novel is about the problems men and women face when they try (and fail) to communicate with each other. In order to bone up on the subject, I read John Gray's *Men Are from Mars, Women Are from Venus* and Deborah Tannen's *You Just Don't Understand.* I thank both authors for writing their books, and I apologize to both for having a little fun with their findings. *Female Intelligence* is intended to be comical in nature, which means that having a little fun is essential.

I'd also like to thank Jean Otte, the founder of Women Unlimited, a company that assists women in achieving parity in the workplace. And thanks to Lois Juliber for the introduction to Jean.

Thanks to my literary agent, Ellen Levine, for always being there for me, personally and professionally, and to Louise Quayle for getting my books into the hands of readers overseas.

Thanks to the people at St. Martin's Press for their enthusiasm for my books and their hard work on my behalf.

Thanks to Renée Young for helping to spread the word about my books and, even more importantly, for making me laugh.

Thanks to Ruth Harris for listening to my ideas for plots and characters and titles and for coming up with smart and snappy solutions every time.

Thanks to Michael Stinchcomb for knowing the dialogue of every Bette Davis movie.

Thanks to Kristen Powers for understanding the mysteries of cyberspace.

Thanks to Kay and John Ziegler for making it possible for me to fulfill a lifelong dream—watching my Yankees win a World Series game from boxed seats on the first base line.

And thanks to my husband, Michael Forester, for loving me even when we don't communicate (*especially* when we don't communicate).

Oh, and thanks to the married couple whom I spotted coming out of a movie theater and who, unwittingly, inspired this book. She said, "Harry, what did you think of the movie?" and he grunted. She said, "I asked you, what did you think of the movie?" and he shrugged. She said, "Why can't you talk to me?" and he said, "About what?"

FEMALE INTELLIGENCE

PROLOGUE

It is a nightly ritual all across this great land of ours, and it has nothing to do with sex. It has to do with intercourse. Verbal intercourse.

What happens is that millions of husbands and wives sit down at the table to eat dinner together. They begin the meal—take a bite of this, a sip of that—and, before you can say, "Pass the salt," there's trouble: The wives attempt to make conversation with the husbands and the husbands act as if they've been cornered; the wives attempt to make more conversation with the husbands and the husbands get that *I-don't-understand-what-she-wants-from-me* look; the wives become angry and frustrated with the husbands and the husbands either assume a ridiculously defensive posture or retreat into their imaginary cave. It should be noted that this nightly ritual is occurring in spite of our awareness of the problem and in spite of generational shifts in attitudes. It is occurring because, like cotton, it is "the fabric of our lives."

No, not every woman is a brilliant communicator and not every man is a blockhead. There are, for example, women who are so unspeakably dull that men have a duty to tune them out, just as there are men who annoy women by *over*communicating.

In the majority of households, however, it's the women who are the more adept talkers and the men who need remedial help. At least, that's the conclusion I came to at the tender age of eleven.

I was a bookish eleven, an intense eleven, an inquisitive eleven who didn't have many friends, probably because I planted myself in the front row of every class and raised my hand to answer all the teachers' questions and didn't care about clothes or boys or making out. A nerdie, know-it-all eleven, in other words.

What interested me more than that kiddie stuff, more than my school work even, was my parents and their inability to get along. Night after night I observed their conversational adventures at the dinner table, studied them as if they were a science project. (My mother: "You never talk to me, Alan." My father: "Not that again, Shelley." My mother: "Yes *that* again. Would it be asking too much for you to share some small shred about your day?" My father: "I told you about my day. I said it was fine." My mother: "*Fine*. Thanks for nothing. How are we ever going to achieve intimacy if you won't communicate with me?" My father, raising his voice: "Enough already with the intimacy, Shelley. The more you talk about it, the more I don't want to achieve it." And so on.) I couldn't make sense of these arguments, couldn't get a handle on them. They seemed so unnecessary.

Sad to report, my parents divorced when I was in high school. Fueled by the certainty that it was my father's failure to communicate with my mother that caused their breakup—and my own failure to identify the problem in time—I vowed to research and find a treatment for this male pattern badness.

And I did. While going for my Ph.D. in linguistics, I confirmed that my parents' situation was far from unique and that, in the overwhelming number of case studies involving conflicts between men and women, women were sharper, more intuitive, more intelligent than men when it came to communication. I thought, if only men were able to talk to women the way women are able to talk to each other, wouldn't the sexes coexist more smoothly? If only men could become fluent in the language of Womenspeak, wouldn't the world be a more harmonious place?

These questions formed the basis for what became the Wyman Method (my name is Lynn Wyman), which I introduced in my dissertation and later expanded upon in my bestselling book. The gist of the Wyman Method was that men could be taught *linguistically* how to relate better to women; that, by making simple adjustments in their speech patterns, by tinkering with their words, and by coaching them on their delivery, even the most clueless, verbally challenged men could, within a few short months, learn to be more sensitive, more forthcoming about their feelings and, best of all, less exasperating to live with.

In a nutshell, the Wyman Method was my therapy for guys who go mute at the dinner table and guys who interrupt in business meetings and guys who tell entirely too many jokes concerning women's breasts. It was my cure for the common cad.

And it made me famous—truly famous—for a time. On the heels of the book followed the radio show and the newspaper column and the monthly appearances on "Good Morning America," plus the very lucrative private practice. I was an important person doing important work until my life took a dramatic dive—a plunge that was breathtaking in its downward trajectory.

But there will be more about my reversal of fortune soon enough, much more. In the meantime, think of me as I was before the fall—a newfangled Pygmalion ("Femalion," as David Letterman dubbed me). Or think of me as Rex Harrison in the movie *My Fair Lady*. Rex was a linguist who taught Audrey Hepburn how to communicate like a lady. I was a linguist who taught men how to communicate *with* ladies. As a matter of fact, think of the story I'm about to tell you as a sort of "My Fair *Man*."

It's a story about language, obviously, and about love, as you've probably guessed, as well as a story about having it all and losing it all and figuring out how to get it all back. And, because it's a cautionary tale, it comes with a warning label: Beware of smart women with a score to settle.

PART ONE

1

"PLEASE TRY THE dinner table script again, Ron. From the top. And this time, speak directly into the microphone."

"Okay, Dr. Wyman."

"I also want you to linger for half a beat on the word 'your.' As in: 'So, Marybeth, how was *your* day?' It's the emphasis on the 'your' that will make your wife feel as if she's the focus of your attention, as if she's getting her turn with you after a long, busy day. Do you understand?"

"Sure, Dr. Wyman. Whatever."

" 'Whatever' is no longer in your vocabulary, Ron. Not when you're talking to women. It sends us an I-don't-care message."

"No 'whatever.' Ever."

"Right. Now, let's hear the line again."

Ron leaned closer to the microphone. " 'So, Marybeth, how was your *day*?' "

"Ron. Ron. You lingered over the wrong word. Listen to how hostile that *daaaay* made you sound." I shook my head disapprovingly as I rewound the tape and played it back to my client. "You gave the impression that you'd rather die than have Marybeth tell you about her day."

"That's because I *would* rather die." His expression was pained. "I have zero interest in hearing about how some secretary in her office lost thirty pounds on the Slim Fast diet. I mean, am I really supposed to give a crap about that, let alone *ask* my wife to tell me about it over dinner?"

"Calm down, Ron. You're the one who came here for help."

"Yeah, because Marybeth threatened to divorce me if I didn't. I don't want her to leave me. I just want her to leave me alone when I'm eating."

"Ron. You've got to keep in mind that Marybeth's chatter is merely an attempt to establish a connection with you. As I told you during your evaluation, communication is crucially important to women. We use words to achieve a sense of intimacy with others. It makes us feel insecure and unloved when men give us back nonresponsive answers or ignore us altogether. If you were to listen attentively to what Marybeth reports about her day and ask pertinent follow-up questions, you would be demonstrating that you care about her and she would respond in kind, and your relationship would improve dramatically. You can trust me on this."

"Oh, I trust you, Dr. Wyman. You wouldn't be so successful if you didn't know what you were talking about."

"Thank you, Ron, but I think I'm successful because I believe deeply in what I'm talking about. There's nothing more satisfying to me than watching men learn and grow as they advance through my program."

"Okay, but there's one thing I don't get."

"Yes?"

"Why is it that men have to do all the learning and growing? Why is everything our fault?"

I smiled. I was hit with that question frequently. "This isn't about blame, Ron. It's about accepting the fact that men and women have different conversational styles. Some people are of the opinion that it's the male conversational style that should be adopted universally, which is why there are women out there taking courses in 'assertiveness,' so they can learn how to talk like men. A total waste of money, if you ask me. I say—and the Wyman Method confirms—that it's the female conversational style that should be adopted universally, because when both men and women do adopt it, *it changes the dynamic of the male–female relationship in a positive way*. Do you understand?"

"I'm trying to."

"You see, we're living in different times now, times that place sensitivity and compassion and the sharing of feelings in high regard. It's a woman's world, Ron, and it behooves men to learn the language. When in Rome."

Ron looked dazed. They all did in the beginning. My program was a difficult one, I admit. I wasn't merely asking men to change how they spoke to women, I was putting them through what amounted to basic training. For example, in addition to tape recording their speech patterns and practicing new scripts with them, I forced them to listen to music composed and performed by actual sensitive men (Kenny G., Michael Bolton, John Tesh). And I took them on field trips for on-site language adjustments, driving them out into the country, getting them lost, and teaching them how to ask for directions. The Wyman Method wasn't for the weak willed, obviously.

"I realize that incorporating these scripts into your daily life with Marybeth may make you a little uncomfortable at first," I said, "but the process will get easier. I promise."

He nodded hopefully.

"Why don't you start again." I pressed the Record button on the tape recorder. "Go."

He cleared his throat. " 'So, Marybeth, how was *your* day?' "

I beamed. "Excellent, Ron. Listen." I rewound the tape and played it back for him. "How did that sound to you?"

"Like somebody else," he said.

"That's because you're becoming somebody else. By the time you've finished the program, you'll be a man Marybeth can talk to, feel close to, and your marriage will be stronger for it."

"If you say so."

"Now, we're going to move on to the next line of our dinner table script. Repeat after me: 'I'd like to share what happened to *me* at work today, Marybeth.' "

Ron looked stupefied. "Me? Share? I don't lead an exciting life. I'm a dermatologist, not a race car driver. Marybeth's not gonna be interested in hearing how I go from examining room to examining room squirting liquid nitrogen on people's actinic kerotosis."

"Please. Let's hear the line, Ron."

He shrugged. " 'I'd like to share what happened to *me* at work today, Marybeth.' "

"That's perfect, absolutely perfect."

And it was. Ron was on his way to becoming another success story.

MY NEXT CLIENT that day was a man who wanted to communicate better with his girlfriend. The client after that was a man who wanted to communicate better with his female boss. The client after that was a man who wanted to communicate better with his mother so he could be written back into her will. He said she was worth a bundle and that he'd give me a piece of the action if the Wyman Method brought her around. I thanked him and said his completion of my program would be reward enough.

At twelve-thirty I dashed out of the office for a lunch meeting with a publisher, one of several who had been offering me large sums of money to pen a sequel to my bestselling book. At three, I raced back to the office to be interviewed by a writer for *Ladies' Home Journal*; I was being included in a cover story called "Women for the New Millennium." And at five-fifteen, I hurried over to the radio station to host my three-hour, drive-time, call-in show that didn't exactly have the audience of Dr. Joy Browne but was creeping up in the ratings.

It was a hectic day, as they all were then. A hectic but invigorating October day during which I was able to teach men the language of Womenspeak and improve the quality of their lives and the lives of the women close to them. The Wyman Method may have had its detractors (*Saturday Night Live* ran a rather tasteless skit where the cast member who impersonated me instructed men how to nag, whine, and fake orgasms—ha ha), but my program worked. It did.

It was eight-thirty by the time I left the parking garage in Manhattan and nine-fifteen by the time I pulled into the driveway of my house in Mt. Kisco, a picturesque hamlet in Northern Westchester just a stone's throw from Chappaqua, the picturesque hamlet in Northern Westchester that Bill and Hillary Clinton either elevated or contaminated, depending on your politics.

My house was rustic yet sophisticated—a stone cottage set on seven leafy, spectacular-for-fall-foliage-watching acres at the end of a dirt road. I had lived in it for five years at that point—paid for it from the advance from my book. I'll never forget how proud I felt the day of the closing. There I was, a single, thirty-three-year-old woman, buying a house in an expensive New York suburb with money I had earned all by myself. No help from a trust fund. No help from an alimony check. No help from either of my parents, who, although divorced, were still too consumed with each other to notice that I had moved.

And then, just when I was beginning to entertain the thought that it would be nice to have a man around the house, a man entered the house—walked right up to the front door and rang the bell, as it happened.

He was a tall, sinewy, exceptionally good-looking carpenter who came to build me some bookcases. He had been recommended by my realtor. His name was Kip Jankowsky and I married him.

Oh, I know what you're thinking. A carpenter, for God's sake. Does the world need yet another story about a highly educated woman having a relationship with a man who's never heard of Joyce Carol Oates? But understand that while Kip was, indeed, a stud muffin and six years my junior and not a college graduate, he made me feel right in tune with all the other career women who were choosing carpenters and cowboys and lawn maintenance workers over dentists. To put it another way, he was easy on my intellect. Instead of challenging me, he appreciated me, which wasn't a terrible thing.

Besides, Kip was an excellent carpenter, an artist, not some run-of-the-mill, high-cracking handyman. The fact that he was also an energetic, extravagantly giving lover—and that, prior to meeting him, I had been sexually inactive for longer than I care to discuss—contributed mightily to his appeal.

But what sealed the deal for me, what boosted him up a notch from hunky companion to husband material, was his ability to communicate, to share, to allow himself to be vulnerable. At our very first encounter, he was surprisingly forthcoming about his conflict about working with his hands for a living instead of being the "suit" his father always wanted him to be. He even choked up, teared up, wiped his eyes, then apologized by explaining that he often became emotional whenever he skipped lunch, due to a chronic low-blood-sugar problem. Perfect, I thought. I've found a man who already knows Womenspeak, a man I don't have to fix. What a relief.

Of course, the media loved Kip and me as a couple, loved the "hook" that my husband was a walking billboard for the Wyman Method, loved that my personal life validated, meshed with, was a shining example of what I preached in my professional life. When I married Kip, *People* magazine gushed: "The woman famous for teaching men how to be sensitive has wed a man who personifies sensitivity." But it was *20/20's* Elizabeth Vargas who put it best when she came to the house to interview us for a piece on "Couples Who

Communicate." "Lynn Wyman," she said, staring straight into the camera lens, "has a husband who isn't afraid to express his feelings."

Lucky me. In the four years that we'd been married, I had never once heard my husband utter the dreaded words: "I don't want to talk about that." He was a great talker, the Kipster.

"Lynn. You're home," he said, rushing to the door to greet me that evening after the radio show. "It's almost nine-thirty. I didn't think you'd be this late. I was getting a little frantic. You could have called."

"What for? There was traffic on the Bruckner, that's all," I said, dumping my bulging briefcase onto the living room sofa.

"You know what a worrier I am," said Kip. "I pictured all sorts of things happening to you."

"That's sweet." I kissed him. He was wearing his uniform—blue jeans and a work shirt—and his wavy dark hair was wet. He looked scrubbed, squeaky clean, as if he had just hopped out of the shower and changed clothes. He had soap in his ears. Like a little boy.

"Well, let's get you something to eat," he said. "You must be starving." He took my hand and led me into the kitchen. "I made lasagna tonight. It reheats well. I'll just pop it into the microwave, then pour us both a drink."

Kip was wonderful about doing the cooking, the shopping, the domestic chores I didn't have time for, given my long hours. He never complained, never balked, never minded when friends teased him about being the "wife," never winced when strangers referred to him as "Mr. Wyman," never even flinched when someone had the nerve to bring up the disparity between his income and mine. He's so evolved, I thought, congratulating myself. So devoted.

While the lasagna was being nuked, we sipped our drinks—a Scotch and water for me, a glass of chardonnay for him. Then, over dinner, he asked me about my day, without any prodding whatsoever.

"And how was *your* day?" I asked him after finishing my recitation.

He told me about his day: how he was building a TV cabinet—an *armoire*—for the newly minted couple down the street; how the wife was extremely friendly and accessible while the husband was aloof and wouldn't make any eye contact; how the supermarket seemed more crowded than usual when he went to buy the ingredients for the lasagna; how he got stuck with a shopping cart that had a bad wheel and felt self-conscious about the squeal it made as he tried to steer it up and down the aisles; how he realized later that he should have just traded the cart in for another one the minute he spotted the bad wheel instead of suffering through the ordeal of having all the other shoppers stop and stare at him; how the girl at the checkout counter reminded him of Britney Spears.

I listened patiently to all this minutiae, never once wishing he'd put a sock in it. We were sharers, Kip and I—a couple of expressers in a world of withholders. Sometimes what we shared was substantive and sometimes it was, well, like the bit about the shopping cart with the bad wheel.

We finished dinner. I offered to do the dishes, but Kip insisted that I relax in a nice warm bath while he did the dishes. Was he a prize or what?

I toddled off to the master bedroom suite, disrobed and turned on the water in the tub. I was pinning up my hair when I remembered that I'd forgotten to call Diane, my assistant, to tell her I wouldn't be in the office until eleven the next morning. (I had a meeting with the programming people at CBS; we'd been kicking around the possibility of my hosting my own daytime talk show.)

I picked up the phone in the bedroom and was about to dial Diane's home number when I heard Kip on the line. And here is what Mr. Communicator was communicating about.

"I love you, too," he was saying, to someone other than me. "It was torture leaving you this afternoon. I can still taste you."

You know, at first I didn't quite get it, get what was going on. Not that instant. You don't if you're not expecting bad news of such magnitude. Instead of getting it, you stand there like a doofus and blink a few times and shake off what you think you heard and tell yourself the old *there must be some mistake*.

"I want to be with you soooo much, Kippy. My body's aching for you," said a female voice I couldn't hear clearly. It was muffled, as if the woman had a pillow over her mouth. Come to think of it, maybe she did. Why else would they call it pillow talk?

And that *Kippy* business. Yech. I mean, it's a cute name for a puppy dog, but please.

"Listen," said Kip excitedly. "I think she's going away next week, to some conference for linguists. We'll be able to spend whole nights together here at the house the way we did last time. She'll never find out."

Well, there wasn't any doubt who *she* was. I had to face the fact that it was *I* who'd been betrayed by the man I'd married.

Actually, I let my body face it first. My stomach lurched, my pulse raced, my cheeks burned with hurt and rage and huge, huge disappointment. I was hot, I was cold, I was nauseous. My husband, everybody's idea of a sensitive guy, had, apparently, been doing a very insensitive thing.

I let them talk, just let them go on and on about their throbbing genitalia. They were so caught up in their disgustingly overheated conversation that they must not have heard the "click" when I'd picked up the extension, must not have heard my labored breathing, must not have remembered that I existed, which made me feel even more ridiculous. Kip's little love affair had been taking place right under my nose—under my roof!—and I hadn't even guessed. Ever since I was a kid, people have been telling me how smart I am, but the truth is, it doesn't matter how smart you are if even one person manages to prove how stupid you are.

They hung up eventually, as did I. Kip went back to doing the dishes, and I remained on the spot where I'd been standing. Numb. Naked. Entranced by the sound of the bathwater running, probably onto the floor by now. Paralyzed.

I honestly didn't know whether I should grab a robe, march out there, and confront the dirt bag, or hide in the bathroom, take a soak in the tub, and try to figure out what to make of this new development. What to do? What to do? I was still stunned. Still stinging. I was used to being in control, used to being in touch with my own power. And yet there I was, about as in touch with my own power as a slice of Swiss cheese.

What if Kip really is in love with this woman? I thought. What if he wants to marry her? What if I end up just like my divorced mother, whose circumstance I've been determined to avoid, which is precisely why I chose the compulsively verbal Kip as a husband instead of a grouchy grunter like my father?

And then another thought broke through. What if people find out that my marriage has turned out to be a sham? What if gossip about Kip's unseemly behavior leaks out? How much credibility will the Wyman Method have if communication expert Lynn Wyman can't get her own husband to communicate with her? How will I be able to earn a living once I go from authority figure to laughingstock?

I decided on the bath, not the confrontation. There was always the chance that I would drown in the tub and escape having to deal with any of it.

2

LYNN? YOU STILL in there?"

It was my *husband*—even the word made me sick now—calling to me as I lay in the tub, my skin pickled from marinating in the hot water for so long.

"Lynn? Everything okay in there?"

Yeah, everything's swell, dick face. I always take nine-hour baths.

"I'll be out in a minute," I said, trying to dry my eyes with my wet hands. A fruitless endeavor.

"Great," Kip said. "I'll come wrap you in a towel." He jiggled the knob on the bathroom door and discovered it was locked. "Hey. What's this? Are we playing games tonight?"

I ignored the question, wrapped *myself* in a towel, and opened the door. Steam poured out of the room, out of my ears.

"There you are." Kip approached me, as if he intended to embrace me, and I recoiled, as if he were a snake, which, of course, he was. "Lynn, what is it? Have you been crying or is it just the—"

"Shut up, Kip," I said, in a notably calm voice. I even smiled a little when I said it, a lip-curling, smirky smile, because the irony of the "shut up" hit me; I was the one who encouraged husbands to talk to their wives and now I was telling my own to zip it. "Just shut up and sit down while I put on a robe."

His eyes widened and he was about to say something but he didn't. He sat on the edge of the bed and waited like a good doggie.

I had planned my speech while I was in the tub, had rehearsed it over and over so I wouldn't cry while I delivered it, wouldn't crumble. I wasn't going to let him see my humiliation, wasn't going to let him know how completely reduced I felt.

Reduced. Yes. Not crushed, but made smaller, cut down. I had always been self-confident when it came to my brains; I'd been the child who skipped grades, the college student who graduated early, the wunderkind linguist who traded academia for multimedia. But what did it say about my brains that I'd picked a rat for a husband? What kind of a dope does that?

Kip's apparent longing for another woman also reduced what little regard I had for my appearance, my immediate conclusion being that he not only preferred hers but was turned off by mine. Oh, I suppose I considered myself somewhat attractive—attractive enough to show up on television regularly—but certainly not drop dead gorgeous. I'm too tightly coiled to be gorgeous, too studious, too intense. To be gorgeous, you have to have a dreamy, languorous look, an insouciant look, a runway model look, a look that says, "I'm gorgeous and you're not and so what." I'm on the scrawny side, like a model, but my look says "rundown" not "runway," thanks to my crazy work schedule. In the "plus" column, I have large, shining brown eyes, remarkably good skin (I hung out in libraries as a kid, not on beaches), even features, and long, curly brown hair that I wear either held in place with headbands or tied back in a ponytail. The point I'm trying to make here is that I'm pretty, but Kip's faithlessness made me feel distinctly unpretty. Reduced, as I said.

You may be wondering if my husband's turning out to be a rat shook my faith in the Wyman Method; whether I regretted choosing a man who communicated; whether I inferred that his adulterous behavior was in some way connected to his ability to express his feelings. Not in the slightest. There are men who communicate and cheat and there are men who don't communicate and cheat, just as there are men who don't cheat whether they communicate or not. I remained as dedicated to my theory as ever. In my mind, Kip was merely a communicator who couldn't keep his Levi's on. No, he put a dent in my self-esteem, but he didn't damage my belief in my program.

"Are you going to tell me what's wrong?" he asked after I sat in a chair across the room. "I'm feeling tremendous discomfort here. I'm feeling the same kind of discomfort I used to feel when my father would—"

"Stop!" I held up my hand to silence him. "I couldn't be less interested in how you're feeling. Just tell me how long you've been popping the little popsy."

"The little what?" He said this with amusement, as if I were joking.

"The one I overheard you plotting with on the phone before," I said. "How long has it been going on?"

Kip feigned surprise and said he couldn't imagine what I was talking about.

"For the third time: How long?" I demanded. "It's late and I'm tired. Just tell me."

"There's nothing to—"

"TELL ME!"

"Three months," he sputtered, plowing his fingers through his thick dark hair in an attempt, I suppose, to appear anguished.

Three months. We hadn't made love in three months. He'd been claiming he had a headache.

"I'll break it off," he pledged, bounding off the bed, over to my chair, and curling up on the floor at my feet. "She doesn't mean anything to me, Lynn. I mean it."

"Who is she?"

"No one. No one important."

"If she's not important, why did you tell her you love her?"

"I don't know. Look, the only reason I got involved with her in the first place was because you've been spending so much time in the city and I've been feeling neglected and—"

"Not the neglected routine." I made gagging noises. He was speaking a dialect of Womenspeak I wasn't crazy about: Pig Womenspeak.

"You do neglect me," he maintained, pouting.

"So you're saying this is *my* fault? Is that your position?"

He could tell from my expression that "yes" would be the wrong answer. "No. Forget that. It's *my* fault," he said. Such a suck up. "Totally my fault. But *she* came on to *me*. I was not the initiator. I want to make that clear."

"Wow. That lets you right off the hook, doesn't it?"

"I'm serious, Lynn. I was the victim here." He took my bare foot in his hand and started to massage it. I kicked him away. "She put the moves on me and I was too weak, too vulnerable, too—"

I held my hands over my ears. Vulnerable! Ha! He was twisting Womenspeak, bastardizing it.

"Okay, okay. Enough of that." He swallowed hard. He was regrouping. "What I'm telling you is that I'm taking full responsibility for what I did. I had a fling. I was unfaithful. I was selfish. But it will never happen again. Never. I'm recommitting myself to you."

"Why? Because you've got a sweet deal living in my nice big house?"

"Sweet deal?" His eyes began to well up at my insinuation; then came the blubbering. *I* was the injured party and *he* was one who was crying. "You're not suggesting (sob sob) that I married you for your money or your fame or any of that, are you (sob sob)? Because I signed that prenuptial agreement. I agreed to all the terms. I married you because you're the woman I want to spend the rest of my life with (sob sob sob sob sob)."

"You want to spend the rest of your life with me but have lovers on the side, while I'm out of town?"

"No!" He shook his head, back and forth, back and forth, back and forth. I kept waiting for him to stop. It was as if it was stuck in the "on" position.

"KIP!"

That seemed to snap him out of it.

"Stop crying and stop shaking your head and stop bullshitting me."

"I'm sorry." He did stop crying but now there was snot hanging from his nose. I didn't tell him it was there. I liked that he looked defective.

"So what now?" I said with a sigh. "Where do we go from here? That's the question."

"I'm going to take care of you and be there for you, just the way it was before," said Kip. "I *have* been a good husband to you, haven't I? Except for this? Think about it, Lynn."

I *had* thought about it. In the bathtub. Kip had been a good husband in all the ways I've already explained, but now he had strayed and I had a decision to make—to accept his mea culpa or throw him the hell out.

I considered the first option. Was I one of those women who forgives the guy his infidelity and bravely soldiers on with the marriage? Was I one of those women who views his cheating as yet another human frailty, in the same category as overspending on a new set of golf clubs? Was I one of those women whose power of denial is so strong she can look at his naked body without wondering where else his *thing* has been? God, no.

On the other hand, was I prepared to divorce him? Was I ready to end up like my mother, miserable and alone? Was I up for the avalanche of publicity our split would trigger—a media circus that would certainly ruin my reputation as an expert on relationships? Was I willing to watch the Wyman Method get trashed because my husband got laid? No again.

Of course, if I hadn't been the level-headed type, the type to reason before I reacted, there would have been loads of other options, including stabbing Kip with one of his kitchen knives, spiking his chardonnay with Clorox, tossing my blow dryer into his Jacuzzi. But I *was* the level-headed type. I needed more time to determine the best course of action.

"I'd like us to do nothing about this for now," I told Kip, who burst into tears of relief that he wouldn't be out on his ass for the moment.

"Oh, thank you," he said.

"I'll sleep here in the bedroom and you'll sleep down the hall in the guestroom and we'll see how it goes."

"It'll go great, I swear."

"You'll call whatever-her-name-is and tell her the relationship is history?"

He nodded aggressively.

"And the two of you will keep quiet about this whole mess?" I added. "I assume that won't be a problem for her since she probably has an unsuspecting spouse too."

"She's—"

"Spare me the details," I said. "Just tell me we have an understanding, an arrangement."

"Oh, Lynn. We do. And you'll be glad you took another chance on me, you really will." He smiled through his tears. "I remember when I was a kid and my father and I had arguments and when they were over and we had found a way to work out a compromise, I felt so secure, so filled with a sense of well-being, so everything's-right-with-the-world. There was one time in particular—I think I was nine or ten—when he came home from the office and, before even saying 'hi' to me, he accused me of not cleaning my room or mowing the lawn, something like that, and I felt horrible because he was right—I hadn't done what I was supposed to do—but I couldn't admit that he was right. Not at first. So I—"

I hadn't wanted to go near Kip now that I knew he had been with another woman—at least not without wearing Latex gloves—but there was no other way to get him out of the bedroom. I took hold of his arm and dragged him out of there. He was still droning on about his father and his feelings and his formative years as he ambled down the hall to the guestroom. I could hear him, even after slamming my door and locking it.

3

THE MEETING WITH the CBS people went well, much better than I had a right to expect, given how out of it I was. I hadn't slept, hadn't eaten, hadn't prepared any notes or graphs or charts, and yet I managed to convince everybody that I had what it took to host my own show. By the end of our little gathering, they were talking pilot. They even suggested that we have a guest spot on the show featuring the lovely and talented Kip, who would demonstrate how he and I incorporate the Wyman Method into our very own daily lives. Yessiree.

"You have tremendous name recognition, Lynn," said one of the executives, immediately after he said I had "edge."

I did have tremendous name recognition, but what I also had were horrendous menstrual cramps that probably had more to do with my edge than anything else. Or was I just feeling lousy about having to lie about my marriage?

"HEY, DR. WYMAN. You don't look good," said Diane McManus, my twenty-seven-year-old assistant. Diane's reason for being was looking good—"good" being a relative term. When I arrived at the office after the meeting, she was sitting at her desk, tweezing her eyebrows.

Diane had been my assistant since I opened my practice, and we were the quintessential odd couple: she wasn't the least bit interested in having a career and I was nothing if not career driven. I didn't love that she took so many coffee breaks and spent far too much time on the phone with her friends and was forever running out to the tanning bed place and the body piercing place and the hair coloring place (since I'd known Diane, her hair had been her natural red, a mud brown, and a strawberry blond with streaks of forest green; her current shade was a blinding platinum), but I couldn't really complain because she got her work done. She showed up every day. She was pleasant to the clients and, most importantly, to me.

"I've got cramps. I'll be fine," I said, continuing to reveal nothing about Kip and me in order to preserve my image. Diane, like the others, held me up as The Role Model of Relationships. I'd be bursting her bubble if I told her that I wasn't immune to the marital problems other women faced.

"You sure you don't want me to cancel your clients?" she asked, glancing at the day's appointment book, which was full.

I shook my head. "But I do want you to cancel my trip to the conference next week."

"Cancel your trip? Really? You never miss one of those conferences, Dr. Wyman."

"I've got matters to attend to here," I said, intending to stay home and address the situation with Kip.

"Yeah. Uh huh." She looked at me skeptically, as if she knew something I didn't, then pointed at me, the frosted blue manicured nail on her index finger glistening under the fluorescent lighting.

"What, Diane?"

"I bet you're not going to the conference next week because it's your anniversary, and Mr. Sensitive up there in Mt. Kisco has something incredibly romantic planned for the two of you. That's it, isn't it?"

God. My anniversary. Mine and Kip's. Our fourth. Diane had remembered it but I had forgotten about it, had even arranged to be away for it. Not good. Not good at all.

It occurred to me that maybe Kip was justified in feeling neglected. Maybe I was partially to blame for his little dalliance. Maybe I'd been unfair to judge him so harshly when it was my commitment to my work that may have pushed him into the arms of another woman.

On the other hand, why hadn't he taken up a hobby if he was so damn lonely? Restoring old cars. Fly fishing. Anything but popping that popsy.

"You guessed it, Diane," I lied, hating Kip again after that momentary lapse. "I'm cancelling the trip because my husband said he would feel a deep sense of abandonment if I were out of town on our special day."

She grinned. "No wonder you have so many clients, Dr. Wyman. You actually got a man to verbalize that."

I grinned back, knowing that I could probably get Kip to verbalize anything. I just couldn't guarantee that he'd mean it.

I WAS GRATEFUL that my radio show was preempted by a postseason baseball game that afternoon. I was too tired to dish out any more advice to people. What I needed was someone to dish out advice to me. So I called my friends—the four women I'd come to spend time with and care about over the years—and asked if they'd meet me for a drink after work. Sensing I was not my usual on-top-of-things self and would never have convened such an impromptu get-together if it weren't urgent, they all said they would meet me, even though it meant postponing a business appointment or arranging for a babysitter or pushing back a dinner reservation. They were busy women with lives full of obligations but they made time for me without hesitation.

My friends. My wonderful friends. The "Brain Trust," we jokingly referred to ourselves. As I've mentioned, I wasn't popular as a kid, so being part of a group, a clique, a support system now that I was in my thirties was a revelation; I realized how important it was to have other women you can depend on.

How did I happen to have these women friends, given that I was such a loner type?

What had begun as a professional association based on networking—the five of us had first rubbed padded shoulders at a Women in Media luncheon—had evolved into a sisterhood of sorts. We were all successful in our areas of expertise and, therefore, had accomplishment in common. We were all comfortable with being successful, which meant that none of us was threatened or intimidated or resentful of any of the others. And we all genuinely liked each other, enjoyed each other's company. I'm not saying we didn't engage in a little competitive banter now and then, particularly after a cocktail or two, but we were just spirited women and there were never any grudges held. None that I was aware of.

We agreed to meet in the lobby bar of the Royalton Hotel, which was right in midtown and easy for everybody to get to.

Penny Herter arrived first. A graduate of the Harvard Business School by way of Bryn Mawr, Penny was the founder and president of PHG (the Penny Herter Group), a public relations firm that specialized in raising the profile of large to midsize companies. A tall, athletic, thirty-six-year-old, she had short, baby fine blond hair, a Kennedyesque overbite and the preppiest wardrobe this side of Talbot's. She was smooth socially, a great one for smiling and shaking hands and pretending to know people she'd never laid eyes on, but underneath the impeccable manners lurked a real operator—a shrewd businesswoman who went after clients with a vengeance, doing and saying whatever it took to land an account. I don't mean to imply that Penny was without integrity. She was just extremely focused, the way a Tomahawk cruise missile is focused. Some people found her overly aggressive, but I got a kick out of her no-nonsense approach to life. She didn't let emotions cloud the picture. She simply assessed a situation, came up with a game plan and went for it. She applied this strategy to her romantic relationships as well, thinking nothing of sprinting right up to men she found attractive, announcing her interest in them, and hitting her target. Bullseye. At first, these men were dazzled by her energy and enthusiasm and forthrightness, but after a period of weeks or, occasionally, months, they would wilt under the force of the same energy and enthusiasm and forthrightness they'd been dazzled by—and bolt. The bottom line was that Penny was still single.

Isabel Green showed up next, wearing all black as usual. She was petite—not just short but small-boned, pale, fragile looking—and her petiteness contrasted dramatically with her jewelry, which was oversized. Huge earrings. Huge necklaces. Huge and incredibly noisy bracelets. They all seemed much too heavy a burden for her tiny body to bear. Thirty-eight, Isabel was an acclaimed, albeit eccentric, photographer whose subject was cats, always cats. She was obsessed with cats, dressing them in human clothing and posing them in human settings, and, not surprisingly, she was perpetually walking around with their hair clinging to her black clothes. She was an unconventional person who quoted obscure, mostly dead writers, consulted with her astrologer before taking on any new project and could go for days without answering her phone (she was the only one I knew without a computer, so you couldn't e-mail her). Her love life, too, was unconventional. She'd been involved with the same man, an art gallery owner, for seven years without a single syllable of commitment from him. She believed that he would marry her eventually but she was perfectly content to wait him out in the meantime. Personally, I thought she was either afraid of commitment herself, and therefore chose an unavailable man on whom to pin her future, or she was incredibly trusting.

Gail Orrick was an Emmy award-winning producer of documentary films of the type that are broadcast on PBS. In other words, she was as plugged in to contemporary life as Isabel was on the fringe of it. She made films about single mothers trying to get off welfare, about heroin addicts trying to stay clean, about endangered whooping cranes trying to survive in a hostile environment. Gail's specialty as a filmmaker was Plight, obviously. She was drawn to anything remotely associated with catastrophes, probably because she had so many catastrophes of her own. They included a widowed agoraphobic mother, a perennially out-of-work husband, and two attention-deficit-disordered children. And then there were her near-death experiences: a kidnapping attempt while she was shooting a film in Lebanon; a bout with malaria after shooting a film in India; assorted car accidents on her way home from the mall. A lot had happened to her in her thirty-four years, but she was definitely the drama queen among us, transforming everyday problems into bona fide horror stories. Oh, and she had a little problem with food. When she was under stress, which was all the time as far as I could tell, she binged but didn't purge, and, as a result, kept jumping dress sizes.

The final member of our group was Sarah Pepper, who wrote a series of enormously popular children's books featuring a magic toothbrush. Originally conceived as a way to coax her own children into practicing better dental hygiene, the books became a phenomenon, formed the basis for a number of animated movies, and made Sarah a wealthy woman who felt she would be wealthier if not for her shabby treatment at the hands of Hollywood. Simply put, she was yet another writer who was both seduced by and bitter toward the movie business. At forty, she was the oldest among us, but she was also the fittest, a genuine beauty who spent a fortune on her clothes and shoes and overall grooming. Slender and sculpted and bosomy, with dark hair that flowed down her back, she looked like the heroine on a romance book cover, give or take a few crow's feet. "I'm not your father's forty-year-old," she was fond of boasting. She wasn't anybody's idea of a children's book author, either, considering that she hardly ever saw her children. She was too busy appearing on panels with the *Harry Potter* author and the *Goosebumps* author and MariaShriverJamieLeeCurtisCarlySimon. (She had no use for celebrities who wrote children's books and displayed this by lumping their names together.) As for her marriage to her high school sweetheart, it was troubled, to put it mildly. Sarah and her husband had been separated and back together more times than even they could count. They were not a couple you'd point to and say, "Boy, what a solid union."

So there we were in the lobby bar of the Royalton. I had assembled my friends and now it was time to tell them why.

"Something very upsetting has happened to me," I announced after we had ordered drinks and exchanged the usual "How are you?" and "How's work going?" and "Did you cut your hair or are you just wearing it differently?"

"Oh my God. You found a lump," Gail said, her eyes darting over my body, in search of the tumor.

"No. It's not a life-and-death matter," I assured her, forgetting that she would assume that it was.

"Then it must be a career dilemma," said Penny, "although I don't see how that could be it. You're at the top of your game, Lynn. Didn't you just meet with CBS about hosting your own show?"

"I'd be very wary of those people if I were you, Lynn," Sarah warned before I could respond. "They take your ideas and then pretend they never heard of you. Predators. That's what those show-business types are. Predators."

"You didn't think they were predators when you were depositing their checks, did you?" said Penny, who was irritated by Sarah's digression.

"I certainly did," said Sarah. "They were predators with deep pockets. But not as deep as they could have been. What they pay writers is chump change compared to what they pay movie stars. And they don't just *pay* movie stars. They give them cars. They never gave me a car. All I got was a coffee mug."

"Is your problem a blockage?" Isabel asked me. "A creative blockage, I mean. Because if it is, I know someone you could see about freeing it up. She lives in SoHo and she does wonderful work with her hands, releases the blood flow to the brain, allows for—"

"No, no. I don't have a blockage, Isabel." This was silly. I was making my friends play Twenty Questions. I took a deep breath and plunged in. "The upsetting thing that happened to me is that Kip has been unfaithful."

There was a collective gasp followed by a long, awkward silence. They were as stunned as I had been, which proved that even *they* had bought into my supposedly storybook marriage.

It was Gail who spoke first.

"Male or female?" she asked.

"What?" I said.

"Is the person Kip's been sleeping with male or female? Or has he been alternating?"

"Gail," said Penny. "There's no need to make this worse than it already is. Fooling around is fooling around."

"He's been having an affair with a woman," I said. "He claims he doesn't love her, that it was just a fling, that he won't see her again, but that doesn't change the fact that he betrayed me."

I started to cry then. Everybody patted me and handed me tissues and said they were sorry.

"Personally, I never trusted him," said Gail, grabbing a fistful of cheddar cheese goldfish. "He was too happy-go-lucky."

"He seemed like an okay guy to me," said Penny. "Not a rocket scientist but sweet."

"*This* is why I photograph cats," said Isabel, throwing up her hands in disgust, a gesture that made her bracelets clang. "They are what they are. No hidden agendas."

"I'm so confused," I said after blowing my nose. "I can't figure out how I want to handle the situation."

"Get rid of him," said Gail, who spoke frequently about getting rid of her deadbeat husband but couldn't seem to. "You can do better."

"I agree, Lynn," said Penny. "You don't have to tolerate behavior like that. It's not as if you'll be out on the street if you two split up. You're the one with the assets."

"I am," I acknowledged. "But if we do split up and the media gets wind of it, I might as well kiss my practice and my radio show and all the rest goodbye. Who's going to take the Wyman Method seriously when I can't even keep my own marriage together?"

Penny nodded. "I see what you're getting at now. Not an easy call."

Everybody patted me some more.

"But let's look on the bright side," she offered, moving into spin mode. "Why would the media have to find out, talk about rocket scientists? They're easy to manipulate, especially if you and Kip came up with some kind of arrangement."

"What kind?"

"Well, maybe in exchange for the generous amount of money you'll unload on him, he'll be discreet and show up at functions with you and pretend to be the ideal husband your audience believes he is. You could just trot him out in public whenever it's absolutely necessary."

"You're suggesting that Kip and I get a divorce but let people think we're still together?" I asked Penny.

"It's done all the time, believe me. For example, I have a client who only sees his ex once a year, at the company's annual stockholders' meeting. She plays corporate wife for the day and he makes it worth her while."

"But that's so dishonest," I protested.

"No more dishonest than what Kip pulled on you," said Gail.

"It's all about protecting yourself, Lynn," said Penny. "Protecting everything you've worked for. Protecting *the Wyman Method*."

"What do you think, Sarah?" I asked. She'd been uncharacteristically quiet since my announcement.

"Well," she said, "I think you should explore your feelings for Kip before making any snap decisions. Do you still love him?"

I shrugged. "Yes. No. I don't know. Maybe I never loved him. Not really. Maybe he was just an accommodation, a warm body, someone to fill a void."

"If that's what you were looking for, you should have gotten a pet," said Isabel. "A cat. Cats never let you down the way men do."

"At least you and Kip don't have kids," said Gail. "It's harder to dump a guy when you're talking about dismantling an entire family. I know from experience."

"It's hard to dump a guy, period," said Sarah. "Why do you think I've stayed married for so long?"

"Excuse me," said Penny, "but this is not about you, Sarah, or you, Gail, or you, Isabel. This is about Lynn. Am I the only one here who's not afraid to address *her* problem?"

We all reached for our drinks. Penny had that effect on people.

"It's too distressing," said Gail. "I thought that Lynn had a good marriage and now it turns out that she didn't. Where does that leave the rest of us?"

"Indeed," said Isabel, who then quoted a Russian poet I'd never heard of. The line had something to do with nothingness. "The fact that perfect Lynn with the perfect husband and the perfect career could have something imperfect happen to her puts me in touch with the possibility that my own romance might be suspect."

"Let's get back to you, Lynn," said Penny, who felt, as we all did, that Isabel's romance *was* suspect. "You're not sure if you love Kip, is that right?"

"Yes," I said. "I hate what he did, but he was a communicator, and we all know what a rare thing that is. And, being a carpenter, he fixes things around the house. I can't stress enough how key that is in a marriage."

"Very practical, but he violated your trust," she said. "There can't be a relationship without trust. Which is why going on with the marriage is not an option, in my opinion."

"Not an option," the others chorused.

"So I urge you to hash out a settlement with Kip," said Penny, "and move on with your life. If you can get him to keep his mouth shut and act the part of Mr. Sensitive Husband, there's no way it'll make the newspapers. As far as the public will be concerned, you two will still be married and you, my friend, will still be a power hitter."

"I'm not sure, Penny," I said. "That kind of a scheme just isn't me."

"Listen," she said, "and listen carefully. Forget how confused you are. Forget how hurt you are. Forget how *schemes aren't you*. Get Kip to agree to 'playing your husband' and hang on to your professional reputation. That's what's important here, isn't it?"

The debate lasted through three rounds of cocktails, plus the appetizers that Gail managed to scarf down before the rest of us had much of a shot at them. In the end, everybody agreed with Penny: I should divorce Kip and keep it a secret. I drove home to Mt. Kisco feeling bolstered by their support but no better about my predicament.

I CONSIDERED WHAT to do about Kip and me during the rest of that week and into the following week but came to no conclusions. I was in emotional gridlock, couldn't think clearly enough to make a decision. Part of me—the part that was a pushover for Kip's attempts at conversation and his offers to cook dinner and his vows of undying love for me—wanted to hang in with him, give us more time, try to get past the hurt. But the other part of me—the part that kept picturing him and his popsy performing sexual acrobatics on my ceiling—wanted to kill him, or, more realistically, coerce him into agreeing to Penny's arrangement.

Every day I drove into the city and saw clients and did my radio show and carried on as if nothing were amiss, and every day I felt like an imposter waiting to be found out. For a person who was used to taking action, being stuck sucked.

There can't be anything worse than this indecision of mine, I fretted, as I lay awake in bed one night.

The second I thought the thought, I knew I was asking for trouble, knew I was done for. There are lots of things that are worse than indecision, of course, and in short order I was about to experience more than my share of them.

4

THE PHONE RANG as I was making coffee and it rang again as I was spooning sugar into my coffee and it rang a third time and a fourth and a fifth as I was actually drinking the coffee, but I was running late so I let the answering machine pick up all the calls.

They're probably from Kip's girlfriend, I muttered, wondering if they really had stopped seeing each other. For the past several mornings, he had gotten up even earlier than I had and vanished. I didn't know what his schedule was anymore and didn't much care.

"Hi, Diane," I said when I arrived at the office minutes before my nine o'clock appointment. "Everything okay here?" As opposed to at my place.

Diane shook her head, and the gesture made more noise than your typical head shaking. She had gone to a beauty salon the night before that specialized in braiding and beading—the Venus/Serena Williams kind of braiding and beading. She looked like a soul sister except that she was Irish.

"You've had a lot of phone calls," she said.

"From whom?"

She perused her note pad. "Your friend Penny Herter called. Your friend Isabel Green called. Your friend Gail Orrick called. Your friend Sarah Pepper called. Then there were the—"

"Hang on a second." I glanced at my watch. It was nine on the dot. My first client was due any time. "I'll get back to everybody later," I told Diane, assuming my pals were probably wondering how I was holding up. Funny that they'd all picked the same morning to check in though. "Right now I'd better head to my desk. We've got wall-to-wall clients today, if I remember correctly."

"We did have them. We don't have them anymore, Dr. Wyman."

"What are you talking about, Diane?"

"Those were the other calls I was trying to tell you about. Some of the clients have cancelled for today."

"Some? How many?" I said, surprised. Sessions with me were hard to come by. I had a waiting list a year long.

"Three."

"Three? That's odd. It isn't snowing. There isn't a transit strike. It's not a holiday. Is there a flu bug going around?"

"The clients didn't say why they were cancelling, Dr. Wyman. But they did say that they understood about having to pay for their missed session since they gave you less than twenty-four hours notice."

"I see. Did you reschedule them?"

"I offered to, but they said they're not coming back."

"Not coming—" I snatched the appointment book off Diane's desk and read the names of the defectors. Ben. Peter. Fritz. Not coming back? Why in the world not? They were doing so well on the program, were making such progress, especially Fritz, a salesman at a local Porsche dealer, who was on the verge of losing his job when he came to me. He had no trouble communicating with male customers, who took it as a given that a Porsche salesman named Fritz would speak with an unintelligible German accent and have a frosty demeanor and answer all of their questions with a look of disdain. But he was hopeless with women customers, of whom there was a growing number, because they expected him to be polite, helpful, solicitous, and when he wasn't they either stormed out of the dealership in a huff or were reduced to tears (and, therefore, did not buy a car). Then he began working with me. Within a few short weeks, he responded beautifully to the Wyman Method, to the point where he was actually able to smile at the female customers and say, "May I offer you a beverage before explaining to you what torque is?"

"Maybe the clients just got busy," Diane suggested with a shrug.

"Busy?" I said, genuinely perplexed. "What could be a higher priority for these men than improving the quality of their relationships with women?"

I SAW THE clients that did show up, including Sam, the owner of a plumbing supply company, whose wife was frustrated by his inability to commiserate with her about her aches and pains—a common problem with men. It's not that they don't care if the woman they love has a nervous stomach or a yeast infection or an arthritic pinky finger that acts up on damp mornings. They just don't want to *talk* about it.

"We're going to spend more time on our empathetic responses today," I told Sam at the beginning of the session. "The goal is to teach you how to show support for Carolyn's medical issues instead of giving her the impression that you're insensitive to them."

"Hey, I'm not—"

"Sam. Sam. There's no point in being defensive. Not in this room. I suggest you just go with what I'll be asking you to say. Now, here's your copy of the script. Let's get started."

He swiped the piece of paper out of my hand. Boy, was he hostile. A lot of them were at first. They couldn't get it through their heads that I was there to help them. But then what do you expect from a species that leaves the toilet seat up, belches out loud and falls asleep after making love?

I turned on the tape recorder. "Repeat after me, okay, Sam? 'Tell me *all* about your symptoms, Carolyn.' I specifically want the emphasis on the 'all.' It will indicate to your wife that you really, truly want to share her pain."

Sam balked. "Doctors say that type of stuff, not husbands."

"Is that right?" I said, nodding. I was used to this sort of resistance. They came around eventually. "Then why don't you tell me what you would normally say when Carolyn discusses her ailments with you."

"I would normally say, 'Do we have any beer in the refrigerator?' Or maybe, 'I'm taking the dog out for a walk.' Something like that."

"In other words, you would change the subject."

"You got it. Who wants to hear her bellyaching?"

"She's not bellyaching, she's *reporting*. She's trying to establish a connection with you because she loves you, Sam, and she wants to feel that you love her too. That's what this is about."

He heaved a sigh. "If you ask me, she's a hypochondriac. Every woman I've ever met is a hypochondriac."

"The script, Sam."

He sighed again, then leaned closer to the microphone. " 'Tell me *all* about your symptoms, Carolyn.' "

"Great. That wasn't so hard, was it? Now, let's move on. I want you to practice the following words over and over: 'I'm sorry.' "

"Why should I practice 'I'm sorry'? I don't make her sick."

I wasn't so sure. " 'I'm sorry' isn't always an apology, Sam. Women often use it as a listening response, to show that they're commiserating with the speaker. When Carolyn has described her symptoms, I want you to nod your head and say, 'I'm sorry,' and it'll work much better than 'Do we have any beer in the refrigerator?'"

"So that's all there is to this communication business?" asked Sam. "I say 'I'm sorry' even if I didn't do anything wrong?"

I smiled. "Why don't you try it at home and let me know?"

SAM WAS MY last appointment of the day, and as soon as his session was over, I returned my friends' phone calls. I couldn't reach anybody except Penny.

"Lynn, how are you?" she said in that concerned way people have when they're addressing someone who's had a death in the family.

"I'm doing pretty well," I said, "under the circumstances." Kip hadn't died; he'd just thrown a grenade at our marriage.

"You are?" she said, sounding as if I shouldn't be.

"Reasonably, yes," I said. "I'm not in the best spirits but I'm functioning. Work is a wonderful tonic. I really can forget my problems when I'm interacting with clients."

"Clients? You mean none of them cancelled?"

I was taken aback by her question. "As a matter of fact, three of them cancelled this morning," I said warily. "Why do you ask?"

"My God, Lynn. You haven't heard, have you?"

"Heard what?"

She groaned. "Let me close my door first, okay?" Without waiting for an answer, she shut the door to her office and came back to the phone. "So nobody's told you?"

"No." I was getting nervous now. "Why don't you tell me?"

"I hate to be the one. Promise me you won't kill the messenger."

"I promise."

"All right." She lowered her voice. "Somebody tipped off the media about Kip's affair. It's out. Your secret's out. And it's been out for days, apparently."

My heart thumped. *Baddaboom.* I could feel my left breast vibrate.

"You were right to worry about the credibility thing," she went on. "The reporter did a total hatchet job on the Wyman Method, suggesting that a man would be crazy to go to you for help when you can't hang on to your own husband."

I couldn't speak at first. I was having trouble breathing.

"Hello? Are you still there, Lynn?"

"Barely." My mouth was so dry my lips were sticking together. I needed water. Or, better, a scotch. "I just don't see how it's possible that this reporter found out about Kip and me. We're still living together, still a couple as far as the outside world is concerned."

"Nevertheless, there's a cover story about the two of you. It's all there in black and white."

"A cover story? I'm not famous enough for a cover story."

"It's in the *National Enquirer*, Lynn. If they don't have dirt on Oprah or Kathie Lee, they take what they can get."

I was on the cover of a tabloid. How dignified. Obviously, Sam and the others who'd kept their appointments with me hadn't seen the story. "So everybody in America will read about me as they're waiting on the supermarket checkout line?"

"I'm afraid so. It's a rotten break but you'll get through it."

"How?"

"You'll issue denials and claim you were treated unfairly and hope the public will view you as a sympathetic figure as opposed to an incompetent one."

"I am not incompetent!"

"Of course you're not. But people may imply that you are, the same way this reporter did. Look, Lynn. I think the work you do entitles you to the Nobel Peace Prize, but it has made you a target. You've set yourself up as the high priestess of communication—the expert of all experts when it comes to teaching men how to be more sensitive—so you're bound to take a few hits about Kip."

"In other words, now that the *Enquirer* has run their story, it'll be open season on me."

"There's sure to be more coverage, yes. I'm sorry, Lynn. So very sorry."

"You have nothing to be sorry about, Penny. The person who should be sorry is the one who gave the story to the *Enquirer*. It was Kip's girlfriend, I assume."

"I doubt it. She wasn't even identified by name. In fact, she was hardly mentioned. The bulk of the story was about you and Kip. You, mostly. There's only one person who could have given them that information, Lynn. One person who could have *sold* them that information. You understand that, don't you? In your heart of hearts?"

"You're saying that Kip—"

"Had to be. He sensed that you were about to throw him out. He knew he was going to need money. He probably figured he could pitch the story to the *Enquirer* and make enough to keep him in screwdrivers for a while."

"Kip." I shook my head disbelievingly. He had seemed so genuine in the beginning, so honest. How could I have misread him so badly, been so off in my judgment? He had not only slept around, he had sold me out. A double whammy.

"Do you want me to hop in a cab and come over there?" asked Penny, whose office was on the other side of town.

"Nope. Thanks," I said. "I've got my radio show to do."

"That should be interesting. If I were you, I'd expect some callers with inquiring minds."

I HAD CALLERS with inquiring minds, all right. They didn't want to talk about their lives; they wanted—demanded—the dirt on mine. Oh, there were plenty of people who hadn't read the *Enquirer* story or even heard about it. There were also a few kindly souls who had read the story but expressed their support for me nonetheless. But, as Penny had tried to warn me, there were troublemakers—busybodies who had read the story and responded by assaulting me with remarks like "Why should we listen to you?" and "You don't know what you're talking about" and "I'm not calling in to this show anymore."

It was that last shot that really resonated with the station manager. As I was packing up and getting ready to leave the studio, he put his hand on my shoulder, said it was too bad that I was having trouble at home and added ominously, "We'll have to keep our eye on this thing."

"Keep our eye on what thing?"

"On whether there's going to be major fallout here. Audiences are fickle, Lynn. When you lose 'em, they don't usually come back."

"But I haven't lost them," I maintained. "I've only shaken their faith in me a little."

I was indulging in some wishful thinking, of course. I was hoping that the *Enquirer* would be the only news outlet that would run the story about Kip and me; that there'd be a flurry of interest in us and then everybody would move on to the next train wreck; that my audience, not to mention my clients, *would* come back.

WHEN I GOT home that night, Kip was in the kitchen, standing at the stove and stirring whatever was in a large pot.

"I made chili," he said cheerfully, "just the way you like it."

I stared at him. He had sold our sordid saga to a tabloid, ruining the reputation I'd spent my entire life building, and he was talking to me about chili? The guy wasn't just a shit; he was pathological.

And I was furious. "You've got it wrong," I said, elbowing past him and grabbing the handles of the pot, which were hot and burned my fingers but who had the presence of mind to think about using potholders. "*Here's* the way I like your fucking chili." I poured all of it into the sink, down the drain, the same place my marriage had gone.

"Lynn! What are you—"

"Get out," I said, as his culinary effort went *glub glub* into the disposal. "Pack a bag and get out, Kip. My lawyer will arrange for you to pick up the rest of your things at some future date."

He started crying, naturally. "But why, Lynn? Why now? I thought you were keeping an open mind about us."

"I was," I said, trembling with anger. "But that was before this." I held up the *Enquirer*. I'd bought a copy on my way over to the radio station.

"Can I see?" he said, as if he didn't have a clue what all the fuss was about. I rolled the newspaper up into a tight little missile and hurled it at him. It hit him in the nuts, poor baby.

I watched as he uncurled the paper and pretended to read the story for the first time.

"How much did they pay you?" I demanded.

"Pay *me*? I didn't have anything to do with this," he protested through his sobs.

"Tell me another one."

"It's true. I didn't give them the story. I'm as blown away by it as you are."

"Sure you are. Okay, then who did give them the story? Your girlfriend?"

"Maybe, but I haven't spoken to her since I broke it off with her, so I can't confirm it."

"Oh, come on, Kip. It wasn't your girlfriend and you know it. She couldn't possibly have had enough specific, intimately detailed, exquisitely *personal* information about me to fill a paragraph, much less a cover story, unless you spent the past three months educating her about my life, which I highly doubt. You two were much too busy screwing each other's brains out to discuss linguistics."

He shook his head, wiped his eyes.

"You sold them the story and now you're getting out of here. I'll arrange to have your things brought to you once you have a new address. Have I made myself clear?"

"I'm going, I'm going." But he didn't make a move. Instead, he just stood there, his eyes still brimming with tears. He kept glancing around the kitchen, a wistful expression on his face, as if he were taking one last look at the room in which he'd spent so many happy hours preparing our dinners.

"What is it?" I said, assuming he was about to burst forth with some expression of his feelings, some anecdote involving his relationship with his father, some awful unburdening.

"I—"

"You what?" I said impatiently.

"I was wondering—" His gaze rested on the shelf of cookbooks. "When you're dividing everything up, would it be okay if I got the Julia Childs, the Silver Palates, and the Marcella Hazans? You know, like just the classics?"

Swell, I thought. Some guys kiss and tell. I picked one who cooks and tells.

What I also thought was that I knew far too much about men at that point to ever let myself fall in love with one. Yes, Kip was different from the clients who came to me for help, but look how he turned out. It was my opinion that, generally speaking, men were clods—simple creatures who farted without apology and left their clothes wherever they fell and assumed that women who took vacations together were dykes. And yet, I wanted to teach them Womenspeak, to enlighten them, to save them. *That* fire continued to burn within me. The question was: were there men out there who would hire me—in spite of this new unpleasantness?

5

UNPLEASANTNESS. TALK ABOUT an understatement.

The next few months were a nightmare and I've tried to block out entire periods of them, but in the interest of full disclosure I'll report the highlights (or, rather, the lowlights) as best I can.

Immediately after the story ran in the *National Enquirer*, I noticed only a trickle-down effect on my practice. A client cancelled here; a client cancelled there. Nothing I couldn't handle. Not a wholesale evacuation, by any means.

Then, just when I'd been lulled into thinking I was going to be all right, the *Enquirer* story was followed by a torrent of bitchy, almost gleeful articles about my marital troubles in the mainstream media. In other words, the same publications that had deified me dissed me. And they not only dissed me, they dissed the Wyman Method, which was even more painful to me. I'd spent my life creating and then refining the program and now, simply because my husband revealed himself to be a jerk, my work was invalid? It wasn't fair. It really wasn't.

Naturally, I tried to counterattack. I begged all the editors in town to let me present my side, but they weren't interested, wouldn't even return my phone calls. Suddenly, I was "over" as far as they were concerned. Washed up. Not worth bothering about.

Why didn't I take advantage of my radio show and my newspaper column and my monthly appearances on *Good Morning America* in order to thrust myself back into the public's good graces? Why didn't

I seize these opportunities to restate my case for the Wyman Method? Because they were no longer available to me. I'd been cut loose from all of them. "You're not credible anymore," is how it was explained to me in a tone of voice you might use to distance yourself from someone with an extremely contagious disease.

It's amazing how quickly you get dropped, cancelled, terminated from these sorts of gigs. Whenever there's a scandal or a controversy or even a perceived misstep on your part, they barely blink before pulling the plug on you. I know I sound like my friend Sarah, the children's book author who was bitter toward show business types, but it truly made my head spin how little time it took before I ceased to exist for them.

Even my literary agent dumped me. I had hoped—foolishly, it seems now—that although my publicist had dumped me and my television and radio agent had dumped me and my business manager had dumped me, I could go back to the arena of my first success: the book world. I'll write another bestseller, I thought—the big important sequel that publishers have been hounding me to write. Well, forget that. My literary agent informed me that, after "testing the waters," she was afraid that the market for any book by Lynn Wyman had dried up. She added that I was free to seek representation elsewhere.

That left my private practice. Happily, I still had a few clients. Just enough clients to keep Diane on salary but not enough clients to keep my house in Mt. Kisco. What with my dwindling income and the alimony I had agreed to pay my scumbag soon-to-be-ex-husband, I wasn't the money machine I once was. The truth is, I was barely managing. I was able to sell the house but was not able to make a profit on it, thanks to the changing tastes of home buyers (they weren't in the market for "rustic" anymore; they were in the market for "casual elegance"). And the rent on the modest garden apartment I moved into sapped most of what I earned from my practice.

I wasn't starving and I had a roof over my head, but what I'm saying is that I went from being a somebody to a nobody and it hurt. I felt like a pariah and I acted the part. I slunk around the streets of New York, as if I didn't belong on the same pavement as all those snappy, purposeful-looking career women hurrying along in their business suits and sneakers. I hid in my office at lunchtime, preferring to watch Diane stencil her fingernails rather than run into the movers and shakers who frequented my old haunts. And I began to neglect my appearance, just stopped washing my hair, putting on makeup, rolling on deodorant. It's a wonder I held onto any clients at all.

A particularly tough moment came when I was standing in the produce section of the grocery store in Mt. Kisco, trying to decide if I should splurge on a head of Boston lettuce for dinner instead of going with my usual cheapo iceberg. The well-dressed man standing next to me (he was buying the Boston) tapped me on the shoulder and said, "Aren't you Lynn Wyman? The one Imus doesn't even bother to make fun of anymore?"

Never mind that the question was as idiotic as it was rude. I was totally humiliated by it. I cried my eyes out that night, the man's words echoing in my brain. But then, while I was taking a break from the crying, I turned on *The Tonight Show* and, lo and behold, there was some self-help author, some Lynn Wyman wannabe, bragging about *her* program for teaching men how to be more sensitive! Instantly, I stopped feeling sorry for myself and got mad. Mad at her. Mad at Kip. Mad at all the people who hailed the Wyman Method as a breakthrough and then jumped on the bandwagon to ridicule it.

Well, the joke's on them, I decided as I tore apart the iceberg lettuce and crammed huge chunks into my mouth, my appetite returning even though my food budget hadn't. I'm not going to let them crush me, not going to let them dismiss the theory I've believed in since childhood. I'll find a way to get their attention. I'll show them.

Of course, I didn't know *how* I would show them, but at least I was thinking positively.

One chilly night in February, not long after I had this change in attitude, I ventured out to Penny's apartment for dinner. She was having the Brain Trust over. Since my friends had been the only bright spot during this otherwise bleak period in my life, each of them spending time with me, distracting me, letting me vent, I was looking forward to seeing everybody.

But when I arrived at Penny's two-bedroom duplex in Gramercy Park, they were all engaged in a lively conversation about work—Penny's public relations business, Gail's documentary filmmaking, Isabel's cat photographs, Sarah's children's books. I felt incredibly left out, as there wasn't much about *my* work that was worth talking about.

I was relieved when the discussion shifted to their personal lives—Penny's latest conquest, Gail's needy husband, Isabel's commitment-phobic lover, Sarah's on-again-off-again spouse—until I realized that I had nothing I wanted to contribute to that subject, either. So much for thinking positively. I was right back down in the pits again.

Eventually, we ate dinner. Since none of us was a cook, we had pizza delivered from the place around the corner.

I wasn't used to ordering pizza. Kip used to make his own for the two of us. From scratch. The dough and everything.

The memory of my faithless husband caused another, deeper dip in my spirits. After dinner, I sat there in Penny's living room and nodded and smiled and threw out a sentence or two if anyone glanced in my direction, but mostly I was out of it, on automatic pilot.

At some point during the evening, I reached absentmindedly into the large wicker basket next to my chair and began to leaf through the magazines that were piled inside. I no longer subscribed to any of them, both for budgetary reasons and because I was boycotting them for having treated me harshly, and so I didn't particularly care who was writing what about whom. Flipping through their pages was just a reflex action, something to do with my hands while the others talked.

And then I spotted the current issue of *Fortune* magazine and pulled it onto my lap. It was the cover story that grabbed me, made my pulse quicken, made me sit straight up in the chair.

"America's Toughest Bosses."

Those were the words printed in bold black letters at the top of the cover page, followed by: "Find out what makes these men and women a major headache to work for."

Okay, I thought. You hooked me.

I opened the magazine to the story and read on. First, there was an actual list, the way *Fortune* lists "America's Most Admired Companies" and "The 50 Most Powerful Women in American Business" and, of course, "The Fortune 500." And then there were the descriptions and biographies and photographs of the moguls themselves.

I scanned the list. Scattered among the hot shots were such notoriously tough bosses as "Neutron" Jack Welch of GE, Michael Eisner of Disney, Steve Jobs of Apple Computer, Ronald Perelman of Revlon, and Linda Wachner of the Warnaco Group.

But I wasn't interested in them. Nope. Before I even opened the magazine I knew instinctively which tough boss I wanted to read about: the guy whose picture was on the cover; the guy whom *Fortune* put in the numero uno position on their list; the guy who, according to the editors, was the biggest pain-in-the-ass in corporate America.

His name was Brandon Brock and he was the president and CEO of Finefoods, Inc., makers of breakfast cereals, snack foods, frozen food products, soft drinks, and, following the company's recent acquisition of Bakewell Industries, cookies, cakes, and candy bars.

According to *Fortune*, while the forty-five-year-old Brock was a brilliant businessman who had turned Finefoods into a lean, profitable, well-run machine, he was a handful in the personality department—a charmer when it suited him and an arrogant, insensitive, imperious brute when it didn't. (His motto? "I don't get ulcers. I give ulcers.") He was described as an alpha male with a quick temper, a low tolerance for those who didn't put in the hours he did, and—get this—*an inability to communicate with the women who worked for him*.

Isn't that last characteristic interesting, I mused, suddenly feeling more alive than I had in months. So he's got a problem communicating with women. Not a good thing for a boss in this day and age. Not a smart thing.

I'd never met Brandon Brock, only faintly recognized the name, but judging by the magazine's assessment of him, I'd met hundreds of men like him and I knew how they operated, knew how they ticked, knew how they *talked*. The only difference was that, unlike my clients, Brandon Brock was extremely visible, someone with a high profile, someone in the public eye. Which meant that if he were ever taught how to communicate with women—by me, for instance—it would make news. *I* would make news.

Yessss, I thought as a concrete plan began to take shape in my head. This guy could be my ticket back, my "I'll show them." All I've got to do is get him to submit to the Wyman Method and—bingo!—he'll become a more effective boss and I'll rise from the ashes.

Of course, I didn't have a clue how I would even make contact with Mr. Brock, but when you're as desperate as I was, you don't worry about tiny details. You just go for broke, which is what I was. Well, not broke, but almost.

"Everybody!" I said excitedly, waving my arms in the air, bursting in on my friends' conversation. "I think I've found a solution to my problem."

"Which problem?" said Gail. "You have more than one."

"Yes, but they're all related," I said. "And, with a little luck, they're about to disappear."

"How?" asked Isabel.

I held up the magazine. "Because of this."

"My copy of *Fortune*?" said Penny.

"Right. Take a look at the man on the cover," I said, barely able to contain myself.

"It's Brandon Brock," Penny said. "He runs Finefoods. The company's done well since he took over, although there are some who think he's in hot water with his board of directors."

"So it says here," I remarked.

"Apparently, his management style isn't the greatest," Penny went on. "He's not a warm and fuzzy type, let's put it that way."

"Which must be why he's number one on *Fortune*'s list of America's Toughest Bosses," I said.

"Exactly," Penny said. "And he beat out a lot of assholes to get there. I hear he treats his people like total underlings. Whenever he goes on a business trip, he lands at the airport, hops into a limo and takes off, while one of his minions has to wait for his luggage and bring it to the hotel in a taxi."

"He's not bad looking though," said Isabel, moving closer to get a better angle of the cover shot. "He has amazing eyes, mystical eyes."

I turned the magazine over to see what she was talking about, having been too caught up in the article to actually study the photograph.

Oh. So *that's* Brandon Brock, I thought, more than a little curious about the man who, God willing, would save my life.

I had to admit that the eyes were amazing (I wasn't so sure about "mystical"), but only because they were so deeply set, so hollowed out. And blue. A steel blue. A hard blue.

The other startling aspect of his face was his hair. It was blond, a tawny, golden blond that you don't often see on men unless they're named Lars. His eyebrows, too, were this light khaki, and they were substantial, bushy, or did they only seem outsized, in contrast to the almost hidden, deep-socketed blue eyes?

He had a long, pronounced nose and a solid chin and lips so thin that the top one seemed to disappear into his skin, speaking of which, his complexion was ruddy, high colored, as if he were an outdoorsman, a weekend warrior. And, judging by the broad shoulders visible in the head shot of him, he was a large man, a beefy man, Paul Bunyan in a Brooks Brothers suit.

He wasn't conventionally handsome, obviously, but there was a presence about him, a strength.

"So what does this guy have to do with your situation, Lynn?" Penny asked.

I swallowed, tried not to lose my nerve. "The article maintains that he has trouble communicating with the women who work for him. Well, I happen to know someone who can help him change that."

"You?" Penny said.

"Me," I said. "Brandon Brock is going to become my client—my most famous client. And once he completes my program and becomes fluent in the language of Womenspeak, he's going to be a walking endorsement for the Wyman Method and put me back on the map."

Nobody spoke. They all stared at me. I couldn't tell if they thought I was a genius or a wacko.

It was Penny who broke the ice. "It's an interesting idea," she said diplomatically, eyeing the others, "but a little ambitious, don't you think, Lynn? I mean, how in the world would you convince him to become a client? How would you get a meeting with him, for starters?"

"The same way you land your accounts," I said. "You zero in on them and go for the kill."

"But you and Brandon Brock don't travel in the same circles," Penny said. "You're not a member of the business community."

"No, but you are, Penny. Maybe you'll help me get a meeting with him. Once my foot is in the door, I'll do the rest."

"It's just not that simple," she said. "These CEOs have layers and layers of people to penetrate. Besides, the companies I work with are large to midsize companies. Finefoods is a mega-company. I don't have any contacts there."

"I'd be glad to put you together with my astrologer," said Isabel. "She'd be able to tell you the best day and time to approach this man."

"I appreciate that," I said, "but I'm going to do it the old fashioned way: pester the guy into submission. And once I do, I'll get my radio show back and my newspaper column and my appearances on *Good Morning America* and maybe even that pilot that CBS was so high on and then dropped."

"I told you those people were predators," Sarah muttered. "They've probably taken all your ideas and found some former Miss America to mouth the words. Shallow bastards."

"Let me ask you something, Lynn," said Penny. "I have to ask it because I'm a publicist and it's my job to anticipate how an idea like yours might backfire with the media."

"Go ahead."

"What if you actually do coax Brock into becoming a client and then the Wyman Method doesn't work on him?"

"Doesn't work?" I shook my head, refusing to even contemplate that possibility. The Wyman Method would work and I would get my career back on track and that was all there was to it.

"We're on your side, Lynn," said Gail. "It isn't that we're not. But you've been through hell this year and we'd hate to see you have to deal with more failure."

This was frustrating. They didn't understand that I was beyond worrying about failure. I was focused on picking up where I left off, on regaining my self-esteem, on subsisting on more than iceberg lettuce.

"Gail's right," said Penny. "You *have* had a rough year. It's terrific that you've recaptured your zest for your work and feel up to launching a comeback, but wouldn't it make more sense to take it slowly? You could go after less controversial businessmen. I'll get you some names, if you want."

"What I want is Brandon Brock," I said firmly. "He's the key to my comeback. I just know it."

There was more silence and a lot of looking down at the floor. Clearly, they thought I was bonkers.

"Listen. All of you," I said. "You're skeptical about this plan of mine and I don't blame you. You're probably wondering how a person who has stopped washing her hair intends to snag the CEO of Finefoods as a client. But I'm going to wash my hair. I'm going to pull myself together. I have a reason to pull myself together now. Can't you see that?"

"Of course we can," said Sarah, running her fingers through her own gorgeous hair. "It's just— "

"So, since you *are* skeptical," I continued, "let's do this. Let's make a bet."

"A bet?" asked Gail with alarm. Her deadbeat husband had a gambling problem. It was on account of all his *bets* that he was sponging off of her.

"Yes," I said, my voice rising with my enthusiasm. "A friendly little wager. Here it is: if I can't turn Brandon Brock, the CEO of Finefoods, Inc., into a man who communicates with women, then I'll scrap the Wyman Method and you'll never hear me utter another word about it."

"You're serious?" asked Sarah.

"Very," I said. "I'll move on with my life and find another way to earn a living."

"How long are you giving yourself to accomplish this minor miracle?" said Penny.

"Six months," I said, pulling the number out of my head. "Within six months, Brandon Brock will be a pussy cat and *I* will be the one on the cover of a magazine."

"Not a pussy cat," said Isabel, who didn't like people to use cats' names in vain.

"Sorry," I said. "How about a teddy bear?"

"Much better," she said.

"Do we have a bet?" I asked expectantly.

No one had the heart not to go along with me.

Sure we have a bet, they all agreed, humoring the mental patient.

We clasped hands and hugged, everybody wishing me luck and complimenting me on my grit and saying they'd be rooting for me. For the first time in months, I was optimistic about the future. I only hoped that Brandon Brock wouldn't get himself ousted from his company before I had a crack at him.

6

OVER THE NEXT couple of days, I read and reread the section of the *Fortune* story that focused on Brandon Brock. I also searched the internet for anything else I could find on him. Here's what I learned. He was born and raised in tony Grosse Pointe, Michigan, the middle son of a General Motors executive and his homemaker wife. Not an impoverished childhood, obviously.

He went east to boarding school at Choate, to college at the University of Pennylvania and to business school at Wharton, then worked his way up in the corporate world, moving from Colgate-Palmolive to Nestlé and, finally, to Finefoods, where he'd been the company's chairman and CEO for just over two years—at forty-five, the youngest leader in Finefoods' history.

Married to the former Margaret Covington, a Grosse Pointe Junior Leaguer from whom he was now divorced (no children), he was a passionate sports fan who had a suite at Madison Square Garden for the Knicks and Rangers games, a box at Yankee stadium for the Yankees games, and front row seats at the U.S. Open tennis tournament, of which Finefoods was a sponsor. In fact, it was through tennis that he displayed his own athleticism. He was a fierce competitor, according to a *Business Week* profile, who expected to win every time he stepped onto the court and was not a pleasure to be around when he didn't (what a surprise).

As for his much-talked-about management style, he was described in every article as a shrewd, innovative marketer whose notoriously short fuse was mitigated by his keen eye for trends. Profits were up at Finefoods since he took the helm, but morale was down, particularly if you weren't a member of his "inner circle," which did not, according to *Fortune*, include women.

He really sounded like a throwback, a guy's guy who either didn't believe that women (he probably called them "gals") were as capable as men, or didn't feel comfortable around them (unless he was coming on to them), or both. I practically salivated at the thought of getting him into my office and putting him through the program. He was the perfect candidate for the Wyman Method. The trick would be to persuade him of that.

I decided to begin my campaign by taking the traditional route. I picked up the phone and called his office at Finefoods, whose headquarters were in White Plains, only twenty minutes from Mt. Kisco.

"Mr. Brock's office," answered a nasal-voiced woman of a certain age. I could picture her. There was no doubt in my mind that she was in her fifties, presentable but not pretty, and totally, doggedly, slavishly devoted to her boss. Brandon Brock, I was sure, would never hire a secretary who called attention to herself and away from him, never choose some uppity wench who might ask for a raise, ask for a promotion, ask for a long lunch. He would employ one who stayed late without a single sigh of complaint, who did his Christmas shopping, who picked up his dry cleaning, who made his life smoother at the expense of her own. She would be a throwback, just as he was. A woman he could dominate. And, I guessed, she was not his only secretary. He probably had several.

"Yes, good morning," I said. "I'd like to speak to Mr. Brock please."

"And whom shall I say is calling?" Yup, a throwback. Today's secretaries ask, "And *you* are . . . ?"

"Lynn Wyman," I said. I waited a second or two for her to recognize my name, but she didn't. Oh, how the mighty had fallen.

"Mr. Brock doesn't know me personally," I pressed on, "but once he's been made aware of my résumé, I think he'll speak to me."

"If you're inquiring about a position at Finefoods," she said, "I'll be happy to transfer you to our human resources department and they can advise you as to where to send your résumé. Please hold."

Before I could protest, she was gone. Since I had no interest in chatting with the human resources department, I hung up and called back.

"Mr. Brock's office," said the secretary, even more crisply and efficiently than the first time, unless I was imagining things.

"Hello, this is Lynn Wyman. I called a minute or two ago, hoping to speak to Mr. Brock, and you transfered me to Human Resources. But I'm not calling about a job at your company. I'm calling to schedule an appointment with Mr. Brock."

"I see. What is the nature of your business with him?"

None of your beeswax. "I'd like to discuss his possible participation in an internationally acclaimed program involving men and communication."

"Ah. Then let me transfer you to our corporate public relations department. They handle all queries regarding Mr. Brock's availability for lectures and seminars."

She was gone again. I hung up and called back. Nobody gets anywhere in this world without persistence, right?

"Mr. Brock's office," she said, a little wearily.

"Hi. It's Lynn Wyman. I hate to keep calling, but I guess I didn't make it clear that I'd like to come in and meet with Mr. Brock."

"I'm sorry, but Mr. Brock is tied up," said his gatekeeper, trying to hurry me off the phone. I could tell she thought I was a stalker now. For all I knew he had lots of them—rejected girlfriends who couldn't accept reality, women who all looked like Glenn Close in *Fatal Attraction*. Scary, in other words.

"He must be very busy," I said, "but would you just take a peek at his calendar and tell me when he has an opening? I'd really like to speak to him about becoming a client."

"A client," she said with new understanding. "Then you're with one of the agencies competing for the Finefoods account. I'll transfer you to our advertising department."

I was sent yet again into telephone netherworld. So much for taking the traditional route.

Okay, I thought. Now what?

For my next act, I wrote Brock a letter, a very professional letter laying out my credentials, hyping the Wyman Method and its impressive rate of success, spelling out the ways in which I felt it could make him an even more effective chief executive. I added that it was the *Fortune* piece on him that had brought his "communication issues" to my attention, and I predicted that if he did become a client and underwent the program, he would never again be the recipient of such negative publicity.

I called his office to get his fax number but, not wanting to piss off Ms. I've-got-a-stick-up-my-nose, I disguised my voice.

She gave me the number. I thanked her and hung up. And then I faxed the letter and waited by the phone for the rest of the day. I knew full well I'd never get a response so fast, but I didn't want to leave the house, just in case. It was after five when Sarah called to invite me over for an impromptu dinner. With only a carton of milk and a loaf of bread in my refrigerator, I was very grateful.

SARAH PEPPER LIVED in a castle. Well, not a castle, but an impeccably restored, nineteenth century colonial fit for a queen—the queen of children's books. Set on twenty or so acres in South Salem, a horsey, bucolic town near Mt. Kisco, "Dogwood," as the house had been named by Sarah and her husband Edward, rested regally at the end of a winding, mile-long driveway, its sweeping front lawn dotted with—you guessed it—dogwood trees. The Peppers kept an apartment in Manhattan, but Dogwood was their primary residence, their pride and joy, the tangible evidence of their success, of Sarah's success. It mirrored her personality too. It was grand, well tended to, had good bones. It was showoff-y, occasionally nauseatingly so, but it was also beautifully appointed, just as Sarah was.

It was Justine, the Peppers' longtime "house manager," who let me inside and then accounced me. Sarah, who had a lady-of-the-manor complex as well as a paranoia toward Hollywood, always made Justine announce people. She also made Justine wear a black uniform with a white apron, refer to guests as Mr. or Ms. So-and-so, even if they were children, and refer to Sarah herself as madame or, when she was speaking *of* Sarah but not directly *to* her, *the* madame. Penny, Isabel, and Gail made fun of our friend's highfalutin' side—Sarah was trailer trash from Kansas before coming to New York and striking it rich in children's publishing—but I had come to sympathize with it, now that I, too, was trying to reinvent myself.

"There you are, Lynn," said Sarah as she descended the staircase, her manicured hand moving gracefully down the banister. She was a knockout in her clinging red sweater and skin-tight black capri pants, her blue-black hair combed straight down her back.

She kissed me hello and we walked arm in arm into the library, its shelves filled exclusively with her own books—U.S. editions, foreign editions, book club editions, movie tie-in editions. There was no escaping whose dominion this was.

"Will Edward be joining us?" I asked after Justine had served us drinks and a few nibbles from a silver platter. I knew that the Pepper children wouldn't be around; they'd been shuttled off to boarding school in Europe.

"God, no," said Sarah. "We're on the outs again. He's staying at our place in the city. Probably has a babe with him."

"Are you saying that he's seeing someone else?" What was it with men anyway? Now that they had their Propecia and their Prozac and their Viagra and were, therefore, no longer bald, depressed, or impotent, they acted like idiots.

"Who knows," she said with a disinterested shrug. "We have a Don't Ask, Don't Tell policy around here. What we do during our time-outs we keep to ourselves. We don't have the kind of marriage you had with Kip, Lynn."

It was my turn to shrug. "I'm not sure what kind of marriage I had with Kip." I felt my shoulders sag, my spirits too. "But let's get back to you. Do you think whatever's going on with you and Edward will blow over, the way it usually does?"

"I suppose. The main problem is that we're both selfish. He wants what he wants when he wants it and so do I. When our wants aren't in sync, he goes off and does his thing and I go off and do mine."

"And you've never considered divorce?"

"Why? We're perfectly suited for each other. Who else is he going to find to put up with him? Who else am I going to find to put up with me? The marriage works for us in a cockeyed sort of way."

After a few more back-and-forths about the Pepper marriage, Sarah moved the conversation to the new book she was writing, another installment in her popular series. And then she asked me how I was coming with my Brandon Brock project. I explained that I'd struck out trying to get past his secretary but that I'd faxed him a letter.

"You'll never get an answer," she said. "Or if you do, it'll be one of those generic Thank-you-for-your-interest-in-Finefoods letters. A kiss off. I know because that's the kind of letter I send out. Or, should I say, Justine sends out."

"You don't answer your own fan mail?"

"Lynn. I get letters by the truck load. I don't have time to write back to every single one of those people. Besides, how would it look? I'll tell you how: it would look as if I were sitting by the mailbox with nothing to do. I have a reputation to maintain."

I smiled. Sarah was so full of it.

"If you really want to get to Brandon Brock," she went on, "you should skip the letters and calls and just place yourself in his path."

"You mean, show up at his office and bully my way in?"

"Of course not. I mean, find out where he eats, lives, plays squash."

"Tennis, not squash."

"Fine. Find out where he plays and go there. Put on an adorable tennis outfit and talk to him without his entourage around."

"I don't have an adorable tennis outfit. I never learned how to play tennis. I was too busy studying."

"You can borrow one of mine."

I laughed. Sarah had D cups. Mine were A minus. "We're not the same size, Sarah."

"I forgot about that." She thought for a minute, giving me the once-over. "I bet you'd fit into Vanessa's clothes. I'll run up and look in her closet. Be right back."

Vanessa was Sarah's teenage daughter. Her skinny, flat-chested teenage daughter. And yes, I was her size, I'm embarrassed to tell you. One of her pert little tennis dresses fit me perfectly.

"So you'll find out where he plays and when his regular game is and you'll go there," said Sarah.

"But he must play at a private indoor club. They'll know I don't belong and throw me out."

"Then you'll have to get Brock's attention quickly, before they do. Just talk fast and make sure you slip your business card into the pocket of his tennis shorts. I really think you'll have a better chance with him away from his office, in a more relaxed setting."

I WAITED ANOTHER day for a response to my fax. When there was none, I realized I had to switch gears and try another tactic, Sarah's tactic. Six months was all I had, according to the wager I'd made with my friends, not to mention all I could afford, thanks to my pitiful bank account. I had no time to waste.

I pulled out the Manhattan Yellow Pages, found the listings for the few remaining indoor tennis clubs in the area (there used to be more in the days before people abandoned tennis for golf) and started calling them. Having spoken to Brock's secretary three times in the past twenty-four hours, I had her nasal voice down pat. I was a linguist, after all, and linguists make very good mimics.

"Good morning," I said to the attendant at the first club. "I'm Brandon Brock's secretary, and I'm afraid he won't be able to make his seven o'clock game tomorrow morning." I figured Brock was one of those crazies who gets up at the crack of dawn, does six thousand push-ups in his "home gymnasium," then sweats for an hour on the tennis court before heading to the office.

"Whose seven o'clock game?" he said.

"Brandon Brock's. He's signed up for seven, isn't he?"

"Nope."

"What about later in the day? Later in the week?"

"No again. I've never heard of the guy."

"Oh. I must have the wrong club. Sorry."

I tried the next number listed in the phone book and went through the same song and dance. No dice. I didn't get anywhere with the third club or the fourth and was beginning to wonder if Finefoods might have an indoor club of its own where His Highness played. Then I hit paydirt.

"Racquet Club," answered a young man at what had to be the most exclusive of the city's tennis establishments. I say "had to" because it was the only club listed that did not run a separate ad—i.e., it didn't need to advertise.

I did my thing with the attendant.

"Oh, hi, Naomi," he said cheerfully, clueing me in to my new best friend's name. "Mr. Brock is down for six tomorrow morning, not seven. He's playing singles with Peter Ogden. Are you calling to cancel?"

The guy played tennis at six o'clock in the morning? What an animal. "Actually, let me check with Mr. Brock just to be doubly sure. Please hold." I kept the kid hanging for a full thirty seconds—one Mississippi, two Mississippi—then came back on the line. "I'm terribly sorry to have troubled you. It seems as though Mr. Brock's early meeting has been postponed for tomorrow morning and he will, indeed, be able to play with Mr. Ogden at six a.m. as scheduled."

"No problem. Have a good one, Naomi."

"And you as well." Whoever you are.

I eyed Vanessa Pepper's tennis dress, which I'd left dangling on a hanger on my bedroom door knob, and realized that I was not about to waltz into the Racquet Club in that skimpy thing, masquerading as someone I wasn't, wearing a costume. I would go dressed in one of my business suits, looking like the professional I'd always taken pride in being. So Brandon Brock wouldn't mistake me for a Wimbledon champion. Big deal. I wanted him to talk to me about Womenspeak, not women's sports.

Yes, I thought. I'll just be myself and see where that takes me.

7

IT WAS DARK when the alarm went off, but then it's always dark at four o'clock in the morning, isn't it? I wasn't used to getting up so early, not since my once-hectic schedule had slowed to a crawl. It was also cold that morning. February-in-the-Northeast cold. The kind of cold where the last thing you want to do is get out of bed.

Still, I was on a mission. I threw the nice warm covers off of me, drank of a cup of coffee, and showered and dressed and fixed myself up. I did a pretty good job of it too, even if I did have to use a vat of concealer on the circles under my eyes. Before I left the house, I took a final glance in the mirror and thought, Okay, Lynn. This is it. Your big chance for a comeback.

By five, I was on the road, driving south on 684, freezing to death thanks to the fact that my car had no heat and I couldn't afford to get it serviced. By six, I was numb from the cold, my extremities about to break off, but I managed to pull the car into a parking garage on East 63rd Street, grab my briefcase and head over to the Racquet Club, which was on the corner of 62nd Street and York Avenue. I had hoped to arrive a few minutes after Brandon Brock showed up, just as he was emerging from the locker room, but by the time I pushed through the club's revolving door, he was already on the court.

"Can I help you?" asked the same young attendant to whom I'd spoken on the phone. To whom Naomi had spoken on the phone.

I tried to answer, but my lips were like blocks of ice. What's more, my nose was running. I could feel it. It always ran in cold weather.

I reached into my purse for a tissue, gave myself a few seconds to regroup, then responded to the man's question. "I'm here to have a word with Mr. Brock," I said finally.

He wasn't convinced. I wasn't a member of the Racquet Club, he'd never seen me before, and it was six o'clock in the morning. I couldn't blame him for being a tad suspicious.

"Naomi told me I would find him here," I added. "She was the one who suggested I come."

"Oh," he said, warming up a little. I wished I would. "Mr. Brock's on the court now. He'll be out there until seven. Do you want to wait?"

"Yes," I said. "Is there someplace where I could sit and watch him play?"

"Right over there," said the attendant as he pointed to a nearby lounge overlooking the club's three courts. "We've got coffee and juice and muffins. Help yourself."

I thanked him, shivered my way over to the lounge and practically dove for the muffins. So far so good, I thought as I wolfed down a blueberry goodie. A meeting with Brandon Brock and free food too.

When I was sufficiently satiated—I polished off another couple of muffins, a cinnamon raisin and a cranberry apple, as I figured this would be breakfast *and* lunch—I turned my attention to the match going on below: Brandon Brock versus Peter Odgen.

I couldn't get an up-close look at Brock from my perch in the lounge but I could certainly recognize him from his photograph, recognize the golden retriever hair and the golden retriever body. Actually, he looked very fit for a big man. Not on the level of those maniac muscle men with their washboard abs and rippling delts, but not the least bit flabby either. I figured him to be somewhere around six feet and 185 pounds, with most of the weight in his shoulders. He had a swimmer's body, I decided, and was probably a champion breast stroker (in and out of the pool) at his fancy shmancy prep school. For a guy of his size he was quick, agile, which was a good thing, considering that he was doing a lot of running around on the court, up and back, side to side. Since I wasn't a tennis aficionado, it took me a few minutes to realize that the reason he was doing all that running was because he was not in control of the match, was letting his opponent dictate play, and was losing.

And then I remembered something one of the articles had said about Brandon Brock: He didn't like to lose. I began to root for him. I wanted him in an upbeat mood when he got off the court, in a receptive mood.

I drank more coffee, perused the courtesy copy of the *Wall Street Journal*, nodded at the club members who came and went, and waited. It was five after seven when he and his pal finally mounted the stairs and entered the lounge. I didn't see them coming. I heard them coming. Heard Brock coming.

First, there was the snap of a towel as he punished one of the empty chairs with a little whip action.

Then, there was the snap of his voice, the booming voice of someone accustomed to hogging center stage. "Was I a joke or what, Peter? I couldn't get any momentum going. Didn't hit out on my shots. Wasn't aggressive. I sucked. I mean, I really sucked."

So much for the receptive mood I was hoping for. Brock was in a foul mood, a sore loser mood. While his tennis partner poured them each a glass of orange juice, he continued to berate himself, his face red with exertion and emotion.

"I kept serving up these sitters for you, just couldn't hit deep. I had so little pace on the ball you'd think I was a goddam *girl* out there."

The downside was that he was crude, as advertised, but the upside was that he was, indeed, the perfect candidate for the Wyman Method. I chuckled to myself as I imagined the techniques I would use on him. There would be no more of that *girl* business once I was through with him.

"Hey, hey, Brandon. Take it easy," said his friend, who must have witnessed plenty of his temper tantrums. "I was having a good day, that's all. You'll get me next time, buddy."

"And it wasn't just my hitting," he kept it up. "My mobility was for shit. I couldn't make my legs move to the ball. I felt like a lard ass."

Yes, I thought. I would eliminate the swearing, too.

Brock sipped the juice but it didn't shut him up. "You know, Peter, the balls we were using were dead. That new can you opened must have been defective."

A common male response, I mused. If blaming yourself doesn't do the trick, blame an inanimate object. That's what my father always did. *I would have been home on time, Shelley, but the car needed gas.* Excuses, excuses.

"And the courts," he said, shaking his head. "They were as chewed up today as I've ever seen them. I didn't get a decent bounce the entire second set."

Blah blah blah. Was this guy predictable or what? I even had a hunch what was coming next: A speech about how hungover he was from the night before and how *that* was the reason he lost the match.

"And then there was that second martini I had last night. It didn't exactly help my concentration."

So? Did I know men like Brock or didn't I? And they accuse women of being whiners.

Peter Ogden gave him one of those manly-man pats on the butt and went to the locker room to change. The others in the lounge had long since disappeared onto the courts, which meant that I was now alone with my prey.

As he continued to stand there, sulking about his defeat, I took a deep breath, rose from my chair and walked over to him, arranging my face into an expression that was cordial, not unctuous. My intention was to land him as a client, not shine his shoes.

"Hello, Mr. Brock. I'm Lynn Wyman. How are you this wintery morning?"

He glanced up from his orange juice and stared at me, his hard blue eyes boring in on me, his thin-lipped mouth forming the beginning of an actual scowl. I had intruded on his "space," I guessed.

Undeterred, I reached out, grabbed his hand and pumped it vigorously. He had a large hand, a strong hand. And no, I did not wonder about the implications of that.

"I'd like to talk to you for a minute or two," I said.

"About what?" He arched one of his bushy golden eyebrows.

Okay, I thought. No dancing around the subject. There isn't time. Furthermore, you're not the type to make idle chitchat. Give it to him straight. "About communication," I said. "More specifically, about the ways in which you communicate with women. I understand that you have problems in that area and I'd like very much to help you with them."

"Run that by me again?" Apparently, I had given it to him too straight. He was annoyed, and I should have anticipated that he'd be. Men claim that they like it when you're direct with them, but the truth is that they only like it when you're direct with them if what you're direct with them about involves a big, sloppy, ego-inflating compliment.

I repeated my pitch, then placed one of my business cards on the granite-top counter against which he was leaning.

He picked it up, examined it, set it back down. "I have no idea where you get your information, honey, but I don't have problems communicating with women."

"Oh, but you do," I said. "Take that last sentence, for example.

It's not politically correct for men to refer to women they've only just met as 'honey,' Mr. Brock. 'Honey' is what one would call his wife. Or, perhaps, his daughter. It's a term of endearment, in the same category as 'darling' or 'dear' or 'snookums.' "

" 'Snookums'?" He picked up my card and gave it another glance, then set his glass of orange juice on top of it. "Look, what's all this *really* about? Are you a reporter or something?"

"No, Mr. Brock. As is made quite clear on my business card, which, I notice, you have just converted into a coaster, I'm a linguist with a private practice here in the city. My clients—all of whom are men—come to me for corrective work on their verbal interactions with women. Some people refer to the kind of coaching I do as sensitivity training, but it's far more specialized than that. The Wyman Method is a unique program in that it focuses on speech patterns. I believe—and I have proven—that by teaching men to become fluent in Womenspeak, I can turn acrimonious relationships between men and women into harmonious ones."

His scowl morphed into a smile. "Okay, okay. You nailed me." He held up his hands in mock surrender. "This is some kind of a joke. My ex-wife paid you to come here and harangue me, right?"

"No, Mr. Brock. This is not a joke. Turning acrimonious relationships between men and women into harmonious ones is serious business."

He laughed, still not getting it. "I don't know who you are or what your game is but I've got a bulletin for you: Relationships between men and women are supposed to be acrimonious."

"That's been your experience, in other words?"

"Mine and every other guy's. Show me a harmonious relationship between a man and woman and I'll show you a man with only one word in his vocabulary: yes. Who wants to be that kind of a doormat?"

"You're awfully cynical, Mr. Brock."

"No. Realistic. Are you married, honey?"

I let the "honey" go for the moment. "Yes, I am." Technically speaking.

"Then tell me: How's your relationship with your husband? Is it *harmonious?*"

It used to be. "My relationship with my husband is not the issue here. We were talking about you, about your communication problems with women. I was explaining to you about the Wyman Method and how it could help you."

"Right, right." He rolled his eyes. "Where in the world did my former wife find you? You're out there in woo-woo land with these off-the-wall theories of yours."

"Actually, I've never had contact with your ex-wife, nor am I out there in 'woo-woo land.' I'm out there in the mainstream. Why don't you have your secretary check the archives of the *New York Times Book Review* and you'll discover just how mainstream. My book expounding on the Wyman Method was on their bestseller list for eleven consecutive months."

"Is that so?" He appeared amused now, as if I were a harmless nuisance, an entertaining nuisance. "If you're so mainstream, why haven't I heard of you?"

"Maybe because you haven't been listening. Men do precious little listening, unfortunately, but we'll work on that once you become my client."

"*We* will?" He laughed again. He was making light of my program, of me, but at least he was engaged in the dialogue. I had expected him to bolt for the locker room by this time.

"Yes. And we'll work on teaching you Womenspeak."

"Womenspeak. What the hell is that, if I may be permitted to reveal my ignorance?" He said this in a high, squeaky voice meant, I assume, to mock the way women speak.

"Men and women have different conversational styles, Mr. Brock. Womenspeak is merely the language that women employ. My theory is that when men adopt it as their own, the male/female conflicts that plague our society are reduced considerably."

He scratched his head while he laughed, as if he found all this both confounding and comical.

His reaction is a defense mechanism, I thought, determined not to be thrown by it. He can't bear to believe that his view of the world isn't the only view. Men are children, when you get right down to it.

"Now," I continued, "regarding the step-by-step program I intend to use in order to help you—"

"I already told you: I don't need any help."

"I'm afraid you do. Did you notice how you interrupted me just then?"

"I didn't interrupt you."

"You certainly did. Let me replay the interaction for you. I said, 'Regarding the step-by-step program I intend to use in order to help you—.' And you cut me off with, 'I already told you: I don't need any help.' "

"Oh, come on. That wasn't interrupting. That was stopping you before you made an ass of yourself." He laughed, slapping his thigh.

"Men interrupt frequently, Mr. Brock," I said, while he continued to congratulate himself on what he considered to be his priceless comeback. "We'll work on that too, once you become a client. We'll also work on preventing those dreadful tirades of yours."

"Dreadful tirades?"

"All that moaning and groaning over losing a tennis game. Honestly."

"I don't like losing. So what? Or is that a problem too, according to you?"

"It's what you say after you lose that's the problem. Instead of expressing feelings—disappointment, sadness, embarrassment—men tend to become loud, even vulgar, because their superiority has been threatened. Once you're a client of mine, we'll work on that, on getting you to express your feelings. I'll give you scripts that will enable you to respond differently to future losses."

"For Christ's sake!" He threw up his hands in frustration. "You make it sound as if I lose matches all the time. And I don't. I'm better than ninety-nine percent of the members at this club."

"Ah, and there's yet another problem area: the *I'm better than they are* mind-set. Men are so desperate to one-up each other."

"And women aren't? One of my favorite pastimes is watching them check each other out at a party. You think they dress up and get their hair done and put on all that makeup for the men? Wrong. They do it to impress the other women, to one-up the other women. It's hilarious."

A riot. "As I was about to say about today's tirade, Mr. Brock, if you had been fluent in Womenspeak, you would have returned to the lounge after your match, put your arm around your friend and said, 'Good job, today, Peter. Sorry I didn't give you more competition.' "

"Why would I say something as wimpy as that?"

"It's not wimpy. It's conciliatory. Which prompts me to ask: When was the last time you used the word 'sorry'?"

"Right now. I'm *sorry* I ever let myself get sucked into this conversation." He haw-hawed at that one. "Now, I really have to hustle over to the office. It's been fun but I think you should peddle your stuff to some other poor bastard."

He removed his sweatbands from his wrists and tossed them into his tennis bag. He was leaving. I couldn't let him.

"But Mr. Brock," I said quickly. "I was under the impression that you were enjoying our conversation. I was hoping—"

"I was enjoying your legs," he interrupted. "If you weren't some cute thing in a short skirt, I would have walked away the second you started lecturing me, trust me."

God, he was disgusting. His remarks were totally offensive, completely inappropriate, utterly without respect for me or my intelligence. Still—and I feel guilty and ashamed and incredibly hypocritical even now as I tell you this—nobody had admired my legs in ages, if ever, and I didn't hate it.

"Please give me another few minutes," I said as I watched him pack up. "According to the current issue of *Fortune*, you really do have difficulties in communicating with your female colleagues at Finefoods. It's all there in black and white. There's no point in denying it."

Suddenly, the scowl returned. The red face too. He was angry. The mention of the magazine article had made him angry, had changed the dynamic between us. I was no longer an entertaining nuisance or a "cute thing." I was the enemy. And yet I didn't back down. I had to go out with a flourish.

"I came away from the *Fortune* piece, Mr. Brock, with the sense that you're an excellent CEO who would be even more effective if you got in touch with your feminine side."

"*My feminine side.* I wish people would give that crap a rest," he snapped.

I pressed on. "If you agree to become a client of mine for six months—six short months—you will accomplish that goal, and you'll be able to say goodbye to all the negative publicity you've been subjected to. How does that strike you, Mr. Brock?"

He polished off the last of his orange juice and wiped the pulp off his mouth with the back of his hand. Classy.

"Here's how it strikes me," he said as he zipped his tennis bag closed and lifted it by the straps. "I think that you and *Fortune* magazine and everybody else who's on my case about this communication shit should get a life and stop messing around in mine."

So hostile. So typical. I let him rant, hoping he'd cool off and realize that what I was proposing had merit.

"Do you have any idea what I'm doing today while the rest of you are talking nonsense?" he asked, jabbing his finger in my general direction. He was not cooling off. Just the opposite.

"Not a clue, Mr. Brock, but then, a mere three seconds ago, you asked me to stay out of your life," I reminded him.

Boy, was he steamed. Men don't appreciate being called on their inconsistencies.

"Well, here's what I'm doing today," he announced. "I'm meeting with the President of the United States. You heard me. And do you know why? Because we're putting the finishing touches on a new program that *I* spearheaded, a program whereby Finefoods, Inc., is donating several million dollars' worth of food to the needy, a program which, unlike my supposed communication problems, will *not* be publicized in the media. Now, which do you think is a higher priority for me, Dr. Whatever-your-name-is: Finding a solution for feeding poor people in this country or worrying about every fucking syllable I say around women?"

He didn't wait for my answer. He just brushed past me and left. And he didn't take my business card with him.

Gee, that went well, I thought, and popped a muffin into my briefcase for the long, cold drive home.

8

SO YOU AMBUSHED him at six o'clock in the morning?" said Penny, who bought me lunch the day after my debacle with Brandon Brock. We sat at her power table at New York's trendy Gotham Bar & Grill and ate vertical food: grilled salmon resting on top of smashed potatoes resting on top of portabello mushrooms resting on top of wilted spinach resting on top of several slices of prosciutto. I needed a step ladder to cut into the thing.

"It seemed like a good idea at the time," I said.

"It was a good idea, but did you have to ambush him by telling him he has a problem?" She shook her head disapprovingly. "That's not the way to land a client, Lynn. It's fine to be aggressive, but you've got to romance people, flatter them, make them love you and *then* move in for the kill."

"I'm not one for all that foreplay, I guess. Besides, I knew my time with Brock would be limited and I wanted to make the best use of it."

"Weren't you even the least bit intimidated by him? I mean, he's not some average Joe. He runs one of America's genuine megacompanies."

"I *was* intimidated at first. When I saw him down on the tennis court with his big racquet and his big shoulders and his big reputation, I started to get shaky, wondering how someone like me was ever going to convince someone like him of anything. But then he finished playing and came into the lounge and started cursing and stomping around and doing an imitation of a two-year-old, and I thought, Gosh, he's like all my other clients. When I realized that, I wasn't afraid of him or awed by him or any of it."

"Interesting," she said. "What's your next move?"

"I'll go back to square one and try to set up a meeting with Brock at his office."

"Forget that. He'll only blow you off. You have to infiltrate his inner circle."

"How do I do that? You said you don't have any contacts at Finefoods."

"I don't."

"But maybe someone at your agency does. Maybe one of your publicists used to work there. Think about it."

She thought about it. "No. I'm running down everybody's résumé in my mind and I can't come up with a connection."

"Then what about your media contacts? You must know business reporters who've covered Brock."

"Sure I do, but what help would they be? From everything I've read, Brock is suspicious of media people. He doesn't cozy up to them the way a lot of CEOs do. What you need, Lynn, is someone he does cozy up to. Someone he trusts, depends on. That's the key to getting to him: getting to the person closest to him."

"And who would that be?"

"How about his girlfriend?"

"Does he have one?"

"I have no idea, but I could make a few calls and find out. That's where my media contacts would come in handy. If he does have a girlfriend and you got chummy with her, you'd have an ally."

"Penny, that sounds like a scheme and I'm not into schemes, remember?"

"Look, it's time to take off the nun's habit, Lynn. You're desperate. You want your career back. You need Brock as a client. If I were you,

I'd do whatever's necessary to make that happen—including sidling up to his girlfriend, if he has one."

I nodded resignedly. I *would* do whatever was necessary. I owed it to all the women out there who no longer had an expert to turn to when their men clammed up at the dinner table.

"If I'm lucky, he's dating someone local," I said.

"In any case, we'll find out who she is and where she is and you'll convince her to convince Brock to hire you. End of story."

Right. I didn't know how I would approach a girlfriend of Brandon Brock's, but I hoped I'd do a better job with her than I did with him.

"Now. Enough about me," I said, not wanting to monopolize the conversation. "How are things with you, Penny? Business good?"

"Great. I'm so busy I'm turning clients away."

"I'm so glad. What about men? Seeing anyone?"

"I wish."

"Nobody?" I found that hard to believe. Penny may have had problems finding men who would marry her, but she didn't have problems finding men who would fool around. It was just that the fooling around got old quickly—for the men. She exhausted them, used them up, sucked all the life out of them, so to speak, and then they dumped her. For a smart woman, she made foolish choices. But I wasn't one to talk.

"Nobody," she repeated. "I'm on hiatus from men."

"You?"

"It's true. I— Oh, never mind."

"Come on, Penny. You were about to tell me something."

"No I wasn't."

"You were. You can trust me. Go ahead. What is it?"

She sighed. "Just that I'm tired, Lynn. Tired of having my teeth kicked in." As Penny had that enormous Kennedyesque overbite, her use of the expression "having my teeth kicked in" was unfortunate. "I fall for a guy and then he leaves me and I fall for another guy and then he leaves me and on and on. I fell especially hard for the last one who left me."

"Oh, Penny. I'm so sorry. Who was he?"

She shrugged, her eyes revealing an ever-so-slight glint of tears, which, for Penny Herter, was a veritable outpouring of emotion. "It's not worth going into."

"Of course it is. You're in pain. I'm here for you."

"I appreciate that, Lynn. But I'm not ready to talk about it. Really."

I wasn't about to bully the story out of her, but I was surprised by her reluctance to discuss this man. Normally, she discussed her men with the specificity of an anatomy professor.

"Moving right along," she said with forced gaiety, as if to block further inquiries into her failed relationship, "how about dessert?"

I declined. I hadn't even made it down to the second-to-last tier of my entree.

PENNY CALLED A few days later to say that one of her pals at *Business Week* not only confirmed that Brandon Brock was dating a woman, but identified her. She was Kelsey Haines, a model–turned–yoga instructor–turned–massage therapist–turned–interior decorator. Apparently, Brock was into women with long legs and short attention spans.

Immediately after hearing of her existence, I dialed Manhattan information and got her phone number. My plan was to lure her up to my apartment in Mt. Kisco, pump her for a few decorating tips, and ask her to put in a good word about me with Mr. Big Shot.

And then I realized how absurd that was. My apartment was neat and tidy but a pit compared to the sort of places that get *decorated*. Kelsey wouldn't deign to come near it.

So where would she deign to come near?

I had the answer: Dogwood, Sarah's colonial. Yes, the house had already been "done to death," as they say, as well as photographed for *Architectural Digest*, but Kelsey wouldn't have seen the article.

She was a novice at swatches and swags, didn't understand the difference between curtains and draperies, I figured. She probably thought window treatments were the doses of sunlight you give people with Seasonal Affective Disorder.

My idea was not to pose as the owner of Dogwood, but merely to be the helpful friend of the owner. I called Sarah to get her permission to use her house as a prop. She was reluctant at first.

"I won't be home, Lynn. I'm leaving for Europe in a couple of days for a six-country book tour."

"Won't Justine be taking care of Dogwood while you're gone?" I said, referring to her house manager. "She could let us in."

"I suppose, but the thought of having strangers tromping through here doesn't thrill me," she said.

"It won't be strangers," I said. "It'll be one stranger: Brock's girlfriend. And I'll be there with her."

She relented, being the good buddy that she was. Which left me to make contact with this Kelsey person, who was surprisingly easy to reach.

"Hello," I said after she picked up her own phone. "My name is Lynn Wyman. I'm looking for a decorator and I was given your name by—" I blanked for a second or two. "By Peter Ogden." Well? Why not Brock's tennis partner? I didn't know anyone else in his social set.

"Peter recommended me?" said a teeny weeny little voice that made Melanie Griffith's sound husky.

"Very highly," I said. "He indicated that you were new to the business but extremely talented."

"Gee, that was nice of him," she squeaked.

"Actually, I'm calling on behalf of my friend, the children's book author, Sarah Pepper."

Silence. Obviously, Kelsey wasn't familiar with Sarah's work. I would not tell Sarah that.

"Sarah's got a magnificent house in Westchester," I continued. "It's in fabulous condition, structurally, but it could use a bit of freshening up in terms of the decorating. Would you be interested in driving up from the city for a consultation?"

"I don't see why not?" she said excitedly. "As Peter told you, I'm just getting started as a designer. The truth is, I don't have a single client, which means your friend would be my first."

"Great," I said, feeling guilty about dragging this honest, decent woman up to Westchester under false pretenses. On the other hand, I felt sure that she would be receptive to the Wyman Method once I explained it to her, even grateful to me for offering to put an end to her boyfriend's chauvinistic behavior.

"What's great is that Peter wants me to work on your project," she said, after taking down Sarah's address and the day and time of our appointment. "I love it when men want me to do something for them and I'm able to do it. I must have been a geisha in a past life."

Okay, so maybe male chauvinism didn't bother her. I would just have to take a different tack with her.

THE FOLLOWING TUESDAY morning, Kelsey arrived at Sarah's house in South Salem in a big black Mercedes—a snazzy car for someone who had no clients.

I had imagined that she would be tiny, because of the tiny voice, but she was an amazon, and it seemed to take forever for her to extricate her mile-long legs from inside the car and plant them onto the driveway. She was blond, which didn't surprise me, given that Brock was blond and egocentric types like him tend to fall for mirror images of themselves. And she was a beauty, which didn't surprise me either, given that Brock was a power guy and power guys tend to have their pick of beautiful women, even the power guys who are less fortunate than Brock in that they're fat and ugly and have cigar breath.

"Kelsey," I said, greeting her in the foyer so Justine wouldn't have to announce her. She was dressed very professionally, in a gray wool business suit, and carried a black leather portfolio. I wondered what could possibly be in the portfolio since she had never decorated anybody's house. "I'm Lynn Wyman. Thanks for coming."

We shook hands. "Wow. This place is gorgeous," she said, taking Dogwood in. "Who's the owner again?"

"Her name is Sarah Pepper and she's the author of bestselling children's books. In fact, she's off in Europe promoting the books as we speak. She asked me to meet with you in her absence."

"An author." She shook her head as if to marvel at the wonder of it all. I noticed that there were dark roots along the part of her otherwise golden streaked hair. "I've always wanted to be an author. I still might try to be. I've led a really fascinating life and people tell me I should write my memoirs."

Kelsey couldn't have been more than twenty-eight. A little young for memoirs, I thought, but then didn't that famous scribe, "Ginger Spice," write hers at twenty-five? As for Kelsey's "really fascinating life," I had my doubts. Being a model–turned–yoga instructor–turned–massage therapist probably has its moments but it isn't exactly the stuff of *Angela's Ashes*.

"Well, why don't I give you a tour of Dogwood and then we can sit down and have a nice chat," I suggested.

She agreed and we wandered throughout the house. I could see that she wasn't a complete dim bulb when it came to interior decorating—she could tell an oriental rug from a dhurrie, for example—but she committed the unpardonable sin of referring to Sarah's dining room draperies as *drapes*. I was on the verge of correcting her when I reminded myself that it was her boyfriend whose language I was intent on correcting.

"Obviously, the house is in mint condition," I said when we had completed the tour and were seated together in Sarah's sunny breakfast room, sipping the coffee that Justine had served us. "And it doesn't need that much in the way of redecorating. Maybe just a tweak here or there."

"More than a tweak," said Kelsey. "To do the house justice, I'd want to redecorate it from top to bottom."

"Why?" As I've said, Sarah's taste was impeccable.

"It's totally not my vision. I'd go ultra contemporary with it."

"But it's a colonial," I said. "It was built in the early 1800s."

"It looks it."

"It's supposed to, Kelsey."

"Only if you're into rules, and I'm not. That's why I'd go modern with this house. For the shock value. Who wants to walk in here and get just what they expect? Wouldn't it be more fun to walk in and go, 'Wow. I never would have thought there'd be track lighting on the ceiling.' "

She was a moron. A pleasant enough moron, but a moron nonetheless. Why do bright men like Brandon Brock choose dopey women like Kelsey Haines? Guess.

I let her go on about how she'd do this and that to Sarah's house, then swooped in to change the subject. I wasn't particularly subtle, but here's how it went.

"I promise I'll pass along all of your ideas to Sarah as soon as she's back from Europe," I said, "but in addition to hearing about your decorating *vision*, she'll want to know more about you personally."

"Like what?"

"Well, let's see." I made believe that what came next was utterly spontaneous. "How about telling me how you know Peter Ogden? I'll tell you how I know him: We go to the same dentist."

"But Peter *is* a dentist."

Caught. "That doesn't mean he doesn't *go* to a dentist. He can't do root canal on himself, for example."

"No, I guess he can't."

"Anyhow, that's how I know Peter. How do you know him, Kelsey?"

"He plays tennis with my boyfriend."

"Is that right?" I nodded vigorously. "So you have a boyfriend. That's lovely. Is he a decorator too?"

She laughed. "No, he's the CEO of Finefoods."

"Brandon Brock?" I said with feigned astonishment.

"That's my guy."

"Is it serious between you two?"

She shrugged. "Am I serious about him? You bet I am. Is he serious about me? Who knows? Brandon's not a big fan of sharing his feelings."

I tried to contain myself, but she had just handed me the perfect segue. "It's interesting that you mention that, Kelsey, about his not being a fan of sharing his feelings, because I'm an expert on that subject."

"On what subject?"

"On teaching men how to share their feelings, teaching them how they can become more sensitive human beings. To put it another way, I work with them on communicating better with women."

"So you're a therapist?"

"No, I'm a linguist. Actually, maybe my name will ring a bell now. Lynn Wyman."

Nothing.

"I wrote a bestseller and a newspaper column."

Nothing.

"And I appeared once a month on *Good Morning America*."

A flicker of recognition.

"And I had my own radio show where I'd talk to callers about the Wyman Method, my program involving Womenspeak."

"Oh my God. You're *that* Lynn Wyman."

"I am." I bowed my head in an ostentatious display of modesty.

"Actually, Kelsey, this is an amazing coincidence, my meeting you under these circumstances," I said, launching into my pitch. "I was just reading about your boyfriend in *Fortune* magazine, about how he has difficulties communicating with the women at Finefoods, and I thought, I wish I could convince him to undergo my program and help him become an even more effective chief executive. And now here I am with you! What luck!"

"You're *that* Lynn Wyman," she repeated, because she was a bit starstruck, I assumed. "The one who was all over the *National Enquirer*. The one who couldn't communicate with her own husband. You're still in business after that whole fiasco?"

So much for starstruck. I was taken aback—well, downright insulted—by her reaction. I kept forgetting that there would be those who would remember me for the Kip saga, not for the Wyman Method. "Of course, I'm still in business," I said, trying to stay on message. "And I wonder if you'd consider putting in a good word about me with Brandon Brock. You must have noticed how he's stuck in that macho, alpha male posturing of his. Well, I could change that, change him. You said it yourself: He's not big on sharing his feelings. But if he were to become a client of mine, he would share his feelings, Kelsey. With *you*." I paused here before delivering what I hoped would be my knock-out punch. "He would share his feelings by telling you he loves you and admitting that he wants to spend the rest of his life with you. Those are the words you've been longing to hear, isn't that right? I could make that happen for you, Kelsey—if you'll convince Brandon to become my client."

She rose quickly from her chair. Not a good sign. "Look, Lynn. I feel bad about what happened to you, about how your career went down the tubes and everything. I'd like to help you out, no kidding, but the thing is, Brandon isn't the kind of guy you suggest things to. What I mean is, he likes to be the boss, you know?"

"Sure I know. But what do *you* want, Kelsey? I'm hearing that you want him to open up to you more."

"Not enough to complain about it. I may not be the smartest girl on the block but I'm not the dumbest girl on the block either. Brandon Brock's a major catch, and I'm not gonna do anything to screw things up between us. When he feels like telling me he loves me, I'll be ready. Until then, I'm keeping my mouth shut. Besides, I like us just the way we are. He runs the show, and I bat my eyelashes and say, 'My hero.' "

Yup. There was no point in going into the male chauvinism bit.

"Now. How about the decorating job?" she asked, then winked at me. "Or *is* there a decorating job?"

No, she wasn't the dumbest girl on the block. "There isn't a decorating job," I admitted since she'd figured it out. "I got you up here so I could talk to you about Brandon. I apologize for the ruse, Kelsey."

She looked at me as if I were truly pathetic. Either that or she didn't know what "ruse" meant.

"Maybe you should try to get Peter Ogden to take your *course* or whatever you call it," she said. "He's the worst when it comes to communicating with women, completely hopeless. Since you two use the same dentist, you might have an easier time signing him up."

Okay, she *was* the dumbest girl on the block, not realizing that I had conned her about the Peter Ogden thing too. But I had just failed miserably in my latest attempt to snag Brandon Brock as a client, so what did that make me?

9

FOR MY NEXT trick, I sent Brock a copy of my book as well as the audiotape version (in case he wasn't a big reader), along with a letter restating how much I thought I could help him if he became my client. He didn't write me back and say, "You're hired," but he didn't return the package unopened either.

I discussed the situation with Gail one night on the phone. She had just come through yet another calamity. She'd thrown caution to the wind and eaten shrimp, thinking she'd grown out of her childhood allergy to shellfish, only to have her face blow up and then her sinuses dry up, thanks to the Benadryl she'd been taking.

"Sounds to me as if you haven't done enough research," she said. "Before I go out to shoot a documentary, I research my subjects thoroughly."

"You're not suggesting I bone up on Brock's breakfast cereals, are you?"

"No. That's not what I meant. When I do research, I interview people, get close to them so I can better understand the subject."

"But I did get close to Brock's girlfriend. Or tried to."

"Then try somebody else. What about his secretary?"

"Naomi? She's about as easy to talk to as her boss."

"Maybe she's different away from the office."

"Maybe, but to tell you the truth, I'm uncomfortable with the 'scheme' approach. I can't pretend to be someone I'm not. Not again."

"Who's asking you to? Approach the secretary the way you would anyone else—professionally. Call her up and invite her to lunch. Explain who you are and what your goal is. Emphasize that you'd like to meet with Brock but that you understand how important she is in terms of the screening process. Make her feel important. It's very possible that she'd love it if somebody paid that kind of attention to her."

I considered Gail's idea but I was distracted. Through the phone I could hear her hyperactive kids screaming and tearing around their apartment and sending objects and each other crashing to the floor. "Is everything all right there?" I asked.

She sighed. "Everything's fine. It's just another day in the Orrick household. God forbid my lazy husband should give me a hand."

"Why doesn't he?"

"Well, we sort of have this deal. When I'm out traveling for work, Jim watches the kids. When he's out looking for work, I watch the kids. So it's my turn tonight."

"What kind of work could he be out looking for at this hour?" It was ten-thirty.

"None. He's either playing poker or manifesting some other addictive behavior. He's a sad case, Lynn. You know that."

I did know that and was about to ask Gail why she stayed with Jim, but I knew the answer. She was a drama queen, as I've said. She seemed to enjoy the constant adrenaline rush of bailing her husband out of this jam or that rehab, seemed to enjoy the sense that she was coming to his rescue, seemed to enjoy the "high" she got whenever something—especially something involving EMS technicians—was going on. Jim was a sad case, but so was she. It amazed me how competent she was in her professional life and how screwed up she was in her personal life. But then I could say that about Penny and Sarah and Isabel too.

And about myself, although I would never have perceived my personal life as being screwed up. Not until recently. I thought I had the perfect marriage, a marriage so unlike that of my parents that it couldn't possibly go sour, a marriage that met my needs.

But now I wasn't so sure what my needs were, wasn't so sure of anything the way I used to be.

I CALLED NAOMI, Brandon Brock's executive secretary, the next morning. She remembered me.

"We received your materials," she said in that nasal tone of hers. Hold your nose and talk and you've got her down.

"Did Mr. Brock have a chance to look over them?" I said hopefully.

"Not that I'm aware of."

"Not even the audiotape? I figured he might have time to listen to it on one of those transatlantic flights CEOs are always taking. It's pretty entertaining—much better than the movies they show on airplanes these days."

"Mr. Brock flies on Finefoods's corporate jet," said Naomi. "There are no movies on board, as the plane is used for business not pleasure."

She was a humorless person. Worse than I was.

"Let me ask you this," I said. "Did you have a chance to look at my materials?"

"Did *I*?"

"Yes." Maybe Gail was right about Naomi. Maybe she wasn't used to having anyone ask for her opinion.

"I glanced at them," she said. "Before I placed them in Mr. Brock's in box."

"And what did you think?"

Silence.

"Did you relate to any of the problems described by the women quoted in the clippings? Identify with them? Find the Wyman Method interesting?"

"I must admit that I did feel a sense of déjà vu about—"

"About what, Naomi? May I call you Naomi?"

"You may."

"So, what was it about the material that you connected with?"

"Well, I suppose I connected with the woman in the article who complained that her male boss never *asked* if she would mind working late; he just *informed* her that she was working late."

"You connected with her because you've had experience with that sort of behavior?"

She hesitated before replying. "Don't misunderstand me, Dr. Wyman. Mr. Brock has been very, very good to me and I would never cast him in a negative light."

"But?"

"But—" Another pause. "But he has been known to toss a handful of tapes onto my desk, just as I'm about to leave the office for the evening, and say, 'I'll need these transcribed and ready for my signature by nine o'clock tomorrow morning.' He doesn't say, 'I hate to ask.' Or 'I hope this won't be a bother.' Or 'I'm sorry to do this to you.' It's as if he takes me for granted, Dr. Wyman, as if I'm a piece of furniture, as if I have no feelings, no heartbeat, no blood coursing through my veins."

Hello. Look what I had unleashed.

"There are times," she went on, growing more and more agitated, "when I want to rise up out of my chair and pump my fist in the air and tell him straight to his face, 'I'm a person too,' but of course I do not. I must not. Mr. Brock is my employer and I did not attend Katherine Gibbs Secretarial School in order to get myself thrown out onto the street on my derrière."

"No. But you could express your displeasure more subtly and, in doing so, inspire a change in Mr. Brock. A change for the better."

"How?"

"By scheduling an appointment for me to come in and talk to him. You see, I'd like very much for him to become a client of mine, Naomi. I believe that if he were to undergo the Wyman Method, he would emerge as a more effective CEO as well as a kindler, gentler boss."

"You're not suggesting I put you down on his calendar without advising him, are you?"

"It's not the worst idea I've ever heard."

"Perhaps not, but I cannot do it. My loyalty is to Mr. Brock, however oblivious he may be to my emotions."

"Then how about just putting in a good word with him about me, about my program? You could tell him you think it's important that he meets with me."

"Tell him *I* think it's important?" She scoffed. "I already explained to you: My opinion is of no consequence to him."

"Maybe you're underestimating how much he depends on you, Naomi. He may not show it, but I'll bet he relies on you heavily."

"Well, I don't know about that."

"Of course you do. How long have you worked for him?"

"Six years. I came over with him from Nestlé."

"You see? He does value you, otherwise he wouldn't have taken you with him to Finefoods. Please say you'll at least mention to him that we've had a conversation," I urged. "Do it for yourself, for your self-esteem, for the collective self-esteem of all womenkind." I know. I was laying it on a little thick. But we were in the home stretch. I could feel it.

She let out a little sigh, a little gasp, a little sucking sound. "All right. I'll do it," she said as if she were about to enlist in the military. "By golly, I'll do it."

THAT AFTERNOON, AFTER seeing my one client for the day and complimenting Diane on her new look (she had colored her hair again; this time the shade was pumpkin), I took a cab downtown. Isabel had invited me to her studio in SoHo, where she was shooting a series of photos for *Vanity Fair*'s annual Hollywood issue. When I arrived, there were dozens of people milling around, dressed in black, holding clipboards, looking terribly serious. I found this seriousness amusing as the subjects being photographed were cats, remember. There was a "Cary Grant cat" in tux and tails, a "Rita Hayworth cat" in red wig and evening gown, even a "Groucho Marx cat" in glasses and mustache. What can I say? One person's art is another person's lunacy.

Also present at the studio was Rita, Isabel's astrologer, who was there, presumably, to sanction that the shoot was being conducted on an auspicious day.

While the others busied themselves setting up, Rita chatted with me about the planets and their mysterious movements. She spoke of Mercury going retrograde and Venus squaring Pluto, and the Moon waxing, then waning, or was it the other way around? None of it made much sense to me. I was a woman of science, after all. My actions were based on empirical evidence, not heavenly bodies. I was grounded. I was practical. I was realistic. I was also floundering, and so I pricked up my ears when Rita said to me, "Communications with a man you are seeking to impress will proceed better if you or your surrogates wait two or three days before approaching him."

I panicked as I imagined Naomi speaking to Brock on my behalf that very afternoon. Too late now.

I also wondered why it is that astrologers' predictions always come out sounding so stilted, as if English isn't their first language.

The shoot lasted for several hours and it was only during a break for green tea, which, incidentally, smelled like the inside of my sneakers, that Isabel had a few minutes to spend with me.

"Are you having fun?" she asked, her jewelry clanging as she lifted her arms to hug me. "I hoped you might be. I wanted to offer you something to take your mind off your situation."

I wasn't sure which situation she was referring to, but I thanked her.

"No thanks necessary," she said. "We're friends, Lynn." Then came a quote about friendship from an Irish playwright I'd never heard of. She used a thick brogue as she spoke it, so I didn't understand a single word, and I didn't have it in me to ask her to repeat it.

She was quite involved with her monologue on the nature of friendship, particularly friendship between women, when she said suddenly, out of the blue, "I'm breaking it off with Francisco." She was referring to her long-time boyfriend, the marriage-phobic gallery owner.

"You are?" I said. She'd been with him for seven years and had seemed inclined to go another seven. "What happened?"

"I had an epiphany." This statement was accompanied by another quote, from a dead Roman this time.

"What kind of an epiphany?" I said. With Isabel, you never could tell what might trigger an insight.

"I've come to realize that he's not the only person on the planet." Which planet she didn't say, nor did Rita, who had joined us by that time. "There are others who are more demonstrative, more sensitive, more giving."

"Isabel," I said. "This is a major turnaround for you. Have you found someone else? Is that what we're talking about here?"

She glanced over at Rita. I assumed they had discussed Isabel's relationship with Francisco and that Rita had given her celestial seal of approval to her client's change of heart. "Yes," she said. "I think I have found someone else."

"Who?" I asked eagerly.

"It's not for sure, so I don't want to put a hex on it," she said with a secretiveness that didn't jibe with the above speech about our friendship.

"But it's 'for sure' enough to break up with Francisco?" I asked.

"Yes. Yes it is. I'm sorry, Lynn."

"What are you sorry about?" It was a strange thing to say, even for Isabel. Why should I mind if she met a man who made her happy?

Before she could answer, she was being summoned by the magazine's art director. One of the cats—the Rita Hayworth cat—had thrown up a hair ball on the Cary Grant cat's cummerbund. I took that as my cue to go home.

WHEN I GOT back to my apartment, I saw that there was a message on my answering machine. One single, pitiful message. I shook my head ruefully as I recalled those high, heady days, when I'd come home from work and find more messages than the machine could handle.

But okay, I thought, rewinding the tape. At least somebody out there loves me.

I made myself a scotch, sat at my desk and hit Playback.

"This is Brandon Brock" boomed the voice that had haunted me in my sleep.

I was so stunned—both surprised and ecstatic—to hear from him that I spilled my drink on myself.

God bless Naomi, I cheered silently, dabbing at my now-wet skirt with a napkin. She actually convinced him to meet with me. But for him to pick up the phone and call me himself—Well, that was beyond my wildest dreams.

"I would have had my secretary contact you," he said, sounding so much more polite, so much more respectful, than he had at the tennis club. I guessed he was showing me the charming Brandon Brock as opposed to the boorish one. "But, alas, she was unable to."

Alas. How gallant.

I waited for him to continue but he stopped talking, as if to gather his thoughts. And while he did, I took a long, lazy sip of my scotch, let the amber liquid just glide down my throat. If it's possible to smile while you sip, I was doing it. I couldn't recall ever feeling so victorious, so validated, so pleased that I had gone the extra mile, because it had been worth it. I'd accomplished my goal. I'd snagged the CEO of Finefoods, Inc., as a client.

"As I was saying," Brock continued, "my secretary was unable to place this call herself. And do you have any idea why, little miss linguist?"

Little miss linguist? Had I celebrated prematurely?

"BECAUSE SHE SEEMS TO HAVE BEEN BRAINWASHED BY YOU, *SNOOKUMS*!"

Brock said this so loudly that I expected the answering machine to explode.

"Apparently," he went on, lowering his voice to a normal growl, "you put the notion in my secretary's head that I wasn't the sensitive and caring boss that I should be—and that I should avail myself of your services in order to learn how to communicate with her and all the other snookumses who work for me. I said to myself: You know what, Brandon? This is the same bullshit that the pretty-but-preachy Ms. Wyman—excuse me, the pretty-but-preachy *Dr.* Wyman—was shoveling at me at the Racquet Club the other morning. What a coincidence."

There was a thud. It took me a second before I realized that Brock had dropped the phone while he was leaving his delightful message. Perhaps he was flustered, the way men often get when they're attempting to express their feelings but end up insulting someone instead.

"So here's the situation, snookums," he recovered. "You have delivered your last speech to me. You have delivered your last speech to my secretary. You have delivered your last speech to my girlfriend—and yes, I know all about that stunt with Kelsey; good try. There will be no further efforts to try to turn me into some wuss or whatever it is you believe men are supposed to be. IS THAT CLEAR?"

Then came a click and he was gone. Without even so much as a "Have a nice day."

10

I WAS MOPEY after getting Brock's message, completely down in the dumps. How was I ever going to restart my career if I couldn't even persuade him I was for real?

I dragged myself into my office the next morning for a session with a man named Louis, a hairdresser at one of the trendy salons in the city. He was having trouble connecting with his female clients, who expected him to share gossipy stories about his other female clients when what he really wanted to do was concentrate on their hair. Within a few short weeks, I'd taught him the language of Womenspeak, of which gossip is a popular dialect. Yes, yes, I know I set myself up for a bashing by feminists when I say that. Well, sorry, everybody. It's true. Women do gossip—i.e., talk about people, especially people they've never met—more than men do, but what of it?

After my session with Louis was over, I had Diane reorganize our filing system. (I had to justify her salary somehow.) And then, because it hit me yet again that I was washed up around town, with nothing to do for the rest of the day and no one to do it with, I left the office in total gloom, got into my heatless car, and drove back to Westchester. I was so depressed that when I reached the Mt. Kisco exit on I-684, I didn't turn off. I kept going, just kept heading north, staying on 684, merging into 84 and then picking up 87 (aka the New York State Thruway). I was bound, I suppose, for Canada. I had the radio tuned to a classical music station and they were playing entirely too much Wagner, which only made me more depressed. As a matter of fact, here's how depressed I was: The car's left blinker was on and I didn't even know it. People were probably driving behind me and saying to each other, "Boy, what a bozo. She's oblivious to what's going on in her own car."

And I wasn't depressed in some amorphous, nonspecific way. For the bulk of the trip, I was focused on Kip, finally allowing myself to *feel* his betrayal. It wasn't just that he had slept with another woman. That was a knife in the heart, no question. It was his selling the story to the tabloid that I absolutely couldn't, didn't want to, let go of. I hadn't seen or spoken to him since we'd signed our separation agreement, hadn't even *gossiped* about him with my friends. The subject was too raw, too unresolved. I was so angry about how he ruined my career that I spent an inordinate amount of time fantasizing about how I would pay him back, how I would exact emotional justice. Yes, that was the need that ate away at me, that depressed me instead of galvanized me.

At some point during my flight from reality, I noticed that my car was nearly out of gas, which meant that I had to get off the highway or risk being stranded and left for dead. (I considered the latter option briefly, then rejected it as being too melodramatic. I was a scientist. For me, just driving without a destination was melodramatic enough.)

I had no clue where I was—somewhere south of Albany, I guessed—but I pulled off at the exit for a town called Coxsackie. I chose it because it sounded like Cocksucker, which, of course, was what Kip Jankowsky was.

But, not really caring where I was, I missed a turn, ended up on Route 9 and found myself and my heatless, gasless, useless car in a town called Omi, which was even more appropriate to my situation than Coxsackie because, as the gas station attendant informed me, Omi was pronounced "Oh my."

Perfect, I thought glumly. Maybe the next town I stop in will be called "Woe is me."

"Is there any place around here where I could get a soda?" I asked the heavily tatooed man filling my car and washing my windshield. No self-serve pumps in Omi. Not much of anything in Omi, as far as I could tell.

"Inside," he said, nodding at the small building behind us but electing not to make eye contact with me. Well, men were men. Even Omi men.

"Thanks," I said.

"If I was you, I'd buy myself a couple of bags of chips too."

"Why? Are they made right here in Omi?" I said, thinking that perhaps I had inadvertently landed in the very town where chips were manufactured and that this gas station guy wanted me to sample the local product.

"No," he said. "You're leaking oil and your front right tire's about to go flat and it's gonna take me a while before I can do anything about it. I'm alone here today."

Oh, excellent, Lynn. Good move taking the car out for this little spin. "So you're saying I can't drive it the way it is?"

He laughed. There weren't a lot of teeth in that mouth. Not a lot of teeth you'd want to go near, anyway. "Not if you want to get where you're going."

Where *was* I going? Nowhere. I was running away from home, like some poor, miserable kid. But I wasn't about to tell that to a stranger. "I'm going to Mt. Kisco in Westchester County."

"Then I wouldn't chance it," he said. "You'll break down somewhere along the line."

I had already broken down, it seemed to me. Otherwise, I would have been in Mt. Kisco that afternoon instead of in Omi.

I went inside the gas station, bought a can of Coke and a bag of Cheez Doodles, picked up the only magazine in the place, a dog-eared catalog selling farm equipment, and waited. I don't remember how long it was before I finally got out of there, but it was too long.

During the interminable ride home I kept the radio off. The last thing I needed was more Wagner.

By the time I chugged into the driveway and inside the apartment, I was exhausted—depression will do that to you—and so I made myself some tea and went straight to bed. It was only seven o'clock but I was ready for the day to be over. I was so ready for the day to be over that I didn't check for messages on my answering machine. Why bother, I figured as I pulled the covers over my head and augered in. Who in the world would be looking for me?

THE NEXT MORNING I stayed in bed until noon, since I had no clients scheduled and was still in the mood to hide. It was hunger that finally roused me. On my way to the refrigerator I glanced at the answering machine and saw that I did, indeed, have a message from the day before.

"Okay. Who are you and what do you want?" I said wearily as I hit Playback.

At first, there was no sound coming from the machine, as if the person had already hung up and left me with dead air. Or maybe he was the type who derived sick pleasure out of breathing into the phone as opposed to speaking into it.

Swell, I thought. I get one lousy call and it's either a wrong number or a pervert.

And then I heard something on the tape, heard someone. A clearing of a throat. A clearing of a male throat. And then an actual voice.

"Hey, there. I bet you'll never guess who this is, snookums."

I stood absolutely still. I knew exactly who it was, obviously. The question was: Why had he called? To bawl me out again?

"I've decided I'm going to hire you."

What?

"I'm going to let you teach me how to act like one of those big cry babies everybody seems to want me to be."

Is this really happening? I thought after allowing myself a squeal of excitement. Has Brandon Brock, the same man who told me in no uncertain terms to take a hike, actually changed his mind about me? In only twenty-four hours? And if so, why the sudden about-face?

"No, Dr. Wyman, this is not a joke," he said as if reading my mind. "I'm very serious. Well, as serious as anyone can be about a subject as ridiculous as whether or not I should be crucified for complimenting a woman on her legs."

So it was true. He *was* hiring me. I still didn't know why, but now I didn't care.

"I'd like us to start with your system or your method or whatever it is you call it as soon as possible," he went on. "Tomorrow, I'll have your old pal Naomi try to reach you at either your home or your office, since you gave us both numbers, and she'll hammer out a schedule with you for my appointments."

This was incredible! Miraculous! My worries were over! I had snagged the biggest client of my life! I was back! Dear God, I was back!

I didn't even pay attention as Brock continued to yammer away. I was too busy plotting my publicity campaign—my announcement to the media that I had turned America's Toughest Boss into America's Most Sensitive Boss. I quickly imagined the offers from book publishers, the meetings with television development people, the cavalcade of new clients, the purchase of a house in the upscale neighborhood where I used to live. I also pictured the groveling, the sniveling, the I-never-stopped-believing-in-you's from the hypocrites who'd been shunning me for months.

This is too wonderful, too delicious, I thought. Everything I lost—everything Kip stole from me—will be mine.

After the answering machine beeped, indicating the end of Brock's message, I hit Playback. I was compelled to listen to it all again, every syllable this time.

"Hey, there. I bet you'll never guess who this is, snookums. . . ."

Okay. You heard this part. I'll pick up with the part you didn't hear.

". . . Oh, and another thing, Doc. Before we embark on this little adventure together, I'll need you to agree to one condition: confidentiality. There will be absolutely no mention in the media that I'm a client of yours. Not a whisper to an editor. Not a blind item in a column. Nothing. We don't have a deal without your word on this. As I'm sure you've figured out, I'm not coming to you because I have this burning desire to get pussy whipped. I'm coming to you because I intend to save my ass at Finefoods. My board of directors had a meeting this morning and the first order of business was their problem with the way I 'relate to women,' as they put it. We lost our big gun in Eastern Europe recently—she said she didn't like working for me, can you fathom it?—and there are a few other gals who are making noises about leaving the company. As if that's *my* fault, right? Well, my board members think it is. They want me to take a course in—Lord, help me—sensitivity training, and I told them I knew a linguist who specialized in that. So here we are. But you can't go running to *Fortune* magazine or any other outlet. No reporters, or I entrust my sensitivity to somebody else. Got it?"

I sank down into a chair, my exhilaration from a moment ago reduced considerably.

The good news was that I had accomplished the impossible: I had gotten Brandon Brock to become a client.

The bad news was that I couldn't use it to resurrect my career, which was, after all, the point.

In other words, I'd be stuck with this Neanderthal for six months without anything to show for it.

I was contemplating the rich irony of the situation when my phone rang. It was Naomi.

"Hello, Dr. Wyman," she said, clearly more upbeat than she'd been in the past. "I was thrilled when Mr. Brock asked me to place this phone call to arrange for your sessions together. You must be thrilled, too."

"I can't begin to describe how I feel," I said dully.

"I'll never forget that beautiful speech you made," she clucked, "when you said that if Mr. Brock were to undergo the Wyman Method, it would benefit all womenkind."

"Well, I was exaggerating just a—"

"And you said that he would become a kindler, gentler boss, Dr. Wyman. I'm really looking forward to that, I don't mind telling you. And I'm not alone in that sentiment. There are others at Finefoods who will be forever in your debt."

Debt. Taking Brock on as a client would fatten my bank account a bit, I reminded myself. Another check to deposit each week.

"Oh, it's all so exciting," Naomi said breathlessly. "I simply cannot wait to see Mr. Brock's metamorphosis. Of course, he'll be a challenge for you, Dr. Wyman, perhaps your greatest challenge thus far. Your task will be akin to turning a lion into a lamb."

It was *that* reference that got to me, woke me up, snapped me out of it. The lion/lamb thing. When I was in graduate school and the Wyman Method was in its infancy, one of my professors—an obnoxious skeptic—said with a sneer, "You expect to change a man's character by changing his speech? Ha! That's as preposterous as trying to turn a lion into a lamb."

His were fighting words, and, rather than deter me or discourage me or cause me to lose faith in my theory, they spurred me on. And now, here was Naomi using the very same analogy, and the effect on me was equally energizing.

Of course I'll take Brock on as a client, I thought, grabbing a pen and my appointment calendar. So it won't be about money and fame and higher ratings than Dr. Joy. It'll be about my work, about helping people, about what I know to be true, which is that men *can* be taught to be more sensitive by fiddling with their language.

Okay, maybe it *was* about money, just a little. A paying customer was a paying customer.

PART TWO

11

NAOMI AND I were hashing out the dates for Brock's sessions when The Titan himself picked up his extension and busted in on our conversation, interrupting without remorse as was his thoroughly irritating habit.

"Listen, don't box me in with this schedule," he bossed both of us. "I'm out of town at the drop of a hat, remember."

"The Wyman Method is a six-month program," I replied crispy. "Therefore, you'll come once a week for six months, Mr. Brock, commencing this month and concluding in September, after Labor Day."

"I just told you," he barked. "I don't keep bankers' hours. I can't stick to a schedule like that."

"Of course you can," I countered.

"No, I can't," he said. "I'm a CEO with meetings all over the world, not a salesgirl who can duck out on her lunch break."

God. He was going to be heavy sledding. "I'm willing to allow for some flexibility within the schedule," I conceded. "If you absolutely have to miss appointments, you can make up the time by seeing me on weekends or evenings."

"Not possible," he said. "I have what is called a *private life* on evenings and weekends."

"Mr. Brock," I said. "You led me to understand that your board of directors has asked you to take immediate action here. You indicated that they're concerned about female executives leaving Finefoods because of your management style. Perhaps they're also concerned about female executives *suing* Finefoods because of your management style." I don't know where I was getting all this nervy attitude, but I guess I figured that he was the one with a lot to lose and I was the one trying to help him, which put me in the one-up position with him for a change.

"What's your point?" he said resignedly.

"My point is that I'm offering to see you on weekends and evenings in order for you to complete the program, satisfy your board of directors, and hang onto your job. If I were you, Mr. Brock, I'd take me up on my offer."

There was no sarcastic comeback from him, just a hang up, which Naomi and I took as a gesture of acquiescence.

I CALLED MY friends and reported to each of them my amazing news, saving until the end the part about my not being able to alert the media and then swearing them to secrecy.

"What's the point of landing Brandon Brock as a client if you can't promote it?" was Penny's immediate response. "The whole idea was for you to use him to rebuild your career."

"I know," I said, "but I really feel that I'll be doing a good thing by working with him. And when you do good things for people, the good comes back to you."

"Please. That sounds like something Isabel would say," Penny scoffed.

Actually, it *was* something Isabel would say and she did say it, right after I gave her the bulletin about Brock. She also quoted from an ancient Buddhist monk and then blessed me.

Gail was alarmed at first. "You're going to see this guy at night?"

"If he has to make up a session, yes."

"Then I'd be *very* careful, Lynn."

"Why?"

"Because you said he's an animal. Well, if he's an animal, you don't want to be alone with him at night when there'll be no one around to hear you scream."

"Gail." I smiled at her leap into melodrama. "I only meant that he's a high-testosterone type who makes inappropriate remarks about women's legs. I think I can cope with that."

"I really respect you for what you're doing," said Sarah when I told her about Brock. "I certainly wouldn't want to tangle with 'America's Toughest Boss.' I'd find it too intimidating."

"We won't be tangling. We'll be working toward a common goal," I maintained. "Besides, I don't let any of my clients get to me. It's not personal with them. It's business."

I honestly believed that. I did.

I TOOK A different approach when I told Diane, my assistant, about our new client. I simply advised her that his name was Brandon Brock and that he would be coming in at noon on Tuesdays. Period. I assumed she wouldn't know who he was, so there'd be no need for all the hush-hush stuff, and I was right.

"I should write him down in the book for twelve noon on Tuesdays?" she confirmed, showing less interest in Brock than in her freshly polished nails, blowing on them before putting pen to paper.

"Yes. Occasionally, his secretary may call to cancel at the last minute, because he travels a lot, but noon on Tuesdays will be his standing appointment."

And so it was. Before he arrived for his initial session, I was oddly jittery, expectant. I dusted the furniture in my office, placed fresh flowers in a vase on the table next to the recording equipment, set a copy of my book on my desk, smoothed my hair, my skirt and whatever else I imagined needed smoothing.

At noon on the nose, he appeared in the waiting room. Diane

buzzed me to tell me. I went out and said hello, shook hands with him, asked him to follow me back to my office. He was wearing a dark gray suit and a green tie and a white shirt, which, together with his blond hair and blue eyes and ruddy complexion, made him look very vivid, very Technicolor. And since I had only seen him in tennis clothes previously, he looked very dressed up, very I'm-an-important-businessman-albeit-a-boorish-one.

I closed the door behind us and said, "Please have a seat, Mr. Brock," pointing to the chair opposite the one where I always sat.

He sat, his broad shoulders broader than the back of the chair, which made him seem even more awkward and out of place than I was certain he already felt. In fact, I was actually on the verge of offering to switch seats with him, my chair being a cushy wing chair and his being a more conventional visitor's chair, but then he surveyed the room and said in his insufferably disrespectful tone, "So what do you call this office of yours, snookums? The Wimp Factory?"

"I beg your pardon?" I replied with disgust. I was supposed to remain impartial, objective, clinical with regard to my clients, but, going by my early exposure to him, Brandon Brock personified everything I despised about men.

"You heard me. Is this the Wimp Factory? The assembly line where you turn out men whose idea of good television is the Lifetime network instead of the Playboy channel?"

"I'm sure you intended that to be amusing," I said, trying to appear unfazed, "but by the time you've completed the Wyman Method, you may, indeed, be watching the Lifetime network."

"And swapping recipes with my friends?"

"Possibly."

"And discussing inexpensive and all-natural ways to keep the inside of the refrigerator smelling fresh as a daisy?"

"If that's what interests you."

"Yeah, it interests me. About as much as estrogen therapy interests me."

"Mr. Brock," I said, reaching for my notebook and a pencil. "I'd like us to get started here."

"Fine. We'll get started. I'm just telling you: I refuse to come out of this program acting like those guys who're always moaning about their *issues*. And forget about trying to get me off sports. I love sports."

"My goal is not to diminish you in any way. My goal is to give you the tools to be the best CEO that you can be. The catch is, in order to accomplish that goal, I'm going to teach you how to speak differently."

"Like a woman."

"Yes. So that you can improve your one-on-one interactions with the women who work at Finefoods, among others."

He rolled his eyes. "All right. Go ahead."

"Thank you," I said. "We'll begin with my doing an evaluation, which will enable me to target specific problem areas. I'll ask you some questions and you'll respond as honestly as you can. Are you ready?"

"I'm on the edge of my seat."

"Question one: What words would you use to pay your secretary a compliment about her appearance?"

"No words. Naomi's a good secretary but she's a dog in the looks department."

I glanced up from my notebook. "Mr. Brock. Are you even aware that that sort of description is extremely adolescent, never mind mean-spirited?"

"You asked me to be honest. Naomi's a sweet gal but she's got the kisser of a bull terrier and tits that droop so low she practically trips over them."

I know, I know. You probably think there aren't men who talk like that anymore. You've read about the Promise Keepers and the At-Home Daddies and you believe that the landscape has changed, that men have grown up, that men have become *feminized*. And some of them *have* gotten their act together, I grant you. But there are still plenty of Brandon Brocks out there—brilliant, successful businessmen who inexplicably speak like Beavis and/or Butthead. If you're married to one, you're nodding right now.

"And I wasn't being mean-spirited," he added defensively. "It's not as if I'd ever say that stuff to her face."

"Then what, precisely, would you say to her face?" I asked.

He thought for a second, then shrugged.

"Nothing?" I prompted. "Not even a 'That's a pretty dress, Naomi'?"

"Hey, wait a minute," he said, waving his big hands in the air. "I thought the reason I was here was because it's not *politically correct* for me to compliment the women I work with on their clothes, their legs, all of that."

Dense. Was he ever dense. "It's perfectly acceptable to compliment a woman on her dress, as in, 'That's a nice color on you, Naomi.' Just as it would be fine for a woman to say, referring to your attire, 'That's a nice tie, Mr. Brock.' "

He smiled as he fingered his own green silk necktie. "Shucks, Doc. I wore it today, just for you."

I ignored that. "But it's not acceptable for you to compliment a woman on her attire, as in, 'Wow. That dress makes you look good enough to eat, honey.' "

Brock laughed. "That wasn't a bad impersonation of me."

"I'm thrilled that you enjoyed it. You see, it's the sexual innuendo in the remark that's inappropriate," I said. "You can compliment a woman on her dress as long as it's crystal clear that you're not coming on to her."

"So I can compliment a woman on her dress—minus the sexual

innuendo—but I can't compliment her on her legs? That's a little arbitrary."

"Nevertheless, when you compliment a woman on her legs, the sexual interest is implicit and you risk getting slapped with a lawsuit, especially if the woman whose legs you're complimenting finds your attention unwanted or even disturbing."

"Do you find it unwanted or disturbing when I say, 'You've got great legs, Dr. Wyman'?"

"Of course I do," I said. Well, that time I did. We were in a business meeting, not at a tennis club.

"Then explain this: If you don't want me to notice your great legs, why the short skirt?"

Not that I need to justify my wardrobe, but, for the record, my skirt was not short that day; it was merely a few inches above the knee, as was fashionable.

"Let's move on, shall we?" I said, tugging on the hem of the skirt, willing it to lengthen. "I'm trying to establish for you the difference between language that might provoke a sexual harassment lawsuit and language that is complimentary but benign."

"Please. I'm not a complete idiot. I already get the difference. I just don't get what the big deal about it is, why everybody runs around crying about it, why my company instituted all these rules concerning what seems to me to be a matter of common sense. Why, for instance, would a woman find it disturbing to be complimented, flirted with, given the idea that she's desirable?"

"Because she's in a *work* environment. She wants to be complimented, praised, valued for her business acumen, not for her ability to arouse a man sexually."

"What if she likes the guy? She'd rather arouse him than repel him, wouldn't she? Even if they do work in the same company."

"As I already indicated, it's the man's *unwanted* expressions of sexual interest that are troublesome."

"Why? All the woman's got to do is tell the guy to buzz off and that's the end of it."

"Really? What if the guy is you, Mr. Brock? How many women would feel secure enough in their job to tell their CEO to buzz off?"

"I don't have a clue, but if they did, I certainly wouldn't fire them, for Christ's sake. A woman tells me to buzz off, I buzz off."

"That's very noble of you, but once you've completed this program, you'll no longer be putting yourself or the women who work for you in that uncomfortable situation."

"And the world will be a far, far better place," he said wryly.

"Let's move on to another question: You're in a meeting, sitting around the conference table with your people, and one of your female executives presents an idea. How do you respond to her?"

"I cut her off in mid sentence."

"You interrupt, in other words?"

"Sure, because if I don't, the meeting will go on forever. Have you ever listened to how a woman presents an idea in a meeting?"

"Well, naturally I've—"

"Trust me, it can be pure torture. Here's how a man presents an idea: 'I have a great idea for this product.' Short. Sweet. Done. Now here's how a woman approaches it: 'I'd like to share with you what I think might be a good idea for this product. It may sound like a dumb idea at first and I may be the only one who supports it, so call me crazy if you want to, but it just might work.' Blah blah blah. I mean, why can't they get to the point and shut up? Why can't they just say what they have to say without all the disclaimers?"

"Because they know they'll be cut off, put down, dismissed by men like you, which makes them feel insecure."

"That's *their* problem."

"No, it's *your* problem or you wouldn't be here. You have to learn how to speak their language so they won't take their insecurity—I mean, their talent—to some other company."

"God forbid."

"Let's try another question," I continued. "When was the last time you told a woman how you really felt?"

"About what?"

"About anything. When was the last time you shared your feelings?"

"A few minutes ago. I told you I loved sports."

"I remember, but I was thinking of something a bit more revelatory. When was the last time you expressed fear, for example?"

"I don't know, but I'll express it right now: I'm *afraid* the Yankees won't win the World Series this year."

I jotted down the fact that Brandon Brock had an aversion to appearing vulnerable. And then I posed the rest of the questions that comprised the Wyman Method's evaluation, noted his responses, and found—unsurprisingly—that he scored poorly in virtually every category.

"Our time is up for today," I said at the end of the session. "Once I've studied your evaluation, I'll make up scripts for us to practice and we'll begin the actual teaching of Womenspeak."

He groaned.

"I know it seems like an uphill climb," I said, rising from my chair, "but in six short months, you'll be a sensitive CEO, your board of directors will be pleased, and women will be clamoring to come to work at Finefoods."

"And we'll all live happily ever after." He stood, straightened his tie, and looked at me. "Before I go, I'd like to ask you something, snookums."

"All right, but our time *is* up," I said hurriedly, as if I had another client waiting, which I didn't.

"Then I'll make it fast. Do women really want men to talk like they do?"

I walked over to my office door and opened it. "Let me answer your question this way, Mr. Brock. What women really want is for men *not* to talk like you do."

12

THE FOLLOWING TUESDAY morning at nine, Naomi called my office and told Diane she was terribly sorry but Mr. Brock wouldn't be able to keep his noon appointment that day.

"She said he had a bunch of important meetings that would last until about five o'clock," Diane informed me.

I had expected this, but I was annoyed. I had made the supreme sacrifice of agreeing to "fix" Brandon Brock. The least he could do was show up.

"Call her back and reschedule Mr. Brock for another day this week," I said to Diane.

"I already tried that but she said he was flying to South America tomorrow and would be gone until Sunday night."

The skunk. Well, he could run but he couldn't hide. "She said his meetings today would be over by five or so?"

"Right."

"Then call her back and reschedule Mr. Brock for some time after five."

"Tonight?"

"Yes."

"But you never see clients at night, Dr. Wyman."

"Look around this reception area, Diane. Do you see people lining up waiting to have a session with me?"

"No."

"Okay. Now look at *me*, Diane. Do you see a woman yearning to rush home to her loving husband in Mt. Kisco?"

"No." She lowered her eyes, her cheeks flushing. She didn't like to talk about Kip, because of what he did to me, I guessed. I assumed she was embarrassed for me.

"Then you understand why I'll see Mr. Brock tonight. Call his secretary and try to get him in here. He's just starting the program. I think his progress would be impeded if he were to skip a week."

Diane placed the call. After what must have been serious resistance on Brock's part, Naomi confirmed that her boss would arrive at my office at seven P.M.

IT WAS ONE of those early April nights, when the nip of winter has all but lost its bite. There was, as there always is for me in April, a hint of hope in the air, a smell of spring, a sense of possibility. And so, although I was ravenously hungry and would have greatly preferred a dinner out with my friends to a fifty-five-minute session with America's Toughest Boss, I was upbeat, ready to rumble.

Brock, on the other hand, was in a foul mood. He stormed into my office, pouting like a bratty kid, grumbling about the date *I* had forced him to cancel with Kelsey.

"How is she, by the way?" I asked cheerfully, refusing to be held accountable for the fact that he would not be getting laid by some half-baked interior decorator that evening.

"Who?" He was in a navy blue suit this time, with a pale blue-and-white-striped shirt and red-patterned tie. He was even more multihued than before, even more entertaining to behold. I say "entertaining" because he was so colorful, literally, what with the vividness of his hair and eyes and skin and clothes, and because his face was expressive and his body a bulky presence. To sum up, he wasn't conventionally handsome, as I've indicated, but he was hard to look away from, as only certain people are.

"Kelsey," I said. "How is she?"

"Pissed off about my coming here tonight. That's how she is."

"Then she's not very forward thinking," I said. "After all, she's going to be among the beneficiaries of the changes in you, Mr. Brock."

"She likes me the way I am. And there are plenty of others who like me the way I am." He stuck his chin out after he said this.

"Of course there are," I said soothingly (okay, patronizingly). "Now, shall we get started?"

"It's your show, snookums."

"Actually, why don't we begin by doing away with the 'snookums.' I think it's run its course, don't you?"

"Fine. What'll I call you then? Doc?"

"No. You should call me Dr. Wyman, just as all my other clients do." I put some emphasis on the *all* because I used to have a great many clients and because I wanted him to believe that I still did. "Your tendency to fall back on nicknames suggests that you like to put yourself above others, to poke fun at them and, therefore, to distance yourself from them."

"Oh, lighten up. There's nothing wrong with giving people nicknames."

"I see. Then you don't mind that your employees at Finefoods have given *you* one: Bran?"

"Bran?" He looked mortified. Apparently, this was news to him.

"Yes. Because your name is Brandon and you sell all those fiber-rich cereals. I read about it in a magazine article about you."

He shook his head vigorously. "Nobody at Finefoods calls me Bran. Nobody."

"So you don't care for the nickname?"

"Of course I don't care for it. It makes me sound like a goddam laxative. It's a stupid nickname."

"Not unlike *Doc*, which makes me sound like a wizened old physician in a western movie—the drunk who tries to save the hero after he's been shot at the saloon."

Brock's scowl receded and I detected the beginning of a smile. "You want me to call you Dr. Wyman? I'll call you Dr. Wyman."

"Perfect. And I'll continue to call you Mr. Brock." It was odd that I gravitated instantly toward the "Mr. Brock," since I usually called my clients by their first names. I suppose I felt my own need for distance between us. "Now, I've prepared several scripts for us to practice." I turned on the tape recorder and moved the microphone closer to Brock's face. "Today's script will teach you how to use Womenspeak in business meetings in order for you to communicate better with the women you work with. I'll speak a line of dialogue and then you'll repeat it into the microphone, and then we'll speak another line of dialogue, and so on. Once you've repeated these lines numerous times and memorized them, you'll incorporate them into your daily conversation and in doing so, you'll change your behavior. Do you understand?"

"Do I understand what you just said? Yes, because I'm an educated man and my hearing's good in both ears. Do I understand why a man is supposed to learn to speak like a woman? No, because it should be the other way around."

I sighed. "But your board of directors didn't send you to a linguist so you could learn to speak like a man, did they, Mr. Brock?"

"No."

I nodded. "The setting for the script is a conference room. You have arrived a few minutes early for a meeting and you find yourself alone with one of your female executives."

"I know, I know. I don't say a word about her legs."

"Right. What *would* you say in that instance, in an attempt to make pre-meeting small-talk with her?"

"I'd probably tell a joke."

"An off-color joke?"

"Is there any other kind?"

"And you think telling that kind of a joke puts the woman at ease?"

"It's not my job to put the woman at ease. If she can't take the heat, she should go back to the kitchen."

"My, what an amusing twist on the old expression." Not. "But must I keep reminding you, Mr. Brock, that it *is* your job to put the woman at ease, now that your behavior has provoked so many capable women to leave Finefoods? That it's incumbent upon you, as the company's chief executive, to turn that trend around? Can't we at least acknowledge the problem and move on, before we waste any more time here tonight?"

"Alrt."

"What was that? You were mumbling."

"I SAID 'ALL RIGHT'!"

"Good. The way to put the woman at ease is to talk to her about something she'll relate to, to find a way to *share* with her."

"I think I'm gonna be sick."

"Here's the line of dialogue I'd like you to repeat. 'Good morning, Susan—' "

"I don't have any women who work for me named Susan," he interrupted.

"Play along, would you, Mr. Brock? 'Good morning, Susan. I don't know how *you* metabolize desserts, but that chocolate mousse cake *I* had last night went straight to my thighs.' "

Brock leaned back in his chair and roared with laughter. When he was finally able to compose himself, he said, "If that's Women-speak, I'm fucked."

I did not permit my nostrils to flare in righteous indignation—I hate stories about women whose nostrils flare in righteous indignation—but I did allow my lips to purse. "Let's dispense with the 'fucked' along with the nicknames, shall we?"

"Sure. But you don't really expect me to say that stuff about my thighs."

"What I expect, Mr. Brock, is that you'll try your best to say the lines of dialogue I ask you to say. Studies have shown that women feel comfortable talking about food, especially in conjunction with their weight. Imagine how much more at ease 'Susan' will be if her boss is engaging her in an anecdote about his fattening dessert instead of cracking a joke in which the word 'pussy' figures prominently."

He laughed again. "You do seem to be well acquainted with my verbal habits, Doc— tor, Wyman."

"It's my job to be well acquainted with them, Mr. Brock. Let's go. Directly into the microphone. 'Good morning, Susan. I don't know how *you* metabolize desserts, but that chocolate mousse cake *I* had last night went straight to my thighs.' Note the extra beats on the words 'you' and 'I.' They'll make Susan feel as if you're truly sharing with her."

Brock shrugged, moved closer to the microphone and delivered the line.

"Excellent."

"Was it? I thought I sounded like—"

"Yes?"

"A woman."

I beamed. "Exactly."

A dazed but slightly euphoric expression came over his face. They all took on that look after their first little success. Remember when you tried to speak a foreign language for the first time and it actually sounded authentic?

"What happens after I say that line to Susan?" he asked.

"She'll probably respond with her own food story and you two will strike up a nice conversation and then after the meeting she'll go back to her friends and say, 'We were wrong about Brandon Brock. He's very human, very down to earth, very easy to talk to.' "

"But what if she doesn't respond with her own food story? What if she just nods at me and plays with her laptop?"

"Then you'll try the next line in the script. You'll say, 'You know, Susan, my car mechanic was incredibly hostile this morning.' "

He guffawed at that one. "Why the hell would I say that to her?"

"Because women often exchange tales of hostile car mechanics and distracted supermarket checkout personnel and self-absorbed baby sitters who show up late if at all. These are the little dramas of a woman's life and you'll be tapping right into them."

"Tapping right into them."

"Yes."

"I'm just wondering, are these *your* little dramas, Dr. Wyman?"

"What—"

"The hostile mechanic and the rest? Do you have personal experience with these daily irritations?"

"Well, yes, with the exception of the self-absorbed baby sitters. I don't have children."

"But you have a husband."

"Not presently."

"No? That day at the Racquet Club you said you were married."

I was surprised that he remembered. "I was married then. I'm not now."

He sat back in his chair and appraised me, the smugness returning. "Let me guess: Your husband told one too many off-color jokes so you gave him the boot. Or maybe he wouldn't quit slobbering over your great legs and that's why you gave him the boot."

"Actually, I gave him the boot because he wouldn't quit slobbering over his *girlfriend's* great legs."

That wiped the smirk off his face. Of course it was only later, in the middle of the night, in fact, that I realized that by admitting that my husband had betrayed me, I was resurrecting the dreaded issue of my credibility as a relationship expert. But, oddly enough, Brock didn't seem to connect the two, or if he did, the information didn't send him running out of the office.

"So you're divorced?" he asked.

"Legally separated. But I'd really rather get back to—"

"I'm divorced," he interrupted.

I didn't say anything. I was not a therapist, he was not on the couch, and our agenda was his speech patterns not his marital woes. Still, I wasn't un-curious.

"Let me guess," I said, echoing him. "You left her for a woman half her age."

"Nope. She left me for a man half her age. Our pool guy."

"Oh."

"I just don't get women," he mused, scratching his blond head. "I honestly don't know what they want. I don't even think *they* know what they want."

"Studies show that they want men with whom they can communicate," I said, hoping to move us back on track. "So why don't we finish today's script, Mr. Brock."

He hesitated for a moment, as if still contemplating the mysteries of the universe, then nodded. We finished the day's script. When our time was up and I was walking him out of the office, he stopped, turned toward me and did the most unexpected thing. He said, "Sorry about what happened with your husband. If anyone knows how that feels, it's the guy you're looking at."

He was gone before I could react.

No, it wasn't as if what he said was brilliant or original or ringing with insight. What was striking was that a man who appeared not to have been born with the "empathy" gene suddenly used the words "sorry" and "feels" in the same sentence!

I drove home to Mt. Kisco thinking my six months with Brandon Brock might not be as trying as I'd feared.

13

IT WAS SARAH'S birthday over the weekend, so I actually had someplace to go instead of sitting in my apartment doing crossword puzzles. Her husband, Edward, with whom she had patched things up temporarily, was throwing her a party at Dogwood and I was invited, along with over a hundred other revelers.

I hadn't been to any big parties since Kip and I had separated, and while I was looking forward to Sarah's, I was apprehensive about it too. Yes, I had always been an independent woman, and yes, I attended plenty of professional functions on my own, but when it came to social gatherings (not counting little get-togethers with my friends) I was oddly tongue-tied.

Yeah, sure, you're probably thinking. How can someone who tells other people how to communicate be tongue-tied? The answer is: I don't know. Put me in a business meeting and I was as glib as a politician. Put me at a birthday party and I was a dud.

This dichotomy of personality, this quirk, was due, I suppose, to a feeling of inadequacy on my part, a sense that I had less control in social situations than I did when I was *Dr. Lynn Wyman*. The truth is, I was all about my identity as a linguist, and once you stripped that away, there was nothing there. Or so I felt. Naked. Vulnerable. Scared. Blame it on some chemical screw-up in my brain. Blame it on my parents' divorce. Blame it on the fact that I was a bookworm as a kid as opposed to a prom queen. However you look at it, I was a bit of a head case or, at the very least, a woman who wasn't always the take-charge dame she seemed.

When I arrived at Dogwood on Saturday night, the party was in full swing. Crowds of celebrants were moving about the house, laughing and gesturing and nibbling on the hors d'oeuvres being passed by the tuxedoed catering staff the Peppers had hired for the occasion. After Justine took my coat, I entered the living room, searching for a familiar face.

"Lynn! Over here!" Penny waved from the other end of the room.

Relieved, I squeezed my way through the crowd. I gave her a hug when I finally reached her. "No date?" I asked. She was rarely without her escort du jour.

"No date. I'm solo tonight."

"Because you're still upset about the man you'd been seeing? The one that got away?"

She looked surprised.

"The one you told me about," I said, in case she'd forgotten she'd mentioned him to me. "You were sort of licking your wounds when we had lunch that day."

She tossed her head back and laughed. "Oh, him," she said. "I'm over him. Totally. He's a shit, and I finally realized that."

"Who was he?" I asked, figuring she'd be more forthcoming about the guy now that she was so over him. "Someone you met through work?"

"No," she said. "Someone I met through a friend."

"Not a blind date," I kidded her, knowing how she detested blind dates. She preferred to engineer her own matches.

"No. I met him through this friend and it was completely platonic at first, but one day we ran into each other, without my friend around, and the relationship took a romantic turn."

"I'm sorry it didn't last. What do you think went wrong between you?"

She smiled. "It wasn't a problem with communication, if that's what you're wondering, Dr. Wyman."

I smiled too. "There are other things that can wreck a relationship. I ought to know, huh?"

She patted my shoulder. "Enough about me. How are you doing, Lynn?"

"Fine."

"Dating anybody?"

"No. Just concentrating on getting my career back on track."

She huddled closer. "So how's everything going with Brandon Brock? Is he pure hell?"

"Not exactly. I think there might be a person in there. I just have to keep plugging away and see."

She was about to ask me another question about Brock when Gail and her husband Jim approached us. Gail was on crutches, having fallen in the woods of California while shooting a documentary about the woman who lived in the tree for two years. Jim, too, looked as if he'd been in a war. His right eye was swollen and bruised after having fought off a persistent loan shark.

"How's the Brandon Brock project going?" she whispered, while Penny made conversation with Jim.

"It's still early in the game, but I'm optimistic," I whispered back. "Everything okay with you? Relatively speaking?"

She maneuvered herself closer to me. "I'm thinking of leaving Jim."

"Really?" I tried to look stunned by this remark, but Gail had been thinking of leaving Jim for as long as I'd known her.

She nodded. "I've started dieting too. I've lost six pounds already." She said this as she eyed a tray of hors d'oeuvres and bit her lip in response to the temptation.

"That's great, Gail. It's important to take care of yourself."

"That's my goal: To look out for *me*. I've spent entirely too many years sacrificing my needs for everybody else's. So I'm losing weight, changing my hair, maybe even getting my nose fixed."

"There's nothing wrong with your nose." True, she had broken it a couple of times, along with countless other bones in her body, but it wasn't crying out for cosmetic surgery. I wondered what had triggered this latest self-improvement kick.

The four of us continued to chat, eventually spotting Isabel who had brought along Rita, her astrologer.

"Did you ever break it off with Francisco?" I asked her. "The last time I saw you, you said you'd met someone else."

"I did break up with Francisco and I have met someone else," she said. "One of these days, without all these people around, I'll tell you about it."

"Good," I said, agreeing that a noisy party wasn't the place for a serious conversation.

I was about to ask her how the *Vanity Fair* shoot worked out when Sarah made her way over to us. She looked spectacular in a turquoise blue silk dress that hugged her body. We congratulated her on her birthday and said we were glad she and Edward were together again. She inhaled our compliments and best wishes and then took off, leaving behind a trail of some divine perfume.

After a while, Penny drifted away from our group so she could shake a few hands, score a few contacts—her usual networking ritual. Isabel and Rita wandered off too, to step outside on Sarah's stone terrace and gaze at the full moon, which, according to Rita, was the brightest in over a hundred years and full of omens for Isabel's birth sign. Even Gail and Jim limped away at some point, to find a comfortable place to sit, I think.

So there I was, alone in the crowd, wishing I could mingle as effortlessly as Penny did. I was downing a stuffed mushroom cap when one of Sarah's guests, a man in a navy blue sport jacket, backed into me, spilling his red wine on my beige shoes.

"Oh my gosh," he said, wheeling around. "We're all so tightly packed in here I didn't see you."

"Don't worry about it," I said, worrying desperately about the shoes, which I hoped weren't ruined.

He continued to apologize and I continue to reassure him, and it went on like that for several minutes before it dawned on me that he was drunk. Not in an obnoxious way, just a little sloppy, slurry. Finally, he got off the wine thing and asked me how I knew Sarah.

"We're old friends," I said. Obviously, he hadn't recognized me. As more and more time passed since the radio show and the television appearances and the book tours, fewer and fewer people recognized me. I could be a lap dancer instead of a linguist for all they cared.

"She and I are old friends too, although I haven't seen her in ages," he volunteered. "I've been living overseas."

"Oh." See? I wasn't much of a chitchatter at social gatherings.

"Yes, I was the president of Far East operations for Finefoods."

"Oh," I said again, with a lot more interest now. If Sarah had an old friend who was an executive at Finefoods, why in the world hadn't she told me? Strange. "Then you worked for Brandon Brock?"

"Still do, actually. Why? Do you know Brandon?"

"No. No, I don't. I've read a number of articles about him, that's all." The last thing I needed was for it to get back to Brock that I was blabbing about him at a birthday party.

This man, who eventually introduced himself as Greg, shook his head and wagged his finger at me. "Don't believe all that crap in the magazines. Brandon's not the monster they make him out to be."

"*Fortune* did name him America's Toughest Boss."

"Yes, and there are people who think he's a nightmare to work for, I admit it. But I can tell you that he's been nothing but terrific to me."

Yeah, that's because you're a *man*, Greg. You two speak the same language. "What do you do at Finefoods now that you're back in the States?" I asked, warming to this conversation.

"Nothing, at the moment. Well, that's not completely true. Brandon got me a consulting deal with the company."

"He got it for you?"

"What I'm saying is he made the deal happen and he didn't have to."

"Then why did he?"

Greg polished off what was remaining in his wineglass. "Look, I've had a lot to drink and I get much too talkative and over-the-top sentimental when I've been hitting the grape juice. But you asked, so I'll tell."

"I don't want to pry." Damn right, I do.

"When I was headquartered in the Far East, my daughter—my only child, by the way—was diagnosed with leukemia. I wanted her to be treated at Sloan Kettering here in New York, so I asked Brandon—who had only just joined the company and didn't know me from Adam—for a leave of absence. Without the slightest hesitation or objection, he put somebody else in my spot and flew me, my wife, and my daughter back home. He paid me a full salary while I stayed away from the office to spend time with my daughter. And when she died last year— "

"I'm sorry."

"Thanks. When she died last year, I told Brandon I wasn't ready to come back to work. I was pretty messed up about her death—so messed up that my wife and I split up, because I wasn't much of a husband by that point. So I lost my daughter and my wife, which really *was* a nightmare, worse than anything they say Brandon can dish out."

"Again, I'm terribly sorry, Greg. But it sounds to me as if you're pulling your life back together with this consulting position you mentioned."

He smiled ruefully. "The consulting thing is bogus. I'm not ready to throw myself into my job yet. Brandon knows that and he appreciates how I feel. But he doesn't want me to starve, so he put me on the payroll as a consultant on Far East operations."

"I don't understand. How is that bogus?"

"Because this is the extent of our consultations: He calls me up once a week and says, 'How're you doing, Greg?' and I say, 'Pretty good, Brandon. How about you?' That's it."

"So you don't even discuss Far East operations?"

He shook his head, his eyes welling up. "Contrary to popular opinion, he can be quite a compassionate guy."

"No wonder you're in his corner," I said, attempting to make Greg's image of Brandon Brock jibe with mine.

"I'd do anything for him," he went on, sounding like a football player willing to die for his coach. "Sure I did a good job for Finefoods before he got there, and sure he wants me back as soon as I can hack it. But he didn't have to help me out. I'm not indispensable. What he did was a big-hearted, generous thing."

Big-hearted. Generous. *Compassionate*. Impressive adjectives, right? It was hard not to wonder if Greg and I were talking about the same man.

But we were, of course. I was just getting another glimpse of my client, a glimpse that seemed to confirm what I had sensed after our last session—that Brandon Brock was a bad boy but not utterly without redeeming features.

14

THE NEXT SEVERAL sessions with Brock were tugs of war, with the occasional breakthrough. Take the session where I had him listen to an entire Michael Bolton CD and then verbalize what he was feeling.

"Nauseous," was his answer.

"And why is that?" I asked, hoping for a response pertaining to his emotions, not his stomach.

"Because all the guy does is whine about love. Men don't relate to that."

"No, but we're working on what women relate to. And they relate to men who are up front about their feelings, especially their feelings about love."

"Baloney. They relate to men who keep them guessing. I'm not exactly without experience on this, Dr. Wyman. Women *say* they want us to fawn all over them, but what they really want is for us to treat them like they don't exist. It makes us a challenge."

"Certainly there are *some* women who prefer men who withhold, but studies show that most women respond to men who aren't afraid to express their feelings, the way Michael Bolton does in his music."

"Please. He's not expressing his feelings. He's wailing like a cat in heat. How does he get his voice to go up that high anyway? He's a guy, right?"

"Yes, Mr. Brock, and you may not be his biggest fan, but he does manage to appeal to women with his sharing. Of course there are other singers who appeal to women for the same reason, but when it comes to putting feelings out there in a thoroughly brave, albeit overwrought, way, Michael Bolton's the Man."

"Ah. I get it. So you want me to walk up to this fictional Susan who works for my company and start howling about how I wanna be her 'soul provider'? What the hell does that mean, to be someone's soul provider? Is he talking about religion? Money? What?"

I smiled. "He's talking about being a soul mate to a woman, about experiencing transcendent love."

His eyes widened. "You're serious. You actually like this guy's music. I bet you have every record he ever made. Come on, 'fess up."

All right, so I did own a couple of his records. Who said I had to admit it? "Why don't we forget about the kind of love Michael Bolton 'howls' about. You once told me you love sports. I'd like you to describe, in the no-holds-barred style you've just been listening to, specifically *how* you love sports, how sports make you *feel*."

"I don't have to sing my answer, do I?"

"Just speak it directly into the microphone, Mr. Brock."

He resisted at first, but after a little pestering he leaned in toward the recorder. "When I'm watching a baseball game, sitting there on the first base line, looking out over that green grass, smelling the beer and the hot dogs, hearing the crack of the bat and the pop of the ball, I feel—"

"Go on, Mr. Brock. You feel what?"

"Oh, Lord. This is stupid."

"You feel what, Mr. Brock?"

He cleared his throat. "I feel happy, giddy as a kid. I love the unpredictability of the game, love how there's no time clock, love how one stroke of the bat can turn the score around, love how the players are human beings from all walks of life, guys who aren't the size of a truck. When I'm at the ballpark, there's no place I'd rather be—with the exception of this office, naturally."

"Skip the sarcasm and keep going."

"Okay. To sum up, I'd say I feel joyous when I watch baseball, among other sports. Joyous. Glad to be alive. *Transcendent*. Does that answer your question, Dr. Wyman?"

"It certainly does. Thank you." Not a huge breakthrough but a breakthrough nonetheless.

At another session, I focused on getting Brock to observe small details about his surroundings and then comment on them, the way women do. Men are pitiful when it comes to noticing things (not counting a woman's breasts), and so teaching them how to practice the art of noticing was crucial to their mastery of Womenspeak.

"Here's the script, Mr. Brock. You and Susan are having a business lunch outside the office. You're sitting at the restaurant, eating, and you glance over at Susan's plate and say, with a concerned expression, 'Susan, I just noticed: You ordered your salad with the dressing on the side and yet it came soaked in balsamic vinaigrette."

"I'm gonna fire Susan."

"What?"

"How competent could she be if she didn't send back her salad when it didn't come the way she ordered it?"

"You're missing the point."

"So enlighten me."

"The point is for you to *notice* that she didn't get the salad the way she ordered it, to show that you're being attentive to her, as opposed to ignoring her. You see, Mr. Brock, if two women were having lunch and one of them didn't get what she ordered exactly the way she ordered it, the other one would notice it and comment on it, because that's how women establish intimacy with each other."

"By talking about salad?"

"Yes."

He shrugged. "Personally, I never order salad at a restaurant. They don't even call it salad anymore. They call it *field greens.*"

"I'd like us to get back to the script."

He honed his blue eyes on me. "You really think I'm from another planet, one of those Mars guys, don't you?"

"No. Absolutely not. I don't subscribe to that particular theory. I just think you need to become more sensitive, more in touch with your feminine side, as I've said over and over. And you'll get there, Mr. Brock. I promise you." I made a bet with my friends that you'll get there, buddy. "Now. Give me the line. 'Susan, I just noticed: You ordered your salad with the dressing on the side and yet it came soaked in balsamic vinaigrette.' "

He gave me the line, then asked, "Has anyone ever told you you'd make a great dominatrix?"

"Yes."

After a few weeks, I decided Brock was ready for his first on-site training trip. When he arrived at my office for his Tuesday appointment at noon, I said, "It's a beautiful day in May. Why don't we wander over to Bloomingdale's and buy your secretary a gift."

He looked totally bewildered. "Why should I buy Naomi a gift? It's not her birthday."

"When is her birthday?"

"How should I know?"

"You should know because you're her boss and you've been her boss for a number of years now. Once you've completed the Wyman Method, you'll not only know when her birthday is, you'll be able to say without any prodding whatsoever, 'Happy Birthday, Naomi. I'd like to take you out for lunch today to celebrate.' "

"Naomi never goes out for lunch. She has a *salad* at her desk. At least, she had one yesterday."

I beamed. "I'm very pleased, Mr. Brock."

"What for?"

"You noticed what she ate for lunch yesterday. That's progress."

He shrugged, as if it were nothing, but he was pleased, too. I could tell.

"So we'll walk over to Bloomingdale's and you'll pick out a present for Naomi, a Thanks-for-being-such-a-good-secretary present. She'll be delighted."

"But I wouldn't know what to buy for her. She's the one who buys all the gifts. I give her a list at Christmas and she takes care of everybody."

"That's why we're going on this little outing," I said. "It's time you learned how to take care of your own personal errands. No more distancing yourself from the people who matter to you."

He bitched and moaned but off we went.

It felt wonderful to be out of the office on such a mild, spring afternoon. Even Brock shed his scowl as he strolled next to me. It seemed that everyone in Manhattan had chosen to be outdoors during their lunch breaks; such were the crowds of men and women basking in the warm sunshine.

"It's nice out, isn't it?" I asked as we walked down Third Avenue.

"Very." He smiled at me, placed his hand on my back, and then, *noticing* my reproachful body language, stuck the hand safely into his jacket pocket.

"That was a smart decision on your part," I said, referring to his aborted touching of me. "It's inappropriate for a man to have that sort of physical contact with a woman in a business setting."

"Yeah, fine. I was just—"

"Yes?"

"Nothing."

"Right."

What I'm leaving out here is that, despite how I scolded him, I *liked* that Brandon Brock had placed his hand on my back. There was nothing the least bit inappropriate or unnatural or sleazy about it. It was an innocent gesture, and I knew it. But I was trying to change the way he interacted with women, and I couldn't do that if I didn't remain consistent and, most importantly, maintain my distance.

When we entered the department store, he looked genuinely lost.

"What's the matter?" I asked.

"I—"

"Yes?"

"I don't know how to buy something for Naomi or any other woman," he admitted, more belligerently than bashfully.

"Nonsense. Surely, you've shopped for Kelsey." That day up at Sarah's house, his girlfriend had been wearing enough expensive jewelry to weigh down an elephant.

"I've shopped *with* her. I've never shopped *for* her."

"Oh, come on, Mr. Brock. You've never bought her a present?"

"I've paid for her presents—lots of them—but she's always picked them out herself. So I've never had to think about it."

"Good. Then picking out something for Naomi will be an even more useful exercise."

"*Picking out what for Naomi?*" He stomped his foot, like a kid having a tantrum. It didn't take a genius to figure out that Brandon Brock wasn't comfortable when he wasn't in charge.

"How about trying to figure out what she might like? This will encourage you to think about her in a caring, supportive way, as opposed to viewing her as a machine. The idea is to remind you that she's a person too."

"I already know she's a person. A person who does my shopping so I don't have to."

I told him to can the backtalk and follow me.

I led him to the escalator, which we took to the designer sportswear department.

"How about buying her one of those lightweight cotton sweaters?" I suggested, pointing to the counter behind which the sweaters were folded.

"If we've ruled out the black negligee," he retorted.

I paid no attention. We walked over to the counter. "Now," I said, beginning my coaching. "The gist of the script is that you're going to ask the saleswoman for help."

"I don't like asking women for help. Never have."

"I'm aware of that. Nevertheless, you're going to wave that saleswoman over here and say, 'Excuse me, Miss. Could you help me with these ladies' sweaters?' "

"She'll think I'm a cross dresser."

"Stop it. Now, give me a practice line."

He looked around, to make sure no one was watching, and whispered, "Excuse me, Miss. Could you help me with these sweaters?"

"These ladies' sweaters. You forgot the 'ladies.' "

"Sorry."

"All right. After you've delivered the line and she says she'd be glad to help you, I want you to explain to her what you're looking for."

"But I don't know what I'm looking for!"

"Just say to her, 'I'd like to buy a gift for my secretary,' and then describe Naomi's size—oh, and leave out the bit about her tits being so low she trips over them."

"Okay, okay." He swallowed hard, then waved the saleswoman over.

She didn't see him immediately, so instead of waiting a few seconds, God forbid, he put his fingers in his mouth and whistled for her, nearly destroying my hearing.

"That's no way to get her attention," I hissed disapprovingly. "What do you do in restaurants when the waiter doesn't appear the instant you need him? Snap your fingers?"

"Sometimes."

"You'd think you never learned any manners, Mr. Brock."

"I learned them. I just bypass them."

"Well don't bypass them in the future. Now, here she comes."

The saleswoman hurried over to us. Brock stood there, fingering his tie.

"Let's have the line," I whispered, urging him on. "Go."

"Excuse me, Miss. Could you help me with these ladies' sweaters?"

"I'd be glad to," she said. "Which one were you interested in?"

Brock looked at me, the proverbial deer in the headlights. I leaned over and whispered the next line of the script in his ear.

"I'd like to buy a gift for my secretary," he managed after several awkward beats.

The saleswoman turned her gaze on me, looked me up and down. "Something in a small then? Or maybe an extra small?"

It was a completely understandable assumption on her part—that I was the secretary in question—but I wasn't crazy about the way she automatically dubbed me an extra small, without even measuring me.

"Oh, she's not my secretary," Brock said, nodding at me. "She's my—" He was stumped. And I couldn't blame him. We hadn't discussed ahead of time what would happen if someone recognized him, recognized me, or simply questioned the nature of our relationship. It was a given that he didn't want his sessions with me to become tabloid fodder, but I didn't anticipate any problem there. People rarely recognize CEOs (except George Steinbrenner, Ted Turner, and Rupert Murdoch—celebrity CEOs, in other words). And people rarely recognized me anymore.

"I'm his shopping advisor," I said, putting the matter to rest.

"Right," he said, relieved.

"Then what size is your secretary?" the saleswoman asked him.

He hesitated. I thought he was actually going to backslide and blurt out the "her tits are so low . . ." answer. He seemed to be struggling with exactly how to describe Naomi's chest size. Finally, he settled on, "She's pretty large on top—not big-boned, but a full cup of java, if you know what I mean."

I shook my head at him, pulled him aside. "That was most definitely *not* Womenspeak," I whispered. "Try to remember what your goal is in all this, would you please, Mr. Brock? Try to imagine what a woman would say in this situation."

He nodded.

"I'm fairly sure I have the general idea, sir," said the saleswoman, who was trying to keep a straight face. "We're talking about a large size for the sweater. Now then. In what color?"

Brock needed another conference with me. This from a man who made decisions on behalf of a multi-billion-dollar company. "What's *your* favorite color?" he whispered.

"Yellow," I whispered back. "Now come on, Mr. Brock. Before your next exchange with this saleswoman, I want you to summon up everything you've been learning in my office and bring it to the surface. I want you to call upon every single bit of information you've absorbed thus far. I want you to succeed at the Wyman Method. Right here, right now."

He nodded again, with more determination this time. I held my breath.

"I'd like to see the sweater in a yellow," he instructed the saleswoman. "But not a screaming, school-bus yellow. I'd prefer a softer, lemony yellow for my dear, tender-hearted secretary, more of a pastel shade, actually. Pastels are lovely for summer, don't you agree? Especially pastel yellow. It's sort of a sunshiney soul provider."

I didn't know whether to laugh out loud or do a victory dance.

"Did you like that?" he said after the saleswoman trotted off to find the sweater. "I hoped you would." He was grinning, enjoying himself immensely.

"Your Womenspeak was excellent," I commended him, forcing myself to remain coolly professional. "Flawless, in fact. Which leads me to believe that the Michael Bolton session had an effect on you after all."

He shook his head. "It was you, Dr. Wyman. You had an effect on me. Or aren't I supposed to say that?"

I felt myself flush slightly, shyly. "Of course you can say that, Mr Brock. I'm enormously gratified that I've been able to help you. It's my job to help you. The Wyman Method is a wonderful, wonderful program. I think you can see that now."

"Right." He glanced at his watch. "Uh-oh. I've got to get back to the office for a lunch meeting." He reached inside his pants pocket, pulled out his wallet and shoved a credit card in my hand. "Here's my Bloomies charge, Dr. Wyman. When the saleswoman comes back with my sunshiney soul provider sweater for Naomi, give her the card, have her bill my account, and then hang onto the sweater for me until I see you next week. What do you say?"

Before I could even sputter a reply registering my acute displeasure, he was gone.

15

LYNN? IT'S PENNY. Did I wake you?" It was eleven o'clock on Wednesday night.

"No. I was in bed reading." Yes, she did wake me. I don't know why people always lie about that. "Everything okay?"

"Yes. More than okay. That's why I'm calling. I'm really, really close to signing up Feminax as a client."

"What's Feminax?"

"Obviously, I did wake you," she said dryly. "Feminax happens to be the hot new manufacturer of tampons everyone's talking about."

I wasn't talking about it. Why would anyone talk about tampons, given the choice?

"Feminax is poised to take a huge market share away from Tampax," she went on. "And the president of the company is poised to hire PHG to do its public relations."

"That's great." And the point of this call at such a late hour is?

"His name is Matthew Cuddy and he seems like a good guy—not a lot of ego, more of a Just-the-facts-ma'am type. Anyhow, I've been trying to get face time with him outside the office, in a more social environment, so I can wheedle a commitment out of him. Well, he called this afternoon to say he's got four tickets to the Yankees game on Friday night and would I like to go!"

"That is good news," I said, my thoughts immediately landing on Brandon Brock. I was still fuming about his abandoning me at Bloomingdale's the day before, but when I remembered his worshipful and,

I assumed, honest declaration of his love of sports, especially baseball, I couldn't help wondering if he'd be at the game Friday night.

"So Matthew and I are going," said Penny, "and Matthew's top financial officer at Feminax, Seth Plotnick, is going. Which leaves one ticket that's not spoken for. I'm hoping—oh, please say yes, Lynn—that you'll round out our foursome."

"Me?"

"Yes. You don't have anything to do on Friday night, do you?" She asked this as if it were a no-brainer.

"Am I supposed to be this Seth Plotnick's date?" I said, not relishing the thought.

"Not necessarily, although he is single and it wouldn't kill you to put yourself back in circulation."

"I don't know, Penny. I'm not sure I'm ready to start dating again."

"Why? What are you waiting for?"

"I'm not waiting for anything. I just don't have the energy."

"Fine. So it won't be a date. Just come with us, please? You're my last shot. I've tried everyone else I know and they're all busy."

Gee, that made me feel great.

"You'd be doing me a big favor," she pleaded. "I want this Feminax account, Lynn, and you know how I am when I want something." Yeah, yeah, like a Tomahawk cruise missile. "So help me keep the boys happy on Friday night, okay?"

Why not, I figured. It won't be a date. Penny will be talking about tampons with Matthew, trying to close her deal, and I'll be sitting there with Seth, trying to act like the sort of flexible, plucky woman who's always up for a good time even when she isn't.

OUR SEATS WERE in the first row of the second level at Yankee Stadium—not the nosebleed section but not the best block in the neighborhood either. Maybe once Penny had raised Feminax's profile, the company would be able to afford better tickets.

"This okay?" asked Seth Plotnick, as we settled into our seats. He seemed nice enough—very gentlemanly and courteous—but he was old enough to be my father and wore a big, disgusting pinky ring and said "bee-yut-ee-ful" instead of beautiful, all of which were not the stuff of horror movies but not exactly turn-ons.

"Yes, fine," I said, nodding. The seating went Matthew, then Penny, then me, then Seth, who, after he'd had a couple of beers, suggested that I call him Nick.

"Nick?" I said. "Is that a middle name?"

"No. Plot-*nick*," he said. "Get it?"

I got it. Seth was a Jewish accountant who'd been watching too many episodes of *The Sopranos*.

The Yankees were playing the Minnesota Twins, who, according to Nick, wouldn't be much of a match for the home team. "The score will probably be lopsided, but it'll be fun anyway."

I smiled, wondering how in the world it would be fun. I didn't like baseball. I didn't like Nick. And by the third inning, I didn't like Penny or Matthew, who were huddled together discussing not only tampons, in general, but cotton cords, biodegradable applicators, and degrees of absorbency, in particular.

"Hot dog?" asked Nick.

"No, thanks," I said, Penny and Matthew having put a dent in my appetite.

"How about a beer then?" said Nick. "I'm having another one."

"Sure." I hated beer but didn't want to seem totally standoffish.

Nick and I chatted about this and that—nothing worth going into, trust me. At one point, he stopped talking so he could watch what was happening in the game. Apparently, the bases were loaded and one of the Yankees was about to score. Or something like that.

"Want to borrow the binoculars?" he offered, after looking through them himself.

"Great. Thanks." I reached out for the binoculars, just to be polite.

It took a few seconds before I could focus my eyes properly and really see anything through the lenses—I actually zoomed in on my own lap!—but once I got the hang of them, the binoculars were quite useful and I was able to view the action on the field in a way that was rather involving. In fact, I was enjoying them so much that I held onto them for a while, checking out the players' uniforms, checking out the food and beverage vendors, checking out the people watching the game.

It was during my casual perusal of the spectators—I swear I wasn't looking for him; well, maybe not *swear*, but I wasn't looking for him, not consciously—that I spotted Brandon Brock, spotted his blond head and his broad shoulders and his ruddy face. He was sitting down on the field near the first base line, his girlfriend Kelsey sitting right there next to him, feeding him the tip of a hot dog and then licking the mustard off his lips. Yech.

I put down the binoculars.

"Anything wrong?" asked Nick. He really was a nice man. Just stupefyingly dull.

"Oh, no," I said quickly. "The binoculars got too heavy, that's all."

"Of course they're heavy for a bee-yut-ee-ful little thing like you. Let me take them—"

"No!"

I didn't mean to overreact. But I wanted to see Brock, had to see how he was interacting with Kelsey. He was my client, for God's sake. It was my job to observe him. "I just—do you think I could hang onto them for a bit longer? It would help me get into the game more, Nick."

"Yeah, okay. Be my guest." He shrugged and ordered some popcorn.

I picked up the binoculars and found my targets again. Yes, there they are, I thought, trying to hold my grip steady. Look at the lovebirds. How sweet.

Brock was on his feet now, cheering for his team, and Kelsey was all over him, draping herself and her long legs around him like a clingy vine. Every time he'd yell something onto the field, she'd plant another smacker on his cheek. She certainly was the affectionate type. Not that he didn't reciprocate. When the Yankees finally scored, he literally swept her up in his arms and lifted her off the ground, the joy on his face unmistakable even at a distance.

I lowered the binoculars then and stared straight ahead, glumly, distressed, as if I'd just been given bad news. There was something about his picking her up, something about the spontaneity of it, something about watching this bear of a man encircle her in his arms that rattled me, plunged me into a funk. But what, Lynn? I asked myself. What's this all about? Where's your clinical detachment with regard to this client? Why do you care what he does with his girlfriend? He only grabbed her and picked her up because he's a macho jerk who thinks he can paw women whenever and wherever he wants to. Why should that bother you?

I tried to answer my own questions while Nick, having given up on me as a conversationalist, leaned across me and talked tampons with Penny and Matthew.

Why *did* Brock's lifting Kelsey up bother me? Because Kip used to lift me up and now he was gone?

Or maybe what got to me was the expression on Brock's face when he lifted Kelsey up. Because it was so free of conflict, so uncomplicated. Because it was such a silly, smiley, *happy* face.

But then, why should it bother me that Brandon Brock looked happy? I was the one he'd hired to help him curb his anger—the ranting and raving I'd seen at the tennis club, the short fuse he was famous for at the office. I should have been proud of him and proud of myself and my program. So why wasn't I?

Well, let's think about this some more, I prodded myself. Could it really be his happiness that was gnawing at me? If so, that wasn't very charitable of me. But maybe it was the disparity between us that struck me that night; the fact that he was having a swell time and I was not; that he had a capacity for playfulness and I did not; that I was a communicator who was, contradictorily, more than a little buttoned up when it came to displaying or even experiencing pleasure.

Nonsense. I enjoyed my work and I showed it; enjoyed coming up with new techniques for the Wyman Method; enjoyed watching the men I coached complete the program successfully. True, the sort of enjoyment I felt was tempered by my seriousness, my restraint. It wasn't a playful enjoyment, like Brock's, wasn't a childlike enjoyment. It had never been that, not even when I *was* a child.

Okay, I told myself. That's all this is. You're feeling competitive with this client. You're pissed off that even though he has the sensitivity of a doorknob, he knows how to have fun and you don't.

Or—and I only allowed myself to linger on this thought for a nanosecond—was it that I was jealous? Of his feelings for Kelsey?

Gag. See what beer does to me on an empty stomach?

"All finished with the binoculars?" Nick asked after he and the others had wound up their debate on whether Feminax should expand their product line with diapers for women of a certain age.

"Yes. Thanks," I said, handing them over.

"Good. Time to go," he said, sliding them back into their black case.

"Why? Is the game over?" I said, so caught up in my musings that I'd lost track of the score.

"Oh, it's over all right." I wondered if he might be referring to our budding friendship.

ON TUESDAY, BROCK came in for his session. I was more than coolly professional this time. I was downright unprofessional in my frostiness but I couldn't do anything about it. Didn't want to.

"Uh-oh," he said warily as he took his seat. "You're still mad about our excellent adventure at Bloomingdale's."

Was that what I was mad about? "I would rather characterize my feeling as disappointment," I said. "I was under the impression that you had made progress that day and then it became clear that you had not."

"Hey." He laughed. "I did make progress. You got me to go into that department store and ask the saleswoman for help with the sweaters and then to *share* with her what color I wanted. That was real and I couldn't have done it without your coaching, Dr. Wyman. I was just having a little fun with you at the end."

"Having a little fun," I said, sounding incredibly uptight to myself. "Is that all you think about, Mr. Brock? Having *fun*? When you're not barking orders at your employees, that is?"

He looked amused. "No, it's not all I think about, but it sure beats the hell out of being miserable."

"Are you saying that *I* prefer being miserable?" I squeaked, and then, hearing myself, modulated my voice and repeated the question.

"Of course not," he said. "What's up with you today anyway?"

"Nothing's *up* with me. I just didn't appreciate your leaving me to pay for Naomi's gift, since the whole idea of the exercise was for you to buy it for her."

"Come on. I did buy it for her. I just ducked out at the end, to have a little fun with you, as I said. If I tell you I'm sorry, can we let it go and move on?"

Well. What was this? *He* was telling *me* to "let it go and move on?" That was rich. And how about the "I'm sorry"? Was this actual Womenspeak? Had he really made progress?

There was one way to find out: Put him through more Wyman Method exercises.

"We've worked on your responses to the women at Finefoods," I began. "Why don't we work on your responses to the woman in your personal life." Okay. So I wanted more information about the lovebirds. So sue me.

"You're talking about Kelsey?"

"Yes. Unless there are other women in your personal life."

He smiled. "There used to be an entire harem of them, but now that you've shown me the error of my ways, Dr. Wyman, there's just poor, lonely Kelsey."

Very funny. "I'll ask you some questions about your interactions with her and then I'll come up with a script that we can practice in future sessions."

"If you say so, but I don't see what my relationship with Kelsey has to do with my communication issues at Finefoods."

His communication *issues*? This from the guy who swaggered into my office for his initial session bragging: "I refuse to come out of this program acting like one of those guys who's always moaning about his *issues*?" My God, he *had* made progress!

"Women are women," I explained, buoyed by this positive turn of events. "How you relate to one spills over onto how you relate to others."

"Makes sense."

"First of all," I said, "have you been practicing your noticing exercises on Kelsey?"

"Oh, absolutely. The other night at dinner, I said, 'Honey'—she doesn't mind that I call her honey—'Didn't you tell the waiter you wanted that grilled salmon with the dill sauce on the side?' "

"And what did she say?" I asked expectantly.

"She said, 'No. I like my salmon swimming in sauce.' "

I smiled. "Sounds like Kelsey doesn't watch her cholesterol."

"No, but I get points for trying the Womenspeak on her, don't I?"

"Of course you do. Now, how else have you used it with her?"

He thought for a second. "The morning after that dinner, we were getting dressed— " He pretended to say this shyly, modestly, lowering his blue eyes on the word *dressed*—"and I remarked, 'Kelsey, I don't know how *you* metabolize desserts, but that apple cobbler *I* had last night went straight to my thighs.' "

"And her response?"

"She said, 'I don't remember you having the apple cobbler last night, Brandon. I thought you had the blueberry tart.' " He shook his head. "If you ask me, Dr. Wyman, she's the one who should be practicing your noticing exercises."

"You're my client, Mr. Brock. I'm pleased that you've been doing them. Very pleased."

"Thank you."

"Now I'm going to ask you those specific questions about your relationship, so I can write up the new script I mentioned."

"Be gentle."

"Do you and Kelsey have a special song?"

"Oh, come on." He cringed. "No, we do not have a special song."

"Why not? Women like having a special song with the man they love. I suggest you think of one."

"Okay. Got it. How about 'Happy Birthday'? "

I sighed. "A song that is special to you and Kelsey, Mr. Brock. A song that holds meaning for the two of you. Surely there must be one."

"Nope. No special song. Next question."

"All right. Why don't you tell me this, Mr. Brock: What do you say to Kelsey when she shares her feelings for you and then asks you to share yours?"

I know. This, too, was a personal area, but I asked all my clients the same question. Really.

"I wing it."

"You wing it?"

"Yeah." He shifted uncomfortably in his chair.

"So you say what to her, exactly?"

"I say, 'You're a great gal, honey.' "

"She tells you she loves you and you tell her she's a great gal?"

"That's pretty much the way it goes, yeah."

I noted his answer. "Next time we'll work on a script in which you'll tell her you love her too. Getting you to share your feelings is the key to mastering Womenspeak."

No response.

"As a matter of fact, I think I'll also have you watch a clip from the movie *Jerry Maguire.*"

"The one where Tom Cruise plays the sports agent?"

"Yes. Did you see it?"

"Sure."

"Good. Do you remember the words Tom Cruise's character uses to tell Renee Zellweger's character he loves her?"

He shook his head. "I must have put my hands over my eyes at that point. I do that when movies have scary parts."

"Well, be brave, Mr. Brock, because here is what he said: 'You complete me.' Do you think you could say that to Kelsey?"

"No."

"Why?"

"Because it's just a sappy line some screenwriter dreamed up. Real men don't say, 'You complete me' to women. They say, 'I'll call you.' "

"And they never do. Okay, Mr. Brock. Here's another question: What do you say when Kelsey brings up the subject of marriage? Studies show that women bring up the subject far more often than men do."

"What do I say? The same thing I say when she tells me she loves me. 'You're a great gal, honey.' "

"So you're evasive."

"I'm evasive."

"Fine. I'll work the marriage angle into the script too."

"Hey, hey. Just a second." His face was flushed and his bushy blond eyebrows were raised. "What if I don't want that stuff in any script?"

"Why not?"

He puffed and squirmed and then answered, "Because I don't want to marry Kelsey."

"Then why don't you just tell her that?"

"Because I don't want to hurt her. She's—"

"I know. A great gal."

"Right."

"But don't you think it's important to be honest with people?"

"Oh, you mean the way women are honest with people?" He was the one getting testy now. "Look, Dr. Wyman. You're trying to teach me how to talk like a woman, and I can appreciate why you're doing it—to save my ass at Finefoods. But women do not—I repeat, *do not*—have a patent on honesty. Take it from me. My wife lied to me over and over, played me for the biggest chump in the world. You may be an expert on how men say this and women say that, but I'm here to tell you: Honesty is not Womenspeak."

"Okay," I said backing off when I saw how upset he was. "Okay."

And it *was* okay, because I knew full well that women can be just as dishonest as men. Unfortunately for me, it wouldn't be long before I would discover precisely how dishonest.

16

THROUGHOUT THE SPRING, Brock continued to make progress in our sessions. He still gave me a hard time now and then (more *now* than *then*), but I was beginning to realize that his fits of resistance weren't always juvenile attempts at mocking me; sometimes they were legitimate challenges to my point of view. In other words, our sessions evolved into often spirited, even stimulating discussions as opposed to the dogfights they were initially.

I was explaining this one Thursday night in June to my friends. I hadn't seen any of them in over a month—Penny had been too "crazed" with the Feminax account to get together; Gail had been too busy interviewing divorce lawyers (she claimed she really did want to divorce Jim; she just hadn't told him yet); Isabel had been in East Hampton photographing cats—at the beach, at cocktail parties, at the notoriously restrictive Maidstone Club (they didn't permit Jews on the premises but apparently cats were another story); and Sarah had been in L.A., both battling and allowing herself to be romanced by the intrepid producers who had purchased the rights to her most recent book.

"It sounds like you're getting through to 'America's Toughest Boss,' " Sarah marveled as we sipped drinks on the terrace of her pied-à-terre, which appeared to have been renovated since the last time I'd been to the apartment. New kitchen cabinets, new mirrored bar, new built-ins for all her bestsellers.

"I hope I'm getting through to him," I said, then suddenly remembered what I'd been meaning to ask Sarah. "Shifting gears for a minute, Sarah, at your birthday party, I met a man named Greg who works for Finefoods. Why didn't you tell me you knew someone who knew Brock?"

The question seemed to throw her off balance. "A man named Greg? At my party?"

"Yes. He told me he ran Finefoods' Far East division until his daughter got sick and his wife left him. Now he's a consultant to the company."

"How curious" was how she responded. "Maybe he's a friend of Edward's. I certainly don't know him, or if I ever did, I had no idea where he worked."

Well, it did seem plausible that this Greg person could be a friend of Edward's. And since Sarah and Edward rarely saw each other, it was more than likely that they moved in different social circles.

"Getting back to Brandon Brock, you're saying he's less ferocious than he was when he made the cover of *Fortune*?" asked Isabel, who, for the first time in memory, was not wearing black. She had on a faded blue work shirt and blue jeans. I was so startled by her change of costume that I almost didn't recognize her.

"Still feisty but less ferocious, yes," I said proudly.

"What about his offensive behavior toward women?" asked Gail, who had lost more weight and looked healthier than I'd ever seen her. "Has he improved in that area?"

"Definitely," I said. "I've been pounding into his head the do's and don't's of how to deal appropriately with women in the workplace. If he only learns one thing from my program, it will be how to speak to his female employees in a manner that will earn their loyalty, not their wrath."

"That's quite a change then," said Penny, a little skeptically. "Or are you just getting used to his hitting on you?"

"He doesn't hit on me," I said, more hotly than I'd intended.

"Oh sure, he doesn't," she said, winking at the others.

"No, really. He's pretty much stopped that kind of talk. It turns out, he's not that bad a guy. He's sort of funny, actually."

"*Funny?*" They all said this at once.

"Well, yes," I said defensively, feeling their eyes on me. "Of course, there's still the side of him that growls at people—the Type A side, the side that earned him the Toughest Boss label. But there's also a side that's childlike, playful, and it's that side that has emerged in our sessions. As a matter of fact, he's had a very interesting transformation thus far. The more sensitive he's become, the less I've seen the belligerence. And the less belligerent he's become, the more I've seen the humor. You know, the other day he told me a joke about a traveling salesman, and I laughed so hard I—"

I clammed up when I realized that my friends were staring at me.

"What?" I said. "What's wrong?"

"Let's talk about *your* transformation," said Penny.

"Mine?"

"Yes. You hate jokes," said Gail.

"That's ridiculous," I said. "Nobody *hates* jokes."

"You never tell them," said Isabel. "You're a very serious person, Lynn."

She should talk. They should all talk. "Okay, so I don't tell jokes. I'm simply saying that Brandon Brock is not the bane of my existence. He's got a quick sense of humor and he knows how to enjoy himself—knows how to embrace life, if you will—and, considering that he heads up a very successful company, he's very bright, very street smart. In short, he's not a horrible person."

"Would everybody get a load of this," Penny said with a smirk. "Lynn's sticking up for the guy."

"He's my client," I said, the adrenaline pumping for a reason I couldn't immediately identify. "I stick up for every single one of my clients. I'm their advocate."

"Bullshit," she said. "You always talk about the men who undergo the Wyman Method as if they're still on all fours."

"I—"

"Penny's right," Sarah chimed in. "You like this one, don't you, Lynn."

"Like him? Well, I suppose I *like* him, as opposed to *not* liking him."

"And you laughed at his traveling salesman joke?" said Penny. " 'Men are such simpletons,' you've told us over and over. 'Their idea of communicating is telling a joke. How pathetic.' Obviously, something—or someone—has changed your thinking, Lynn."

"My thinking is that you're twisting what I said," I countered. "I'm just doing my job with Brandon Brock, just trying to win our bet, remember? You didn't believe I could feminize him in six months and I'm proving I can."

That shut them up for the time being. But while they moved on to other topics, I couldn't help but wonder silently about my true feelings toward Brock. Did I care about him in the same way that I cared about Fritz, the Porsche salesman, and Sam, the owner of the plumbing supply company, and the rest of my clients who, by the end of the program, had learned the language of Womenspeak? Or was it remotely possible that I cared about Brandon Brock in an actual romantic sense; that, as he was becoming more attuned to the sensitivities of a woman, he was also becoming more appealing to me as a man?

IN JULY, BROCK went to Europe on business and had to cancel two sessions as a result. I suggested to Naomi that we reschedule him for one double session instead of trying to make up the two.

"I would have asked for a double session anyway," I explained to her, "because we're far enough into the program for me to take Mr. Brock on another field trip."

"Oh!" she said excitedly. "That sounds intriguing."

"Hopefully, it will be instructive too," I said, getting a kick out of her enthusiasm. If it hadn't been for her, I wouldn't have landed Brock as a client.

"You know, Dr. Wyman, I've seen remarkable changes in Mr. Brock since you started working with him," she said.

"Have you?" I said. "How?"

She giggled shyly. "The other day, he complimented me on my dress. He said it was a lovely color on me."

"Good. Very good," I said, extremely pleased to hear this.

"But what really surprised me was what he said next," she went on. "He laughed in a rather self-deprecating way and said, 'Well, you may be wearing the perfect dress today, Naomi, but I simply couldn't decide what to put on this morning. Nothing fit. I don't know how *you* metabolize desserts, but that crème brûlée *I* had last night went straight to my thighs.' I'm telling you, Dr. Wyman, I nearly fainted when he came out with that. It was so, so—"

"Similar to what a woman would say?" I offered.

"Exactly. I responded immediately and we had a nice little chat about food and weight gain—the sort of conversation I never dreamed I'd have with Mr. Brock."

"Excellent." So he really was practicing his scripts.

"But he made the most startling comment of all just before he left on his trip to Europe."

"What was it?" I said eagerly.

"He stopped by my desk, looking a little worried. I assumed whatever was bothering him was a Finefoods matter, having to do, perhaps, with our European operations. In any case, I didn't expect him to share his feelings with me—Brandon Brock share his feelings with his secretary? Ha! When all of a sudden, he gazed right into my eyes and said, 'Naomi, I'm concerned about leaving the country because of my sister's condition.' I was flabbergasted. I knew Mr.

Brock had a sister but only because she's on his Christmas gift list every year."

"Go on," I urged.

"So I asked, not wanting to pry but thinking he might view me as callous if I didn't, 'What is your sister's condition?' He leaned in and said softly and with great sensitivity, 'She has menopause.' "

Has menopause. Still, I was delighted. Brock and I had spent almost an entire session on women's health issues.

"And I'm not the only one who's noticed the difference in the way he speaks," Naomi continued. "All the women in the office are talking about it. It's as if he's developed an entirely new vocabulary. He's actually been using words like 'hopes' and 'hearts' and—here's the one that really touches us—'children.' "

"And it's only going to get better, Naomi," I pledged. "He still has another month or so before he finishes the program."

She sighed. "Imagine what he'll be like by then."

I did imagine it. In fact, I spent entirely too much time imagining it.

HOW'VE YOU BEEN?" Brock asked as he sauntered into my office after returning from his two weeks abroad. He looked tanned and fit, not the least bit jet-lagged.

"I've been fine, thanks," I said approvingly. Asking a woman how she's been, like asking a woman how she feels, shows a real proficiency in Womenspeak. "And your trip went well?"

"Fair," he said. "I was upset about how one of our distributors spoke to me during a meeting. He was really hostile."

Yes, I thought, nodding. He's come a long, long way.

"Well," I said, getting down to business. "As you know, we're going to take another field trip today."

"Not to Bloomingdale's, I hope," he said. "According to Kelsey, they're having a summer sale at Saks. I really think we should go there instead."

I laughed. "Is that one a joke or are you actually trading shopping tips with Kelsey now?"

"That one was a joke," he said with a grin. "So where *are* we going today?"

"Out of the city," I said cryptically, gathering my purse and my briefcase. "My car's in the garage. Shall we?"

We said goodbye to Diane, who was adhering a fake beauty mark to her upper lip (she was in her Cindy Crawford phase), and left the office.

"Why don't I drive?" Brock offered, as we approached my car.

"Nope," I said, waving him over to the passenger's side. "This exercise has to do with you not driving, with you not being the one in control, with you allowing yourself to appear vulnerable."

"Sitting in the passenger's seat of your car will make me appear vulnerable?"

"Let me ask you this, Mr. Brock: Who drives when you and Kelsey are going someplace in her car?"

"I do."

"I rest my case. Studies show that men feel passive when they're being driven around by a woman, because they're so accustomed to being in charge. Today, you will experience what it's like *not* to be in charge. Today, you will sit where the woman usually sits: in the passenger seat."

"So I'll sit in the passenger seat." He shrugged, as if this were no big deal, and lowered his bulky frame into my Nissan.

I pulled the car out of the garage and headed toward the FDR Drive, en route to the 'burbs.

We drove along in awkward silence. Brock was definitely twitchy, squirmy, stuck there in that passenger's seat without the steering wheel as an anchor. It was rather comical, actually. He was incapable of just sitting there and being driven. He tapped his feet on the floor, played with his tie, fidgeted. At one point, he leaned over and adjusted the thermostat on the air conditioner.

"What did you just do?" I asked as I drove.

"Turned the air up," he said. "It's as hot as a bitch in here."

I gave him a disapproving look.

"Sorry. What I meant to say is, it's as hot as a just-out-of-the-oven tuna noodle casserole in here."

I reset the thermostat to where it had been before he'd changed it.

"Hey," he said, reaching over to turn the thermostat back down and, in the process, brushing his hand against mine as I was reaching over to turn the thermostat back up.

There was a moment of genuine awkwardness then, as we both let our accidental touching, let this clumsy physical contact between us register. I can't speak for him, of course, but I found the incident both unnerving and exhilarating, one of those things you can't wait to do again but feel you shouldn't.

"It really is too hot in this car," said Brock, whose already ruddy face was even more flushed. "I'm sweating my brains out."

"Well, I'm not," I said, regaining control of myself. "Women feel the cold more keenly than men do."

"Oh, yeah? What happened to women who have menopause and all those hot flashes you've been coaching me to talk about?"

"When women are *in* menopause, many of them do experience hot flashes, but there's an entire population of women who are not in menopause, Mr. Brock, and many of them work at Finefoods. In fact, another line of Womenspeak dialogue for you to practice at the office, when you walk into a meeting, is: 'Gee, is it cold in here or is it just me?' The nonmenopausal women in the room will really relate to that."

"So I should pretend to be cold when I'm hot?"

"It's not so much pretending as it is simply speaking the language, Mr. Brock. When you say, 'Parlez-vous Francais?' you're not *pretending* to be French. You're just *speaking* French. Do you understand the concept now?"

He looked at me and laughed. "How in the world did I end up with you in my life, Dr. Lynn Wyman?"

"Excuse me?"

"I've never met anyone like you, you know that? In the beginning I thought you were a nag whose saving grace was her legs, but at this stage?" He shook his head and smiled.

Clearly, these were all rhetorical questions, so I didn't answer them. Still, I sensed that he was enjoying the program now, maybe even enjoying me, and the knowledge made me wildly happy.

I kept driving until we got to the town of Pelham Manor, about twenty minutes from the city, depending on traffic. I exited off the Hutchinson River Parkway, made a number of turns and finally stopped the car at the Pelham Manor train station.

"What are we doing here?" asked Brock, who was unfamiliar with the town, as I suspected. While his office was in nearby White Plains, he lived in Manhattan. I figured the landscape between home and work would be uncharted territory for him, and I was right.

"We're lost," I said, turning off the ignition.

"Lost?" He pooh-poohed that idea. "We're five minutes off the parkway."

"Yes, but can you get us from here to Oak Street?"

"Where the hell's Oak Street?"

"Exactly." I smiled. This was going to be fun. "Oak Street is a small side street in Pelham Manor. It can't be far from here, judging by this map." I held up the AAA map that I'd retrieved from my briefcase and handed it to Brock.

He batted it away, didn't even glance at it. "Maps. Who uses maps?"

"I'll tell you who uses them, Mr. Brock. Women."

"That's because they have no navigational skills."

"No, it's because they aren't afraid to admit they need help."

"Help? Have you ever tried to unfold and then refold a map? It's worse than trying to untangle Saran Wrap."

"Nonetheless, here's the map, Mr. Brock. I suggest you find Oak Street on it. Oh, and please keep in mind that we're on a tight schedule here. We've got to get you back into the city in two hours."

"Damn right. I've got a meeting."

"Then read the map."

He read the map. "I can't find Oak Street," he whined after a few minutes, "but I found Oak Circle. Must be near Oak Street."

"If you say so. Why don't you tell me how to get there?"

"No problem."

I started the car and waited for his instructions.

"Make a right at the light," he said, running his finger along the map. "Then, at the next light, make another right. Then continue down that street until it forks and take the left fork, then another left."

I did what I was told. We drove around and around until Brock finally, reluctantly, begrudgingly confessed that he didn't have a clue where Oak Street was or how we might find it.

"Then I guess you'd better ask someone for directions," I said, arriving at the point of the exercise.

He looked as if he were about to have an aneurysm.

"You can do this," I said reassuringly, knowing what a big step he would be taking. Studies show that men have fantasies of being the master of their domain. Making them ask for directions is like telling them they're not.

"But I—"

"Just roll down your window, Mr. Brock," I coached, "so you can call out to passersby."

Now he looked plain mortified. "I am *not* asking for directions," he said, as if drawing a line in the sand.

"Why not?"

"Because there's no reason to. The person I ask will probably give us the *wrong* directions and we'll be worse off than we already are."

"Oh, I see," I said, having heard that one before.

"Besides," he said, "if I had more time, I'd find the damn street on my own."

"But you don't have more time," I reminded him. "So ask that woman over there how to get to Oak Street. Go ahead."

"I bet she won't know," he grumbled.

"Ask her, Mr. Brock. You won't complete the program successfully unless you do."

He sighed and leaned his head out the window. "Miss?" An elderly woman approached the car. "Do you know how to get to Oak Street?"

She cupped her ear and asked him to repeat the question. He wasn't thrilled. The indignity of it all.

"DO YOU KNOW HOW TO GET TO OAK STREET?" he said again, louder this time.

"No, I'm afraid I don't," said the woman, who then ambled away.

Brock glared at me.

"Ask that woman," I suggested, motioning to another passerby. "But when you ask her, try not to bark at her, Mr. Brock. In other words, try to make her *want* to give you the directions. Women respond much more sympathetically when there's a human-interest slant to a situation—much more so than they do to straight commands or questions. So this time, add a little information to your presentation. Say something like: 'We were driving up from the city, because it's such a lovely summer day, and decided to see the sights here in Pelham Manor. Would you tell us how to get to Oak Street, please?' "

"Human interest." He relaxed a little. He was feeling less threatened, I could tell. He just had to be *eased* into the exercise; they all did. "Okay. How's this?" He leaned out the window. "Oh, miss?" The woman approached the car. She was a pretty young redhead in shorts and a sleeveless top that exposed her midriff, among other treasures.

"Yeah?" she said, between chomps on her bubble gum. She was eyeing Brock in a sexy, seductive way while completely ignoring me. I did not experience the bond of sisterhood with her.

"We were driving up from the city today," he began, sounding very jaunty. "We wanted to be out in the country on such a lovely summer day and smell the air, smell the flowers, smell the essence of the season." God, he was laying it on a little thick. "Speaking of smells, that's a wonderful perfume you're wearing, miss."

"Thanks," she said. "My boyfriend bought it for me."

"And a lucky guy he is."

I cleared my throat, hoping he'd get the hint to stay on message.

"Anyway, our destination was Oak Street but instead we ended up here."

"So you're lost," said the redhead.

Brock took a deep breath before admitting he was. "I was wondering if you could give us directions."

"Nope," she said. "I've never heard of Oak Street. Sorry."

She turned and strutted back up the road.

"I think you were overdoing it," I said, unable to resist. "Womenspeak does not involve drooling."

He grinned. "I wasn't drooling, Dr. Wyman. I was just trying to arouse her . . . sympathy."

Yeah, yeah, yeah.

He managed to get the directions to Oak Street out of the third passerby, a man in his fifties.

"Good job," I told Brock. "This was a difficult exercise today and you came through it very well."

"Then it's on to Oak Street we go," he said cheerfully, pleased to have passed this latest test.

"No, it's back to the city we go," I said, starting the car. "It's getting late."

"What about Oak Street?"

"There is no Oak Street. That's why you couldn't find it on the map."

"But that man just gave me directions to it, unless I'm totally out of my mind."

I smiled. "Men would rather die than have other men think they don't know something. He wasn't about to let you think he didn't know where Oak Street was, so he gave you bogus directions."

"You mean the guy was one-upping me?"

"He was talking Menspeak to you. Same thing."

Stunned, Brandon Brock sat back against the seat of the car and regarded me. "Are you like this with all men or just with me?"

"Am I like what?"

"So *in command.*"

I laughed to myself, remembering those months after Kip left when I felt anything but. "I'm not in command," I said. "I've just been doing this kind of work for a long time. I have my area of expertise, that's all."

"I'll grant you that, especially after seeing you in action today. As a matter of fact, I'd love to hear the story of how you came to be interested in the different languages that men and women speak—if you have the time to share the information, of course. I'd really enjoy listening to the genesis of the Wyman Method and the steps you took to market the program, as well as how you've helped so many men to become sensitive, caring individuals who are *there* for the women in their lives. I, for one, still have a lot to learn on that score."

I stole a quick glance at him as I drove, just to be sure that the man sitting next to me, the man who had just addressed me in impeccable Womenspeak, was the man who had once called me snookums.

"Yes, Mr. Brock," I replied, my voice quivering ever so slightly. "You do have a lot to learn, but not nearly as much as you think."

17

DURING THE RIDE back to the city, I told Brock about myself—because he'd asked and because we were stuck in traffic. I told him about my father's inability to communicate, about my parents' bitter divorce, about my graduate work in linguistics, and about my book and how it turned me into a media darling. I even told him about Kip and how he sold me out to the *National Enquirer. That* I told him not just because he'd asked, but because he was such a good listener.

Brandon Brock? A good listener?

You must think I'd lost all perspective with regard to him, but he *was* a good listener that July afternoon, and no one was more surprised by that—more proud of that—than I was. There was no doubt that the Wyman Method had changed him. He didn't interrupt me. He didn't try to switch subjects on me. He didn't even make jokes whenever there was a lull in the conversation. (Well, except one. He asked me if Kip and I had ever had a special song. Ha ha.) What's more, he posed perceptive questions and made comments that weren't frivolous.

"Maybe you should spend some time with your father and hear his side of the story," he said after I had described the acrimony between my parents. "It might sound different to you after all these years. It might occur to you, for example, that the reason he didn't communicate with your mother at the dinner table was because he was unhappy, not because he was *male*."

"I didn't base my entire career on the failings of my own father," I protested. "Study after study shows that a huge segment of the male population has problems communicating with women."

"I'm only suggesting that your father's 'failings,' as you call them, may have been his way of dealing with your mother, with whatever was wrong between them. Why don't you have a talk with him and see?"

After we were done with my history and were still crawling down the FDR Drive, I asked Brock to give me a thumbnail sketch of his. He told me about his mother, who was beautiful but remote; about his father, who was a task master and had no use for a son who didn't excel; about his sister, who still lived in Michigan, was the wife of a G.M. executive like her father, had three children, and thought it was high time her brother remarried and had kids of his own.

"Do you like kids?" I asked, trying to picture him changing diapers.

"Yeah. As a matter of fact I do."

"And Kelsey?" I said, trying to picture *her* changing diapers.

"What about Kelsey?"

His tone confirmed what he'd told me in a previous session. He had no intention of marrying Kelsey. He didn't love Kelsey.

It won't shock you to learn that I was not broken up by this news.

The more Brandon Brock and I talked that day in the car, exchanged personal information as well as the occasional quip, the more I realized that we were engaging in real communication, not the sort of gratuitous, empty chatter that Kip and I were famous for.

What I also realized was that I was going to have to admit to myself what my friends already suspected, to confront what every reader of this tale has already guessed. Yes, I was going to have to face the fact that my feelings for my client had evolved, over the course of nearly six months, from contempt, to tolerance, to affection, to heart-pounding, pulse-racing, can't-eat-can't-sleep-can't-wait-to-see-him-again passion. To put it another way, I was falling in love with the guy, and I didn't know what to do about it.

I DID NOTHING about it. Not right away. I just went on with my routine. I continued to see Brock, of course, continued to coach him and go over scripts with him and teach him new Womenspeak phrases and expressions. But I never let on that I was counting down, ticking off the days until that first Tuesday after Labor Day, his final session and the moment I was now dreading; never gave him an inkling that the thought of him disappearing into his life and out of mine was painful.

There was one afternoon with him that was especially difficult for me. We had just wrapped up a session in which he had learned that women want men to express understanding, not dispense advice, when he made a point of thanking me.

"For what?" I said, as we stood at the door to my office. He was planting his blue eyes on me. I was trying to look as if my insides weren't churning.

"For being tough on me, not letting me bulldoze you," he said, positioning himself at a respectable distance from me but not so far from me that I couldn't smell his cologne.

"Oh, well," I said with a phony little laugh. "It's just my job. I'm a dominatrix, remember? I'm tough on all my clients."

"I know, but there's something extra you've done for me."

"Something extra?" I said.

"Yes. When I first signed on here, I asked you to promise that you wouldn't go running to the media about it."

"And I haven't gone to the media. I kept my promise."

"I know, Dr. Wyman. That's the 'something extra' you've done for me. See, I know how tempting it would have been for you to tip off a columnist about my coming here. Your career had taken a downturn. You needed clients, needed good publicity. Getting the word out that the CEO of Finefoods—*Fortune*'s poster boy for bad behavior!—had hired you to help him would certainly have heated things up for you. But you did keep your word and I assume you'll continue to keep it. I respect you for that, and I thank you for it."

Boy, that sounded like a goodbye, didn't it? A nice goodbye, but a goodbye nonetheless. And I didn't want to let him go, didn't want to have to get my Brandon Brock fix by reading about him in the business section of the *New York Times*. But what was I supposed to do?

"Tell him," said Penny when I finally caved in and admitted what she'd already surmised.

"I can't," I said. "He's my client. It would be highly unprofessional for me to blurt out my feelings in the middle of a session."

"He's almost *not* your client," she said. "Wait until his last session and then blurt out your feelings."

"Tell him," said Sarah when I confided in her.

"I can't," I said. "He's involved with someone."

"You mean that nitwit decorator you brought to my house?" She laughed. "The one who wanted to paint all the rooms red?"

"Kelsey, yes."

"He doesn't love her. She's not the kind of woman men love. She's the kind of woman men flaunt at their high school reunions, to show everybody they're still getting laid."

"Tell him," said Gail when it was her turn to hear about my dilemma.

"I can't," I said. "He's a successful, high-profile guy. He'll think I'm after him for his money."

"What's wrong with having a little money? If Jim would get his ass out there and earn some, maybe I wouldn't be so quick to divorce him." So quick. They'd been married for years.

"Tell him," said Isabel after I laid out the scenario for her.

"I can't," I said. "What if he doesn't love me back?"

"Then get a cat," she suggested, as she had so many times before.

At each and every remaining session with Brock I struggled with whether or not to tell him I loved him—with whether or not to even hint that I had more than a professional interest in him—and ultimately couldn't find the words. Talk about another irony. There I was, an expert at getting men to share their feelings, and yet I was proving to be incapable of sharing my own.

Surprisingly, it was Diane, my assistant, who provided the solution; Diane, who had never struck me as a student of my work; Diane, who had seemed so superficial, shallow, interested only in her appearance; Diane, who turned out to be the most perceptive of anybody.

I was packing up my things one afternoon, tidying up, when she knocked on my office door, holding up that day's edition of the *Wall Street Journal*, which a client must have left behind in the waiting room.

"Look, Dr. Wyman," she said excitedly, pointing to the front page. "It's your client, Mr. Brock."

Apparently, the newspaper had done a piece on Finefoods and adorned it with a line drawing of Brock. As it was in black-and-white, the portrait didn't do him justice.

"I'd like to read it," I said, after thanking Diane for bringing it to my attention.

"I didn't know he was *famous*," she gushed, her lips painted in that dark brown shade that some women find attractive but I do not. "I mean, I knew he was a big-shot businessman but not, like, a celebrity or anything."

"You knew he ran Finefoods," I reminded her. "That's a major company. So he's in the news a lot."

"It's still awesome," she said, "the fact that he's famous *and* hunky."

"Hunky?" I'd never thought of Brock in that light, exactly. Brawny, yes. Attractive, yes. Golden, yes. But hunky? Well, maybe.

"Way hunky," she said. "And he's gotten much nicer too, since he's gone through your program, Dr. Wyman. He says hi to me now. He even told me the tube top I had on the other day was a 'lovely color' on me."

"Did he?" I said, choking up suddenly.

"Yeah, and he did something else that was cool. I was eating a Hershey Bar at my desk and he stopped and said, 'Don't worry about your complexion, Diane. It's a myth that chocolate makes a woman's skin break out.' Isn't it incredible that a man would say that?"

My eyes misted. Brock and I had spent a recent session on the relationship between women and old wives' tales.

"Is everything okay, Dr. Wyman?" Diane asked, noticing that I was on the verge of a meltdown.

For some reason—maybe because she had been with me since the beginning and had borne witness to my rise and fall and had never once shown anything but loyalty to me—I chose Diane as the person to whom I would unburden myself.

"No," I replied. "Everything isn't okay."

And then I let it out, just started blubbering, just hurled my normally held-together self into her arms and unraveled.

"Oh my God, Dr. Wyman," she said, obviously stunned to have The Boss slobbering all over her.

"I'm sorry, Diane," I said, sobbing into her shoulder, which had been buffed and toned to that of a body builder's. "But you're the only one I can really talk to, the only one who knows Brock the way I know him."

Don't ask me what that meant. It just sounded right at the time. I needed to bond with Diane in a way we had never bonded.

"So this is about Mr. Brock?" she said, patting my back. Her acrylic nails kept catching on my cotton sweater.

"Yes," I said. "Oh, Diane. I've fallen in love with him but I can't find the words to tell him."

That brought forth a torrent of tears from me and an actual gasp from her.

"You?" she said, clearly unnerved by this. "You're in love with Mr. Brock?"

I nodded. "But I can't tell him. I don't know how to tell him."

"You?" she said again. I was hoping she'd be a tad more articulate, given the significance of the situation.

"Yes, *I*," I said, a little impatiently. "*I* am in love with Brock. I don't know if he's the slightest bit interested in me, but I won't find out unless I tell him how I feel. The problem is, I'm blocked on this, totally blocked. Every time I even imagine sharing my feelings with him, I freeze up, can't compose a sentence, can't speak. I don't understand what's the matter with me. I've never been like this. Never."

"Dr. Wyman?" said Diane.

"What?"

"You've always been like this."

I picked my head up off of her. "What are you talking about?"

She took a seat, in the wing chair in which I customarily sat, then motioned for me to sit in the other chair, the client's chair. "Why don't you relax and I'll explain what's going on."

She would explain? Warily, I sat. This was a new Diane, a Diane who smelled a shift in the balance of power.

"Okay," she said. "Here it is." She crossed her legs, made herself comfy. "You've been my boss for a long time and you've always been so . . . so uptight. You never showed any emotion, not even when your husband dumped you, not even when he sold your story to the *Enquirer*, not even when your business went down the toilet. Not a tear. Not a rant. Just the stiff upper lip. Just the same old Dr. Wyman."

I winced. I guess it was the "old." No, it was the bluntness.

"You've been so busy being the inventor of the Wyman Method," she continued, "so busy teaching men how to talk like a woman, that you've forgotten how to talk like one yourself."

I winced again. This wasn't fun. "Is that true?" I said, genuinely taken aback by her impression of me.

"Sure it's true. Think about it."

I tried to think about it but she was on a roll and wouldn't be quiet.

"If you ask me," she said, "you talk just like the men who come to you for help."

"I most certainly do not!"

"Oh yeah? You interrupt. You order people around. You make me buy your Christmas gifts instead of getting out there and buying them yourself."

"I did that once. Once! And only because I was away at that conference in Arizona."

"Once, shmonce. The point is, you did it. Not only that, I never heard *you* say that a top I was wearing was a lovely color on me, the way Mr. Brock did."

"Never?"

"Nope. And speaking of him, listen to how you call him *Brock*, instead of Mr. Brock or Brandon or whatever. Only men call each other by their last names, Dr. Wyman, which is more proof that the language you speak is Menspeak."

Ouch! She was taking bluntness to a new level. But was it possible that she was onto something? Had I been so consumed with my work that I hadn't practiced what I'd preached? Had my command of Womenspeak gotten rusty? Did I need to get back in touch with my own feminine side? My friends didn't complain about the way I spoke, didn't accuse me of withholding. They accepted the fact that my personality was on the reserved side and cared for me unconditionally. On the other hand, they were pretty self-involved and may not have even noticed that I wasn't the most emotional person on the planet.

"But Diane," I said weakly, reeling from the notion that my own communication skills might be flawed and, therefore, eager to stick up for myself. "Haven't I at least been a good boss to you? Treated you fairly? Behaved professionally toward you?"

"Oh, you've behaved real professionally," she said in a way that suggested there was more to her answer. I braced myself. "You kept me on here at the office, even though you hardly had any clients. You paid me on time, no matter what. You let me set my own hours, go to the gym, the tanning place, whatever. But on a one-to-one basis, you acted like I was your doormat. 'Do this, Diane. Do that, Diane.' Without any of the human stuff."

"What kind of 'human stuff?' " I said defensively.

"You've never asked me about my family or where I live or whether I'm a Republican or a—"

"I hardly think it's my business to grill you about your private political beliefs."

"See how you interrupted me just then, Dr. Wyman? Did you *hear* yourself?"

"Oh." God, she was right.

"You've never stopped to find out who I am," she went on. "And you never, ever shared your feelings with me."

Yikes. What a cold, heartless bitch she was describing. But I wasn't that bad. Cold, maybe. But not heartless. No, not heartless.

"Have you ever seen the movie *All About Eve?*" said Diane, who was a fan of "movies from the olden days," as she put it.

"Yes," I said. "Bette Davis was wonderful in it. But what does that movie have to do with my situation?"

"Plenty. Remember the speech Bette makes when she's stuck in the car with Celeste Holm?"

"No," I said, wondering where this was going.

"She takes a drag on her cigarette and says something like, 'Funny business, a woman's career. The things you drop on your way up the ladder. You forget you'll need them again when you go back to being a woman. That's one career all females have in common, whether we like it or not: being a woman. Sooner or later we've got to work at it.' She paused, having done a pretty good Bette Davis. "Does any of that ring a bell, Dr. Wyman?"

"Well, yes," I acknowledged. "Actually, it does." So I had forgotten how to be a woman. How had I allowed that to happen?

"Getting back to the problem with Mr. Brock," she said, leaning forward in the chair, my chair. "If you can't share your feelings with a nobody like me, how do you expect to share them with him?"

"You're not a nobody," I said, wiping my eyes. "Don't sell yourself short, Diane."

"I won't if you won't."

"What do you mean?"

"I mean that you shouldn't sell me short. You should let *me* put *you* through the Wyman Method."

Now it was my turn to go monosyllabic. "You?"

"Why not? I can help you. I've been here long enough to get the gist of how the program works. You've had me transcribe zillions of tapes and type zillions of scripts. And I've read your book."

"Have you? I didn't know that, Diane." A touching moment in an otherwise nightmarish interaction.

"That's because you never asked me. You never asked me anything about myself."

"I'm sorry," I said. Was I ever.

"Anyway, I think I can teach you how to talk Womenspeak, Dr. Wyman. We can do a shortened version of the program, just a quickie refresher course so you'll be able to tell Mr. Brock how you feel about him by the time his last session comes around. Since you don't have a lot of clients, we can work as much or as late as you want."

"Diane." I reached out to squeeze her hand. I was overwhelmed by her generosity, particularly in light of how I'd behaved toward her. "I'm very grateful to you for having the courage to say these things to me today and for offering to take me through an abbreviated application of the Wyman Method. But there's a big difference between expressing my feelings—incorporating the 'human stuff' into my conversations—and actually telling a man I love him."

"Yeah, but you can't get the love part down until you've gotten the basics down. First things first, Dr. Wyman."

"You have a point."

"So how about it? I can help you, I know I can."

I got up from the chair and hugged her—and not just because I was trying to win her over; because I *felt* like hugging her. "I accept your offer," I said, tearing up again. "I think it would be very stimulating to undergo my own program, to turn my supposed female intelligence on myself. But I have to ask, Diane: What will you get out of this?"

"What will I get? A flesh-and-blood woman for a boss instead of an ice queen," she said, then smiled for the first time since she came into my office. "And if I do a good job on you, maybe you'll promote me," she added. "You didn't know this, but I'm much more ambitious than I look."

18

MY FIRST SESSION with Diane was scheduled for the very next morning, and my first taste of what it would be like to have her as my teacher hit me the minute I walked into the office. I stopped by her desk, as I always did, and said, "Good morning, Diane. Any calls?"

"No calls," she said, handing me a piece of paper. "But here's your script, Dr. Wyman. I came in early to type it up and print it out for you."

"That's very industrious of you," I said, "particularly since our session isn't for another hour."

"True, but I think it's important to get a jump on things. For example, did you hear what you said to me just before?"

"What *I* said?"

"Yeah. You said, 'Good morning, Diane. Any calls?' "

"So?"

"So where was the 'How are you this morning?' or the 'Did you get a patch for that nail you broke the other day?' or the 'I love where you pierced your left eyebrow.' Nothing human."

"Whatever was I thinking."

"The point is, we should start right in with the script," she said. "I'm going to speak one of the lines of dialogue in it and I'd like you to repeat it for me immediately afterwards. Are you ready?"

"Diane," I said with a tolerant chuckle. She was a pretty decent mimic of me, I had to admit. "Let's not go overboard with this arrangement. I haven't even had my coffee yet."

"Your coffee will have to wait," she said firmly. "Look, Dr. Wyman. You only have a few more weeks until Mr. Brock finishes the program. That means you don't have much time before you have to tell him how you feel about him. If I were you, I'd get off my high horse and get down to work."

"ALL RIGHT!" I said, foregoing the coffee. "What's the line of dialogue?"

"Listen carefully."

"I'm listening with every fiber of my being."

"There's no need for sarcasm, Dr. Wyman."

"No. Of course there isn't." I know. I sounded like Brock, when he was starting the program. Condescending. Defensive. A jerk, in other words.

"The line is: 'Good morning, Diane. Did you have a good time with your boyfriend last night? I'm *dying* to hear all about it.' "

"I didn't know you had a boyfriend, Diane."

"Duh. You don't know anything about me, but we're going to work on that, Dr. Wyman. We're going to teach you how to pay attention to the little girlie details that are the *hallmark of Womenspeak*, as you would say."

"The little girlie details?"

"Yeah. Now give me the line."

I shrugged. "Good morning, Diane. Did you have a good time with your boyfriend last night? I'm dying to hear all about it."

"I didn't catch the emphasis on the word 'dying.' That's key. It's the emphasis that tells me you really, really want to establish intimacy with me."

I wasn't sure I did. But okay. I said the line the way she instructed me to. "Now what?"

"Now I tell you about my date and after that you say the following line: 'Since I don't have a man in my life, thanks to my dirty rotten husband, who cheated on me and then ruined my career, *I* spent last night alone, watching *Touched by an Angel,* eating ice cream right out of the container, and crying my eyes out.' "

"Whoa, whoa, whoa. Why would I say a mouthful like that?"

"Because it's something a woman would say."

"Not this woman. I don't watch *Touched by an Angel.* I don't eat ice cream out of the container. And I don't cry."

"You don't cry?" She smirked. "What about yesterday? Or was that somebody else snarking all over my shirt?"

"Fine. I do cry. But the bit about Kip is over the top."

"Is it? Aren't you mad as hell at him, Dr. Wyman?"

"Well, yes, but it wouldn't be appropriate to—"

"To what?"

"Whine about it."

"You wouldn't be whining about it. You'd be expressing anger about it, sharing your feelings about it. Come on, Dr. Wyman. The idea behind the line is to let others see your vulnerability. We want Mr. Brock to see your vulnerability. Right now, all he sees is your masculine side."

My masculine side. Not a turn-on.

I said the line, word for word.

And that was only the warm-up act. An hour later, Diane and I sat down in my office for the actual session—she in my chair, me in the client's chair. She may not have looked the part I had played for so many years, but she knew what she was talking about when it came to the Wyman Method. And, most importantly, she understood the task at hand: to help me be more forthcoming about my emotions.

During that first session, which was a marathon, by the way, since my schedule was wide open, we practiced all sorts of scripts, covering everything from the deeply personal ("I wish my parents hadn't gotten divorced" . . . "I'd like to kill my ex-husband for what he did to me") to the mundane ("I'm mad at myself for finishing that whole turkey sandwich" . . . "I really love Celine Dion").

In fact, we accomplished quite a bit that day, at the end of which I was thoroughly drained.

"We'll do more work on you tomorrow," she said as we were locking up the office.

"I've got Brock coming in tomorrow," I reminded her.

"You've got *Brandon* coming in tomorrow," she corrected me. "Say it."

"What?"

"His first name. Say it."

I clutched. It was difficult for me to say his first name. If I called him Brandon, I would be losing my professional distance—the wall I had so scrupulously erected between us. At least, that's how it felt to me.

"Come on, Dr. Wyman," Diane coaxed. "I know it's a big step for you to call him by his first name, but it's just the two of us and he's not going to hear you and if you want to keep calling him Mr. Brock when you're in a session with him that's up to you. But let's kill the last-name thing."

"Okay, okay," I said. "I've got *Brandon* coming in tomorrow."

"Good job. So you'll see him tomorrow and we'll have our session after that. Or maybe we should have our session before you see Mr. Brock. That way you could practice some of our scripts on him."

"Whatever you say, Diane. You're the boss."

She smiled and told me I was dismissed.

AT ELEVEN O'CLOCK the following morning, I had my next session with Diane. She made me practice a script in which I was, yet again, forced to articulate my feelings, particularly my feelings of vulnerability. I repeated such lines as "I'm so embarrassed" and "I don't know anything about that," and "I feel bloated."

"When Mr. Brock comes in today," said Diane, "I want you to use each of these phrases in conversation with him."

"I will not say 'I feel bloated' to him or any other client. Forget about it."

"Maybe you're right. Save that one for your friends. But say the other two."

"I'll try, but I think it's highly unethical for me to practice *my* scripts during *his* sessions."

"Listen, do you want this guy or not, Dr. Wyman?"

She was tough. "I want this guy," I said, painfully aware that my days with him were numbered.

BROCK—SORRY BRANDON—was a few minutes early for his noon appointment. He was chatting animatedly with Diane when I walked out to the waiting room to get him.

"Hey, did you cut your hair, Dr. Wyman?" was how he greeted me.

"Yes," I said, pleased at how proficient he'd become at his noticing exercises. I was about to leave it at that and lead him back to my office, when I caught Diane giving me a disapproving look. "I—uh—was supposed to have a trim," I improvised, trying to incorporate some of her "human stuff" into the conversation with him, "but it ended up being much shorter than I'd intended. *I'm so embarrassed.*" There, Diane. Satisfied?

She beamed and gave me a thumbs-up.

"Well, I think it's very flattering on you," said Brandon. "As a matter of fact, I could use a trim myself." He fingered his golden locks. "When it gets this long, I can't do a thing with it."

Now, tell me: Was this a changed man or what? And not hard on the eyes, either. He was wearing a summer-weight khaki suit, with a pale blue shirt and dark blue tie, and the entire package just got to me. It's not possible that I won't see him again after he completes the program, I thought. I simply can't let that happen.

Once in my office, Brandon and I got to work on a script involving

Susan, the fictional Finefoods employee. I was totally engaged in helping him, really I was, but I was equally as conscious of wanting to follow Diane's instructions, of needing to follow them. And so I said again, apropos of nothing this time, *"I'm so embarrassed."*

"About your haircut?"

"No." Enough with the hair talk. I had to think of something else about which to be embarrassed. "About my lack of knowledge of your company, Mr. Brock. Of the products that Finefoods manufactures and sells. *I don't know anything about that.*" There, Diane. Another one.

"Oh," he said politely. "What would you like to know?"

What would I like to know. Good question, since I truly didn't know anything about the food business. "Let's see," I said. "I've always wondered about breakfast cereals."

"Is that right? What have you wondered about them, Dr. Wyman?"

"I, well, there are so many areas, so many mysteries. *I feel humbled by my ignorance* when it comes to breakfast cereals."

He smiled, rather affectionately it seemed to me. Perhaps the changes, in me, although modest at this early stage, were having an effect on him. "I'd be glad to *share*," he said in perfect Womenspeak. "Ask away."

"Right. Okay." Come on, Lynn. Ask him something. Anything. "Specifically, Mr. Brock, what, exactly, is riboflavin?" Sorry, but it was the first thing that came to mind. "It's listed among the ingredients on every cereal box and yet *I feel so uneducated about it.*"

"Please. Don't be so hard on yourself, Dr. Wyman." He leaned toward me, cocking his head in an absolutely magnificent display of empathy. "Riboflavin is a growth-promoting member of the vitamin B complex."

"Great, thanks."

"Any other questions? Or should we get back to the Wyman Method? I don't have many more sessions to go, don't forget. Pretty soon, I'll be on my own out there in that big, scary world full of women."

So he, too, was counting down. He, too, was thinking how dismal life was going to be without me. Or was he simply eager to get on with the day's session and then beat it?

"Yes, Mr. Brock," I said, my mind racing. I wanted to reveal something of my emotional shift toward him, something that would prepare him for The Big Speech I was gearing up to deliver on his last day of the program. "Of course we should get back to the Wyman Method. But first, may I say that I feel—"

"Yes?"

"I feel—"

"Tell me, Dr. Wyman."

"I feel—"

"You feel what?"

"Bloated."

He laughed. "I know, I know. I'm supposed to say that sort of thing to Susan while we're sitting in the conference room together before a meeting, right?"

"Yes, that's it."

Well? It was the best I could do. I wasn't ready to articulate even a hint of my feelings for him. I wasn't ready to say that I had enjoyed working with him, or that I had found him an occasionally contentious but always challenging client, or that I would miss him. I was, therefore, not remotely close to being able to tell him I loved him. But there was still time for Diane to whip me into shape. At least I hoped there was.

19

DIANE AND I really poured it on in the waning days of the summer. We'd have a session, break for lunch, have another session, break for her to pop over to the tanning bed place, have another session, and break for an early dinner, which wasn't much of a break at all, seeing as she used these forays out to restaurants for on-site language adjustment.

It was at our dinners that I got to know Diane and she got to know me. She may have pierced her body in six hundred places whereas I hadn't pierced mine anywhere, not even my ears, but we had more in common than we had imagined. Her parents were divorced when she was a teenager, as were mine. She wasn't popular in school just as I wasn't, although for different reasons (the kids in my homogeneous suburb ostracized me for being nerdy; the kids in her homogeneous suburb ostracized her for having tri-colored hair). And, like me, she'd been betrayed by a man (her former boyfriend had claimed he managed a rock and roll band when what he really managed was a Colombian drug cartel).

We shared and shared and shared until I was bleary-eyed with sharing. The result was that we developed a mutual respect for each other, not to mention an actual fondness. But was I ready for the moment when all our hard work might pay off? Was I ready to share my feelings with Brandon Brock? Not quite. I still needed more practice—and I got it over Labor Day weekend.

Isabel, who had been spending a lot of time in East Hampton, rented a house there for the month of August, her lease also including the holiday weekend. Generous friend that she was, she invited Penny, Gail, Sarah, and me to spend the four days out there with her.

I was delighted to escape my garden apartment in Mt. Kisco for a wonderful old shingled place in the Hamptons—and, of course, to spend quality time with my pals. There would be no husbands, no boyfriends, no children, and no astrologers. Just the Brain Trust.

The weekend got off to a festive start as Isabel threw a little party for us on Friday night, introducing us to some of her neighbors, many of whom were members of the Hamptons' arty set. Saturday was a beach day, and Saturday night was a movie night. On Sunday we hung around the house, read, relaxed. Which brings me to Sunday night, our last night, as we were all heading home on Monday.

As I believe I've said, none of us was particularly gifted in the kitchen, but we decided that for our final dinner we would *try* to create a meal together.

Our menu, which was rather ambitious, considering the dearth of culinary talent, consisted of steamed lobsters, roasted potatoes, fresh asparagus, garlic bread, and a salad.

"We can do this," Penny said, rolling up her sleeves and then assigning us each a task. She put herself in charge of the lobsters and Gail in charge of the potatoes and Isabel in charge of the asparagus and Sarah in charge of the bread and me in charge of the salad. I got off easy, I thought, and therefore, drank numerous glasses of champagne while I washed the lettuce and chopped the tomatoes and crumbled the gorgonzola. By the time dinner was served, I was smashed.

We placed the food on the picnic table outside, lit some citronella candles, and sat down.

"Toast! Toast!" I said, my champagne glass in the air. "Before anyone eats a morsel of this bounty, I'd like to share my feelings." I should add that I was asked to repeat all that; my speech was seriously slurred, apparently.

"Uh-oh," said Penny, winking at the others. "This should be entertaining."

"Glad you think so, Penny. I'll start with you," I said, then raised my glass even higher and my voice even louder. "To Penny Herter, who always gets her man — into bed!" I laughed energetically. No one else did. "I've always admired how you go after the guys you want, Penny. I feel envious that you have no compunction about sleeping with them on the first date. What I'm saying is, I *love* that you're in touch with your inner slut."

I expected my friends to respond positively to my expressions of admiration and envy and love for Penny, but they didn't. Instead, they seemed stunned by my attempt at sharing, and, in my drunken state, I couldn't figure out why.

"Okay, Isabel. You're next," I said, after I took another belt of champagne. "To Isabel Green, who would have us believe that she's wacky — excuse me, *eccentric* — but is really the smoothest operator of us all!" Again, I was the only one laughing. "I'm in awe of how you've created such a media-friendly image for yourself, Isabel, and I think your photographs are pure genius. But — " I giggled, took another sip — "I have to share with you the fact that your cats make me sick."

I didn't mean anything malicious by *that* remark either. I was only saying that I was allergic to cats, hers included, and that when I was around them, I couldn't breathe without wheezing.

"Now for my toast to Gail," I said, oblivious to the lack of enthusiasm for my performance. "To Gail Orrick, who is forever fixated on the adversities of life, most of them her own." This drew out-and-out boos, which I mistook for oohs. "I love your flair for the dramatic, Gail. Love how everything is a crisis with you, how everything is a soap opera." I blanked for a second at that point. Where *was* I, anyway? "So here's to you!" I said, recovering. I punctuated the sentence with a hiccup.

"I think that's enough, Lynn," said Penny, who rose from her seat and tried to swipe my glass.

"Hey!" I said, swaying a little, polishing off the fizzy golden liquid that was left in the glass. "I haven't toasted Sarah yet!"

"Why don't you eat something instead," said Sarah.

"Why don't you let me share my feelings?" I said petulantly. I raised my empty glass. "To Sarah Pepper, who is the diva of children's books! I love how you keep writing about that magic toothbrush, Sarah. It's so fitting because your marriage is magic. Presto—you have a husband. Presto—you don't. Presto—you do again. Presto—you don't. Isn't she something, everybody?"

No sooner had I spoken those words than I tipped over and fell to the ground. (The others described it as sort of a swoon.) Sarah grabbed one arm and Penny grabbed the other, and they propped me up and led me inside the house to the bedroom I was sharing with Gail. "Take these," said Penny, depositing two Advil into my palm and then waiting until I'd swallowed them with the water she'd brought me.

"But I'm not ready to go to sleep," I protested as Sarah turned off the light.

"Maybe not, but *we're* ready for you to," she said as the two of them left me all by myself.

Needless to say, I felt horribly guilty the next morning—and hungover. I didn't remember precisely what I had blurted out during my toasts, but from the look on my friends' faces it wasn't the stuff of Hallmark greeting cards. I spent most of Monday apologizing, and by the time I went home everybody had forgiven me. When I arrived at the office on Tuesday morning, which was not only America's first day back to work after the holiday weekend but Brandon Brock's graduation day, I was eager to tell Diane what had happened.

"I don't understand it," I wailed. "You spent hours and hours helping me to loosen up, getting me to be able to share my feelings, and it seemed as if all those hours were paying off. But then I drove out to the Hamptons and shot my mouth off, and it almost cost me four friendships."

"Come on, now. There's a moral to this story," said Diane, as she applied her mascara.

"What is it?"

"Never *share* when you've had too much to drink."

"Right, but all this doesn't bode well for my talk with Brandon today. I had hoped that being with my friends over the weekend would give me the opportunity for a dress rehearsal, and it didn't."

"You've got nothing to worry about today, Dr. Wyman. You're ready for Mr. Brock. Your Womenspeak is terrific. And you look beautiful."

"Do I?" I had changed my outfit four times that morning before settling on the yellow dress. Yellow being "our" color, Brandon's and mine. In my mind, anyway.

"Yeah, you do." She patted my shoulder. "You'll be great. You'll tell Mr. Brock how you feel and he'll be so excited to hear it he'll take you in his arms and ask you to marry him."

I smiled. "You're quite a romantic, Diane."

"I can think of worse things to be, Dr. Wyman."

BRANDON WAS A few minutes late for his noon appointment, which gave me more time to pace nervously around my office, imagining any and all of his possible reactions to my declaration of love. When he finally did show up, he didn't merely walk in; he limped in, with the help of a pair of crutches.

"What happened?" I asked as he lowered himself into the chair, his right foot tightly wrapped in an ace bandage.

"I sprained my ankle on the tennis court over the weekend," he said, wincing in pain as he was trying to find a comfortable position. "I was running for a shot and tripped over a ball. The ankle went one way; the rest of me went the other."

"I'm sorry," I said, concerned about his injury but pleased that he had merely reported it as opposed to cursing about it, which he would have done in the old days.

"No, I'm the one who's sorry," he said with one of his killer grins. "I wanted to look my best for our final session, get my appearance just right so your lasting impression of me would be a positive one."

I laughed hollowly. What was there to laugh about? "Not to worry, Mr. Brock. You look fine." Better than fine.

"Thanks. So. What happens on this momentous occasion, this day of all days? Is there something special that you do when a client makes it to the finish line of the Wyman Method? Some sort of ceremony that you preside over?"

"No. Nothing like that," I said, continuing to wear what must have been a ridiculous-looking, pasted-on smile. I almost couldn't bear to meet his eyes, couldn't bear to think of his never coming back, couldn't bear to face that, unless I shared my feelings with him, he would walk out of my office—limp out of my office—and that would be the end of that. "What happens is that I do an exit interview, where I ask you questions and then compare your answers to those you gave me at our very first session. This allows me to assess the changes that have occurred."

"It sounds like a final exam."

"I suppose it is, in a way."

"Do you think I'll pass?"

"Yes." Yes, I do take Brandon Brock to be my lawfully wedded—

I stopped myself—I was worse than Diane—and got on with the exit interview. I asked him questions relating to his former tendencies to interrupt, to be abrasive, to be arrogant, to be adolescent, to be defensive, to be stubborn, etcetera. And I probed other areas that had posed problems for him, particularly those where he had put himself at risk for a sexual harassment lawsuit, the chief concern of his board of directors.

He answered all my questions without a single misstep—it was hard to imagine that he had once been dubbed America's Toughest Boss. The more he talked, the more clear it was that he really had mastered the language of Womenspeak, really had become the kind of man any woman would want to work for (or marry).

Of course, if I hadn't been so caught up in my romantic feelings for him, I would have allowed myself to feel a tremendous sense of pride and satisfaction for what we had accomplished, for what *I* had accomplished. Brandon Brock was proof that the Wyman Method was sound. And whether or not I ever landed another client, whether or not I ever found my way back to *Good Morning, America* or the radio show or the bestseller list, nobody could take that away from me.

"I know you're probably not finished," said Brandon, interrupting my private pep talk, which didn't count as an offense, "but there's something I'd like to tell you, Dr. Wyman."

"Oh?" I did make eye contact with him then, let myself be ensnared by his remarkable blue eyes. He had something to tell me. Could it be the same something I wanted to tell him? I swallowed hard. "Please, Mr. Brock. Go ahead."

"Okay, but what I'm going to say is off the record. Not part of your exit interview, in other words. So no demerits if I veer off into Menspeak. Promise?"

I smiled expectantly. "Promise."

"Now." He cleared this throat. "When I first came to see you, I was only doing it to keep my board off my back."

"I'm aware of that."

"And I was very, very skeptical of this program—and of you."

"I'm aware of that too."

"And while there are still aspects of the program that I think are way, way out there—no demerits, remember?—I respect what you're doing. I respect that there's a need for men to learn how to communicate with women. I respect that you didn't try to change me; instead, you tried to change my perspective. It's distinctly possible that I'll go into a meeting tomorrow and tell an off-color joke, but the difference will be that I'll have the sensitivity to realize that I may have offended someone and I'll apologize. It's also possible that, in a weak moment, I'll slip and call our buddy Susan 'honey,' but I'll understand what I've done and use my infinite charm to make it up to her." He smiled. "To sum up, Dr. Wyman, I've gotten a lot out of the program. I sincerely believe that I'm a better man today than I was when I showed up for my first session."

I waited. Was that it? Was his speech over? Did he have nothing to add? Was he not going to say that as *he* had grown over the months, he had grown to love *me*?

Apparently not. I thanked him for his words of praise for me and the program and said that I was gratified to have worked with him and to have watched his progress. Blah blah blah. My heart was clanging in my chest, my brain urging me to share my feelings. So what if he wasn't the first one to say "I love you?" *I'd* be the first one to say it then. I could handle that, couldn't I? Hadn't Diane trained me to be able to say it first? Maybe all Brandon needed was a little encouragement from me, because he was a man and, fluent in Womenspeak or not, men don't like to be rejected. Yes, maybe his speech was meant to be *my* encouragement to speak openly about my feelings for him. Maybe he was sitting there right that very minute hoping I would say the words he longed to hear.

"Dr. Wyman?" he asked after there had been several seconds of silence. "I know you weren't finished with your exit interview when I sounded off there. So please. Say whatever you were going to say."

Okay, Lynn. He's just given you an opening. This is where you tell him you love him and alter the course of your relationship. Tell him. Now.

"Mr. Brock," I began, my voice quivering like some pathetic wuss. "What I'd like to say—what I'd like to *share*—is that I—" I faltered.

"You what?"

Here we go again. No! I would get the words out if I had to reach down my throat and yank them out.

"I think you're a very special man." All right, so it wasn't poetry. It was a start.

"Hey, thanks. I appreciate that."

"It's true. You have humor and a wonderful capacity for play, plus you're a shrewd businessman, obviously."

He seemed very surprised by my comments, puzzled by them.

"And you've probably been told this a million times," I soldiered on, "but you have incredible eyes. Mystical eyes."

His puzzlement turned to amusement. Yes, he was wearing a great, big, happy smile, and I took it as my cue to proceed, to let my emotions pour forth at last.

"This is hard for me," I said, "because I don't know what your reaction will be, but what I'm trying to say, Mr. Brock—Brandon—is that I have feelings for you, feelings that extend far beyond our work here in the office, feelings that—"

I cut myself off because now he was laughing. Laughing! What the hell was so funny?

"You're good, Dr. Wyman," he said, trying to catch his breath between guffaws. "I mean, you're really, really good."

"Good at what?" I said, utterly confused. Of all the reactions I had envisioned, laughter was not one of them.

"Putting your clients through the paces, straight through until the bitter end." Ha ha ha ha ha ha. "Here I thought I was off the hook, about to graduate with an A+, and you ambush me with another pop quiz." Ha ha ha ha ha ha.

I didn't know what to make of this, was absolutely flummoxed by his response. I had gone out on a limb—had shared my fucking feelings—and he thought it was a scream?

"Actually," he said, calming down, "I should have been better prepared, since you've been beating the sexual harassment thing into my head all these months. I should have figured you would test me, as sort of a final exam. Still, the bit about my mystical eyes. . . ." Ha ha ha ha ha ha. "You almost had me there, Dr. Wyman. But then it dawned on me that you were only coming on to me to trip me up—to see if I'd take the bait and come on to you right back. Well, I didn't, because I've learned that I'm not allowed to make overtures to women in a work environment. So I guess I passed your final exam with flying colors. I'm not a naughty boy anymore."

My God, I thought. I've created a monster. I summon up all my courage and tell the guy how I feel about him, and he assumes it's just that evil genius, Dr. Lynn Wyman, making him undergo yet another wild and crazy experiment.

"Does this wind up your exit interview with me?" he asked, still chortling.

"Yes," I said, trying to pull myself together, to bring my blood pressure back to normal. "Our time is up for today, which means we're finished here, Mr. Brock, finished with our work. It's been a pleasure coaching you through the program. I wish you the very best of luck in your future endeavors."

I know. I couldn't have sounded more detached, abrupt, matter-of-fact, like my old self.

I rose from my chair, reached for his hand and shook it perfunctorily. He took a few minutes to get up, because of the ankle and the crutches, and when he was finally standing, he said, "Would it be inappropriate for me to give you a hug, Dr. Wyman? As a thank-you to my teacher?"

I was so out of it by this point that I said, "Yeah, sure, whatever," and let him hug me. So what? Who cared? Why not? I was numb from all the energy I'd expended during that single hour, totally sapped.

But suddenly, when he removed his arms from around me and limped out the door of my office, I was anything but numb. I was alone.

He may have been the one with the sprained ankle but I was the one with the collapsed ego. Obviously, he didn't care about me. If he did, he would have said "I have feelings for you, too" or "I want us to start dating now that our professional relationship is over" or even "To hell with sexual harassment! Come 'ere, baby," which would have been followed by a lusty and long-anticipated embrace.

No, Brandon Brock was gone and he wouldn't be coming back. If I ever saw him again, it would be on the cover of a magazine. "America's Most Sensitive Boss," the headline would read.

Swell, I thought. Just swell.

20

SO? TELL ME what happened?" said Diane after Brock (I was back to calling him that) had left the office.

"Nothing." I shrugged listlessly. I felt as if I'd been run over by a sport utility vehicle. "I did my best, Diane. He didn't go for it."

"What do you mean?"

"He thought I was coming on to him, as some sort of a test, to see if he'd take the bait and flunk his 'final exam.' I coached him so well on the subject of sexual harassment that he wouldn't let me sexually harass him. It was a disaster."

"Wait. Don't say that, Dr. Wyman. It sounds like it was just a miscommunication, the kind that always goes on between men and women. You know the routine: She loves him but he doesn't realize it, and then he realizes it but now she's too proud to admit she loved him in the first place."

"Aren't I supposed to be too smart to get stuck in those miscommunications?"

"Why? You're human, remember? We worked on getting you in touch with your human side."

"A lot of good it did me."

"Stop it. You've got to stay positive. I have a feeling that once Mr. Brock has had a chance to think things over, he'll call you."

"Why should he?"

"Because he'll miss you. The same way you'll miss him. You'll hear from him, no doubt about it."

I had plenty of doubt about it, and I was right to. The entire month of September went by and there wasn't a peep out of Brock. I had a call from Naomi once, to thank me yet again for turning her boss into a sweetie pie (her term), but nothing from The Titan himself.

I pined. I really, really missed him. I missed him so much that whenever Diane would run out to do errands, I would skulk into my office, pull out the tape recordings of Brock's sessions, and listen to them. I'd sit in my chair, straining to catch every nuance of his speech patterns as he practiced his scripts, and I would pretend he was there with me, in body as well as voice. Yes, I agree that there was something slightly masochistic about this, but as I said, I really, really missed him.

October arrived and so, at last, did my divorce from Kip. There hadn't been a peep out of him, either, not in many months. I had thought about him from time to time, wondered if he was with someone, but only in the way you wonder about a person you're glad you don't have to see or talk to and can, therefore, wonder about without obligation.

"Let's have a 'Lynn's divorced' party," said Isabel when I told her the marriage had been officially terminated.

"Thanks, but I'm not in a celebrating mood," I said. I was pretty melancholy, due to the Brandon/Kip combo, plus I remembered what had happened the last time I'd partied with my friends.

No, I buried myself in my work, such as it was, coached the few clients who came to the office.

Oh, and I paid a visit to my father, just as Brock had suggested I should during our car ride back into the city after that last field trip. In recent years, I had seen my mother regularly, but had kept my distance from dear old dad. He and I weren't estranged, exactly; it was more that I had written him off as the "bad guy," had sided with my mother in their ongoing battle over which of them was responsible for their divorce, had decided that he was a lost cause who wouldn't or couldn't be helped by the Wyman Method and was, therefore, not worth my trouble.

But one Sunday in early October, a day when I'd been in serious mooning-over-Brock mode and replaying every single syllable he'd ever said to me, I decided to show up on Alan Wyman's doorstep.

He lived in Hartsdale, less than a half-hour from my place in Mt. Kisco. He lived alone—for the moment. (While he'd had several long-term relationships since the divorce, he'd never remarried.) He lived quietly, without pets scurrying around or the television or stereo blaring. And, the owner of a small printing company, he lived modestly.

Naturally, he was surprised to see me. I was with him for most of the afternoon, but here's the *Cliffs Notes* version.

"Lynn? Is that you?" he said, peering from behind the front door.

"The one and only," I said. "I know I should have called first. Is this a bad time?"

"No. No. Come on in." He hugged me. I let him.

"You're sure you're not busy?" I said as I walked inside the house, into the living room, which was freezing. He had the air conditioner on, even though it was a chilly fall day.

"No, I was just reading the paper," he said. "I wasn't expecting company, that's all."

I was company instead of family. I found that very sad.

As we sat on the sofa together, making the requisite chatter about his health and my health and that old standby, the weather, I observed that he was still a handsome man, with his dark hair and prominent jaw and large brown eyes. He was just thinner than I remembered. Shorter too. And nervous about my being there, clearly uncomfortable. I could hardly blame him, though, given that he probably viewed me not only as "company" but as an emissary from the enemy camp.

"Something to eat, Lynn? Or drink?" he asked.

"No, Dad. I came to talk."

"Uh-oh. The 'T' word," he said, managing a little smile. "You and your mother have a thing about that 'T' word."

"I guess we do," I said, not wanting to scare him off. "But, speaking of my mother, I'd like to ask you about your marriage, if you don't mind. And that doesn't mean I want to put you on the spot or make you dredge up old wounds or cast blame on you."

"I find that hard to believe," he said with a rueful chuckle.

"It's true, Dad. I know I've blamed you in the past but I'm here today to learn about myself, not to pass judgment on you."

"What does a woman like you have to learn? You're as smart as a whip. Always were."

"Maybe not as smart as everybody thought. You see, Dad, I came here because I've been taking a good look at myself and my relationships with men, and in doing so I've wondered about your relationship with Mom."

He winced. "You already know about that. We were oil and water, she and I."

"Yes, right. But tell me about the communication problem you two had. Tell me why it was so hard for you to talk to her. I'd really like to know, Dad. Not to blame. Just to understand."

"Lynnie." He patted my knee. "We've been over this many times. I don't want to cause any more hurt."

"You won't. I swear. I'm going to listen with an open mind."

"Okay, but don't say I didn't warn you."

"Go ahead, Dad."

He sighed. "Why was it so hard for me to talk to your mother? Because I couldn't stand her, that's why. Could not abide the woman, don't have a clue why I married her. She was always on me, right from the beginning, always nagging me, always pushing and pushing. She never eased up on me, never. Even when she was out of the house, she didn't let up: She'd leave me notes telling me what to do; she'd call me every seven minutes telling me what to do; she'd have *you*, my own daughter, telling me what to do."

"*I* told you what to do?" I had no memory of that.

He nodded. "In the same exact voice as your mother. You were some mimic." He shook his head. "It was like having two harpies going at me twenty-four hours a day. As much as I loved you, honey, I couldn't take it."

Honey. I thought of Brock then. My *snookums*. Where was he on that Sunday afternoon while I was with my father in Hartsdale? With Kelsey? On a business trip? Working at his apartment? God, how I missed him, missed having him walk into my office on Tuesdays at noon, missed having him in my life. I wished I could tell him he was right about my father, that Alan Wyman had been an unhappy man, not just an uncommunicative one.

"I can imagine how awful that must have been for you," I said, "but why didn't you ever talk back to Mom? Why did you withdraw and withdraw and withdraw until she couldn't get a word out of you?"

"Lynnie." He sighed again. "Your mother was relentless. The way she spoke to me wasn't communication. It was a harangue. I realize that you've made a name for yourself with your theory that men should learn how to communicate with women by talking like women, but talk is not the answer to everything. Sometimes—as in my case—it's better to keep your mouth shut, bide your time, and then get the hell out."

"That's what you did?"

"That's what I did. I kept my mouth shut until I felt you were old enough not to be traumatized by a divorce. And then I got the hell out."

"Oh, Dad. You really were miserable all those years."

Naturally, I got choked up at this juncture in the conversation. I felt terribly sorry for him. Sorry for the three of us. And guilty for not hearing his side before, really hearing it. But I suppose I hadn't been ready to hear it. I was too consumed with my own idea of what had gone wrong in their marriage. I had clung to that old idea, because it had formed the basis for the Wyman Method, the program that had defined me, made me famous. Letting go of it would have meant letting go of my career, of my identity.

"It's true that I wasn't the greatest talker in the world," my father went on. "To be honest with you, Lynnie, the other women I've been with have had their own complaints on that score. But when it came to your mother and me, it wasn't about a lack of communication; it was about a lack of love. Big difference."

Big difference. "Okay, so here's the long and short of it," I said, trying to come to some sort of conclusion about what he'd told me. "Your position is that you can't have communication without a good relationship but you can't have a good relationship without communication."

He laughed. "Now that's what I call a vicious circle—emphasis on the 'vicious.' "

I laughed, too. "Okay, how about this: What you're saying is that relationships are a bitch, any way you look at it."

"That's what I'm saying, honey."

I SAW MY father more frequently from then on—we had decided to "get to know each other better"—but mostly I worked, went about my business, kept on.

And then one day, clear out of the blue, Brock called.

I was walking a client out of the office when the phone rang. Diane picked it up and began gesturing wildly to me.

"What?" I said when the client was gone. "What on earth is the matter with you?"

"It's Naomi," she squealed, her hand over the mouthpiece. "She says she's got Mr. Brock on the line for you."

I stood absolutely still.

"Did you hear me, Dr. Wyman? *He's* on the phone. Snap out of it."

I nodded. Still, I was rigid with excitement, anxiety, expectation—all of the above.

"Go," she urged. "Take it in your office—and hurry. He's a busy guy."

"Right." I dashed into my office, closed the door and sat down at my desk. I took a couple of deep breaths and, tentatively, lifted the receiver. "Hello?"

"Hi, Dr. Wyman," said Naomi. "Please hold for Mr. Brock."

More deep breaths. In—two, three, four. Out—two, three, four.

"Hey, Dr. Wyman," he said buoyantly when he came on the line. "It's Brandon Brock. Remember me?"

No.

"Of course, I remember you," I said. "How are you, Mr. Brock?" My tone was friendly but not fawning.

"I'm great. The ankle's healed. I've been doing a ton of traveling—we have a couple of positions at Finefoods that we haven't filled, so until we do *I'm* filling them—but everything's been going well. You'll be happy to know that I've been Mr. Sensitive around the office. People come to me and tell me their problems and I listen and nod and say, 'I can only imagine how you must feel.' "

"I'm glad to hear you're using your Womenspeak, Mr. Brock. Very glad." Okay, okay. So why are you calling?

"You don't sound glad," he said. "See? I notice everything now."

I smiled to myself. "I *am* glad. I'm busy at the moment, that's all."

"Oh. Then I won't keep you. I was wondering—"

"Yes?"

"I'm hesitating because I don't know how you'll react."

"The best thing to do is just come out and say what you have to say." Yeah, it sure worked for me.

"Good. Then here's the new script I've been practicing. Ready?"

"Ready."

"Since it's been a while since I finished the program—enough of an interval to make this invitation appropriate, I hope—I was wondering if you'd go out with me, Dr. Wyman. If you even date former clients, that is."

Invitation. Go out. Date. So it was happening. My wish had come true. I had waited for those words, yearned for them, and now he had uttered them. It was a miracle.

"Scripts aside, I've wanted to ask you out for some time," he said more soberly, "but I thought you might hate the idea. And then there was the complication of Kelsey."

"I take it she's no longer a complication?" This was fabulous. Amazing. I had the impulse to jump for joy but decided to wait until after we hung up.

"No, she's not. We're history."

"Oh. What precipitated your breakup, if I'm not being too personal?"

"Too personal?" He laughed. "You know more about me than anyone. The story is, we were out for dinner one night. I said to her, 'I don't know how *you're* going to metabolize that alfredo sauce, but *I'm* having mine on the side.' She glared at me, threw her napkin at me, said, 'I liked you better the old way,' and stormed out of the restaurant. I haven't spoken to her since."

"I'm sorry."

"Are you?"

"No."

He laughed again. "I meant what I said before. I've been close to calling you a million times, Dr. Wyman, but whenever I'd pick up the phone I'd get cold feet. You always seemed so unapproachable."

"I'm approachable. Approach me and see what happens," I said after rejecting the notion of playing hard to get. This was my big chance and I wasn't about to blow it. Besides, I was a graduate of the Wyman Method. I knew how to express my feelings. "And please, call me Lynn."

"*Lynn.*" He paused. "It feels strange to call you by your first name."

"I understand that completely, *Brandon*."

He exhaled. "I'm so relieved. I didn't have a clue how it would go if I called you, and I was pretty worried about it. Naomi kept saying, 'Oh, call her, call her, Mr. Brock.' But it was Diane who gave me the nudge I needed."

"Diane? *My* Diane?" I hadn't expected that piece of news anymore than I'd expected to hear from Brandon.

"Sure. I thought she would have told you. She stopped by the office last week, to see Naomi, I guess, and when she saw me passing by in the hall she said, 'Dr. Wyman misses you and is dying for you to call her.' "

"She actually said that?" I was mortified.

"She did, but I'm sure she was only exaggerating."

No, she wasn't, but that was beside the point. She was a little sneak! "She never mentioned that she'd seen you," I said, trying to calm down, to focus on the positive. I suppose it was sweet of Diane to intercede on my behalf. I just would have preferred that she'd tipped me off.

"Well, we have her to thank for this call. As I said, I was planning to get in touch with you anyway, but she made it happen faster."

"Fine. I'll give her a raise."

He laughed. "So *was* she exaggerating?"

"Oh, you mean—"

"About you missing me?"

I gave this a second or two before replying, just for a tiny bit of drama. "No."

"Hey, that's easily the best news I've had all day," he said. "I've missed you, too. Boy, have I ever. I really do want to see you, Lynn. As soon as possible, in fact."

The urgency in his voice made my body turn to mush. I had never had a serious boyfriend in high school or college and had certainly never felt this way about Kip. No, whatever was going on inside me was the real thing. For the first time in my life.

"What do you have in mind?" I said.

"What are you doing tomorrow night?"

"Not a thing."

"Perfect. You're going with me to Yankee Stadium for Game 3 of the World Series. I've got the best seats in the house—down on the field at the first base line."

I flashed back to the night I went to Yankee Stadium with Penny and the two duds from Feminax, the night I spotted Brandon through the binoculars, sweeping Kelsey into his arms. Yes, I knew exactly where his seats were. I just never thought I'd be sitting in one of them.

"I'd love to go," I said enthusiastically. "I don't know much about baseball, though, so you'll have to explain things to me."

"I will, but there's one thing you already know about the game: How I feel about it. Remember all those months ago when you asked me to share my feelings about something, anything, and all I could come up with was baseball?"

"I remember." I'd listened to the tape of that session over and over.

"Then you remember how much fun I get from watching the game, how much pleasure it gives me. Let's see if I can get you to experience that pleasure too."

I'm already experiencing it, I thought, my heart soaring. More than you know.

SO YOU'RE NOT mad?" said Diane after I'd come flying out of my office and given her a complete account of my conversation with Brandon, including his report of her little behind-my-back visit to Finefoods.

"No, I'm not mad," I replied, hugging her. "I'm too happy to be mad. I'm getting the chance I've been dreaming about. It's a new beginning for me, Diane, a fresh start. After all I've been through with the split from Kip and the publicity and the career problems, I finally see the light at the end of the tunnel, finally have a sense that my future looks bright." I gave her another squeeze. "Everything's all right now," I said. "And it's only going to get better."

21

BRANDON DID MORE than just invite me to the World Series. He rolled out the red carpet for me. He arrived at my apartment in his chauffeur-driven Mercedes, escorted me into the car, had the driver, an amiable fellow named Liam, drive us straight to Yankee Stadium (no crowded subways for us, no sir), and then led me through the throngs of fans into the stadium and down to our seats, which, by the way, *were* the best in the house.

"How's this?" he said proudly as the usher showed us to Section 15, Row 50—right smack on the field, on the first base line.

"Incredible," I said, referring to the seats *and* the royal treatment I was getting. Cinderella had nothing on me.

"Good. Get comfortable. I'll order us something to eat." He waved a young man over. Apparently, the best seats in the house came with a private waiter (no ordinary vendors for us, no sir). We could have selected one of the trendier items from the menu but went for hot dogs and beer. "The food is half the fun," said Brandon, his face lit up like a kid's at Christmas. Clearly, he hadn't been conning me when he'd described his love for the game all those months ago. One look at him told the story. The first pitch wasn't for twenty minutes, but he was already as excited as I'd ever seen him.

And he seemed to know everybody around us, or, rather, everybody around us seemed to know him. There were a lot of "Hey, Brandon, great to see you"s and "The Yanks are gonna do it tonight"s and "It wouldn't be a game without you here"s. He shook hands and slapped backs and high-fived anyone and everyone. He was in his element. For six months, he had been in my element, on my turf, playing by my rules. That night, he not only knew the rules, he knew the language.

"Teach me some Baseballspeak," I teased after the game had gotten underway. "What, for example, is a balk?"

He told me. I learned about balks and bunts and bases on balls. I learned the names of all the players—coaches and managers, too. I learned the difference between a sinker and a slider, a fastball and a forkball, a sidearm curve and a slurve. In other words, I gained an entirely new vocabulary.

The game was a tight contest, and while I did get caught up in it, I couldn't take my eyes off Brandon for very long. He was too much fun to watch, with all his whooping and hollering and unapologetic rooting for the home team.

I don't mean to suggest that he was so involved with the game that he neglected me. On the contrary. By nine o'clock, the temperature at the stadium had dipped down into the forties, and he kept asking me if I was warm enough, kept taking my hands in his and rubbing them, kept putting his beefy arm around me.

"You sure you're okay?" he said during the seventh inning stretch.

"I'm fine," I assured him.

"Just checking," he said. "Now that I've persuaded you to go out with me, I don't want you thinking you made a mistake."

"I didn't exactly need persuading," I reminded him. "You asked me out. I said yes."

He cocked his head at me. "Now that you mention it, you *were* an easy 'yes,' " he said. "Why was that?"

"Because I've wanted to go out with you for a long time," I said, about as straightforwardly as I'd ever said anything.

His blond eyebrows arched in surprise. "Then why in the world didn't you ever tell me, Lynn?"

"I did tell you. At your last session. You didn't believe me."

Now he looked puzzled. "You don't mean—" He stopped, replayed the conversation in his mind. "When you were saying you thought I had mystical eyes—"

"Actually, it's my friend Isabel who thinks you have mystical eyes. I think you have just plain beautiful eyes."

He smiled. "So when you were saying you had feelings for me that went beyond our professional—"

I nodded.

"You weren't testing me, to see if I'd mastered Womenspeak?"

I shook my head.

"I walked out of the office totally clueless?"

I nodded.

"And you let me?"

Enough with the pantomime. "What was I supposed to do? I figured that if you'd had feelings for me too, you would have said so."

"But I did have feelings for you. I've had feelings for you since that day at the tennis club when you marched over to me and launched into your speech. From the second I laid eyes on you I've wanted to—"

"What?"

He decided to show, not tell. He grabbed me by the shoulders and kissed me on the mouth. First tentatively, then, when he could see that I was hardly resisting, more ardently. We'd *still* be kissing if a foul ball hadn't come careening into our section, nearly decapitating us.

"That was close," I said.

"*We* were close," he said, pulling me to him. "I liked that."

"So did I."

"Then how about an instant replay?" He kissed me again. It was a gorgeous, hot-breathed, fulsome kiss, and it brought cheers from the fans sitting directly behind us.

"This is going to be great," he said, clutching my hand.

"What is?" I said, feeling happier than I thought possible.

"We are. You'll see."

I DID SEE. After the game, which the Yankees won in extra innings, Liam drove us back up to Mt. Kisco. Brandon told him to wait a few minutes while he walked me inside the apartment.

"What about tomorrow night?" he murmured, after kissing me in the stillness of the dark foyer. "We could skip the crowds and have dinner at my apartment, just the two of us."

"Are you a cook?" I asked as he nuzzled me. I loved the smell of him, loved the feel of his skin against mine, loved the way he combed my hair back with his fingers, loved how he ran his lips along the side of my neck. This is how it's supposed to be, I thought, remembering that the sex with Kip had been athletic but not involving. With Brandon, every part of me was involved, every muscle, every nerve ending, every brain cell. I was wholly in the moment when I was with him, was as aware of his body as if it were an extension of my own. I realize that sensations always feel heightened, more intense, at the beginning of a relationship and that the sort of excitement I was experiencing is typical of good chemistry on a first date. But I knew—just knew—that what was going on between Brandon Brock and me was not merely a run-of-the-mill first date. It was a connection that had formed gradually, over the course of six months, a connection that nothing and no one could break.

"Am I a cook?" he said in response to my question. "No. You may have taught me how to *talk* about food, but all I know how to *do* with it is eat it. I hope that's not a problem."

"Hardly," I said, thinking of my ex-husband, the chatty chef. "I'm not much of a cook either. So how will we have dinner at your apartment if neither of us cooks?"

"You leave that to me. Just say you'll come. I'll have Liam pick you up at your office at seven and bring you over. And then, when it's time for you to go, he can drive you home. Or not."

I looked at him, spotted the twinkle in his eyes. "It's a date," I said, thinking I'd bring a change of clothes to his apartment. In case I decided on the "Or not."

AT SEVEN O'CLOCK on the dot the next evening, Liam was parked outside my office waiting for me.

I practically leapt into the Mercedes, counting the traffic lights until we got to Brandon's building, which, it turned out, was a four-story brownstone on the corner of Second Avenue and Eighty-first Street on Manhattan's Upper East Side. I chuckled to myself as we pulled up alongside it. I had envisioned him living in a penthouse apartment in a high-rise—a swinging bachelor pad decorated (by Kelsey) in an ultracontemporary style. But his building was an historic structure, built, perhaps, around the turn of the twentieth century, and, from the look of it, magnificently restored and maintained.

"You made it," said Brandon, who was standing at the door to his home, beaming.

"Liam took good care of me," I said, floating up the steps, into Brandon's arms, where I remained, by the way, for several stirring minutes. It sounds sickeningly romantic, I know, but neither of us wanted to let go of the other. You'd think we were a couple who'd just been reunited after a long and tragic separation instead of people who'd spent hours together the night before at a baseball game.

Eventually, we went inside. Brandon poured us drinks, then gave me a tour of the place, describing in excellent Womenspeak the pedigree of each antique and where and when he fell in love with it. For a man who'd been infamous for his bad taste in jokes, he had exquisite taste in home furnishings.

"I would never have figured you for a guy with an eighteenth century English commode for a night table," I kidded him.

"Which goes to show that Dr. Wyman doesn't know everything," he said smugly.

"Obviously," I said. "Any other surprises for me?"

"Dinner," he said. "Follow me."

He guided me into a richly panelled dining room, its table set with silver and china and crystal, not to mention laden with platters of fruit and cheese, smoked salmon and black bread, grilled shrimp and curry sauce. This was the same man with whom I had pigged out on hot dogs and beer?

He pulled out my chair, a sturdy antique from the Louis-something-with-a-Roman-numeral period, poured us each a glass of wine and sat down next to me.

"Shrimp?" he asked, passing the platter.

"Yes, thank you," I said.

"Curry sauce? *Or would you prefer yours on the side?*"

"On the side," I said wryly, delighting in the way he was poking fun at me, sensing that we were on the verge of the sort of intimacy based on a shared history as well as a mutual respect. "Where did you get all this delicious food?"

"From the gourmet place down the street," he said. "I bought it and brought it home and put it out. Not a big deal. As I told you, I'm not a cook."

"You don't hear me complaining, do you?"

After we finished the first course (yes, those were only appetizers), Brandon emerged from the kitchen with filet mignon wrapped in bacon. "I don't know how *you* metabolize beef, Lynn, but whenever *I* eat it, it goes straight to my arteries."

"Okay, Brandon," I said, recognizing another parody when I heard one and enjoying the affectionate tone that accompanied it. "You can relax now. You've already graduated from the program. You don't have to prove how sensitive you are. You don't have to prove anything to me anymore." I touched his arm, yearned to touch every inch of him. "We're way past all that, aren't we?" I added with a new note of seriousness.

"You bet we are." He leaned over and kissed my cheek.

That innocent kiss led to another innocent kiss, which led to a series of kisses that were anything but innocent. These things happen when two people are in the throes of new love, as anyone who's been there knows. But it also happens when you've spent six long months fighting a sexual attraction to a guy and the fight's finally over. The truth was, we weren't two kids on a first date; we were a couple of adults who had discovered, over time, that we really mattered to each other. As a result, we abandoned all pretense of being even remotely interested in food and fled the table for the master bedroom, where we immediately got horizontal.

"It occurs to me that you never taught me how to use Womenspeak during sex," he joked as he was feverishly trying to unbutton my blouse. "Not even one script to practice."

"A huge oversight on my part. Repeat after me," I said as I was feverishly trying to unbuckle his belt. "I don't know how long *you've* been fantasizing about this moment, but *I've* been thinking about little else for months."

"That's a good script," he said breathlessly, his hands having just made contact with my bare breasts, "a very good script. But what about this one. I *notice* that you have a luscious body, and I want to *share* with you that I'm incredibly eager to be inside it."

I was helping him pull off his pants now, freeing his willy. "How about this script?" I said, my own breathing coming in spurts. "I *feel* what you're *feeling*."

We were both buck naked at this point, tangled up in each other, poised to do the nasty. "I like it," he said, exploring me everywhere, igniting me everywhere. "But I have a script I know you'll be crazy about. Ready?"

"I couldn't be more ready."

"Okay," he said as he climbed on top of me, assuming the position. "The script is: Oh, miss? Could you help me with directions? I'm lost."

"Forget that script," I said. "You're not lost. You're exactly where you're supposed to be."

"You too."

We made love like beginners; as if we had never done that and that and that with anyone else; as if the very act of lovemaking had been invented by us alone.

On the other hand, we made love like veterans; as if we'd been together forever and, therefore, didn't have a single awkward, insecure, Am-I-doing-everything-right moment.

In other words, when we made love, we had the best of both worlds, which isn't a terrible way to kick off a relationship.

22

THE NEXT FEW weeks were straight out of a romance novel. Brandon and I were inseparable, except, of course, when he was out of town on business. Even on those occasions, there was considerable touchy-feely, kiss-you-miss-you talk over the phone, plus a bouquet of flowers here, a bottle of perfume there. (I should note that at no time did Brandon dispatch Naomi to purchase gifts for me. He really was a changed man without losing the brashness, the colorfulness, the outsized personality that had attracted me in the first place.) There was no doubt that there was a serious courtship of me underway, a campaign for me in progress, and I sat back and let myself enjoy every second of it.

It was on the night that he returned from London, bearing boxes of souvenirs from Harrod's, that he told me he loved me. He had arranged for Liam to drive me to Kennedy airport, so that when his plane landed, I would be there to meet him. We had been apart for three days and enough was enough.

"Hey, is it ever good to see you," he said, encircling me in his arms after making his way inside the terminal. "Miss me?"

"Not a bit," I kidded, bombarding him with kisses.

"That's what I thought. Love me?"

"Not that either."

He pulled away. "No?"

"No what?"

"You don't love me?" He looked as if he'd been punched in the stomach.

"Oh. I didn't know we were being serious. Are we being serious?"

"I was. In case I haven't mentioned it, I love you, Dr. Wyman. Madly."

I smiled, because by finally telling me he loved me after knowing me for nearly eight months, he was confirming what I'd already sensed. By contrast, Kip had told me he loved me the first week we met (in the midst of one of his tearful unburdenings about his relationship with his father) and I'd never truly believed it. "No, you haven't mentioned it," I said.

"Well, I do love you," said Brandon. "That's okay with you, I hope."

"It's not okay, it's imperative," I said. "Otherwise I'd be the only one doing the loving, and that can be a pretty sticky situation."

He embraced me then, as if to solidify our emotional commitment to each other. We were a couple. A couple in love. A couple with a future that promised rewarding careers and incredible sex and, with any luck, a brood of kids. Yes, I was getting ahead of myself, but I had every reason to be optimistic and no reason not to be.

BRANDON AND I saw each other every night that week following his trip to London, in spite of the fact that it was an extremely busy period for him at the office. Finefoods' cereal sales had slipped in the last year, due in large part to the growing tendency among Americans to skip breakfast in favor of getting to work in a hurry. To shore up profits, Brandon was unveiling a new "convenience food" division of the company—snack food spin-offs of its trademark cereals with names like Crispi Treats and Cheeripops and Nutri-Chewy Bars. It wasn't just a hectic time for him; it was a high-profile time for him as he was constantly making himself available to the media in order to ensure the line's successful launch.

While he was hardly a fan of reporters—he avoided them when he didn't have to be out there plugging a new product—he was a terrific spokesman for his company, the vividness of his appearance and the straightforward delivery of his message a compelling combination. I was very proud of him, very proud of the way he was able to marshal his communication skills and tackle what was, for him, the least appealing part of his job.

I was also very grateful that he took a few hours out of his jam-packed schedule to have dinner with my friends, all of whom had been hounding me about finally getting a chance to meet him. I had prepped him about each of them beforehand, explained how I'd never really had women friends earlier in my life and, therefore, had a special fondness for Penny and Isabel and Gail and Sarah, despite their quirks. When the evening came, he was the perfect gentleman to all of them—didn't call a single one of them "snookums." I could tell by the way they looked at me that they were not only stunned that I had transformed America's Toughest Boss into such a prize catch (and won our wager so convincingly) but were green with envy that I had charmed the prize catch into falling in love with me. To put it another way, their tongues were hanging out.

As for Brandon, he was lukewarm about my friends. When I asked, "So what did you think of them?" he shrugged and said, "They're very entertaining but I'd watch my back around them if I were you."

"What do you mean?" I said, more than a little surprised by his appraisal.

"Nothing," he replied, thinking better of his remark. "If you find them supportive and trustworthy, that's all that matters. I guess I've just been in the corporate jungle too long. I see everyone as the enemy. Pay no attention to what I said."

And so I paid no attention. Brandon loved me. He didn't have to love my friends.

And he did love me. He showed me his love over and over, night after torrid night, one night in particular.

"Do you remember when you asked me, during a session, how I responded to Kelsey whenever she'd bring up the subject of marriage?" he said as we lay in bed together, spooning.

"I do remember," I said. "You told me you were evasive, because you didn't want to marry Kelsey."

"Right. But here's the funny thing." He hesitated. "If *you* brought up the subject I wouldn't be evasive."

My eyes flew open and I bolted up in bed. "Run that by me again?"

"I said," he replied calmly, as if he were discussing the weather, "if *you* brought up the subject of marriage, of the two of us ever taking the plunge, I wouldn't be evasive."

"You wouldn't? Then what *would* you be?" I said, regarding him intently. I had more than a passing interest in his answer.

"I would be excited about the idea."

I was speechless. Despite our frequent and fervent declarations of love, the last thing I expected was a marriage proposal. Not this soon, anyway.

"What you're saying is, Brandon—Have you really been thinking that you might—Are you suggesting that you and I—"

He laughed. "And I paid *you* to teach *me* how to talk?"

I laughed too. "Forgive me, but I'm a little shaken up here. What, specifically, are you telling me?"

He reached for me, cradled me in his arms. "What I'm telling you," he whispered in my ear, "is that I want to marry you, Dr. Wyman. It doesn't have to be this minute. It doesn't have to be this year. I'm just saying that the feeling, the desire, the intention, is there."

"Oh."

"Oh? That's the best you can do? *Oh?*"

I kissed him. "I meant, *Oh*! As in: I would love to marry you. It's just that I never expected to remarry. Honestly I didn't."

"Why not? You're not exactly over the hill."

"No, but when you and I met, romance was the last thing on my mind. My focus was on getting my career back on track, on reestablishing my professional reputation."

"I know, I know. And you could have gotten your career back on track if I hadn't held you to that confidentiality agreement. You could have run to the media about me becoming your client—could have gotten a lot of great publicity for yourself at my expense—but you didn't. You stuck to our agreement instead of using me to hype the Wyman Method. I told you before: That's why I trust you, Lynn. You keep your word. Do I understand that you still want to boost your career back up there where it used to be? Of course. Will I help you in every way I can? Absolutely. I just can't help you by coming out publicly and saying I was your client. That would make my board of directors very jumpy, not to mention my stockholders. They like to think there's a stable guy at the helm, not some asshole who offends women every time he opens his mouth."

"Brandon, there *is* a stable guy at the helm. And I would never have reneged on my promise to you, just like I won't renege on this promise."

"What promise?"

"That I'll always love you."

He kissed me. "Even if I slip and call our pal Susan 'honey'?"

"Yup."

"Even if I interrupt her in a meeting?"

"Even then."

"Even if I tell her she has great legs?"

"You tell her she has great legs and I'll break yours."

"Fair enough."

I WAS IN my office the very next morning, consulting with Diane about our new client (I was letting her do the evaluations now), when the phone rang. "Could you get that?" she said. "My nails are wet."

I shot her a look and picked up the phone. "Dr. Wyman."

"Good morning, Dr. Wyman. It's Naomi. I have Mr. Brock on the line."

Gee, he *is* a lovesick fool, I thought, feeling the familiar flip-flop in my stomach that came over me whenever I heard his name. I only left him twenty minutes ago and he's calling me already! "Put him on, Naomi. And have a nice day."

"I'll try," she said. "But judging by the way it's going so far, I'm not hopeful."

Before I could ask her what she meant, she put me on hold.

"Is that loverboy calling?" Diane teased while I waited.

"Who else?" I said with mock nonchalance. I was thinking I was glad he was calling, because I had forgotten to ask him what time he'd be home later. And then I heard his voice.

"Lynn?"

Something was wrong. I could tell immediately, just from his tone as he said my name. He sounded odd, not his ebullient self at all.

"Hi, Brandon. What's up?"

"I need to see you. Right away."

He really did sound awful. He was barking the words at me, the way he used to in the not-so-good old days. "I have a client scheduled in about forty minutes but I could meet you for lunch or—"

"I said *right away*," he interrupted. "I'm working out of my apartment this morning. I'd like you to meet me here as soon as you can get here."

"What is it, Brandon? What's happened?" Clearly, something had. I was beginning to worry.

"I find that question not only an insult to my intelligence but a commentary on your own."

"What—"

Click.

"Is everything okay?" asked Diane, as she gazed up at me. "You're totally pale."

I didn't know how to respond. I was stung by the way Brandon had spoken to me, by the way he'd ordered me, by the way he'd patronized me. What had provoked him to behave so boorishly?

"Dr. Wyman?" Diane prodded.

"I've got to go," I said, trying not to panic. "Hold down the fort for me, will you, Diane?"

"Sure," she said. "I'll take care of—"

I was out the door before she finished her sentence.

I CAUGHT A cab and made it uptown to Brandon's apartment in ten minutes. I mounted the steps to his brownstone, reached for the brass knocker, and knocked.

He appeared at the door just as Naomi was exiting it. Neither of them looked ecstatic to see me.

"Okay. Now what's this all about?" I said when he and I were alone in the house. I was really concerned now. He hadn't made a move to kiss me or touch me, which was extremely unusual. He was nothing if not physically demonstrative.

"Here," he said with disgust, handing me that day's edition of the *New York Post*—at arm's length, by the way, as if the mere thought of my coming within a foot of him was abhorrent to him.

Reeling from his dramatic change in attitude toward me, I reached for the newspaper. It was opened to "Page Six," the *Post*'s widely read gossip column. It only took me a second before I spotted both of our names—in the column's headline!—and a few seconds more before I figured out why Brandon was so hostile toward me. There, in black and white, in full view of his board of directors, his stockholders and the rest of the world, was a story about how he had secretly been paying me to feminize his personality in order to prevent women executives from leaving Finefoods in droves for rival companies. (They referred to me as "Lynn Wyman, the has-been celebrity linguist," but that was the least of my problems.) The piece was highly critical of Brandon, describing him as a high-testosterone monster who was so close to losing his job that he was forced to undergo my "treatment."

"Never mind that I come off sounding like a nut case," he snapped. "Never mind that this will send everybody at Finefoods into a tailspin at a particularly crucial time for the company. Never mind that a zillion other media outlets will grab this story and run with it, creating an avalanche of negative publicity for me, personally, and a huge distraction for my public relations people, who've been working tirelessly to get the message out about our convenience-food division. NEVER MIND ANY OF THAT!" He stopped, his voice having risen to a roar. Yes, he was shouting at me, red-faced, tight-lipped, eyes blazing. He was the Brandon Brock I'd seen at the tennis club, the yeller and screamer I had bet my friends I could tame.

"Brandon, I—"

"I'M NOT FINISHED!" he interrupted at high volume. "As I was about to say, never mind about all of us poor bastards. The good news is that Lynn Wyman is back in the press!" He was the sarcastic Brandon now, the hurtful Brandon. "She landed the CEO of Finefoods as a client, taught him how to speak like a fucking girl, and saved his ass. Let's hear it for Dr. Wyman, a media darling once again!" He put his hands together and began to clap.

I hated that he had reverted to Menspeak. I knew he was only using it to taunt me, because he was furious at me. "Look, Brandon," I said, my mouth as dry as the Sahara, "I had nothing to do with this story, if that's what you're thinking."

"Save it for some other sucker."

"It's true. I gave you my word I wouldn't tip off any reporters about our arrangement and I kept it. You even thanked me for that, as recently as last night, for God's sake."

"Yeah, so imagine my surprise when I bought the paper today." He shook his head. "When I think that you just sat there while I was going on and on about how trustworthy you are, just smiled and blushed and lowered your head modestly, fully aware that the story would be appearing in a matter of hours! I mean, I knew you were determined to rebuild your career, but I didn't know *how* determined."

He was being so unfair, so quick to condemn me for something I hadn't done. "Brandon," I said, struggling to maintain my equilibrium. "You're assuming that I planted this story and I didn't."

He laughed scornfully. "Of course you planted it. You're the only one who benefits from it, not counting the dig about being a has-been."

My head was spinning. How could he suddenly have such a low opinion of me after telling me he loved me, after telling me he wanted to marry me? How could he automatically dub me the villain? I was deeply wounded, but I had to get a grip, had to keep trying to defend myself, to reason with him, to make things right between us.

"If I planted this story as you believe I did," I said, "why did I wait so long to do it? If I was so desperate to rebuild my career, why wouldn't I have given the *Post* the tip about you months ago?"

"Who the hell knows? Maybe you decided it was better to give it to them *after* I'd completed the program, because you figured that if the story broke while I was still your client, I'd drop out midway and you'd be left without an ending, without a successful *case study*. Maybe you're writing another book, with me as the main character, and your deal with the publisher was that I had to finish the program. Maybe this, maybe that. The point is, you broke your promise and blew apart everything we had together, *Dr. Wyman*."

This was too much to bear, these attacks on me more than I could tolerate. *I* was angry now, steaming. "Did it ever occur to you, *Mr. Brock*, that someone within Finefoods might have leaked the story?"

"Nice try. The only person at Finefoods who even knew that I was your client was Naomi, who is the most loyal woman I've ever come across." He glared at me, as if I were the least loyal woman he'd ever come across. "Oh, and my board members knew, naturally. They were the ones who sent me to you in the first place, remember? But they did it because they support me and would like me to continue running Finefoods. I make money for them. I do a good job for them. The last thing they're going to do is deep-six me."

"Well, how about someone else at Finefoods?"

"I JUST TOLD YOU! NO ONE ELSE AT FINEFOODS HAD A CLUE I WAS YOUR CLIENT!"

"I can hear you, Brandon. There's no need to shout."

"Yeah, well hear this," he said nastily. "I loved you. I trusted you. I wanted to spend the rest of my life with you. And you betrayed me. You of all people. Your ex-husband did the exact same thing to you. You'd think you'd have learned from that experience. But then maybe what you learned is to look out for yourself. Maybe what you learned is: Lynn Wyman is the only one who matters."

"That's utterly ridiculous, but I'm glad you brought up Kip. He did sell me out in the very same way that you're accusing me of selling you out, and I've told you how devastating it was to me. So why would I turn around and cause you that kind of anguish? Have you forgotten that I love you too? Has it slipped your mind that I want to marry you? What would possess me to sabotage my own happiness?"

"Your almighty career," he said with a mean smirk. "You told me last night that romance wasn't high on your list of priorities; that you were only interested in getting your radio show back."

"That was true when we met," I said hotly, "but priorities change.

After I fell in love with you, *you* became my top priority. I figured I'd refocus on my career once—"

"Once I was a done deal," he cut me off. "Which proves that you did plant the story. It's all making sense to me now. You'd gotten me through your program. You'd gotten me into your bed. You'd gotten me to make a commitment to you. So with all that frivolous stuff out of the way you were finally free to concentrate on the career. And what better way to do that than to create some publicity for yourself, right?"

"Shut up. Just shut up!" I was shaking with rage, couldn't fathom how he could have made up his mind that I was guilty. "Listen to me and listen carefully," I said. "I didn't do this and it will come out that I didn't do it."

"Ah, I'm afraid you're a little late as well as off-the-mark with that prediction."

"What do you mean?"

"I had Naomi call the *Post* and ask them where they got their information."

"A waste of a phone call, since they never give up a source."

"Oh really? They sure gave up their source this time. Naomi was told that 'Lynn Wyman herself provided the information.' What do you have to say to *that*?"

I had nothing to say at first. What could I say? Obviously, there had been some mistake. Naomi had misunderstood. But most troubling of all was that Brandon wasn't willing to give me the benefit of the doubt. Yes, the evidence against me was damning, but where was the trust? Where was the love?

"You're ruining everything, you know," I said finally, softly, defeatedly. "You're trashing our relationship."

"*I'm* trashing it?" This seemed to infuriate him further.

"Yes. What we had was real and special and, I thought, unassailable. We grew to love each other, Brandon. We grew to love each other as we each grew as individuals. We were a good team. I taught you how to be more sensitive toward others and you taught me how to take myself less seriously. And now, in the blink of an eye, we're over, as far as you're concerned. It doesn't seem possible."

"No, it doesn't seem possible." His broad shoulders slumped as he stood propped up against the wall, his arms dangling at his sides. He looked terribly sad, beaten. Clearly, he was as undone by this turn of events as I was.

"I didn't betray you," I tried again, knowing with absolute certainty that he still loved me—in spite of what he'd said, of what he'd read, of what he'd deemed to be the truth.

"But you did," he said, not listening, the way he used to not listen. "I'd give anything if I were wrong."

With that plaintive remark, he walked toward his front door and opened it. He was telling me without telling me to leave his house, to get out of his life.

I know it's a cliché and I'm very sorry to have to use it, but here it is: The minute he opened that door to usher me out, my heart broke. Something inside me shattered into tiny pieces.

"I didn't betray you," I repeated very quietly, as I moved toward the door. "I didn't. No matter what you believe."

I took one last look at him and noticed that he was clenching his jaw, his face a reflection of his desperate attempt to hold in his feelings. I had an impulse to rush over to him and embrace him, in the hope that our bodies might be able to communicate what our words could not.

But then he clamped his mouth tighter and defiantly turned his back to me. And so I didn't rush over to him. Instead, I breathed deeply, gathered myself up, head held high, and made my way out of his house.

"No, I didn't betray you," I whispered once I was outside on the curb, wondering where to go, how to get through the day. "No, I did not."

While I waited for a taxi, I replayed what had just taken place, replayed Brandon's accusations and my rebuttals, all of it. It was after a cab finally pulled up, after I'd settled into the back seat, after I'd instructed the driver to drop me off at my office, that the new thought emerged, the notion that put an entirely different slant on this nightmare.

I suppose it was understandable that I hadn't lit on the idea right away, given the jumble of emotions I was experiencing, but I wish I had. What finally occurred to me, you see, was that while it was inconceivable that *I* could have betrayed Brandon, it was not out of the realm of possibility that someone could have betrayed *me*.

Why not? It had happened before, as Brandon had pointed out, happened when I was married to Kip. Now here I was, an entire year later, and yet another story had just run in a newspaper about me, another story that I hadn't wanted leaked. Coincidence?

The editor at the *Post* had told Naomi that *I* had furnished the paper with the information about Brandon, but that had not been the case. A year ago, I had assumed that Kip had furnished the *Enquirer* with the information about me, but perhaps that had not been the case, either.

Yes, somebody has betrayed me, I decided. Not once, but twice. The question is: who?

If I had a prayer of getting Brandon back, it was up to me to find out.

PART THREE

23

BY THE TIME I got back to the office, Diane had already read the column in the *Post*. She was about to comment on it when I waved her off, mumbled, "I don't want to talk about it," and brushed past her, fleeing down the hall into my cocoon. Don't ask me how, but I managed to see two clients that day without breaking down. It was only after they were gone that I buried my head in my hands and sobbed, all the while wondering who had been screwing around with my life—and why.

By late afternoon, I'd had it with crying and decided to find a more empowering solution to my problems.

I called the *Post* and asked to speak to the "Page Six" editor. I said that I was Lynn Wyman, that I'd read the piece in the paper, and that I wanted—demanded—to know who'd given them the information on which the column was based.

"You did," said a man with a snide laugh. "I took the call myself, Dr. Wyman."

"But I *didn't* call you," I maintained.

"Well, then it was someone who claimed to be you, someone who knew an awful lot about your life, someone who sounded exactly like you, someone who left your phone number in case we had to do any fact checking."

Okay, I thought. So he's convinced I have multiple personality disorder. So what. The main thing is, it was definitely a woman who had set me up. That narrowed the field by fifty percent.

Next, I reached into a filing cabinet in my office and pulled out the *National Enquirer* story about Kip and me that had run the year before. I called the *Enquirer* and asked to speak to the reporter whose byline accompanied the story—something I had never bothered to do when the story originally broke, because I'd been too stunned at the time and because I had assumed Kip had been responsible. When the reporter answered the phone, I explained who I was (naturally, he said, "Never heard of you") and that it was imperative that he tell me how he'd gotten the dirt on me.

"Normally, I don't divulge my sources," he said, remembering who I was, finally, "but since that story ran so long ago and nobody but you gives a flip about it now, I can tell you that it was one of your own people who spilled their guts."

"My own people?" Then it *had* been Kip?

"Someone in your camp. Your agent. Your manager. Your P.R. gal. I can't remember her title at this point."

No, not Kip after all. My P.R. *gal,* he'd said. Can't remember *her* title. Whoever had contacted him was a woman, which suggested that one person must have committed both acts of sabotage. Still, I wasn't taking his words at face value. "I don't see how that's possible," I protested. "Your story presented me in a highly negative light. It put a huge dent in my professional life, as a matter of fact. Back in the days when I actually *had* people in my camp, they had a vested interest in building my career, not tearing it down. Why would any of them have 'spilled their guts' to you?"

"Hey, I don't know why people do what they do," he said. "What I do know is that this person hinted that *you* wanted your story out—anonymously—because you were pissed off at your husband for cheating on you and you wanted to dump him, without having it *appear* like you were dumping him. So we ran it. It's all coming back to me now, Laura."

"Lynn."

"Whatever. Take care, huh?"

Click.

All right. So whoever had leaked the two stories to the media about me was a woman claiming to be in my camp, in my circle, close to me. Well, she'd *have* to be close to me because she knew everything about me, including my secrets. And, if the guy at the *Post* was telling the truth, she had my voice down pat too, was a good mimic.

A *good mimic*. Wasn't that what I'd said about Diane while she was putting me through the Wyman Method? While she was playing my part, assuming the role of the linguistics coach, *impersonating* me?

No. It couldn't be. Not Diane, my loyal, trustworthy Diane. Sure, she was "in my camp," as the reporter had put it, but what motive could she possibly have to ruin my business, never mind my relationship with Brandon? It was ludicrous to even think that she might have—

And yet, she'd said it herself: "I'm more ambitious than I look." She'd been the one to suggest that I promote her from a lowly assistant who booked appointments to a bona fide coach who interacted with clients. She'd been the one who'd expressed a desire to take on more responsibility. What if that desire was so strong that she actually wanted me to fail? What if she'd been plotting to make me look bad in order to be able to say to the world, "Dr. Wyman's out of the picture but I can do whatever she did—and better!" She didn't have a degree in linguistics, but she knew the Wyman Method cold. Perhaps she'd called the *Enquirer*, hoping that the article about Kip and me would be unflattering enough to bring me down, and when it didn't put me completely out of business, she bided her time until she could try again—with the *Post*.

Or, what if this wasn't about her ambition? What if it was about her resentment of me? Hadn't she admitted to feeling talked down to by me? Hadn't she described me as not being respectful of her needs, of not treating her as a human being, of not showing enough empathy over her broken nails? Maybe she was a disgruntled employee and I'd just never realized how disgruntled.

My God, I thought, the veins in my neck throbbing. It was Diane! How could she!

I hadn't always been so impulsive in my thinking, so trigger-happy in my judgments, but the events of that morning had knocked me for a loop. I shot up from my desk and stormed out of my office, down the hall to the reception area. Diane was trimming her cuticles when I confronted her.

"Put down those nippers this instant!" I said, feeling even more tightly coiled than usual.

She glanced up casually. "Why? You need them? That's cool. I've got another set in my drawer."

"I do not want to use your nail paraphernalia," I said, as she was about to hand me her back-up nippers. "What I want is the truth from you, Diane."

"About?"

"About that rag on your desk." I nodded at the *Post*, which was sitting there incriminatingly, opened to the loathsome "Page Six."

"Oh, that," she said. "You want to know what I think of it, is that it? Of how Mr. Brock came off sounding like a crazy person?"

"No, Diane. I want the truth about how Brandon and I made it into the paper in the first place. I want you to admit that *you* planted the story, just like *you* planted the story about me in the *Enquirer* last year."

She dropped her jaw (and her nippers). "Now *you're* sounding like a crazy person."

"Am I? Who else has been working side by side with me? Who else has had access to every detail about my career? Who else has had designs on my Wyman Method, on taking over my business? What do you have to say for yourself, Diane?"

She stared at me, her expression a combination of disbelief and amusement. If she laughs, I'll kill her, I thought.

"You're kidding right?" she said. "I mean, you're practicing a script or something. You're not serious. You can't be serious."

"I'm quite serious. Someone planted the stories in the *Post* and the *Enquirer* and I have a hunch that the 'someone' was you. So why don't you tell me why you did it. Then I'll call Brandon and tell *him* why you did it, and he and I can pick up where we left off."

Diane was angry now. She rose from her chair and got nose to nose with me. The shiny gold ring that was wrapped around her right nostril nearly blinded me.

"Look, Dr. Wyman," she said, jabbing a finger at me. "You're way out of line accusing me of doing something so awful. But I'm going to defend myself, just to put you in your place. Are you ready?"

"Sure, let's hear it," I said skeptically, hands on hips.

"Number one. I couldn't have planted the story about you and your ex in the *Enquirer* last year because I didn't even know the two of you were having marital trouble back then. You weren't sharing your personal life with me in those days. You weren't sharing anything with me in those days. I was totally in the dark about your situation, because you were the ice queen, remember?"

All right, scratch that theory. So I hadn't confided in her about Kip and me. I'd forgotten about that.

"Number two," she continued. "Why would I plant a story in the *Post* that would make Mr. Brock come off sounding like a lunatic? He's a good guy. I helped the two of you get together, or has that slipped your mind?"

"Ah, I'm glad you brought that up. You went behind my back and told him I how I felt about him. Maybe you're in the *habit* of going behind my back. Maybe that sort of behavior comes naturally to you, Diane."

"Listen here, missy." Boy, she was getting really huffy. "If I hadn't gone behind your back and told him you were interested in him, you and he would never have gotten together," she countered. "If I were you, I'd be kissing my ass instead of chewing me out."

I flinched at her vulgarity but conceded that she had, indeed, played a pivotal role in bringing Brandon and me together. Was I way off-base by making her the villain? Probably, but I was on automatic pilot and couldn't stop myself. "How do I know you didn't bring us together just so I'd get caught up in romance and lose my focus on my business?" I said. "Wouldn't that open the door for you to waltz in and snatch the Wyman Method right out from under me?"

She sighed. "You're a smart woman, Dr. Wyman, but that's a stupid idea."

"Is that so?"

"Yeah. If you went out of business, where would that leave me?"

"Free to start your own business—as the new practitioner of the famous Wyman Method."

"I have a bulletin for you: The Wyman Method isn't famous anymore."

"Well, not *as* famous, I grant you."

"Not only that, I have no interest in starting my own business. I was happy working for you—until today, that is. I'm not the type to have my own business. And I'm not the type to do the lowdown, underhanded things you're so convinced I did."

Maybe Diane had a point there too. She had never struck me as being the devious type. Different, but not devious.

"Number three," she went on. "The *Post* said Mr. Brock was *secretly* paying you to put him through the Wyman Method. Well, that was news to me, because you never told me it was a secret that he was your client. You never said a single word about him, except that he was a successful businessman who traveled a lot. So his showing up every Tuesday at noon was no big deal to me, no hush-hush type of thing. What I'm saying is that if you're trying to pin stuff on me, you're wasting your time, Dr. Wyman. What's more, I'm so mad, I quit."

"Quit?"

Good grief. I couldn't let her quit. Not after she had defended herself so articulately. Not after she had *communicated* with me so expertly. What could I have been thinking to come bursting out of my office and blasting her? Clearly, I'd been thrown by the ordeal with Brandon that morning, but to blame Diane for my problems was unconscionable. I didn't believe she was behind the stories any more than I believed she was out to take over my practice. I was just grasping for answers, any answers.

"Yeah, I quit," she said. "Why should I stay?"

"Because I was wrong to accuse you and I'm sorry," I said, hanging my head in embarrassment. "I had no business jumping to conclusions." The way Brandon had jumped to conclusions about me. "It's just that when something like this happens to you, it makes you paranoid, Diane. You start to think you can't trust anybody. Even those closest to you. Especially those closest to you."

She simmered down a little. "I can see why you'd be upset," she said, "but to attack me, of all people—"

"I know," I said. "I'm ashamed of myself. You've been a loyal, devoted assistant—and a supportive friend too. I couldn't have kept the practice going without you. And I certainly couldn't have gotten together with Brandon without you, as you mentioned. He and I may be apart now, but what we had was wonderful while it lasted. I'll always be grateful to you for that, Diane."

"How grateful?" she said, taking me by surprise. I hadn't expected her to digest my speech and accept my apology so quickly.

"Very grateful," I said. "Honestly."

"Okay," she said, nodding her head. "Then I'm thinking that this might be the perfect time to ask you for more money. How does a twenty-percent raise sound?"

24

HAVING CROSSED DIANE off my list, I sat in my office and tried to come up with the names of other women who might have grudges against me. But frankly—and I don't mean to sound immodest when I say this—I couldn't think of any.

Well, except for Kelsey. It occurred to me that she probably wasn't my biggest fan, seeing as I had not only "corrupted" her macho man by making him more sensitive but snared him for myself. Maybe she watched the World Series on television and saw him twirl me around in his arms, the way he'd twirled her, and maybe that made her angry. She certainly knew that he was my client—and that he hadn't wanted our arrangement made public. It was possible that she was the vengeful type who, in a fit of pique, decided that *she* would make the arrangement public, just to spite me.

Of course, if she was the one who gave the *Post* the story about Brandon and me, then the notion of there being only a single saboteur went out the window. Kelsey didn't know me when I was married to Kip, so she wouldn't have had any reason to contact the *Enquirer* a year ago. But she did have a reason to tip off the *Post*, so I didn't rule her out as someone to interrogate.

Yes, I thought. Why not pay her a little visit and find out exactly what she's been up to these days?

The following morning I looked up her address in the Manhattan phone book, drove into the city, and showed up at her apartment—bright and early and without calling first. Rude of me, I admit, but

I was hoping to catch her off-guard, so she'd be powerless to defend herself against my barrage of questions.

She lived in a quaint, non-doorman building on the Upper West Side. I spotted her name in the directory posted outside the building and buzzed her.

"Yes?" she called out through the intercom.

Great, she's home, I thought with relief. "Delivery coming up," I said, lowering my voice. I sounded like a boy going through puberty.

"What sort of a delivery?" she asked.

Hmmm. What sort of a delivery. "Fabric swatches," I said, praying that my favorite model–turned–yoga instructor–turned–massage therapist–turned–interior decorator hadn't moved on to yet another career since the last time I'd seen her.

"Okay. Give me a second," she said.

I figured she wasn't dressed yet and, therefore, needed time to grab a bathrobe. I waited a few minutes, then she buzzed me in. Her apartment was on the third floor of the five-story building. I took the elevator up, got off and snooped around until I found the door with her name on it. I rang the bell. She answered it.

I was prepared for the shocked look on her face; after all, I'd led her to believe I was a delivery boy, not the ex-girlfriend of her ex-boyfriend. What I was not prepared for was the shocked look on *my* face. When she opened the door, I discovered not only that she was barely clothed—the peek-a-boo nightie was straight out of a Victoria's Secret catalog—but that she was not alone. Who was in her apartment, hovering behind her so closely he was practically climbing up her back, was Brandon! My Brandon! No, he wasn't wearing a peek-a-boo anything. He was fully dressed—nattily dressed, as a matter of fact, in a three-piece business suit—but still!

"What are *you* doing here?" Kelsey screeched at me.

"What are *you* doing here?" I screeched at Brandon.

"It's not what you think," he said in perfect Menspeak, opening the door wider so I could enter, since Kelsey hadn't invited me to.

"When a man says, 'It's not what you think,' it's always worse," I replied in perfect Womenspeak. I was sick with jealousy that he had gone running to her the minute my back was turned. "Why don't you explain what you're doing in her apartment so early in the morning."

"You're the one who should explain," said Kelsey, positioning her scantily-clad self between him and me. "I hardly know you and yet you come here at this ungodly hour pretending you're delivering swatches."

"Oh, I get it. It's an ungodly hour for me but not for him?" I smirked, nodding at Brandon.

"I stopped by before work so I could *talk* to Kelsey," he said, his eyes meeting mine. "That's all."

"Well, isn't that cozy," I said. "What have you two been discussing? Breakfast cereals? Riboflavin, maybe?"

"What Brandon and I have been discussing is none of your business," said Kelsey.

"Hang on a second, Kelsey," said Brandon. "It is Lynn's business, to be fair."

"Thanks a million," I snapped at him, "but I need you sticking up for me like I need a migraine."

I marched myself inside the living room and sat down on what I assumed was a sofa. It was leather and it had legs but it was shaped like a kidney and was purple. One of Kelsey's designs, most likely.

"So," I said, settling in, while the other two remained standing. "I hate to break up this little love nest, but I came to ask Kelsey a few questions."

"I have a feeling I've already asked her your questions," said Brandon. "I was just leaving."

Leaving?

Even though I'd caught him in the apartment of his half-naked ex-girlfriend, even though he wasn't taking me in his arms and begging for my forgiveness, even though I was being mean to him and he was being mean to me, I couldn't bear for him to leave. Who knew when I'd have another chance to remind him how magical we were together, how much in love.

"Yes," he said, his thin lips tight. "Since I saw you last, Lynn, I've been feeling guilty about accusing you of planting that story in the *Post*."

"Have you?" I said, crossing my fingers that he had come to his senses and realized his mistake. Then it hit me that if he had come to his senses and realized his mistake, he would have rushed to my apartment, not Kelsey's.

"Let me amend that. I *had* been feeling guilty," he said. "I told you that the only people who knew I was your client were Naomi and my board members at Finefoods, and that wasn't accurate."

"No?"

"No. I should have remembered that there was someone else who knew I was your client: Kelsey."

"Bingo," I said. "That's why I'm here, too. To make her confess to planting the story."

"She didn't plant it," said Brandon. "I showed up here this morning to find out if she'd planted it. I was hoping she had, so that you and I could resume our—"

"Not until you apologize," I said.

"You interrupted me," he said. "Somebody once taught me that it isn't nice to interrupt."

"I'll bet it was somebody who cared about you and then got punched in the stomach for her trouble."

He ignored that. "As I was saying, Kelsey didn't plant the story, Lynn. She didn't even read it or hear about it. She's been out in Los

Angeles visiting her mother for the past three weeks and only took the red eye back this morning. She hasn't been to bed yet."

"You mean, she hasn't been to *sleep* yet." I hated that he was taking her side against me, but not as much as I hated that the two of them used to have sex. "And, by the way, being in L.A. doesn't let her off the hook. They have phones out there, from what I understand. She could have made a long-distance call to the *Post*. She could also be a big fat liar." I glanced at Kelsey, who was the size of a pencil. "Never mind about the fat. I'm just saying that she could be lying about her supposed West Coast trip. People don't usually admit it when they're guilty."

"Am I allowed to speak or is this a two-way conversation?" said Kelsey irritably. "I'm happy to present my plane tickets as evidence, but I think you're both certifiable with all your talk talk talk. You, Brandon, come knocking on my door, wanting to find out if I tried to ruin your reputation. Honey, I couldn't care less about you or your reputation. The night I walked out on you in that restaurant was the night I said to myself, 'Kelsey. Go out and get a *real* man, not some wuss who actually gives a shit whether I order my salad dressing on the side.' "

"Now hold on a minute," I said to Kelsey. "Brandon *is* a real man. An evolved man."

"Thanks a million," Brandon snapped at me, parodying me, "but I need you sticking up for me like I need PMS."

"Men don't get PMS, you jerk," said Kelsey. "See what she did to you with all that Wimpspeak?"

"Watch it," I said. "That's my Wyman Method you're maligning."

She laughed at me—not in a good way. "As for you, why would I waste my time calling a newspaper to ruin your reputation? You don't have a reputation, Dr. Wyman. Not anymore and not for ages."

"That was unnecessary, Kelsey," said Brandon. "Take your jabs at me, but lay off Lynn."

"Well, excuse me," she said, tossing her blond mane around. "If she's so goddamn special, why are the two of you on the outs?"

He didn't answer, probably because it was a really good question.

"So, Brandon," I said, breaking the brief silence. "You believe that Kelsey wasn't the one who planted the story now, but I'm still on the hot seat, is that it?"

He was about to respond but Kelsey beat him to it. "Look," she said. "I'm tired. I've been up since yesterday. How about you, Dr. Communicator, and you, Mr. I-am-woman, taking your act somewhere else so I can get some sleep."

"Why not," I said. "I've been thrown out of better places." I glared at Brandon as I rose from the "thing" I'd been sitting on.

"I didn't throw you out of my house the other morning," he said as we moved passed Kelsey, into the entrance foyer. "I just put an end to our conversation. We had both made our points and I felt that—"

"Have a lovely day," Kelsey said mockingly, cutting us off and then slamming the door in both our faces.

Brandon and I stood outside together for several seconds without speaking.

"How are you?" I managed finally, reaching out to touch his arm. A reflex.

"Fair," he said. "I've got great P.R. people at Finefoods. They've been doing damage control on the *Post* column, so I'm hoping the story won't spread like one of those computer viruses."

"I hope so, too."

"You doing okay?"

"Of course I'm not. I didn't plant the story, Brandon. It's killing me that you think I did."

"Who else if not you?" he said, shrugging his broad shoulders. "I tried Kelsey, as you saw. She didn't do it. I don't have anybody else to point a finger at."

"Maybe you should stop pointing fingers and listen. You weren't very good at listening when you started working with me, remember?"

I detected the slightest trace of a smile. Or maybe it was a grimace. Hard to tell.

"I thought we fixed that problem when you were undergoing the program," I went on. "I thought you became a man who listens and empathizes and shares his feelings."

"I did become that man, Lynn, but you changed. You didn't keep your word."

"That's not true," I said. "Please. Consider this. Isn't it possible that the person who planted the story was someone you don't know?"

"Why would someone I don't know want to hurt me?"

"She wouldn't."

"She?"

"Yes, I believe we're talking about a female who did this. Suppose she wanted to hurt me? Suppose whoever planted the story in the *Post* was the same person who planted the story in the *Enquirer*, and the purpose of both leaks was to hurt me, not you?"

"Doesn't make sense. Sorry. The *Post* story made you look good, let's not forget. You wanted publicity—and you got it."

"But I lost you," I said, my voice catching. "I didn't want that."

He shrugged again. "I guess it was a gamble you decided you had to take."

"But I didn't take it. I didn't do what you think I did." This was so frustrating. He wouldn't get it. "Okay, Brandon. Maybe I'm not explaining it right. Maybe this is just another example of a man and a woman not being able to communicate."

He shook his head. "This isn't a communication issue, Lynn. It's a trust issue."

"Fine. So how do we fix it?"

"I'm not sure we can. Not yet."

Not yet.

I was certain he didn't realize it, but his two little words boosted my spirits. *Not yet* was a far cry from *never. Not yet* implied the much more encouraging *someday*, or the still more heartening *soon*. And, given that I had a major challenge ahead of me—the task of ferreting out my back-stabber—I'd have plenty to keep me busy in the meantime.

25

BRANDON WAS RIGHT when he said the *Post* column was good publicity for me. It generated what I'd been so desperate for: clients. Shortly after the story broke, the phone began to ring off the hook, just like the good old days. And the callers weren't only men seeking help with their communication problems; they were book publishers and television producers and magazine editors—all wanting to meet with me about my "miraculous transformation of Brandon Brock." In a particularly ironic twist, a reporter from *Fortune* magazine called, wanting to do a story on the ways in which the Wyman Method could be spun off and used by human resource departments all across corporate America. In other words, I had risen from the ashes. Brandon had been my ticket back after all. I had revived my career because of him, but I had lost him in the process. Talk about a hollow victory.

I declined all media interviews, in deference to him, but I welcomed the new clients into my practice. Not only was it nice to have the infusion of cash, but it was great to have the guys around again. They made me realize that it was the sessions with them, the one-on-one language adjustment, the *work*, that was much more satisfying to me than appearing on *Good Morning America*.

As a matter of fact, I was so busy at the office that I didn't have a lot of time to devote to the Who's-been-out-to-get-me question. Only at night, when I was home alone in Mt. Kisco in my tidy little garden apartment, did I ponder that. And the answer I kept coming up with was that I needed to track down Kip, needed to begin where my problems began, needed to learn what he knew or, at least, what I could wheedle out of him about what he knew.

The trick would be to find him. When we first split up, I sent him alimony checks every month to a mailing address in nearby Pleasantville. More recently, I stopped sending the checks because he kept returning them. (I assumed he'd had an attack of conscience. Since I was glad to keep the money instead of handing it over to a low-life like him, I never pressed the issue.) Anyway, I hoped he was still living at the Pleasantville address and could be reached at the phone number I had for him there.

When I called one night, I got a recording, saying the number had been changed and providing a forwarding number in the same 914 area code.

So he's moved but he's within striking distance, I thought as I dialed the new number.

This time a man answered, and his voice was unmistakably the Kipster's.

"Hello, Kip," I said, trying to remain calm. So much had happened since I had last seen or spoken to my ex-husband, and while my white-hot anger toward him had cooled during the past year, there was still some residual resentment toward him. Whether or not he'd been responsible for the *Enquirer* story, he had cheated on me with another woman. You don't forget something like that. You get on with your life, if you're smart, but you don't forget.

"Lynn?" He was surprised to hear from me, understandably.

"I was wondering if I could drive over and see you," I said, coming straight to the point, in order to avoid one of his outpourings. "As soon as possible."

"Oh. Well, gosh, yeah. It's been a long time, hasn't it? I've been doing a lot of soul searching since we broke up, and I'd love to share with you how my feelings about our relationship have really evolved and—"

"So you're up for a meeting?" I cut him off. It was self-defense, not Menspeak. But then wasn't that what Brandon had said in an early session? That he cut women off in meetings because they droned on forever?

"I guess we could get together. Sure," he said. "It's just that your phone call is a little out of the blue, so I'm feeling insecure and uncertain and—"

"Just tell me where you live now, Kip. I gather you've moved."

"Yeah. I'm in an old cottage tucked away in the woods, and it has all the cozy charm and rustic style of the house where you and—"

"The address, Kip. Give me the address."

He gave me the address. "Are you free tomorrow night?" I asked. "I could stop by around eight."

"Eight. That sounds okay, I guess. Will you have eaten? Should I make us a light supper? There's a terrific fish market near here and I could see if they've got some fresh—"

"No thanks," I said. "I'll see you tomorrow night."

KIP'S "COTTAGE" WAS twice the size of the house we lived in together. It was set on several pastoral acres and was expensively furnished. Clearly, he wasn't starving without me or my alimony checks. Either the carpentry business was more lucrative than it used to be, or Kip had funds from another source.

"Are you sure I can't get you anything?" he asked, as I took a seat at his kitchen counter. There, on the shelves that he must have built himself, were the cookbooks he'd taken with him after I'd booted him out. Who's he cooking for now? I wondered.

"I'm positive," I said.

"Not even a little something to nibble on?"

"I came to talk, not to nibble, Kip."

"Okay. Fine." He sidled over onto the stool next to mine. "How've you been?"

"I've had my ups and downs," I said. From the look of him, he'd had nothing but ups. He was as comic-book handsome as ever and in great shape, too. Not a guy you'd pass up if you were on the prowl for a pretty face and a hard body. "I'd like to talk to you about my downs, as a matter of fact, starting with the *National Enquirer* story."

"Not the *Enquirer*," he said, raking his fingers through his dark wavy hair. "I know how much pain that caused you, and I'd hate it if you cried while you were here."

I laughed. "Of the two of us, I wasn't the crier, so I wouldn't worry about that. I just want an honest answer. There's no reason for you not to be honest with me now, Kip. Our marriage is over and we've gone our separate ways. Let's wipe the slate clean and tell the truth about what happened."

"So you're seeking *closure*," he said, nodding.

"Right," I said, reminded that Brandon used to make fun of the word. God, how I wished I could be sitting with him instead of with my bimbo ex-husband. "Was some of this"—I gestured toward his swell surroundings—"paid for with the money you got from the *Enquirer*?"

"You still think I sold you out?" Judging by the expression on his face, he found the notion incredibly insulting. "Well, I didn't."

"Okay. I believe that you didn't actually pick up the phone and call the tabloid yourself, because I have new information in that regard. But did your girlfriend make the call? So the two of you could split the money?"

"Oh, Lynn, Lynn." He sighed. "Yes, I cheated on you. Yes, I lied to you. But I never stopped loving you. I love you now. You're beautiful and intelligent and the most—"

"Stop."

"It's true. I love you. That's why I returned your checks. I wanted you to think well of me."

His lower lip began to quiver. Guess what came next.

"Here," I said, reaching into my handbag for a tissue and handing it to him. When he was slightly more composed, I resumed the questioning. "Please tell me, Kip. Did your girlfriend call the *Enquirer* or not? I won't go running after her with one of your fancy Henckel knives, if that's what's bothering you. I just need to know."

"You want an honest answer? I'll give you one," he said after blowing his nose. "The answer is: No."

"How can you be sure?"

"I confronted her about it. I asked her if she did it to get back at you."

"Get back at me? Why would she want to get back at me? You were sleeping with *her*, not with *me*."

"But I loved *you*. She knew that. You had what she wanted: my devotion." I almost puked. "She was extremely upset that even after you found out I'd been having an affair with her, you didn't kick me out. I wondered if maybe she decided to force your hand, to *make* you kick me out, by going to that tabloid with our problems and letting you think I did it."

"But she denied doing that?"

"Absolutely."

"And you believed her?"

"Yeah. She flipped out that I would accuse her of something so underhanded."

I could relate to that. It's not a picnic to have the man you love believe you're a scheming, conniving bitch. "Are you still seeing this woman?"

"No. I told you: You're the one I love."

"Oh, enough with that already. You're saying you two broke up?"

He nodded. "We had quite a scene."

"Sorry."

"I'm not. She's incredibly needy."

"Who is she?"

"Who is she?"

"What's her name, Kip? Since you're not together anymore, you can tell me, can't you?"

"Nope. I don't feel comfortable giving you her name."

"Why not? As I said, I'm not going to drive over to her house in a jealous rage and butcher her. I'm curious, that's all."

He wouldn't budge. "I may be a jerk for being an adulterer, but give me credit for being discreet about it."

Whoopdeedoo. Chivalry is not dead. "Come on. Tell me who she is, Kip."

"Lynn. Why are you doing this? That relationship is over and done with. Why cause yourself unnecessary pain by asking me to tell you her name?"

"Let me explain this one more time. I'm not in pain. I'm *curious*."

"Because of the closure."

"There you go." Brother.

He shook his head. "I can't. I promised her."

You little shit. You promised me too—to be faithful. "Then don't tell me her name. Just tell me if she's someone I know."

He considered this, his lips pursing.

"Is she someone I know or not?" I said impatiently.

"Okay! Okay! Yeah, she is!" he conceded. "But that's all I'm saying about her. Not one more thing."

"Hey, calm down. It's okay." What was he getting so excited about? So he'd been banging the real estate agent in town, the one who'd introduced us way back when. She'd always had the hots for him. No headline there. Or was it the woman down the street? The chick who'd hired him to build her a dinner table and then invited us to dinner so we could try it out? Oh, who gave a shit. "Are you seeing someone new?" I asked, making small talk before I scrammed.

"Yeah, but she and I could never have the kind of relationship that you and I—"

"Did she foot the bill for these swanky accommodations?"

"She contributed." He had the decency to blush.

"Then you've got yourself another good setup. Congratulations. Hopefully, you won't screw it up, the way you did with me."

He hung his head. Back came the tears. I fished into my purse for more tissues. He certainly was a fragile soul.

"Did you ever love me, Lynn?" he said between sobs.

"I don't think so," I said candidly, figuring this was the last conversation I'd ever have with my ex-husband. "When you and I got together, I didn't have the vaguest idea how it felt to love a man. I'd spent years in academia, leading a sheltered existence, focusing exclusively on my work, which was the only source of pleasure I really understood. Marrying you was a conscious act on my part to broaden my concept of pleasure, to have a personal life, a romantic life."

"But now you know how it feels to love a man. You've found someone else, haven't you? I can sense it."

"Yes, Kip. I have." Even though the "someone else" despises me at the moment.

More tears. "I'm happy for you," said Kip. "I may not look it, but I am. I'm as happy as I was the day my father told me. . . ."

I tuned him out as he droned on. He was such a loser. How could I have ever thought he was responsible for the piece in the *Enquirer*? What's more, he and his then-girlfriend, whoever she was, couldn't have planted the *Post* story, since neither of them knew that I was even seeing Brandon as a client.

No, Kip was a dead end. It takes cunning and cleverness to plot someone's downfall, and he didn't have either. He was a lightweight in the brains department, to put it mildly.

Besides, there was the gender issue. Men are basically simple creatures, as I've said before. They're overt in their actions. They don't overthink things. If they don't like you, they tend to let you know. On the other hand, women. . . . Well, we're a different breed altogether. We're more complicated. We're verbal but we often feel one thing and say the opposite. And if we don't like you, we hardly ever let you know.

Yup, it was a woman who planted both of those stories, I reconfirmed as Kip continued to ramble, cry, ramble. As much as it pains me to admit it, one of the most popular modes of communication for women—one of the most common dialects of Womenspeak—is Doublespeak. Which means that my enemy might be sounding very much like my friend.

26

I SUPPOSE YOU think I'm as dumb as a post for not suspecting that a member of the Brain Trust might be my saboteur, but—come on!—we're talking about my friends here. Yes, they were the only ones to whom I had divulged everything, the only ones who knew my secrets, the only ones I'd told about both my problems with Kip and my work with Brandon (and, therefore, the only ones who could have leaked both stories), but the reason I'd told them was because they were my buddies, my staunch supporters, my confidantes, and I trusted them.

Even now, it gives me an attack of the guilts to brand them as betrayers. They were there for me when I was at my lowest. They consoled me when my career went into the tank. And, most of all, they included me.

As I've mentioned, I'd never had close women friends when I was in college and graduate school, so being welcomed into a clique, a social circle, a "sisterhood" as an adult was a unique and thoroughly unanticipated experience for me. Meeting Penny and Isabel and Gail and Sarah and then being taken in by them ("taken in by them" having new meaning for me now) made me feel less isolated, more insulated. But, because I was a beginner at female friendships, I didn't know what to expect from a friend, didn't even know what constituted a friend. As a result, my standards weren't exceptionally high; I think I was fond of Penny and Isabel and Gail and Sarah, in large part, because they seemed fond of me.

So despite the fact that the four of them were privy to precisely the same information that had been printed in the media about me, I didn't connect any of them to the two stories. It wasn't within my frame of reference to connect them. Women don't betray women, I'd thought. Men do.

And yet, as a linguist specializing in the conversational differences between the genders, I had come in contact with Doublespeak. I had researched Doublespeak. I had read through numerous case studies involving Doublespeak. In other words, I was aware that women were capable of treachery, but I didn't apply it to my own situation. You don't, generally. You close your eyes to the possibility that one of your own kind could plunge a knife into your back.

Speaking of backs, as I was driving home from Kip's house that night, mulling over in my mind whether one of my friends might not be a friend after all, I remembered what Brandon had said after meeting them for the first time: "They're very entertaining, but I'd watch my back around them if I were you."

At the time, I'd chalked his remark up to the sort of paranoia that's common among those trying to survive in the "corporate jungle," as he'd put it. But had he been paranoid or prescient? Had he been able to view my friends more objectively than I'd been able to? Was I the better communicator and he the better judge of character?

Well, he hadn't been a very good judge of *my* character, not if he thought I could have coldly and calculatedly broken my promise to him. Still, I decided to call him at the office the next morning, on the chance that he wouldn't mind discussing the Penny-Isabel-Gail-Sarah hypothesis with me. The fact that I was dying to see him also figured into the equation.

"Mr. Brock's office," said Naomi.

"Hi, Naomi. It's Lynn Wyman. How are you?"

"I'm as happy as a lark," she trilled. "Mr. Brock bought me a silk scarf this morning—in yellow—to match the sweater he'd gotten me some time ago."

"That was very sweet of him," I said. "What was the occasion?"

"There was none. He's just a lovable, sensitive, generous man."

Boy, was she singing a different tune, thanks to me. "I'd like to come and see him, Naomi. Does he have any holes in his schedule today?"

She heaved a sigh. "I'm afraid not, Dr. Wyman."

"Not even ten minutes?"

"Not even ten minutes."

"Oh, come on, Naomi. I have clients coming and going all day. If I can squeeze ten minutes into my schedule to see Mr. Brock, surely he can squeeze ten minutes into his schedule to see me, can't he?"

"Not to see you, no."

Now *I* heaved a sigh. "So I've been frozen out?"

"Please don't blame me, Dr. Wyman. This wasn't my idea. I don't believe for a minute that you were behind that *New York Post* column, but Mr. Brock seems to think you were and he's very hurt."

"Did he say that?"

"Yes. You know how good he is about sharing his feelings now. But however hurt he may be, he still loves you."

"Did he say *that*?"

"No, but he does love you."

"How can you tell?"

"He called one of our account executives Lynn yesterday."

"And her name isn't Lynn?"

"No, it *is* Lynn. But he never remembered her name before. That proves that he's pining for you, doesn't it?"

"No, it proves that he's using the tools he learned from the Wyman Method."

"Oh."

"Listen, Naomi. Are you sure you can't get him to see me, just for a quick meeting?"

"I'm sorry."

"But you said he's pining for me. You wouldn't want to stand in the way of true love, would you?"

She considered this. "All right," she whispered. "He's having lunch in Manhattan today. At the Union Square Café at twelve-thirty. Liam will be driving him into the city, dropping him off and waiting for him on East Sixteenth Street, in front of or as close to the restaurant as he can get without being towed. If I were you, Dr. Wyman—and you didn't hear this from me, it goes without saying—I would be sitting in the back seat of the car when Mr. Brock is finished with his lunch."

"Naomi, that's inspired," I replied enthusiastically. "But how do we know that Mr. Brock hasn't given Liam the same instructions about me that he gave you?"

She chuckled. "Liam is only Mr. Brock's driver, while *I* am Mr. Brock's right hand. Need I say more?"

AT TWO O'CLOCK, I spotted the Mercedes parked down the block from the Union Square Café. Liam was sitting in the driver's seat flossing his teeth with a matchbook. I scurried over to the car, tapped on the window and motioned for him to let me in. He waved and, without hesitation, unlocked the door. I hopped into the back seat.

"Dr. Wyman, this is a nice surprise," he greeted me. "You're meeting Mr. Brock?"

"Yes, Liam," I said. "I just need a minute or two with him but I don't want to interrupt his lunch. Is it okay if I wait here?"

"Sure, no problem."

He asked me if the temperature in the car was to my liking, if I wanted to read his newspaper, if I was comfortable. I told him everything was just ducky. And it was, except for the tiny matter of my messed-up personal life.

At two-twenty, Brandon and two Asian men stepped out of the restaurant and strolled down the street. As they neared the car, I caught Brandon saying, "Can I give you both a lift to your hotel?"

Oh, great, I thought, slinking down into the buttery leather seat, hoping he couldn't see me. We're about to have a full house.

Naturally, the two men said they'd be thrilled to have a lift to their hotel. I panicked. Now Brandon would be livid not only that I had ambushed him in his own chauffeur-driven automobile but insinuated myself into his business affairs.

Paralyzed, I sat there like a lump as Liam jumped out of the car to open the back door for his boss.

"No, Liam. I'll sit up front with you, so my friends from Japan can have the back all to themselves," Brandon was saying as his driver opened the door.

I waited silently for the men to discover me as they slid into the seat next to me.

"Oh. Please excuse," said the one who got in first. He was startled by my presence but bowed from the waist up.

"Nothing to excuse," I said brightly, giving him and his friend my best reciprocal bend-over. "Come on in. There's plenty of room."

Hearing my voice, Brandon poked his head into the back seat and did a double take when he saw me. No, a triple take. He looked stunned, then pleased, then, after he reminded himself that he was supposed to be angry at me, absolutely furious. I knew he wouldn't make a scene in front of his associates but I could tell he was dying to.

I warded off a possible "What are *you* doing here?" by making polite but not entirely true chitchat with my new traveling companions, who introduced themselves and handed me their business cards. "I'm an outside publicist handling the Finefoods account," I told the men. "I ride in the car with Mr. Brock now and then, if there are matters we need to discuss and don't want to take up valuable time in the office."

"Save time is good idea," said one of the men. "Very efficient."

"Thank you," I said, wondering why people from foreign countries speak our language better than we speak theirs, not counting the funky accents and the dropping of verbs, modifiers, etc.

By this point Brandon had lowered himself into the passenger seat of the car and told Liam to make a stop at the Waldorf Astoria.

"Yes. Okay. Conduct business," the other man urged Brandon and me. "We stay quiet."

"That's very kind of you," I said. I leaned forward and addressed Brandon. "It's urgent that we talk about those two thorny media stories, Mr. Brock. I have a new theory about the source of them."

He kept his eyes straight ahead on the road—I was speaking to the nape of his neck—but at least he answered me. "What's the new theory? I won't be able to live another day unless you tell me."

Such a wiseguy. "Do you remember when we had dinner with those four women friends of mine and you commented that you found them entertaining but would watch your back around them?" Come on, play along, Brandon. These guys aren't paying any attention.

Wrong. One of them laughed. "Sorry about interrupt, Brandon, but she say you have four women wash your back?" He laughed again. The other one joined him.

"Not wash. Watch," I said to them. "Two different words." Oh, well. What was yet another communication problem?

"I remember," said Brandon, in response to my question. "Now tell me why I care."

"Because I'm wondering if one of the four women planted the two stories," I said. "Obviously, there was something about Penny, Isabel, Gail and Sarah that made you feel they were untrustworthy."

"All women untrustworthy," one of the Japanese men interjected, along with a *hee hee hee*. "That's why we don't tell them things."

"I beg your pardon?"

"They act own way," he said. "It's mystery. That's why we don't tell them things."

"You mean, you don't share your feelings with women? Don't share whether you're happy or sad or hurt or confused?" I know. I should have kept my mouth shut. But this stuff was my bread and butter.

"Confused?" he said. "Men in Japan never confused. Women always confused. Take them to restaurant for dinner and they look at menu for long, long time. Can't make up mind. Men have to make up mind for them."

"My, that's not very sensitive of you," I said, as Brandon whipped his head around to glare at me. I ignored him. "Has it ever occurred to you that the women might feel intimidated by you? That you could change the dynamics of your relationships by making them feel validated?"

"Validated?" the two men said simultaneously.

"Let me ask you something," I continued, figuring they didn't understand. "Do you make conversation with the women while they're taking so long to decide what to eat?"

"What kind conversation?" asked one of the men. "We don't talk to women while eat. We read newspaper or use Palm PDA."

"So you avoid conversation," I said, "and thereby avoid intimacy."

"What she mean?" the other man asked Brandon.

"I can speak for myself," I said. "What I mean is that— "

"Here's the Waldorf," said Brandon when we had arrived at the hotel. "She'll have to tell you what she means some other time."

After a tentative goodbye to me, the men got out of the car and stood with Brandon at the hotel's entrance, bowing and winding up whatever mutual business they had. Eventually, Brandon got into the Mercedes—into the back seat this time—and instructed Liam to take us to my office.

"Tell me you're not mad," I said as we rode uptown.

"Mad about the way you 'coached' my Japanese friends, or mad about the way you found yourself in my car?"

"The latter. The former was beyond my control."

"To be honest, I don't know how to feel about you anymore."

"Sure you do. According to Naomi, you still love me."

"Is that right?"

"Yes. Now please let me try out my new theory on you. Just until we get to my office. Okay?"

"I'm not going to throw you out of a moving vehicle, Lynn."

"Good. So, my theory is that one of my friends may have planted both the *Enquirer* story and the *Post* column. They were the only ones I told about my problems with Kip. And they were the only ones I told about signing you up as a client."

"You told them I was your client? I assumed you only told them we were dating."

"Of course I told them you were my client. You must have forgotten. They were there the night I saw you on the cover of *Fortune*. They were there when I wagered that I could transform you from America's Toughest Boss into America's Most Sensitive Boss. They've been there for me, period."

"Then why are we having this conversation?"

"Because now I'm wondering if they only *appeared* to be there for me. Maybe one of them has been harboring a grudge against me and done a great job of concealing it. Do you have any opinion on this, Brandon, based on your brief exposure to all four of them?"

"The truth?"

"I wouldn't be here otherwise."

"Then here it is. Penny's a shark. Isabel's a flake. Gail's a major hysteric. And Sarah's an egomaniac. That's some bunch you picked out for yourself."

Sure, I was stung by his unflattering characterizations of my friends, but he didn't use words I hadn't used myself to describe them. It was just that I had seen beyond the easy labels, had accepted that there were traits about each woman that were less than appealing, had been so grateful for their unconditional affection that I'd pledged my own in return. But now I didn't know what to think, which was why Brandon's opinion mattered so much.

"Then you agree that one of them might have leaked both stories?" I said.

"It's possible," he said, "but where's the motive? You, on the other hand, had a motive. For the *Post* column, anyway."

"Oh, Brandon. I didn't have a motive and you know it."

"What about your career? You can't deny that you've gotten clients as a result of the column, can you?"

"No."

"See?"

"God, when are you going to let go of this absolute certainty that I broke my promise to you? Usually, it's the woman who plays the martyr."

"I am not playing the martyr!"

"Okay. How about the victim?"

"Not that either."

"But you are holding onto a kind of indignant attitude, which, as I said, is more common in women."

"Probably because I've become so fluent in Womenspeak," he said wryly.

I smiled. At least he was making fun of me again. "Seriously, I think you're playing the victim because you're afraid to trust me. Your ex-wife must have done a number on you, dumping you for the pool guy. You don't want to subject yourself to that kind of hurt again, so you've erected this barrier between us, this false notion that I betrayed you. Can't you just put your emotions aside for a minute and be analytical on this particular issue? I need you to help me figure out if one of my friends could have planted the stories."

He scratched his head. "I really don't get it. I spent six months in your office listening to you preach how I should stop being analytical and expose my emotions, and now I'm supposed to do the opposite?"

"Yes. In order to help me solve this."

"I can't help you solve it. They're *your* friends. You've got to examine your relationship with each of them and figure out what's there—or not there."

He was right, I realized. This was my battle. He had only met the members of the Brain Trust once, had only formed a superficial impression of them. It was up to me to dig deeper.

"Fine," I said. "Then all I ask from you is that you don't write me off. Give me a chance to prove to you that I didn't betray you. And don't—do not!—get involved with some awful Kelsey type in the meantime."

"I couldn't, even if I wanted to," he said, his expression softening. "The Kelsey types don't like me anymore. You've taken care of that, Dr. Wyman."

"Good. And stay away from the Dr. Wyman types, too. This is going to be a tough period for me. If it turns out that one of my friends has been out to get me, it'll be quite a blow. I'll need a shoulder to lean on. A broad shoulder. Your shoulder."

"If it turns out that one of your friends has been out to get you, you'll have more than my shoulder. You'll have my—"

"What, Brandon? What will I have?"

"My profound apology."

"What else?"

"What else do you want?"

"I want what we had before. I want us to get back there, and then I want us to move forward."

His eyes met mine. "It might not be easy."

"Nothing worth fighting for is."

27

I DECIDED THAT my approach with regard to my friends would have to be much more subtle than, say, the strategy I'd used with Kelsey. No showing up on doorsteps unannounced. No confrontations. No badgering. In order to flush out the bitch from among Penny, Isabel, Gail, and Sarah, I'd have to take things slowly, diplomatically, delicately. I'd have to spy, practice covert operations. Yes, that was it; I'd have to employ a different sort of female intelligence.

The first task was coming up with a possible motive, but I couldn't remember ever doing anything that would have provoked one of them to try to ruin me. I was the perfect friend, as a matter of fact. I listened to their problems. I rejoiced in their good fortune. I brought them chicken soup when they were sick (well, except Isabel, who was a vegetarian; I brought her minestrone). The worst that could be said about me as a friend was that I wasn't much of a joke-teller, pre-Brandon, but then people don't try to destroy your life because you're not a laugh riot, do they?

No, there would have to be some sort of simmering resentment I wasn't aware of, some reason for pretending to be my friend while hating my guts.

I ran through the usual bones of contention among women.

Number One: *She's prettier than I am and I want to rip her face off.* Well, as I've indicated, I'm nice looking but not beauty contest caliber. Besides, Penny and the others were attractive women in their own right. No, no one was sticking it to me because they were jealous of my appearance.

Number Two: *She's thinner than I am and I'd like to wire her jaws open and pour gallons of milk shakes down her throat.* While it's true that I am thin—thinner than Gail, especially—and while it's also true that many women who are not thin have a genuine hostility toward women who are, I couldn't imagine one of my friends plotting my downfall over that particular issue.

Number Three: *She's more successful than I am and I want to see her fail.* This was an interesting scenario, definitely worth pondering. On one hand, each of my friends was successful in her chosen field, so there'd be no reason for them to feel inferior to me in that regard. Sure, Penny was always in hot pursuit of new clients, but not because her P.R. firm was in trouble; it was because she couldn't stand to lose clients to other firms. She was just competitive, as scrappy types usually are. And yes, Sarah was forever whining about being cheated by the show business community, but she was the queen of children's books, had achieved a level of success most authors only dream about and, despite complaints here and there about the grind of writing, loved her work. On the other hand, I had been famous in a far more mainstream and diversified way than the others. I had not only written a bestseller; I had hosted a radio show, penned a syndicated newspaper column, appeared on national television, and built a thriving practice. My name and face were everywhere for a time, even on the sides of buses. Maybe one of my friends coveted that kind of fame for herself. Maybe she coveted it to such a twisted extent that, instead of getting out there and trying to increase her own visibility, she decided to put an end to mine—first, by planting the story in the *Enquirer*, in order to knock me off my lofty perch; then, by planting the column in the *Post*, in order to prevent me from climbing back up. Of course, in the case of the *Post*, her plan misfired badly. It was thanks to the column, after all, that I now had more clients than I could handle. Could it be that she had expected the column to cast me in a more negative light than it did? Was it possible that she had leaked the story, intending that *I* be made to look bad, not Brandon, but, as is often the case with the media, she couldn't control what ultimately found its way into print? Was she sitting at home at that very moment, cursing that she'd been foiled again?

Number Four: *She's got more money than I do and I'm envious as hell.* This one was close enough to Number Three that I decided to fold them in together.

Number Five: *She has much nicer clothes than I do and it's not fair.* See above, as this is related to having more money and success. However, I didn't give it much credence because Sarah was the one with the spectacular wardrobe (although since Isabel wore only black, for the most part, and her clothes were always covered with cat hair, it was hard to tell whether they were nice or not). Moreover, clothes, thinness, and beauty were highly charged but nevertheless superficial issues, and I was fairly certain that the motive I was searching for had more substance.

Number Six: *She stole my man and I'm going to make her pay.* I rejected this one immediately, because I hadn't stolen anybody's man. I was the one who'd had my man stolen from me. There I'd been, the oblivious little wifey-poo, who, before taking a soak in the tub one night, picked up the phone and overheard some woman telling my husband she loved him. I call that having my man stolen, don't you? Besides, my friends had their own men most of the time. Penny didn't have a steady guy, but she was rarely without a date. Isabel had spent seven years in a relationship with the gallery owner but had recently found someone new. Gail had a husband—not a prize catch, but a man—and, in spite of her incessant declarations that she was divorcing him, she still hadn't. And Sarah had her husband, her high school sweetheart with whom she had an open marriage. She was very candid about the fact that they each had their flings during their frequent separations, but through it all and for whatever reason they had stayed together. So no, Number Six didn't make sense.

Instead of continuing with my musings about motives, I decided I'd better stop and do some work in preparation for the next day's clients. There were transcripts of tapes to plow through, new scripts to write, research literature to study.

It was while I was poring over a textbook offering examples of women who communicate one thing while feeling another (Womenspeak/Doublespeak) that my mind meandered back to Number Six, the *She stole my man* motive. I began to think about all the stories I'd read over the years, all the anecdotes I'd heard, involving women who "do in" other women by running off with their men. It's quite common, this disgusting phenomenon, this pattern of women who, seemingly without remorse, commit acts of betrayal against their female counterparts.

Come on, you've heard them too. Maybe you've even lived one.

There's the woman who engages in an ongoing, clandestine affair with her best friend's husband—while continuing to pretend they're all a perfect little threesome.

There's the woman who engages in an ongoing, clandestine affair with her next-door neighbor's husband—while continuing to dash over with fresh herbs from her garden.

There's the woman who engages in an ongoing, clandestine affair with the husband of her yoga instructor—while continuing to show up for class in her snappy spandex outfits.

Cases like this are standard issue, sadly—the secretary who sleeps with her boss even though he's married and the nurse who sleeps with the doctor even though he's married and the White House intern who sleeps with the President even though he's married.

Are these faithless husbands to blame? You betcha. But how about the women? What are they thinking, anyway? They don't comprehend that they're hurting their own kind, don't understand the concept of female solidarity, don't buy the whole sisterhood thing? I mean, we're all looking for happiness, but do we have to take each other down to attain it?

I don't know why I was getting myself in such a lather over this subject, except that there was something about it that resonated with me, something I was feeling ominously unsettled about. Maybe it had to do with Kip's former girlfriend, the one he'd been humping when he was supposed to be humping me. When I'd discovered that he was having the affair, I'd been too angry at him to be angry at *her*. I'd forgotten to be angry at her, and that was an oversight. He was the easy target, because he was the one I'd trusted, but she was equally culpable, because she was the one who'd appropriated (or allowed herself to be appropriated by) what was rightfully mine.

Growing more and more uncomfortable with these newly stirred-up emotions, I stood up from my desk, stretched, poured myself a Scotch. And then I sat back down and found myself replaying my recent conversation with Kip. He had been his usual voluble self, I recalled, talking, talking, talking, holding nothing back—except any details about the mistress. He had demurred when I'd asked him her name, and it wasn't like Kip to demur. He was incapable of having an unexpressed thought, didn't have the knack for self-editing. So why hadn't he just blabbed about the woman the way he'd blabbed about his local fish market? Not to spare my feelings, certainly. If he'd cared about my feelings, he wouldn't have cheated on me in the first place. What's more, I'd made it clear that I wouldn't have a heart attack if he told me, that I was merely curious about the woman, the way one is curious about ancient history. And yet, he'd refused to tell me who she was.

Well, I thought, whoever she was, she was cagey. Mt. Kisco is a small town. Word of people's comings and goings gets around. She had managed to conduct an affair with a married man—for God knows how long—while keeping her role a secret. That was a good trick in the suburbs, where everybody knows everybody else's business. She had to be smart as well as cagey. And extremely committed to my not catching on. All the things Kip wasn't. All the things my back-stabber was.

I put down my scotch glass and sat very, very still. I felt cold, suddenly. Prickly, creepy cold. One thought and one thought only throbbed in my head. It wouldn't disappear no matter how hard I tried to distract myself from it, no matter how badly I didn't want it to be there. It stayed and it strengthened and it sickened me as profoundly as it shocked me. And here is what it was:

Not only is one of your so-called friends the woman who's been spilling your secrets to the media . . . she's also Kip's mystery woman.

I know, I know. Boy, do I know. I should have sensed the truth sooner. I should have forced myself to follow my instincts. I should have made the awful leap that it was a member of the Brain Trust, not the real estate agent in Mt. Kisco or the woman with the new dining room table, who was the little popsy who had lured Kip into her bed while he was married to me. No wonder he didn't want to tell me her name! No wonder she had made him promise not to tell me her name!

I pulled my sweater tighter around me. I was trembling now, my body chilled with the hideousness of my conclusion. It wasn't bad enough that one of the women I cared about had planted the two venomous stories in the media? She had to sleep with my husband, too?

No. It wasn't possible. What I was thinking simply was not possible. I knew my friends' voices almost as well as I knew my own. I would have recognized Penny or Isabel or Gail or Sarah if one of them had been on the other end of the phone the night I'd overheard that lovey-dovey conversation.

Or would I have recognized them? Now that I really thought about it, the voice had been muffled. I remembered that distinctly. Furthermore, I had never heard any of my friends speaking while in the throes of passion, passion being a condition that can render a woman's voice high and squeaky or low and throaty, depending. And there had just been that one time I'd overheard them, that one brief time. I'd been too stunned to listen attentively, too upset to try to identify an actual person on the line. So maybe it *was* possible that I not only knew the woman who'd been cooing, "Oh, Kippy"; I knew her very, very well.

But how *could* one of them have been having an affair with Kip without me finding out? How would she have pulled it off? Why would she have wanted to pull it off? I know this sort of stuff happens every day, as I've already made abundantly clear, but not to me. Call me an idiot, but I just never, ever imagined that the old Best-friend-sleeps-with-her-husband nightmare would turn out to be *my* nightmare.

No, I didn't have any hard, physical evidence that one of them had slept with my husband and planted those articles. What I had was deductive reasoning. My friends were the only ones aware of the aspects of my relationships with Kip and Brandon that were to be kept quiet, the only people who could have handed the information over to the media. And if one of them did hand it over to the media, she had a big-time ax to grind against me. And if she had a big-time ax to grind against me, then sleeping with my husband was a nifty way to act it out.

The key question, though, was: why? What triggered the big-time ax to grind? What had I done to embitter her so?

I felt sure that this wasn't about clothes or money or even professional success. I also felt sure that, for once in my life, it wasn't about communication. No, whatever I was dealing with was far beyond my expertise.

28

I BEGAN WITH Penny. "Penny, the predator," as she often referred to herself in fun (ha ha). I began with her because she was the public relations expert among us. She dealt with the media for a living. If anyone knew how to leak stories, it was she, I figured. As for whether she was the most likely of the four to have been Kip's mistress, that was a tough call. Each of my friends had questionable personal lives. On the other hand, Penny was the only one who was aggressively single. She was also the one, I reminded myself, who'd confided several months earlier that she had fallen for a man and been terribly disappointed when the relationship didn't work out, but she hadn't been willing to tell me who he was except to say, "I met him through a friend." Perhaps I was the friend and Kip was the man. Perhaps that was why she hadn't been very forthcoming about the romance. Perhaps I would kill Penny.

But first, I invited her to lunch, my mini-tape recorder tucked inside my purse. She may have been the public relations expert but I knew a thing or two about analyzing speech patterns.

"I'm really glad you suggested this," said Penny after I'd arrived at the Penny Herter Group at noon. "Give me a sec to run a comb through my hair and we'll go."

"Perfect," I said, flashing a fake smile. When I had mentioned lunch to Penny, I'd indicated specifically that we should meet at her office first. I wanted a few minutes to snoop around there, ask around, see if I could link her in any way to Kip.

So while she was in the ladies room, I snuck over to her desk, found her Filofax and flipped hurriedly through the pages in search of the address and phone number of the house in Pleasantville where my ex-husband had lived immediately after moving out of our place.

There was nothing listed under "Jankowsky" or under "Kip." I also tried "Wyman" and "Lynn," in case she'd entered him under my names. I even checked under "C" for Carpenter. Nothing.

For all I know, they have revolting pet names for each other, I thought, looking under "B" for Big Boy and "W" for Wild Thing, and finding nothing there, either.

I opened her drawers and poked around for mementos, maybe even a photo of the two of them, but came up empty. I picked through papers on her desk, a pointless endeavor. Then, I went out into the hall and grilled Penny's long-time assistant, Annette.

"Just between us, Annette," I said in my best us-girls voice, "I've been feeling very guilty about my friend."

"Guilty? Why?" she asked.

"Because I'm afraid she was put in an uncomfortable position."

"Oh?"

"Yes. When my ex-husband Kip and I were splitting up last year, I think he used Penny as sort of a sounding board, in an attempt to manipulate her into pleading his case with me. He did call her here at the office from time to time, didn't he?"

"Gosh. I don't remember any calls from a man named Kip, although she was getting calls from a man named Rip."

No duh. I mean, did the lovebirds really think they would fool everybody by changing one stupid letter of his name? "So he did call," I muttered.

"Yes, but he wasn't your ex-husband," said Annette, sensing I was misreading the situation. "Rip was Penny's Pilates trainer. He was bugging her to do P.R. for his studio in exchange for free workouts.

She's not into bartering, never has been. I kept telling him that and he finally stopped harrassing her."

Okay, so Kip didn't call her at the office. Maybe he called her at home. Or on her cell phone. Yes, that was probably it, I decided. Wasn't that why cell phones were invented? In order for people who are committing adultery to have a little privacy, for God's sake?

"Ready," said Penny, back from the ladies room. "I reserved my usual table at the Gotham Bar and Grill. Being in P.R. is all about seeing and being seen, right?"

Once at the restaurant, she put in an appearance at practically every table, air kissing this one, shaking hands with that one, waving to the chef whom she'd spotted in the kitchen, stuffing a wad of bills into the palm of the maître d'. By the time we got to her table, she'd seen and been seen all right. I was exhausted just from watching her work the room.

"Now. Tell me how you are, Lynn," she said once we'd ordered lunch.

"I'm fine," I said. "Busier than ever thanks to the *Post* column."

I waited for a reaction. A twitch. A blink. A lip curl. Nothing.

"What an irony," she said. "You get the publicity but you lose the guy. How are you dealing with the split with Brandon?"

I'm miserable, but then that's what you wanted, isn't it? "I'm doing okay," I said. "He and I are still talking. I'm trying to convince him that I wasn't the one who planted the column."

"Do you have any idea who did?"

"I might."

"Oh, do tell!"

"Not yet, Penny. Not until I'm sure. Actually, I was hoping not to have to think about Brandon and me for a few hours, to take a break from all that. That's why I wanted to have lunch with you. I'd rather hear what's going on in your life."

"Well, I'm doing a huge promotion on the Feminax account. We've hired Heather Locklear to . . ."

I feigned interest as she regaled me with her efforts to hype her client's product. When she ran out of gas, temporarily, and our food arrived, I asked her about her love life.

"Oh that," she said, rolling her eyes. "I'm seeing an Internet guy. He's very full of himself, having made a bundle by the age of thirty, but he's a sex machine. Always *up* for it, if you know what I mean."

I knew what she meant. "Did you ever hear from that man you were seeing last year? The one you really fell for?"

She continued to chew, didn't even look up, just said, "What man?"

"Penny. You told me about him. You said you'd met him through a friend, that it was strictly platonic at first but became a real romance after awhile and then ended badly."

She kept shoveling her Chilean sea bass into her mouth, didn't flinch at all. "Oh, that one." More chewing, a swallow of Pelligrino. "No, we haven't been in touch. It ended badly, as you pointed out."

"Who was he?" I said, pretending to eat but only pushing my mushroom risotto around on the plate.

"An artist," she said. "Not my usual high-powered type."

"An artist. How fascinating." I had considered Kip to be an artist once. But that was only because he had located my G-spot, not because his woodworking was museum quality. "Did you meet him through Isabel?"

"No. Through a woman I used to work with. She owns a few of his paintings. You don't know her."

Yeah, sure. "Why do you think it didn't last between you and—What's his first name?"

"John."

Good one, Penny. I bet his last name is Smith. Or maybe Doe.

"Why do you think it didn't last between you?" I repeated. "Was John married or something?"

"No, he was single. And he intended to stay that way. The minute he thought I was getting too involved, he cut me loose. The bastard."

"Sorry."

"Me, too. But I've managed to pick myself up, dust myself off and move on. The same way you did after the fiasco with Kip. We women are survivors, right? If we can't hang onto a guy, we go out and find another one."

This line of questioning wasn't getting me anywhere. I decided to stop pursuing a tie-in with Kip and try to determine if Penny had any beneath-the-surface bitterness toward me.

"Penny," I said, "we've known each other for a number of years now. Have I ever done anything to make you angry with me?"

"Why would you ask that, Lynn?"

"I was just wondering. There are times when I'm so consumed with my work and my clients and my research that I may not be much of a hands-on friend. I hope you haven't resented me for that."

"Don't be silly. I'm not exactly sitting around twiddling my thumbs, waiting for you to call."

"I know. But did you ever resent all the attention I got, in the days when my career was going gangbusters? You're pretty competitive. Maybe you wished *you* were the one getting on *Good Morning America*."

She laughed. "Where the hell is all this coming from? I'm the one who books people on *Good Morning America*. If I wanted to be *on Good Morning America*, I'd pick up the phone and get myself on. There are people who prefer the behind-the-scenes role, Lynn, and I'm one of them. I wouldn't trade my career for yours or anyone else's. I love what I do."

Okay, so it's not motive Number Three unless she's lying through her Kennedyesque overbite.

"Of course, there is one thing that's always gnawed at me about you," she added.

I pricked up my ears. "What is it?"

"Your weight. You don't go to a gym. You don't have a personal trainer. You don't even power walk. And yet you stay nice and thin while I have to watch everything I eat." She shook her head. "I don't know how *you* metabolize desserts, but that chocolate ganache *I* had last night went straight to my thighs."

WITH THE JURY still out on Penny, I moved on to Isabel. The following week, I trekked downtown to her loft for a drink after work. When she answered the door, I was startled to see that for only the second time since we'd met, she was not dressed in black. She was wearing a flowing red caftan that was way too much fabric for someone as short as she was, but not a terrible fashion choice in that, unlike her black clothes, it didn't show cat hair. Not that the felines weren't everywhere. No matter where I was about to sit, one of them was already occupying the chair, so I stood during the entire visit.

"What can I get for you?" asked Isabel.

"Scotch would be great," I said, wondering if she could possibly be The Betrayer. If she and Kip had been keeping company, wouldn't he have come home covered in fur balls?

"Sorry. I only have green tea," she said. "Should I make us both a cup?"

"Make yourself a cup," I said, remembering how foul her green tea tasted and wishing I'd brought a flask of Dewar's.

While she busied herself in the kitchen, I scoured her loft in search of the same sort of clue I'd looked for in Penny's office, but found nothing except a couple of dead mice.

"How've you been?" I said, returning to the kitchen as she poured herself the tea.

"How have I been? Really, really at peace with myself now," she said.

Had she been at war? With Kip? With me? "At peace in your work?" I asked. "Or in your personal life?"

"In my internal life," she said. "I'm not in turmoil anymore. I've been liberated." She quoted a dead civil rights leader I'd never heard of.

"Not in turmoil anymore. Sounds to me as if something has been bothering you, Isabel, something you've needed to get off your chest." Like back-stabbing a friend?

"Exactly." She grabbed my hand. "Did you intuit the inner struggle that's been raging within me?"

Talk about language adjustments. Isabel was speaking Nutspeak. I couldn't do much with that.

"No, I wasn't aware of your inner struggle, but now that you're feeling better, why don't you tell me about it?"

"All right." She breathed deeply, let go of my hand. "I was a bad person, Lynn. A selfish, self-deluded person. I wasn't being true to myself or to those closest to me."

Aha. I smelled a confession. This was almost too easy. "Go on," I said. "I'm listening."

"Do you remember how I spent seven years waiting for Francisco to make a commitment to me? How I hung onto that relationship, clung to it, let it become my identity for so long?"

"Yes, but I also remember that you said you'd broken up with Francisco, because you'd met someone new."

"I did meet someone new." She blushed. She was definitely hiding something. "That's where my inner struggle comes in."

I nodded. I had a hunch where this was headed. Right into my marriage. "You didn't just meet this someone new, did you, Isabel? You were having an affair with this someone new, even though you allowed your friends to think you were crazy about Francisco."

"You see? You are an intuitive woman, Lynn. Very intuitive."

And very wary of Isabel Green all of a sudden. "You're saying you were having a relationship behind Francisco's back." Behind *my* back.

"Yes, Lynn. Yes, I did precisely what you suspect me of doing. Please don't be—I mean, I couldn't bear it if you—I'm so sorry for deceiving you."

Deceiving me. So it *was* Isabel.

"The magnetism between us was too strong to resist, the energy too powerful," she said, seemingly filled with remorse about sleeping with my husband. "Judge me if you must—I wouldn't blame you if you did—but understand that my actions resulted from a passionate yearning inside me, a yearning to find my true soul mate. Why didn't I tell you about this for so long? Because I was afraid of your reaction, worried that you wouldn't approve of my behavior."

I stared at her, not with the cold fury I'd expected to feel, but with a sense of bewilderment. I tried to picture her standing next to Kip and couldn't. Since he was a tall drink of water and she was such a shrimp, she probably came up to his belt, which was goofy. On the other hand, maybe her height worked well for them. For him, especially.

You bitch, I thought then, the cold fury hitting me after all. How could you have slept with my husband, planted those stories and pretended to be my friend? How? Why?

I wanted to slap her, slap that beatific smile right off her face, but I wasn't the slapping type.

"Lynn?" said Isabel grabbing my hand again. "You look pale. Are you sure you don't want some green tea?"

I wriggled out of her grasp. "I wouldn't drink anything you gave me, you midget. There might be poison in it."

She appeared stunned. What a good little actress she was. "Poison?"

"Sure," I sneered. "You've been out to get me for over a year. Why not finish the job?"

"Lynn, what are you—"

"How do you live with yourself?" I said, shaking my head at her. "How do you have the nerve to do what you did and then invite me over to your loft, offer me some of your fucking green tea, play the friend?"

"Play the friend? You are my friend," she protested.

"And you are disgusting," I said.

"Disgusting?" She looked as if I *had* slapped her. "I had no idea you'd feel that negatively. I thought you were much more open-minded."

"Open-minded? About what you've done? You're out of your mind."

Tears welled up in her eyes. I was making her cry and I was glad. Glad!

"You're my dear friend and I should have told you about the relationship, because dear friends confide in each other. But it's not as if I didn't want to," she said, her voice choked with emotion. "As a matter of fact, I was all in favor of telling you, of telling you and Penny and Sarah and Gail, but there was another person's feelings to consider, don't forget."

"Forget? How could I forget?" She and Kip had screwed around in my house while I was away at a conference. No, I wouldn't forget that. "You know what I think, Isabel? I think you're sick."

"Sick?" She was crying in earnest now. "How can loving another human being qualify me as sick?"

"You're telling me you two are still in love?" Hadn't Kip said they had split up? And not amicably?

"Very much in love. We're going to live together, have children together. I've been dying to share the news with you before she moved in but I could never find the words."

"She?" Isabel was scarier than I thought. She couldn't even keep her pronouns straight.

"Yes. Rita. She's moving in next week. Oh, Lynn. I wish you could find it in your heart to be happy for us."

Rita? Isabel's astrologer? That's who was moving in with her? That's who had replaced Francisco in her bed? Isabel had been afraid to tell me she was a lesbian? *That's* what we were talking about?

And I was an expert in communication?

Now it was my turn to cry. I threw my arms around Isabel, practically crushed her with my hug. I begged her to forgive me, claimed temporary insanity for the way I'd spoken to her, explained that there had been a giant misunderstanding, and promised to host a wedding shower for her and Rita if they ever decided to tie the knot.

By the time I left, she and I were friends again. Better friends than before.

At least I can cross one of them off the list, I thought as I drove home to Mt. Kisco, feeling dangerously close to being the punch line of a good news/bad news joke.

29

GAIL LIVED IN a two-bedroom apartment on Manhattan's Upper West Side, only a few blocks from Kelsey's place. I rarely visited her, because her kids were so disruptive that it was impossible to conduct a coherent conversation with her, but I went anyway. I wanted to see her in her natural habitat, see if I'd stumble across any leads there.

I had proposed, as I had with Isabel, that I pop over after work for a drink. I knew I wouldn't get stuck with green tea at Gail's; the Orricks enjoyed their alcohol, and their bar was always fully stocked.

"A Scotch for you, a martini for me, and a bowl of nacho chips for both of us," said Gail as she bustled over to the sofa and plopped herself down next to me. She had gained back the few pounds she'd lost and was looking rather chunky. I tried to imagine her and Kip having sex. I wondered if he had located *her* G-spot.

"Is Jim out tonight?" I asked, knowing they took turns staying home with the kids. Perhaps it had been during his turn with the kids that she'd taken her turn with Kip.

She nodded resignedly. "He's playing cards. Probably losing his shirt."

"Are you still thinking about going ahead with the divorce? The last time we talked, you said you'd been to a few lawyers."

"I've been to three lawyers, but every single one of them grossed me out more than Jim does."

"So you haven't moved forward?"

"No. I'm hoping Jim will die in a plane crash so I won't have to."

"Oh, come on, Gail. Maybe you don't really want to divorce him. I mean, it's not as if you're interested in anyone else, right?" Answer that one, sister.

"Me?" She laughed. "I'd love to be interested in someone else, but who has the time? Between my work and the kids, how would I slot in a torrid affair?"

You tell me. Or better yet, let me check out your calendar from last year. "There's always time for an affair, Gail. Look at Kip. He worked, took care of the house, did the grocery shopping, cooked dinner for us, but he managed to sneak in some nookie."

"Well, that was Kip for you, the little shit. I hope he dies in the same plane crash as Jim."

"My, I didn't realize you had such hostility toward my ex-husband. What did he ever do to you?" Besides dump you, you slut.

"It's what he did to *you* that galls me. I don't like seeing my friends' husbands cheat on them, Lynn."

Liar! "I appreciate your support."

"Well, it's true. As a matter of fact, I'm changing my mind about the plane crash. I think Kip should die at the hands of an aging, sex-crazed, former *Sports Illustrated* swimsuit model."

You have to understand that this was vintage Gail. She always spoke in hyperbolic, over-the-top language. Still, I couldn't be sure that she didn't have her own, very personal grudge against Kip and, of course, against me.

I tried to get more out of her on the subject of my ex-husband, but all she wanted to do was conjure up new and ever more horrible ways in which he could die.

"Where are the children?" I said when I realized that Gail and I had actually been chatting, uninterrupted.

No sooner had I asked the question than her two young sons, Danny and Dicky, came bounding into the living room, screaming at an entirely unacceptable decibel level.

"Hey, hey, hey," Gail scolded them as they circled the sofa, one of them trying to mash the other's face in. "Behave yourselves. I have a guest."

"Behave yourselves. I have a guest," said Danny, the five-year-old. He was at that stage where he thought that repeating everything an authority figure said was hysterically funny.

"You heard me," said Gail. "I want you both back in your room, playing quietly."

"I want you both back in your room, playing quietly," said Dicky, the six-year-old. He was at the same stage as his brother, apparently.

"That's it. That's enough." Gail slammed her martini onto the coffee table, spilling most of it, and chased the children into their room. She was only gone a few minutes, which was too bad; I had hoped to wander around the apartment looking for, say, clippings of the *Enquirer* and *Post* stories. Like the others, Gail was savvy when it came to the media. She was a documentary filmmaker who specialized in Plight, don't forget. Maybe the Plight she was really interested in was mine.

"I'm back. Sorry," she said, reclaiming her seat on the sofa. "They're my babies but they make a lot of noise."

"Nonsense. They're adorable." The way boom boxes are adorable.

"Where were we?"

"I was just sitting here wondering, Gail, while you were in there with the boys, have I ever done anything to upset you or make you angry or cause you to resent me?"

She looked surprised by the question. "Absolutely not. Why would you even ask that, Lynn? Is it because we don't see each other that often? As I said, between work and the kids, I barely have time to take a crap."

Thanks for sharing. "It's just a feeling I've had, that's all. I know you're not jealous of my success. I mean, you're the one with all the Emmys, right?"

"Right."

"And you couldn't care less about who wears nicer clothes or makes more money or—"

"I make plenty of money," she cut me off. "I make it and Jim spends it. But that has nothing to do with you, Lynn. That's my cross to bear."

"Then you're not mad at me for any reason?"

"Of course not. I still don't get why you would ask that." Because someone leaked my secrets to the press, and you just might be the psycho that did it. "Although there is something about you that does drive me nuts."

Here we go. "What's that, Gail?"

"How long have we been sitting here?"

I shrugged. "A half-hour?"

"Okay. And have you eaten a single nacho chip?"

Oh, please. Not the weight thing again. I was overdosing on Womenspeak, I had to admit.

"Well, I've practically finished them," said Gail. "Inhaled the entire bowl. Which is why I look the way I do and you look the way you do, and I hate you."

She giggled, then hugged me, which is not what a woman who hates you does unless she's trying to disguise that she hates you. Obviously, I was back to square one with Gail.

When the phone rang and she told me she really needed to talk to the caller, I said, "No problem. Take your time," and ventured down the hall to the boys' room. No, I wasn't a glutton for punishment. I was just desperate for clues and thought maybe they knew something about their mother that she wasn't planning to tell me herself.

"Hi, guys," I said when I entered what was basically a toy store with a double-decker bed in it. I'd never seen so much stuff. "Whatcha doing?"

"Playing," said Danny, who had his brother in a head lock.

"Tell him to let me go!" cried Dicky. "Tell him I wish he'd die in a plane crash!"

They were their mother's sons, clearly. "How about talking to me for a minute?" I said.

"About what?" said Danny, who had released his brother and was now spinning around, trying to make himself dizzy.

"About a friend of your mom's." Her *lover*.

"But *you're* my mom's friend," said Dicky.

"Yes, I am. But I meant her friend who's a man. Have you ever met him? He's tall and thin and has dark wavy hair. He always wears blue jeans and sometimes he carries tools with him, so he can fix things. Ever seen anybody like that around the apartment?"

"Yeah," said Dicky while Danny was still spinning.

"You have seen him?" I said, trying not to let them know how important this was.

"Yeah," said Dicky. "He's the super in the building. He comes here to fix things. He even comes at night, to drink and play cards with my dad. One time he lost a card game and got real mad and socked my dad in the nose, and there was blood all over the floor. When my mom got home she had to take my dad to the hospital."

Was I ever glad I asked. "Stop spinning, Danny," I said after thanking Dickie for his riveting tale. "You'll make yourself sick."

"Stop spinning, Danny. You'll make yourself sick," said Danny as he not only continued to spin but gave me the finger.

I MET SARAH at Dogwood the following Sunday for brunch. Edward was away at a golf tournament in Arizona, so it was just the two of us, which was just the way I wanted it.

When I arrived at the house, Justine announced me as she usually did, then Sarah descended the staircase, making a grand entrance as she usually did. She really was a beauty, with her long raven hair and porcelain complexion and stunning figure. It was hard to imagine that she would have any reason to envy *me*.

Still, I had come in order to rule her in or out as a possible villain, and that's what I was prepared to do. She had contacts galore in the media and, therefore, could have planted the stories without much effort. Plus, she was often estranged from Edward and, therefore, could have engaged in an extramarital affair with my husband without interference from her own.

"Lynn, darling," she said, after kissing me on each cheek. She had just returned from yet another trip abroad and was playing the Lady of the Continent.

"Hi, Sarah. Thanks for having me over."

"I was delighted when you suggested we get together. Come, let's get you something to drink. Justine?"

She called for her house manager and instructed her to bring us each a Bloody Mary.

We sat in her sunroom, a glass-enclosed solarium facing out onto Dogwood's lush, manicured grounds. A beautiful house for a beautiful woman, I thought. A woman who has everything she could possibly desire. A spoiled woman. A woman with a skewed sense of entitlement. A woman who believes that whatever doesn't belong to her should. Kip, for instance.

I asked about her latest book. She said the movie offers were pouring in but that she was holding out for more money.

"Don't you have enough money?" I said, taking in our plush surroundings.

"Don't be naïve, Lynn. It's not about the money. It's about getting what you deserve."

I was all for people getting what they deserved, especially people who pretended to be your friend and trashed you behind your back.

"I guess things are going better for you in the money department," she said. "That's good news."

"Yes, but it's not much consolation if I've lost Brandon. He trusted me not to publicize that he was my client, and then the *Post* column destroyed that trust. If I could only find out who planted the story I could make things right between us."

No reaction. She just sipped her Bloody Mary, which Justine had brought as ordered. "Any ideas who could have done it?"

"Ideas but nothing definitive."

"Well, if you ask me, this Brandon of yours isn't worth the trouble."

"Not worth the trouble? I love him, Sarah."

"Love," she scoffed. "I'm not sure I know what that is anymore. I thought I loved Edward and look at us: a husband and wife who never see each other."

"But you like it that way. You told me you did. You and Edward have your 'arrangement' and it works for you. That's still true, isn't it?"

She sighed. "Neither of us is monogamous. That's what's still true."

Yessss. An opening. "I hope I'm not getting too personal, Sarah, but since you've made no secret of the fact that you've had affairs, I was wondering, are most of the men you've been with over the years married too?"

She laughed. "What a question. Of course you're getting too personal, but the answer's yes. It's much easier for me to sleep with a married man than a single man because I'm in the same boat as the married one. To him, I'm some man's wife. To me, he's some woman's husband. We speak a common language."

A language in which I was not fluent. Would she actually be admitting this if she really *had* slept with Kip? Could she be so twisted? "Doesn't that ever bother you though?" I said.

"Doesn't what bother me?"

"That your lover is 'some woman's husband?' Don't you ever feel guilty about her, about what you're doing to her marriage?"

"No, because I'm not responsible for her marriage. I'm only responsible for my own."

"But I remember that you were outraged when I told you that Kip had been having an affair. You thought it was as despicable as the rest of us did, even though he was 'some woman's husband,' the sort of man you seek out, and even though I was 'some man's wife,' the sort of woman you don't feel guilty about. How do you reconcile the two, Sarah?"

"It's very simple. I was outraged because you're my friend, not because you're some man's wife. In other words, Lynn, I wouldn't sleep with *your* husband."

Well, there it was. An outright denial. What else could I do except say things like "Of course you wouldn't" and "I wasn't implying that you would" and "I'm mighty hungry. How's that brunch coming?"

We ate poached eggs and roasted potatoes and asparagus tips with hollandaise sauce (she had hers on the side). After we finished, I went into the kitchen to thank Justine for a wonderful meal. She was a marvel, that Justine. She not only ran the household, she cooked for the household.

"I did the potatoes differently today," she said proudly. "The recipe came from a cookbook the madame's friend gave her as a gift last year."

"One of Sarah's friends gave her a cookbook?" How silly. Everyone knew that Sarah never cooked. She once tried to make a turkey with disastrous results. Instead of simply rinsing the bird and patting it dry, she squirted Palmolive Liquid into the cavity, ended up with stuffing full of soap bubbles, and never set foot in the kitchen again.

"Yes. A male friend. I didn't meet him, but the madame said he was an excellent cook."

Well, naturally, I thought of Kip. Was this the proof I'd been waiting for?

"Does Mrs. Pepper still see this friend?" I asked.

"That I couldn't tell you, but I can tell you there've been no more cookbooks."

What a pity. "Just curious, Justine, because the potatoes were so delicious: Which cookbook was it?"

She reached for the book sitting on the counter and handed it to me. It was by Marcella Hazan, the great Italian cookbook author, who just happened to be one of Kip's favorites.

No, he hadn't written a mushy inscription inside the front cover. No, he hadn't even signed his name with xxx's and ooo's after it. No, he wasn't necessarily the one who'd given Sarah the damn cookbook. As they would say on those televised courtroom dramas, the evidence was interesting but inconclusive.

30

WHEN I GOT home from Sarah's on Sunday afternoon, there was a message on my machine from Brandon, of all people. He was at the office, he said. He was thinking about me, he said. He would be there until five or so if I just happened to be cruising by Finefoods' corporate headquarters, he said.

The invitation was a touch on the passive side, but I wasn't about to quibble.

I checked my watch. Two-forty. Lots of time.

I jumped back into the car and drove the twenty minutes to White Plains, my hopes soaring. Had Brandon had a change of heart? Did he realize he'd been wrong about me? Was he ready for us to resume our relationship? At the very least, he was reaching out to me. That was progress, wasn't it?

When I got to Finefoods, the building showed no signs of life except for the security guard in the lobby. I told him I was there for a meeting with Mr. Brock. He phoned upstairs to Brandon's office, got the okay, and allowed me to proceed to the elevator.

I rode up to the executive floor, stepped off and hurried down the long hallway to Brandon's cushy corner suite. He was standing behind his desk waiting for me, a Styrofoam container of half-eaten deli food resting on top of a mess of papers.

"Is that a pickle on your platter or are you glad to see me?" I said.

He smiled. "It's not appropriate to tell off-color jokes in the workplace. Didn't anyone ever tell you that?"

"Not that I can recall."

He was dressed in casual clothes since it was a weekend—slacks and a sweater—and he'd had a haircut, which made him look boyish, sweet. I wanted to rush into his arms but restrained myself. I was going to follow his lead on this.

"You got my message," he said, sitting down after pulling out a chair for me.

"Yes. I had just come back from having brunch at Sarah's."

"You were with Sarah? What happened to your theory that it was one of your friends who planted the stories?"

"I'm actively pursuing it. That's why I was with Sarah: To find out if she was the culprit. I thought I'd let her feed me while I was interrogating her."

"Well, how was it?"

"Delicious. She had poached eggs, roasted potatoes, and asparagus tips."

"I meant, how was the interrogation, Lynn. Is Sarah the guilty one?"

"I can't decide. It's certainly possible that she slept with Kip, even though she denied it."

"Slept with Kip?"

"Oh. I haven't told you about that part. The other night, I figured out that the woman who planted the stories was also the woman who had an affair with Kip. Don't ask me to explain. Just trust me."

The second the words were out of my mouth I remembered what Brandon had said the last time we were together—that it wasn't a communication issue keeping us apart; it was a trust issue.

"What I'm saying is, I don't want to take up your time this afternoon leading you step by step through my thought process," I added. "But I'm convinced that one of my friends was Kip's sex kitten. Although, speaking of kittens, I've crossed Isabel off the list. She's a lesbian, it turns out. She's been sleeping with Rita, her astrologer, not with Kip. So I'm down to three candidates."

"You must dread having to cross-examine them all."

"Oddly enough, I don't dread it, because it'll bring me one step closer to getting to the bottom of this mess. Then we can pick up where we left off. Isn't that what we agreed?"

"All I know is that I can't stop thinking about you, Lynn. For six months, you coached me on getting in touch with my feelings and now I'm so in touch with them I can't shut them off."

I smiled. He still loved me. We were home free, as soon as I nailed the bitch who was trying to ruin my life. "I can't stop thinking about you either, and some of my thoughts are pretty X-rated, you might be flattered to hear. In fact, how'd you like to clean off the top of your desk, meet me up there, and have your way with me?"

He laughed at my boldness. "Is this the same woman who said it was criminal to make sexual advances in a business environment?"

"No. I'm not the same woman, Brandon. I'm a woman in love for the first time in my life."

It was true. I felt as if I'd had an attitude transplant. I may have put him in touch with his feelings, but he also put me in touch with mine.

"Getting back to my evil saboteur," I said, "she's Penny, Gail, or Sarah. The problem is, how do I prove which one?"

"By tripping her up."

"Keep going."

"You've got to set a trap for her and then let her walk right into it. For example, if my security people say to me, 'We suspect a Finefoods employee of stealing confidential documents and leaking them, but we can't prove it,' I'll tell them to throw together some phony documents that appear to be confidential, deposit them smack into the employee's lap, and sit back and see what happens. If the documents get leaked, the employee gets canned."

"Interesting. I could do that sort of thing, couldn't I?"

"Why not?"

"Why not." It was a great idea. The perfect idea. The only idea that would tell me definitively who had been stirring up trouble for me. "I'll invent a secret about myself—information that, if made public, would be detrimental to me somehow—and I'll share this secret with Penny, Gail, and Sarah. Then I'll wait and see if it gets leaked to the press, the way the other two stories were."

"Sounds good, but you left out an essential element."

"Which is?"

"You've got to tell them each a *different* secret and then wait and see which one gets leaked. That's the only way you'll know which of your pals has the loose screw—and the loose lips to match."

"You're right, Brandon. The only hitch is that I'll have to think up the three awful secrets about myself and then deal with the fact that one of them will turn up in a newspaper. It's not exactly a picnic having negative things written about you, as you know. Look what happened to my career when the *Enquirer* story broke. Look what happened to my love life when the *Post* column ran. I'm taking a big risk here."

"Not to worry. If you catch this woman and you and I get back together—"

"Not if. When."

"You interrupted. Have you forgotten every single thing you taught me?"

"Sorry. Go ahead."

"*When* you catch this woman and you and I get back together, I'll be in a position to help you. Even if your career takes another dip—and I assume that will be your saboteur's intention, to put you out of commission once and for all—I'll be able to refer clients to you. Hell, I'll make you a consultant to the company if you want. I'll send you all our cavemen and you can transform them into wusses like me."

"It would be my pleasure."

He smiled, leaned forward in his chair. He was about to say something, but changed his mind.

"That's okay, Brandon," I said, understanding that he wasn't quite ready to trust me again, not until the situation was resolved. "We're almost there."

THREE SECRETS. ONE for Penny, the predator. One for Gail, the hysteric. One for Sarah, the diva. Yes, I would dream up three custom-designed tales about myself and then disclose a different one to each woman.

On Monday morning, I called Penny at her office. Annette, her assistant, answered the phone.

"Hi, Annette. It's Lynn Wyman. It's urgent that I talk to Penny. Is she there?"

"She's in a meeting, but—"

"Could you pull her out of it, Annette? It's sort of an emergency."

"Oh. Okay, let me see what I can do."

I waited, did a little whistling, hummed a few bars of "You've got a friend," thought that was funny, under the circumstances.

"Lynn? What's wrong?" said Penny when she came onto the line. She sounded breathless, as if I really had pulled her out of a meeting.

I fake-cried, which was easy enough, having watched Kip in action over the years. "Something terrible has happened," I said. "But before

I tell you about it, you have to swear to me that it'll stay between us. Well, between the members of the Brain Trust. I'm going to tell the others, too, but it's crucial that you don't discuss it, even with them. My whole future depends on it."

"My lips are sealed."

"Promise?"

"I promise. Just tell me."

I sighed, threw in a couple of gulps. "The IRS claims I owe the government a fortune in back taxes, Penny. They're threatening to shut down my business."

"My God! Are you serious?"

"Very."

"When did you hear about this?"

"About an hour ago. These agents stormed into my office and started rummaging through my files. It's been bedlam over here."

"I'll bet. What does your accountant say?"

"Not much. He's the one who bungled my tax returns."

"How about your lawyer?"

"She's going to do her best to keep me out of prison stripes."

"Prison stripes? I don't believe this, Lynn. And just when you finally got your career back on track. What are you going to do?"

"I don't know. The thing is, I'm totally innocent—well, I may have taken a few too many deductions—but proving it is going to be a huge undertaking." I paused, to give her time to digest the story before hitting her with the point of my little exercise. "Of course, even the slightest publicity about the situation before I prove my innocence would not only kill my practice but wreck any possibility of getting back together with Brandon. He won't want a tax cheat for a fiancée."

"Oh, Lynn. I feel awful for you. Is there anything you need from me? Anything at all?"

One final sob. "Just be there for me, Penny. And, as I said, keep this under your hat. I'm going to make sure that Isabel and Gail and Sarah do the same."

"You can trust me, Lynn."

ONE DOWN. TWO to go.

I called Gail at her apartment, as I knew she would be home packing for her trip to California later that day. (She was taking a break from her heavy-handed documentaries for PBS and, instead, shooting a skit for the Comedy Channel showing the dichotomy between northern California, aka Silicon Valley, and southern California, aka Silicone Valley. "I'm more versatile than people in television give me credit for," she'd said.)

When she answered the phone, I did the fake-cry again, although I think I was better at it the first time. "It's Lynn," I said. "You're probably rushing to catch a flight, but something terrible has happened and I just have to talk to you, Gail."

"Oh, no. They found a lump."

"No lump," I said. "But I'm suffering from an extremely rare disease."

She gasped. "What kind of a disease?"

"It's got a really long name, one of those unpronounceable names that ends in -osis."

"What are the symptoms?"

"They're absolutely devastating, let me tell you. First, there's the sore throat—a horrendous sore throat, not just a scratchy sore throat. Then, there's the rash."

"On your face?"

"Everywhere—and I mean *everywhere*."

"Oh."

"And just when you think you'll go insane from the itching, you start to experience this intense ringing in your ears, followed by an inability to speak clearly."

"You sound fine to me."

"The slurring comes and goes."

"So this is a neurological disease?"

"Yes, but it affects the ovaries, too."

"The ovaries?"

"Yes. For some reason that the medical community hasn't determined, the production of estrogen triggers a thickening of the tissue around the ovaries, which is related in some way to the ringing in the ears and the slurring of the speech. Oh, the mysteries of the human body."

"I don't know what to say, Lynn. Is there a cure for this?"

"Not yet. The good news is that it's not terminal. The bad news is that it's putting my career in jeopardy. How can I coach men on their speech patterns when my own are incomprehensible, off and on?"

"This is tragic. Absolutely tragic. If you want my advice, I think you should take your case straight to the news media. March yourself onto *60 Minutes*. Hold a press conference. Demand that the government allocate billions of dollars for research. Do whatever is necessary to call attention to your *plight*."

I couldn't resist a smile. "I'm glad you brought up the media, Gail, because I can't stress strongly enough how big a secret my condition is. I'm only telling you and Penny and Isabel and Sarah about it with the understanding that you are not to say a word—not a whisper!—to anyone, not even to each other. If it leaked out that I was a victim of this -osis thing, it would be the end of my practice, not to mention the end of Brandon and me. He's not going to want damaged goods any more than my clients will."

"Oh, Lynn," she said again. "I'm so sorry. What can I do to help?"

"Just promise me you'll keep my secret."

"I promise."

"Thanks."

"I do have another question though."

"What?"

"Is this disease contagious? I'm only asking because I just saw you the other day and I—"

"You've got nothing to worry about, Gail." If you keep your mouth shut.

TWO DOWN. ONE to go.

I reached Sarah at Dogwood. Justine always screened the calls when *the madame* was hard at work on another novel about the magic toothbrush, but I impressed upon her how critical it was that I speak to our lady of kid lit.

"Lynn? What's this all about?" said Sarah, sounding irritated that she'd been disturbed.

"Something terrible has happened," I said, trotting out the same tired line, as well as the phony tears. "I would never have interrupted your writing if it weren't important."

"That's all right. What's going on?"

I exhaled deeply into the phone, to show how pained I was to have to report my supposedly hideous news. "Do you remember at brunch yesterday, when we talked about your affairs with married men?"

"Yes, Lynn. I may be older than you are but I'm not senile."

"Well, I withheld information from you—information that could cost me everything." Sob sob.

"Don't leave me hanging. What information?"

"I had my own affair with a married man."

"You?"

"Yes. I'm sure you think I'm a complete hypocrite, but I couldn't bring myself to say anything to you, Sarah."

"Why not? I spilled my guts to you."

"This is different. Your men are everyday men. My man is—" I let her twist in the wind for a second—"famous."

"How famous?"

"The-cover-of-*People*-magazine famous."

"You're kidding."

"I wish I were. I've never felt so cheap in my entire life."

"Never mind about that. Tell me who he is."

Another ostentatious exhale, plus several beats of silence, to make her sweat a little. "He's an extremely well-known television personality."

"Gee, that narrows it down."

"With a big hit show."

"And?"

"And he's on the air five times a week."

"His name, Lynn. Tell me his name."

"Sorry, but this is painful for me."

"It's painful for *me*, the way you're keeping me in suspense. Now who is he? Matt Lauer?"

"No."

"Peter Jennings?"

"No."

"Regis Philbin?"

This was much more fun than I'd anticipated. "No."

"THEN WHO?"

I whispered into the phone the name of the celebrity whose face was on my television screen at that very moment.

"Him?"

"Yup."

"I can't believe this. I just can't believe this."

"Neither can I, frankly. We were only together once, but that doesn't excuse what we did."

"Once. Twice. Who cares? How did you meet him?"

"At the gym where he works out."

"You don't go to gyms, Lynn."

"Not usually, but his gym was offering one of those free trial workouts, so I figured, what the heck. The last thing I expected was to strike up a conversation with him and end up in his apartment—in his *bed*—while his wife was out of town. Why, oh why, did I do it? I guess I was lonely, because of the breakup with Brandon."

"I still can't picture you—"

"Listen, Sarah. I told you about the affair because I was dying to get it off my chest, but I'm really embarrassed about it."

"Don't be so hard on yourself. You'll learn from it and go on."

"Only if the media doesn't find out about it. Can you imagine what a field day the tabloids would have with the story? They write about this guy all the time—he must be used to it by now and probably couldn't care less what they print—but how about my reputation? My career would go straight back down the drain. And I could forget about reconciling with Brandon. He'd never speak to me again."

"He does seem rather thin-skinned."

"So I'm begging you, Sarah: Keep my secret. I've told Penny and Isabel and Gail about it, and they've promised not to discuss it with anyone, even each other, so please make the same promise."

"Your secret is safe with me. But before I let you go, I have to ask: Was he any good?"

"Who?"

"Mr. Television Personality. Was he a good lover? Those show business types are so self-involved that I assume he was all about making sure *he* was satisfied and not giving a damn about *you*."

"He was good enough," I said, trying to sound as if I had tons of experience in this area, "but Brandon is the man I care about. Just swear to me that he'll never hear what I did."

"Not from me he won't."

THREE DOWN, NONE to go.

I had set my traps. Let the games begin.

31

I SPENT THE rest of the week working with clients and waiting for the shoe to drop. Whose shoe? That remained to be seen.

Brandon checked in a couple of times to see how I was holding up under the stress. And while I was thrilled that he cared enough to call, I could sense a distance in his tone. He was still protecting himself, I knew, making absolutely sure he could trust me before leaping back into the relationship.

I didn't blame him. He'd spent years being angry at his ex-wife for leaving him, because it had been far easier to be angry at her than to allow himself to mourn the loss of her, to let himself *feel* the pain of her rejection. But that was before he underwent the Wyman Method; before he acquired empathy for and sensitivity toward women; before he had the nerve to look in the mirror and admit that the guy staring back at him could be an arrogant jerk; before he realized that he'd been clueless about what his wife wanted or needed during their marriage and too busy clawing his way up the corporate ladder to ask her. Now he was a man whose emotions were exposed, a man who would experience hurt in a way he never had.

So I understood his reluctance to remove the barriers between us before I proved to him, once and for all, that I hadn't broken my pledge of confidentiality, that I hadn't sold him out in order to advance my career. But I was getting antsy. I was more than ready for my nemesis to reveal herself, ready to proceed with my life, ready to be with Brandon.

Another seven days went by, and there was nothing from the enemy camp. But the week was hardly without drama. Rita had moved into Isabel's loft by then, and the two of them hosted a festive gathering one evening that was a combination housewarming/we're-out-of-the-closet party. Naturally, I was invited, as were the rest of my friends. And naturally, I wasn't keen on going. I had told Penny, Gail, and Sarah each a different fabrication about myself while giving them the distinct impression that I'd told the others the exact same tale of woe. The idea of standing there, schmoozing with all three women, fearing that at any moment one of them might start popping off about the information she assumed the others were privy to, made me queasy. How would I handle it? How would I keep all the balls in the air? How would I manage not to blow the whole scheme?

On the other hand, if I didn't go to the party, the three of them might very well huddle in a corner and gossip about me in absentia, only to discover that I had handed them a bunch of bull. I had to be there, I decided, had to at least take a stab at controlling their conversation.

Besides, I couldn't refuse Isabel's invitation, didn't want her to think that I wasn't supportive of her relationship with Rita.

I went to the party bearing gifts (I bought them matching "her" and "her" bathrobes), figuring I'd put in a quick appearance and bolt.

After greeting the loving couple and congratulating them on their new living arrangement, I mingled with the revelers, hoping to corral Penny, Gail, and Sarah as soon as they arrived and engage them in a lively discussion about politics or sports or food—anything that would deprive them of the opportunity to compare notes about poor Lynn.

I spotted Sarah first and waved. She paraded herself over to me, bestowed a peck on each of my cheeks and narrowed her eyes at me knowingly.

"What?" I said.

"I wanted to see if you'd look more worldly, now that you've slept with a married man. A married television star."

"Shhh. I asked you not to mention it in public, Sarah." My decision to show up was the correct one, I thought, even if it means saying "Shhh" a lot.

"Lighten up, Lynn. It's just us."

"Yes, but someone might overhear."

"Lynn, darling. Be embarrassed if you insist, but don't be paranoid."

"I'm not paranoid. I'd rather not talk about it at this party, that's all."

"Are you still feeling guilty about it?"

She wasn't getting my point. "I said I prefer not to talk about it tonight, Sarah."

"Talk about what?" said Penny, who had made her way over to us. My stomach began to ache. Maybe the decision to come hadn't been so smart after all.

"Can't you guess what we're talking about?" said Sarah, winking at me. "Lynn's deep, dark secret, that's what."

"Oh," said Penny, lowering her voice to a whisper, then turning to me. "How are you handling the situation, Lynn?"

She was referring to my tax issues, obviously, not to my affair with a celebrity.

"I'm handling the situation pretty well," I said, "but, as I was telling Sarah, I'd really rather not talk about it tonight. Not with so many people around."

"Understood," said Penny, her eyes darting here and there, surfing the room for possible clients and/or men to hit on. "Just answer one question: Have you hired a bona fide expert to help you through it? Someone who's had years of experience navigating people through the kind of mess you're in?"

Sarah laughed. "I didn't know there were experts in the kind of mess Lynn's in. Where you do find them? On *Entertainment Tonight*?"

Penny shook her head disapprovingly. "You and your show business nonsense, Sarah. Leave it to you to turn Lynn's dilemma into a made-for-TV melodrama."

"Did someone say 'melodrama'?" It was Gail, talk about perfect timing. She had joined the conversation and had brought along the bowl of soy nuts she'd swiped off the buffet table.

"We were discussing Lynn's melodrama, not one of yours," said Penny.

"Oh my God, yes." Gail's expression grew serious. *She* was referring to my dreaded disease, obviously, not to my tax issues or my affair with a celebrity. "How do you feel, Lynn?"

Like taking a hike. "As well as can be expected," I said.

"I suggested she consult an expert," said Penny.

"Why does she need an expert?" said Sarah. "She'll heal on her own."

"Heal on her own?" said Gail, who seemed outraged by the notion. "I agree with Penny. This isn't something to fool around with. I'd get a specialist, the best person money can buy."

"Right," said Penny. "I can try to get some referrals for you, Lynn. I have a client who went through what you're dealing with now. It was tough on him psychologically, but he managed to hang on to his business, his house, everything."

"He must have had a good insurance policy," said Gail. She studied me for a second, peered at every pore on my face. "I don't see any sign of the rash, Lynn. Does it come and go like the other symptoms?"

"Yes," I said quickly, wondering how long I could maintain this charade. "It comes when I'm upset and goes when I'm not."

"Same here," said Sarah. "I get hives every time I'm in a room full of studio executives, but they disappear as soon as the meeting's over." She tossed her hair back. "I still think you're making much too much of what happened, Lynn. You committed one tiny mistake, one lapse in judgment. It's not the end of the world."

"Lapse in judgment?" said Gail, who was really outraged now. "You sound as if you're blaming the victim, Sarah. I hate it when people do that. It's not as if Lynn brought this on herself, as if she *asked* for it."

Sarah smirked. "She didn't exactly fight it."

"That's because she's in a weakened condition," said Gail. "You can't fight anything when you're not yourself."

"What happened to Lynn could happen to any one of us," said Penny. "I, for one, leave myself wide open when April 15th comes rolling around."

"Everyone does," said Gail. "The weather's so changeable in the spring. It's warm, then it's cold, then it's warm again. It's an easy time to pick up things."

"To pick up people, too," said Sarah with another wink. "Right, Lynn?"

Okay. That was enough. They were dangerously close to finding out that their wires were crossed.

I was about to jump in, to beg them to change the subject (or, more accurately, subjects), when Isabel and Rita stopped by to thank us for coming to the party.

"How is everybody?" said Isabel, looking very happy. And why shouldn't she? She wasn't on my list of bitches. I hadn't set a trap for her. "Having fun?"

"We're having a wonderful time," I lied.

"Under the circumstances," said Gail.

"What circumstances?" said Isabel.

"Well, it was difficult for Lynn to put everything aside and walk in the door tonight," said Gail. "It was very brave of her, if you ask me."

"Why was it brave?" said Isabel, her smile vanishing.

"Why? Because it's hard to be up for a party when you're obsessing about moral values," Sarah taunted me.

"Whose moral values?" Isabel said defensively. *She* was referring to the fact that she was gay, not to my tax issues, my affair with a celebrity, or my dreaded disease.

"Sarah didn't mean—" I started to explain, so that Isabel wouldn't misunderstand, but I couldn't. There was no way to, without getting myself in more hot water.

"Calm down," said Rita, trying to soothe Isabel. "Saturn is squaring Mars today, which is why you're feeling insecure. If Lynn is having problems, it's not our responsibility."

"If she's having problems, it *is* our responsiblity," said Gail. "We're her friends. Friends should be there for each other."

"You would think!" said Isabel, still huffy. "I was hopeful that you would all embrace my new lifestyle, but—"

She was interrupted by a cat fight—literally. Two of her Persians were going at each other and their wailing was loud enough to stop all conversation.

Isabel hurried over to break up the racket, Rita trailing behind her. After several more minutes of chatting—about the cats, not about me, thank God—Sarah, Penny, and Gail each said they had to leave. Penny had a date, Gail had to get home to the kids, and Sarah had theatre tickets. As we bid our goodbyes, my friends wished me well with my "situation," completely oblivious to the fact that they were not on the same page.

I had dodged a bullet. No, I had dodged four bullets. I had made it through the party, bloodied but not beaten. For once in my life, I had witnessed a total failure to communicate and been grateful for it.

32

ANOTHER TWO WEEKS passed. There was nothing in the press about my tug-of-war with the IRS, my tragic battle with -osis, or my affair with a married TV star.

I kept on. I went about my routine. I bought a lot of newspapers, which was a waste of money, as luck would have it. What I hadn't counted on was that, this time around, my enemy had chosen another vehicle for disseminating information about me: the Internet.

Diane came running into my office one morning. "Turn on your computer," she said breathlessly.

"I can't," I said. "I have a client due in five minutes."

"Turn it on," she repeated. "You've got to see what they're saying about you."

"What who's saying about me?"

"Everybody. You're all over the place."

"Oh. You mean the Wyman Method is being mentioned on iVillage or Oxygen or one of the other women's sites?"

"No. That would be a good thing. This is not a good thing."

I took a sharp intake of breath, finally getting it. It hadn't occurred to me that the "secret" might show up on the World Wide Web, even though the Internet had far surpassed the print media as the place of choice for spreading gossip and innuendo. But now that I understood what was going on, I was rigid with suspense. Which of my trumped-up stories would appear on my computer screen? Which of my friends would reveal herself as the back-stabber? Was I really ready to find out? And what would I do when I did find out?

"Are you going to turn it on or do you want to come out and use mine?" Diane persisted.

"I'll come out and use yours," I said, too nervous to sit and wait for my computer to boot up.

We scurried out to the reception area and huddled around Diane's iMac.

"Look," she said, pointing to an item on some Web site I'd never heard of.

I looked, my heart thumping. There it was, one of the lies I'd made up about myself. And there *she* was, not in name, but in deed: my betrayer.

I suppose I'd always known she was the one, always had a hunch, always felt in my gut that there was something a little off about her. But I hadn't wanted to face it, not after all the time we'd spent together, not after all the time I'd spent without female friends.

But now I had to face it, and it hurt much more than I'd expected it to. In the previous weeks, when I'd attempted to guess who was trying to bring me down and why, when I'd kicked around my theory with Brandon, when I'd accused Diane and then Kelsey and then Kip of being the rat, it had been more of an academic exercise, a sort of mental aerobics. All that changed the instant I saw the story on the screen. I felt as if I actually *had* been stabbed, not in the back, but in the heart, as corny as that sounds. My eyes flooded with tears, my mind reeling with "How could she?" and "Why did she?" and, most painfully, "I thought she cared about me." Don't get me wrong. It's no fun being cheated on by your husband, but when your best friend pulls that kind of crap, it's worse, in a way. It completely knocks you off balance, maybe because it seems like a crime against nature, or maybe just because it's such a dirty rotten thing to do.

"Dr. Wyman," said Diane, putting her hand on my shoulder to comfort me. "Does this mean what they're writing about you is true? Is that why you're so upset?"

I was so choked up I couldn't answer right away.

"It's not true, is it?" she said again. "IRS agents aren't shutting down your practice, shutting down *our* practice, are they?"

"No," I managed. "No one's shutting down our practice, Diane."

"Then why are you crying?"

"Because I lost a friend," I said sadly. "And it's going to take me a long time to get over it."

PENNY. PENNY, THE predator. Penny, the P.R. whiz. Penny, the one who'd mentioned recently that she was dating an "Internet guy," which explained how the IRS story wound up there. Penny, the operator who always went after what she wanted.

But what did I have that she wanted? What was there about me that brought out the Tomahawk cruise missile in her? Did she want Kip? Was that what all this had been about? God, every time I let myself picture the two of them together, I felt sick. Penny and Kip. Kip and Penny. My husband and my friend. Yes, "sick" was the right word for it.

And yet if this was about Kip, why the column about Brandon and me? Why the story about the IRS and me? Why the compulsion to watch me suffer?

Obviously, I was going to have to ask her.

I called her at the office. She was in conference with a client, but I left a message with Annette that I needed to see her after work. I said I would meet her at her apartment at six-thirty unless I heard back from her within the hour.

Since there was no call, I headed for her place at six-fifteen. I was not looking forward to this little confrontation. As I said, I hadn't expected to feel as raw as I did, as violated. In fact, I had anticipated that I would be happy once I collared the villain, because it would mean a fresh start with Brandon. But I wasn't happy. Not at all.

SHE WAS HOME when I arrived, acting as if absolutely nothing out of the ordinary was going on.

"Drink?" she said, after she made introductory small talk—how her apartment was messy because she didn't know she'd be having company, how she'd had such an exhausting day, how she was retaining water—"See how puffy my eyes are?"—and didn't know why.

"No, thanks," I said, finding it difficult even to look at her. On the other hand, I couldn't take my eyes off of her. I kept searching her face for some indication of what was wrong with her (besides her water retention problem), but couldn't detect a single clue.

"No scotch?" she said. "That's not the Lynn I know."

"No, and you're not the Penny I thought I knew."

"Uh-oh. What unpardonable sin did I commit? Did I lapse into Menspeak without realizing it? Did I interrupt you? Did I forget to show *empathy*?"

We were standing next to each other in her kitchen. I was close enough to her to kick her in the shins. It was a nice fantasy, but I didn't give in to it.

"No, I wasn't referring to the Wyman Method," I said. "I was referring to my situation with the IRS."

"Right. I forgot to ask about that. I bet that's why you're peeved at me. What's happening? Did you hire a tax attorney? Someone who can get you off the hook?"

"No."

"Why? You can't just let them take everything away from you, Lynn."

"You mean, the way you tried to?"

"What?"

"You tried to take everything away from me."

She appeared puzzled, the phony. "I think you'd better have that Scotch. You're not making any sense. Your beef is with those pit bull IRS agents, not with me."

"There are no IRS agents, Penny. No tax issues, either."

"But you told me they were going to put you in jail if you didn't pay up."

"I lied."

She blinked. "Maybe I'm the one who needs the Scotch." She reached into her liquor cabinet and poured herself a Dewar's. "Now, run this by me again. You lied about what?"

"About the agents ransacking my office and dangling a prison sentence over me. I made it up, Penny. Just for you."

She laughed. "I don't know what's up with you tonight, but I heard you telling Gail and Sarah and Isabel all about it."

"No. I only told you about it. To see if you'd leak the story to the media, the way you leaked the other stories. I set a trap, Penny, and you stepped into it."

She sipped her drink, took a few seconds to regroup. "What, exactly, are you accusing me of, Lynn? I'm getting the impression that you're accusing me of something. Why don't you just lay it out for me, since I must be too stupid to catch on?"

"You're not stupid. You're very smart. That's why it's taken me so long to figure out what you've been up to."

"And what's that, pray tell?"

"You had an affair with Kip, Penny." I willed my voice not to crack as I said this. I also gave her a few seconds for some sort of denial. There was none. "And then you suggested I dump him but play at staying married to him, in order to preserve my professional reputation, remember?" I grew angrier as I relived her treachery. "When I didn't decide right away whether or not to follow your advice, you fed the story to the *Enquirer* and let me think it was Kip who did it. And as if that weren't enough, you struck again, by giving the *Post* the story about Brandon being my client. Why, Penny? Why would you do these terrible things to me?"

She put her drink down, an odd little smile on her face. It was over. She'd been caught and she knew it.

"Lynn," she said. "You're such an innocent in the ways of the world."

"And you, Penny, are a bitch with a capital 'C.' "

She laughed. "Good one. But then words are your specialty."

"And deceit is yours, apparently."

"Not deceit. No, my specialty is fairness."

"Fairness?"

"Yes. Making sure everyone gets her fair share." She was wearing a nasty smirk now. She was manipulating me again. The difference was that she was doing it out in the open this time.

"Where do you get off calling what you've done to me 'fair'?" I said.

"You misunderstood, Lynn. Listen up. I said that I make sure everyone gets her fair share. You had too much. I had to take some of it away. To keep things *fair*."

"Too much of what?" I always knew she was competitive, but I never knew she was crazy.

"Lynn, Lynn. You're not getting this." She picked up her Scotch, sipped it. "You see, when you were married to Kip, you two were heralded as the Golden Couple—the couple who had it all, including the key ingredient in a happy marriage: communication. It was too much, it really was. All those magazine pieces and television shows and newspaper articles raving about what a perfect relationship you had. It wasn't *fair*. Some of us women don't have a husband, let alone a communicative husband, so I had to intervene, to subtract a little from your embarrassment of riches."

"A veritable Robin Hood."

"You could say that."

Talk about bizarre logic. "So you seduced Kip, to take from the rich and give to the poor—the poor being you."

"Sure, but he didn't require a whole lot of seducing. He was ripe for a fling, Lynn. He was *starving* for a fling, to be honest. All I had to do was say, 'That's quite a tool you've got there, Mr. Carpenter,' and he was all over me."

"But he wasn't in love with you, Penny."

"No. And that wasn't fair, either. I had planned to wreck your marriage and leave it at that. But when he told me he still loved you—in spite of our unbelievable sex, by the way—I decided I'd better wreck your career, too. To make sure you weren't benefitting more than the rest of us out there."

She really was nuts. Why hadn't I seen that?

"So there you were, down in the pits where you belonged," she continued. "Everything was going fine until you latched onto Brandon Brock. I thought, Oh well. She'll teach him her precious Wyman Method and that'll be that. But nooo."

"We fell in love."

"Yes, and who would have predicted it? America's Toughest Boss and America's Smuggest Linguist. Not exactly a match made in heaven."

"But it was, Penny."

"And it wasn't *fair*."

That again. "So you felt you had to subtract Brandon from me, the way you subtracted Kip from me, is that it?"

"Precisely."

"And since you figured you couldn't seduce him, given your tendency to repulse men, you decided to subtract him from me by leaking the fact that he was my client and destroying his trust in me."

"Yup, although the 'repulse' business is below the belt, Lynn."

"Not nearly as below the belt as you deserve. How about the IRS story? Did you leak that one for the same reason? So Brandon would believe I was dishonest as well as disloyal? So you could bury our chances for a reconciliation?"

"That's pretty accurate."

"Then this isn't about fairness at all," I said. "This is about love. You've never had a man to love you, so you can't bear it that I've had two. But what made you think you could trick Kip and Brandon into falling *out* of love with me? Love doesn't operate that way. Love lasts. That's what differentiates it from the guerilla tactics you practice. You can't force men to feel what you want them to feel, Penny."

"Save your lectures for your clients," she spat.

"I will. Just get it through your head that your strategy bombed. You tried to take Kip's love away from me and it didn't work. Then you tried to take Brandon's love away from me and *that* didn't work."

"But it did work. You and Brandon are over. You said so. You went on and on about how depressed you were about it."

"Sorry, but we're not over. In fact, Brandon was the one who came up with the trap that ensnared you."

She looked crestfallen. "You're back together?"

I nodded. Well, we would be, once he heard the news. "You see, Penny, after it dawned on me that you were the only ones who knew my secrets—you and Gail and Isabel and Sarah—I conveyed this to Brandon and he suggested that I concoct counterfeit secrets about myself, one for each of you, and then see which of the stories found its way into the public domain."

"Clever guy, that Brandon."

"Yes, he is. He and I love each other and we're going to be together. We're planning a wonderful future—without you in our lives. You'll have to find some other unsuspecting friend to betray."

When she failed to counter with one of her mean-spirited comebacks, I turned to leave, then thought of another question I needed answered.

"Speaking of unsuspecting friends, what about the others?" I said.

"Could you be a little more specific?"

"Gail and Isabel and Sarah. Do they have any idea what you've been up to?"

"Of course not."

"So you never tried to 'subtract' anything from their lives?"

"Why bother? They're zeroes in the love department. Although Isabel seems positively blissful in her new relationship."

"Don't even think about it," I said, reading Penny's mind. "You try one of your schemes on her and I'll make sure Feminax and every other company in town hears about the hell you've put me through."

"My, that sounds like a threat."

"It is."

"Are you finished?"

"Very."

I regarded her one final time. She was a sad case, a desperate case, and yet so capable, so bright. What a pity. But she was not my problem anymore.

"What?" she asked. "You looked as if you were about to say something."

"Just that I'm still wondering how you were able to pretend to be my friend while you were chipping away at my life. How did you manage to keep the act going for so long, Penny?"

"Talent," she said wryly.

"A talent that hasn't gotten you anywhere. You're alone. All alone. That wasn't the result you were after, was it?"

I didn't hang around for another snappy retort. Before she even opened her mouth to reply, I was out the door.

33

BEFORE I DROVE back to Mt. Kisco, I stopped at a phone booth near Penny's apartment and called Brandon. I'd walked out her door feeling pretty blue until I reminded myself that there was an upside to finding out what she'd done to me—that he and I could be together without the trust issue hanging over us—and I was eager to tell him the news. I knew he'd be relieved, supportive, and, most of all, remorseful that he had ever doubted me. We would have an emotionally stirring reunion. Nothing would stand in our way.

Unfortunately, I couldn't reach him either at the office or at home, getting stuck with voice mails in both places. I tried him again later that evening. Still no answer. I had dinner, did some work, tried him once more. Nobody home. I went to bed, figuring I'd catch up with him in the morning.

I slept well for the first time in months, which surprised me. I had expected to have nightmares in which Penny would be chasing me with an ax or poking my eyes out with Feminax tampons or taking a bite out of me with those big Kennedyesque choppers. Instead, my sleep was uneventful—no tossing, no turning, no thoughts of Penny or anyone else. I suppose I was too worn out for dreams. Or maybe it was that I finally felt a sense of peace after all the turmoil of the past year.

In any case, I woke up rejuvenated the next morning, refreshed. As soon as I got to the office, I called Brandon.

"Good morning, Naomi," I said cheerfully. "It's Lynn Wyman. Is he there?"

"I'm afraid not," she said.

"No, really, Naomi. Is he there?" I chuckled, assuming she was still operating under Brandon's previous instructions not to put me through to him. "Mr. Brock and I are on speaking terms again. In fact, I'm calling on the slim chance that he's available for lunch today."

"Oh, but I wasn't giving you the run-around, Dr. Wyman. Mr. Brock isn't here because he's gone away."

"Away?" Swell. "Where?"

"Japan. He flew to Tokyo yesterday."

My heart sank. I'd had visions of a fabulously romantic lunch somewhere, just the two of us. A kiss-and-make-up lunch with champagne and hand-holding and an inordinate amount of "I'm sorry"s on his part. "When will he be back, Naomi?"

"Not for at least a week. Ten days is more like it."

I was terribly disappointed. I had waited long enough to reconcile with Brandon. Ten days felt like an eternity. "Is he seeing those two men who were here in this country recently? The ones I met in the back seat of his Mercedes?"

"You must be thinking of Toshi Yamazaki and Makoto Takahashi. They're in charge of our sales operations in Japan. And yes, Mr. Brock will be meeting with them along with our distributors."

"I'm guessing that means he hasn't hired anyone to run Finefoods' Far East division. He mentioned that he was filling the position himself until he found the right person."

"That's true. He's trying to hire a woman who's currently an executive at one of our competitors, but they haven't completed the negotiations."

"A woman." I smiled. There was a time when Brandon wasn't able to recruit top women, because he didn't know how to communicate with them. All that had changed.

"Yes, indeed, Dr. Wyman. The atmosphere is entirely different since Mr. Brock went through your program. Did he tell you that he allows the employees to bring their pets to work now?"

I laughed. "No, he didn't tell me."

"My gosh, this place is like the humane society! Animals everywhere! And children!" She clucked. "He's set up a day care center off the cafeteria. He doesn't want to discourage young, smart, working mothers from leaving the company. He even sent a memo to our managers, suggesting that they let their people adjust their schedules to meet the demands of their families. Ah, yes. Mr. Brock has come a long, long way."

"And now he's traveling a long, long way," I said, more than a little frustrated by this turn of events. "When he calls in, Naomi, will you tell him I was looking for him?"

"Of course."

"Or, better yet, why don't you give me the number of the hotel where he's staying and I'll call him."

"I'd be glad to."

I SAW CLIENTS the rest of the morning, then sorted through my phone messages while Diane ran out to get us a couple of sandwiches for lunch.

"Well, what do you know?" I said out loud after reading one of the messages. It was from the CBS development person I'd met with the year before, to discuss the pilot for my own daytime talk show.

So he's back, I thought with a quickening pulse. So he wants a meeting. So he's offering me the very opportunity he'd withdrawn.

I couldn't deny that I was intrigued and flattered that he'd called. I mean, it's not everyday that a major television network hands you your own show. The mere possibility of having creative control over a project of that magnitude, of being able to reach millions of women and reassure them that there *is* help for the verbally challenged men in their lives, well, it was all pretty heady stuff.

I know, I know. I said I was only interested in maintaining my private practice. But this was the big time, the big chance, the big move. There was no harm in returning the man's phone call, was there?

Of course not. I called him, expecting to be kissed off, but he actually took the call within seconds. And, following a few pleasantries, he said the magic words: "Lynn, we want to work with you." What was I supposed to do, tell him to shove it?

Well, I couldn't, not so fast and not after all the years of wanting the kind of recognition he was dangling in front of me. No way. Instead, I scheduled a meeting with him for later in the week. CBS's top brass would be there, he pledged. The show would get the green light, he vowed. *I* would be a ratings winner, he predicted.

I hurried out to the reception area to deliver the news to Diane, who had returned with our lunch.

"Do you want to eat it here or in your office?" she said, a large brown bag in her arms.

"Here's fine," I said, too keyed up to even think about food. "Diane, you'll never guess who called."

"I know exactly who called. I took the messages."

"Right." I sat down, ignored my turkey sandwich. "So are you ready for this? I've got a meeting with the CBS people about a pilot for a talk show. Oh, Diane, they want me. They really, really want me."

"They really, really wanted you the last time and look how that turned out."

Clearly, she was not as enthusiastic about the project as I was.

"Yes, but things are different now. My career's on solid ground again. Plus, they've conducted focus groups and the results have indicated a genuine need for relationship-oriented programming."

"Awesome, but I'd rather hear what happened with you and Penny yesterday," Diane said, munching on her tuna salad wrap. "Did you confront her or not?"

"You bet I confronted her," I said and filled her in on the details.

"It's unbelievable what she did to you," she said, finger-combing her hair off her face. She'd dyed it the color of eggplant the week before. (Her hair, not her face.) "That woman needs help."

"Major help," I agreed. "But my focus now is on moving ahead with my life, not worrying about hers."

"Moving ahead with your TV show, you mean."

"And with Brandon. I can't wait to tell him that it was Penny who masterminded our split, although I'll *have* to wait if I want to tell him in person."

"Why?"

"He's in Japan."

"So go there and be with him."

"Diane."

"You just said you couldn't wait."

"You're being too literal."

"No, I'm being sensitive to your situation. How long is he staying there?"

"A week to ten days."

"More than enough time for a nice little rendezvous."

"Please. Japan isn't a ten-minute hop in a cab. It's on the other side of the world."

"That's what makes it cool. And now that I think about it, hasn't it been a while since you took a vacation, Dr. Wyman?"

"Not if you count last year, when I was basically out of a job. I sat home writing and rewriting my résumé."

"Some vacation. The truth is, you never go anywhere except to those linguist conferences."

She was right, I had to admit. I hadn't been much of a traveler, just a grind. Work, work, work.

"You should fly over to Japan, surprise Mr. Brock, and have a romantic adventure," she urged.

I smiled. She was so young. "I have responsibilities here, Diane. They're called 'clients.' It wouldn't be fair to cancel them without giving them some notice."

"I hate to break this to you, Dr. Wyman, but you're not a medical doctor and the men who come to see you aren't going to drop dead if they have to postpone their appointment. You do language adjustment, not brain surgery."

"I'm aware of that."

"And you're forgetting about me."

"I could never forget about you, Diane."

"I'm serious. *I* could see the clients while you're gone. I've been doing a lot of the evaluations anyway." She sat up very straight when she said this.

"I have no doubt that you're capable of seeing the clients," I said, "but there's another, even more practical consideration: A trip like that probably costs a fortune."

"Let me ask you something. Didn't you tell me that Mr. Brock wasn't the only one who changed, because of your relationship? Didn't you say that you changed too? That you're not so serious all the time and you let yourself enjoy life and you're more spontaneous? Didn't you tell me that?"

"Yes. The old me wouldn't even be discussing this."

"Well? Why not just take a chance and go? I mean, you could call him first if you want, to make sure he's staying where he's supposed to be staying, so your surprise doesn't fall flat. But think about it: Is there a better way to show him you're for real? He can't possibly doubt your commitment to him after you've flown nine thousand hours just to be with him."

She had a point. An expensive point. "I can't spend the money."

"Why not? You're doing great now. Your practice is back where it used to be."

"Speaking of which, there's my meeting with the CBS people in a few days. I can't miss that."

"Don't miss it. Reschedule it."

"Oh, Diane. You don't do that with these people. Once you have their attention, you have to hold onto it, take advantage of it, use it to make things happen. Opportunities like the one they're offering me slip away so easily. You've got to grab them while you can."

"What about Mr. Brock? He could slip away, too."

"Not possible. He's my top priority."

"Then prove it. To him. To yourself. Prove that your career is important but that he comes first, that your love for him comes first."

"You're suggesting that by flying over there, I'd be making the Grand Gesture?"

"I'm suggesting that by flying over there, you'd be going to get your man. Mr. Brock broke up with you because he thought you were using him to rebuild your professional reputation. Wouldn't traveling all the way to Japan—and skipping your meeting with the CBS people—be the perfect way to show him that he was wrong? Or aren't you willing to risk blowing your shot at a TV show to do that, Dr. Wyman? Maybe you haven't changed as much as you keep saying."

Sheesh! "I'm not hungry," I said, pushing aside my lunch. "I think I'll do a little work in my office before the next client comes in."

"Mind if I finish your sandwich?"

"It's all yours."

Once back in the safety of my office, I sat at my desk and mulled over everything Diane had thrown at me. The conclusion I came to was that people don't change simply because they *say* they've changed. Change isn't about a script or a line of dialogue. It's about demonstrating a shift through actions and deeds.

I had wanted my own talk show because I'd thought it would validate my work. But my work was already validated on a daily basis by every client who successfully completed the program. I didn't need the show anymore, I realized. What I needed was Brandon.

Yes, I had changed, but Diane was right. If ever there was a time to prove that my feelings for him came first, this was it. I was going to fly to Japan to "get my man," as she had put it.

When she buzzed me to tell me the client had arrived, I shared the good news.

"You're really doing it?" she said.

"Sayonara."

LATER THAT DAY, I called Brandon at the Park Hyatt Tokyo, to double check that he was still booked at the hotel. The surprise would be on *me* if I got there, only to have him registered somewhere else.

"The Penny/Gail/Sarah issue has officially been resolved," I announced when I reached him. In my effort not to blurt out my secret plan, I forced myself to speak *very* slowly, *very* calmly.

"Don't keep me in suspense," he said, sounding happy to hear from me. "Which one turned out to be the bad girl?"

"Penny. What a whorebag."

"Penny, huh? I was leaning toward Sarah."

"Another whorebag, but that's between her and her husband."

"So it's over. We're finished with this awful business."

"Yes. Now, you and I can concentrate on each other," I said, trying to imagine his reaction to my showing up in Tokyo in a matter of hours, praying he would be overjoyed to see me. "That's what you want too, isn't it?"

"It's what I've always wanted. I'm ashamed that I didn't trust you.

I made a mess of the situation. What good was teaching me how to be sensitive to a woman's needs if I couldn't be sensitive to yours?"

"You can be sensitive to mine when you get home."

"I'm not sure I can wait that long."

You won't have to, snookums. I'm on my way.

I BOUGHT A Fodor's guide on Japan and read up on my destination. Then I called United Airlines and booked the 11:55 A.M. flight for the very next morning. What the heck, I thought, as I threw clothes into a suitcase. I've got a passport. I've got cash and credit cards. And I've got the man I love at the other end. Why drag my feet? Besides, it takes fourteen hours to get there. Might as well move it.

I slept for a good portion of the trip, daydreamed for the rest of it. People always complain about how endless the journey to Asia seems, but I viewed my 747 as a miraculous conveyance, not only carrying me from one culture to another, but delivering me to Brandon. No complaints from me.

I landed at Tokyo's Narita Airport at 2:30 the next afternoon, and got my first taste of the Japanese efficiency and attention to detail I'd been reading about. The airport was so spotless you could eat off the floor. Following the suggestion of the guidebook, I hopped onto a bus to downtown Tokyo, arriving 70 minutes later at the magnificent, towering, granite-and-glass Park Hyatt, the epitome of cutting-edge, twenty-first century architecture.

I can't believe I'm doing this, I thought as I took the elevator to the forty-first floor to check in. A batallion of hotel staff greeted me with deep bows and offered their assistance. Never had I felt so attended to. I explained that I had flown all the way from New York to surprise Mr. Brandon Brock, the CEO of Finefoods, Inc., and that I needed them to give me a key to his room. This was not a simple request, I knew, given security concerns, but I did not expect the negotiations to take forever. The Japanese, you see, never say "No," as that's considered an act of aggression. Instead, they smile relentlessly and inscrutably and sidestep an issue, hoping you'll tear your hair out and give up. But I did not give up and they did not back down. What we ended up with was a compromise, which is how negotiations usually end up. Two of them would escort me up to Brandon's room so they could supervise me opening the door and rushing into his embrace.

Okay, I consoled myself. So it won't be the most private reunion in history.

When we arrived at his room, I was handed the key. I breathed deeply as I inserted it in the lock—I was nervous, excited, dying to see the expression on my beloved's face when he caught his first glimpse of me—and then slowly opened the door.

I took a quick look around, but Brandon was nowhere in sight.

I ventured further into the room, which was a suite, by the way, befitting the king of breakfast cereals, and called out to him.

"Brandon? Are you in here? It's Lynn. I've come to surprise you."

My two escorts followed me inside, making sure I wasn't stealing the ashtrays. After another minute, we all heard the water running in the bathroom and realized Brandon was taking a shower.

Oh, great, I thought. He's going to walk out in his birthday suit, talk about a surprise.

I volunteered to tap on his bathroom door, to warn him, but the hotel staff insisted I remain right where I was.

So I waited and they waited and we were all forced to listen to Brandon's humming. (The song was difficult to identify, but I believe it was one of Michael Bolton's.)

At last, I heard him shut off the water. I played with the ends of my hair as I listened to him gargle, spray on the shaving cream, hum a few more bars, open the bathroom door.

Out he came, his torso wrapped in a towel, thank God.

"Surprise!" I shouted, my arms extended.

He clutched his heart as he stared at me. I wondered if I had sent him into cardiac arrest.

"Brandon, honey," I said. "I came all this way to show you how much I love you."

"Lynn?" His face broke into a wide grin. No cardiac arrest. "What are you doing here?"

"I told you. I came to be with you."

"But this is so out of character for you."

"Not anymore."

"Everything all right, Mr. Brock?" interrupted a member of the hotel staff.

"Oh, yes. Fine," said Brandon, recovering enough to dismiss them.

Even after we were alone, he continued to stand there with that dopey grin on his face, running his eyes over me in sheer amazement.

"I wanted to show you how much you mean to me," I repeated, wishing he'd say something instead of just grinning. "Maybe you think it's crazy that I came. But I had to come. Please tell me you're glad I did."

He moved closer to me then. I caught a whiff of his aftershave.

"I realize you're probably still in shock," I yammered on, as he kept inching toward me. "I would be, too. But it would make it easier if you'd tell me how you feel about my being here. Remember how we worked on getting you to express your emotions? To verbalize them? *Do* you remember, Brandon?"

"I remember," he said softly. "I remember every single thing about you." He kissed my cheek. "As for your flying here, it's the most beautiful surprise anyone's ever given me. Because I know it involved a sacrifice for you. I know you don't just pick up and leave your office on a whim. I know you must have intended to prove something to me. But there's something I need to prove to you, too."

"What?"

"That I was wrong to ever doubt you. That I love you more than

I thought I could love a woman. And that I would eagerly get on a plane and fly anywhere you are."

It was my turn to smile. "That's a relief," I said. "Surprises can be tricky. Some people like them. Some don't. I guess you're telling me that you're in the 'like them' category. Is that fair to assume?"

No sooner were the words out of my mouth than he dropped the towel he'd been wearing around his body, letting it fall to the floor. He was now a naked man in a state of serious arousal.

"Does this answer your question?" he asked.

"It does," I said.

HERE'S A TIP for any woman looking for a bang-up way to patch things up with her boyfriend: Fly to Tokyo and have sex with him in his suite at the Park Hyatt hotel. I don't know what they put in the water over there, but Brandon was as frisky as one of Isabel's cats.

Sure, he did a lot of apologizing between the purring—we both did—but the bulk of our conversation that night consisted of "Oh, God"s and "Faster"s and "Yes!"s.

At one point, when Brandon finally started to conk out but I still had my motor running, I straddled him and tried to coax him into one more ride.

"I don't think I can," he said.

"No?" I reached down to fiddle with his gear shift.

"I wish I could but—"

"Look, buster," I said, feeling signs of life in the old shift. "We can make this easy. Or we can make this hard."

"Make it hard."

And so I did.

AT NINE-THIRTY THE next morning, Brandon was conducting a meeting in the living room of his suite while I was still out cold in the bedroom. It was lunch time before I finally emerged and was greeted by my old chums, Toshi Yamazaki and Makoto Takahashi, who offered to be our translators and guides for the afternoon.

In between stops to a few of Finefoods' distributors, they took us to one of Tokyo's numerous noodle bars, where you bring the bowl right up to your mouth and slurp the food down, no utensil required. (Don't make the same mistake I did—i.e., don't wear a silk blouse you care about.) They took us to one of the ubiquitous Pachinko parlors, neon-lit store fronts where Japanese businessmen, housewives, and teenagers play what amounts to an upright version of pinball. They took us to some of the city's famous gardens. And they took us to the lovely Asakusa district, the most traditional section of Tokyo. There, they suggested we visit the Sensoji Temple, where Buddhists and tourists alike come to worship.

"You go in now," said Toshi, indicating that Brandon and I should enter the Temple.

"Aren't you joining us?" I asked.

He smiled. "It's for you and Brandon to enjoy together."

"Very romantic," Makoto added, a twinkle in his eye. "We wait for you here."

Brandon clasped my hand and we ventured inside the Temple. After ambling through the building, which was as mystical as it was magnificent, we found ourselves at a counter where, we were told, we could each buy our fortune. Brandon went first, placing a 100-yen coin into a wooden box and shaking it until a long bamboo stick slid out from a small hole. The stick had a number on it, corresponding to one of the numbers on a nearby set of drawers. He took the fortune from the appropriate drawer and studied it.

"It's in both English and Japanese, luckily," he said.

"Great. What's it say?"

"It says: 'Beware of women who teach men to talk like fools.' "

"It does not."

"No, it doesn't. It says: 'If a mysterious woman shows up at your tennis club one morning, straight out of the blue, marry her.' "

I laughed. "It doesn't say that, either."

"No, but it should."

I regarded him. "Is that so?"

He nodded, his expression becoming serious, earnest. "I want to marry you, Lynn. I made that claim before and then ran for cover. Not something an enlightened, Womenspeaking man would have done, was it?"

"No, sir."

"Well, I'm not running anymore. You're stuck with me for the long haul, through sickness and health, through communication and miscommunication."

"That's sweet."

"It's true. You will marry me, won't you? Within six months or so? Actually, next weekend works for me."

I hugged him. "I love you. I want to marry you. But first—"

"First what?"

"First I have to check *my* fortune."

I dropped the coin into the wooden box, followed the same procedure that Brandon had followed, and out popped my portent of the future.

"What's the good word?" he asked, draping himself over my shoulder to peek.

"It says: 'Never marry a man who used to call you Doc.' "

"Cute. Try another one."

"Okay. It says: 'If a man fulfills you in every possible way, marry the sucker before some other woman gets her hands on him.' "

He smiled. "I take it, that's a yes to my proposal?"

"That's a yes."

He pumped his fist in the air, then lifted me up in his arms, twirled me around, shared his feelings with me *his* way. Every success I'd ever achieved, every ounce of happiness I'd ever experienced, paled in comparison to that moment.

"I love you," I said. "I can't believe how much."

We held each other for a long time, neither of us wanting to let go. It was only when I remembered that Toshi and Makoto were waiting for us outside that I reluctantly pulled away from Brandon.

"We should get moving," I said.

He nodded. "Before we do, I'm just curious. What was really written on your fortune?"

I retrieved it from my pocket. "It says: 'A comfortable chair is good for sitting.' "

He laughed. "I guess it lost something in the translation."

"How about yours?" I asked.

He picked it out from his pocket. "It says: 'A person who speaks to another's heart and soul has a most precious gift.' "

I looked up at him, astonished. "Does it really say that? No kidding around this time?"

"I swear it does, Lynn. Here."

I took the fortune from him and read it for myself. "It's uncanny, isn't it?"

"Scary," he said. "Leave it to the Japanese to sum up the Wyman Method in one sentence. It took you six months to make your point."

"Maybe, but they were the best six months of your life and don't you forget it."

"The best?" He kissed my forehead. "I have a feeling that's still ahead of me."

EPILOGUE

So there we were, filing out of the movie theater. We had just seen what is commonly referred to as a "chick flick," which is a movie that is appealing to women and repellent to men. Men excluding Brandon, that is. Being a Sensitive Man, he is beyond such gender stereotyping and goes to chick flicks without having to be dragged, even though they do not feature car chases.

By the way, he and I have been married for three years, three wonderful years during which our love for each other has deepened and our mutual respect grown. What has also grown is my abdomen, as I am five months pregnant with our first child. Aside from the morning sickness and the breast tenderness and the swelling of my feet at the end of the day, I am ecstatic. So is Brandon. We feel blessed, truly we do.

On the professional front, he is riding high as Finefoods' CEO, with a stable of talented executives working for him. Plus, he has me working for him. Well, I don't work for him, exactly. I work with him. He is my client, just like the old days. The difference is that I'm not making adjustments in his language; I'm tinkering with the speech patterns of his employees—male and female.

"Did she say male *and* female?" you're probably asking. "What's up with that?"

Well, relax. I didn't sell out. I just altered my perspective. I came to appreciate that the Wyman Method, while extremely valuable in terms of its impact on men and their inability to communicate with women, had its flaws. It didn't go far enough, was limited, was restrictive.

It's obvious that men and women have different conversational styles, I thought, so why not encourage them to become fluent in each other's languages? Why not coach men in Womenspeak and women in Menspeak? Why not teach one side how it feels to talk like (and, by extension, walk in the shoes of) the other? Isn't that the best way to foster a spirit of understanding and acceptance? Shouldn't I stop practicing a program of corrective linguistics and instead promote a method for actually bridging the communication gap?

Yes, I concluded, and my work with Finefoods' employees is the result. It has proven not only satisfying but lucrative. I have a new book coming out too—a few months after I have the baby coming out—and I write a syndicated newspaper column every week. But there's no radio show this time around, no appearances on *Good Morning America* and no development deal with CBS. Nowadays, I prefer to devote any extra hours to my expanding family.

Do Brandon and I ever have the sort of communication issues that you have with your partner? Sure. I suppose that's the real "caution" aspect of this cautionary tale—that in spite of how skilled he and I are in the art of communicating, in spite of our mastery of the scripts and the exercises and the use of words like "share," in spite of our genuine desire to be responsive to each other's needs, we fall into the same traps you do.

As an example, let's go back to the little anecdote I was about to *share* with you a minute ago. Brandon and I were leaving the movie theater, and I turned to him and said, "So what did you think of it?"

He shrugged, stuck his hands in his pocket.

"What did you think of the movie?" I repeated. When they don't feel like answering, they pretend to be deaf.

"I thought it was a waste of money."

"Why? The acting was good. The jokes were amusing. The ending was uplifting. What more do you want out of a movie?"

"A decent story. My idea of a good time isn't watching three divorced women laughing and crying and saying, 'You go, girl.' "

"Oh, Brandon. That's silly."

"Why is it silly? I hated those women and their revenge plot. I was rooting for their philandering ex-husbands."

"Come on, there was more to the movie than the revenge plot. You're being pretty judgmental."

"No, Lynn. You're the one who's being judgmental."

"*I* am?"

"Yeah. You're criticizing my review of the movie. Who made *you* Roger Ebert?"

Okay. I'll stop right here, before it gets ugly. I just wanted to give you a snippet, demonstrating how even a man who willingly watches chick flicks and doesn't mind critiquing them afterwards and a woman who has studied everything there is to study about male/female interactions can stumble into trouble talking to each other. Why? Because there are simply times when men are unable to connect with women and vice versa. It can't be helped. They're wired differently than we are.

Given these preordained circumstances, we women have to stay focused on the big picture. And the big picture is this: Since we can't expect perpetual harmony in our relationships with men, we have to be grateful for those momentous occasions when they say "How was your day?" and "Are those earrings new?" and "I see your point," and remember that they're only doing the best they can.

CPSIA information can be obtained at www.ICGtesting.com
Printed in the USA
LVOW08s1305220714

395478LV00002B/182/P